My Loving VIGIL Keeping

D0724928

My Loving VIGIL Keeping

CARLA KELLY

BONNEVILLE BOOKS
AN IMPRINT OF CEDAR FORT. INC.
SPRINGVILLE. UTAH

ISBN 13: 978-1-59955-897-4

Published by Bonneville Books, an imprint of Cedar Fort, Inc.
2373 W. 700 S., Springville, UT, 84663
Distributed by Cedar Fort, Inc., www.cedarfort.com

LIBRARY OF CONGRESS CATALOGING-IN-PUBLICATION DATA

Kelly, Carla, author.
  My loving vigil keeping / Carla Kelly.
    pages cm
  Includes bibliographical references and index.
  ISBN 978-1-59955-897-4 (alk. paper)
  1. Women teachers--Utah--Winter Quarters--Fiction. 2. Mormons--Utah--Winter Quarters--Fiction. 3. Coal mines and mining--Utah--Winter Quarters--Fiction. I. Title.

  PS3561.E3928M9 2012
  813'.54--dc23

                                  2012021335

Front cover photograph courtesy of the Western Railroad and Mining Museum, Helper, Utah
Cover design by Angela D. Olsen
Cover design © 2012 by Lyle Mortimer
Edited and typeset by Melissa J. Caldwell

Printed in the United States of America

10 9 8 7 6 5 4 3 2 1

Printed on acid-free paper

In memory of the 200 men and boys who died in the Winter Quarters [Scofield] Mine Disaster, May 1, 1900.

Until we meet again.
Hwyl fawr.
Näkemiin.

ALL THROUGH THE NIGHT
(AR HYD Y NOS)

Sleep, my child, and peace attend thee,
All through the night.
Guardian angels God will send thee,
All through the night.
Soft the drowsy hours are creeping
Hill and vale in slumber sleeping,
I my loving vigil keeping
All through the night.

Love, to thee my thoughts are turning,
All through the night.
All for thee my heart is yearning,
All through the night.
Though sad fate our lives may sever
Parting will not last forever,
There's a hope that leaves me never,
All through the night.

Chapter 1

꧁꧂

"Good-bye, Della. Write and tell us all about your new school, and come back for Christmas," Della Anders said out loud as she stood for a long moment in the foyer of her uncle's house. "We'll miss you."

No comment; she expected none. The foyer was empty of everything except Della Anders and her luggage. Even though everyone knew she was leaving for her new teaching assignment, Aunt Caroline had taken her two daughters to ZCMI to buy last-minute necessities for their European tour. Uncle Karl was in his office downtown, oblivious as always.

Della picked up her carpetbag, the same shabby thing she had brought with her into the house in 1888, when she was twelve and sad. She had already sent her trunk ahead to the train depot, plus one box of books—all she needed or wanted.

She had her hand on the doorknob when she remembered the pasteboard carton she had leaned against the foot of the stairs and her promise to deliver the fox fur stole to Amanda Knight in Provo. She opened the box for another look, chuckling to see the skinny fox face with the beady eyes that adorned each end, feeling some sympathy for the foxes.

Della closed the front door quietly behind her, tucking the pasteboard box under her arm. Her carpetbag was heavy, crammed with a book to read on the train, a change of clothing, and oddments that wouldn't fit in the trunk, but she was going to carry it only a few blocks. She looked back at the Anderses' house, three stories of Queen Anne splendor with a porch swing for Sunday afternoons.

Della thought of Christmases and birthdays in the house—strange, lopsided affairs—and graduation parties for her cousins. In a few days, she knew her cousins and aunt were headed in all their splendor to the depot, the first stop on a continental tour.

When the trip was announced last winter and anticipated through an endless spring and equally tedious summer, Della had known she wasn't included. She was deep in her second year of teaching at Westside Primary School and had more on her mind than which was better, two weeks in Paris or a week in Paris and a week in Bruges. When she made it home in time for dinner, she had listened with half an ear and knew most of their plans. From painful experience, she knew what was coming.

The day after Della announced she had signed a contract for another school year, her aunt had come to her with a sad face, the one she wore when she wanted to let down her niece easily at no pain to herself.

"My dear, how unfortunate! We were hoping you could accompany us on this European trip, but you have signed another school contract," Aunt Caroline had said. Her voice was softly reproachful, as though it was Della's fault for being so thoughtless as to overlook the possibility, however remote, that she might be included this time. Aunt Caroline was complicated.

Della set off at a brisk pace for the taxi stand, resolved not to look back. She had done something so impulsive after her aunt's little fiction. Maybe she had wanted to take this European trip; maybe it was the culmination of years of hurts and slights. It had taken a long time, but maybe her cup just finally ran over.

Whatever it was had sent her to the education department at the University of Utah to find a teaching position far from Salt Lake City. She felt it now, almost liberating. She knew there were women who boldly struck out on their own, but until that moment, she had not numbered herself among them.

There in the education department, she had calmed her nerves with a prayer, then looked at the positions-open board. It was already late summer, and most teachers—including herself—had received appointments for the 1899–1900 school year. All desirable posts were filled; there were no yellow cards tacked anywhere on the Wasatch Front portion of the Utah map or in Cache Valley. Della had glowered at the board, but all the stares in the world weren't going to make a miracle. She was turning away when she noticed a fluttering of yellow in that space of canyons and mountains. She had looked closer and then slowly removed the tack from the yellow card.

It had been there awhile. She could tell because the card was punched with numerous tack marks when hopeful teachers had pulled it off for a closer look, as she was doing, then tacked it back, obviously not impressed. *Winter Quarters School,* she read to herself. *Teacher with Second Grade Certificate and one year's experience wanted. Located in Pleasant Valley, altitude 8,000 feet.*

Della nearly tacked the card back to the map. She would have, if she hadn't kept reading. For the first time in years, she felt something in her heart, some stirring that twelve years living on the sufferance of relatives hadn't entirely squelched.

Winter Quarters is a coal mining camp, located one mile beyond Scofield, she read. *Salary for a nine-month school is $25 a month, with living quarters furnished. Only morally upright educators need apply.*

Della had held the card in her hand, staring at the words "mining camp," remembering *her* mining camp, *her* father, *her* loss. Standing there, she realized for the first time in years how deep she had buried her mining camp memories, mainly because none of the Anderses wanted reminders. When she was twelve and hurting, they had always stopped her when she tried to talk about the Molly Bee, embarrassed at her roots.

But there it was, a coal mining camp. Papa had been a hard rock miner. Coal wasn't as glamorous, but it would do. She carried the yellow card to the front desk. "This position," Della began, looking at the student worker. "Has it been filled?"

He looked at it. "No one wants to go there."

"I do."

Della could tell it was on the tip of his tongue to ask her why she was interested in Winter Quarters. He didn't, so she was spared the need to explain that her father had been a miner and that she missed mining camps. When she told him her name, he looked at her with respect.

"Anders? *The* railroad lawyer?"

She nodded. Karl Anders's name had been in all the newspapers recently, after his masterful settlement of a labor dispute in the railroad's favor.

The secretary wrote the address of the school district on the back of the card and handed it to her. "You can do some good among those less fortunate, Miss Anders," he said, respect in his eyes. "I call that commendably philanthropic."

Embarrassed, Della left quickly. No need for the secretary to even suspect that her own relatives considered her among the less fortunate.

A week later, she had a contract. She withdrew from Westside School, which hadn't been impressed with her philanthropy, since she had to be replaced on short notice. Aunt Caroline had not been impressed either.

"Have you taken complete leave of your senses?" her aunt asked, when Della announced her news at dinner. "You, of all people, to willingly go to a *mining* camp? I am speechless."

No, she wasn't speechless, which was another reason

Della was happy enough to be leaving so soon, and even grateful for the diversion of that upcoming European trip. Now it was her turn; after twelve years, she took it.

"Aunt Caroline, it wasn't all bad in that mining camp. I remember good times." She had never said that before, but it was true. Della smiled at the serving girl when she set the filet of sole in front of her, the girl's eyes filled with terror at someone crossing Aunt Caroline. Even Uncle Karl never did that. "Thank you, Ellie."

Uncle Karl had broken the silence first. "My dear, I thought you were going to Europe with your cousins."

Della had regarded him with something close to sympathy. *Poor Uncle Karl, for a railroad lawyer, you never have suspected that your wife has bamboozled you over my care and upbringing*, she thought. Still, he meant well and he did resemble her late father. No point in ruining his evening. After all, he had to live with Aunt Caroline well into the eternities, and Della only had to get through dinner and two weeks.

"Uncle, now that I have been earning my living, I find it quite to my taste. I'll see Europe another time," she told him, giving him all her attention, even though he had given her none. She dared a glance at her aunt, still silent, her knuckles white around the fish fork—just another dinner at the Anderses' house.

No more of that ever, Della thought as she settled in for her ride on the interurban to Provo. She looked out the window as the little towns of Murray, Sandy, and Draper passed in review. The wheels seemed to say *never go back, never go back*, and Della found it soothing. The rhythm of the wheels took her back to her own Colorado mining town, tucked in a narrow canyon deep in the Sangre de Cristos. Papa had told her when they took the train to Pueblo for her baptism that the wheels were saying *Della dear, Della dear*. Maybe narrow-gauge rails sang a different song.

5

"Della dear," she whispered to her image in the window and turned her attention to the *McCall's Magazine* she had bought at the depot. She smiled to see an article about "Venice the Beautiful," thinking how much money Aunt Caroline could save on travel if she just read something as common as a women's magazine.

I believe I will subscribe, Della thought. *Even if I am on my own, fifty cents a year for a subscription won't break the bank. McCall's can send it to Della Dear Anders.*

She decided to subscribe as Della Olympia Anders, her real name, the one Aunt Caroline winced to hear. It was the name her father had given her after Olympia Stavrakis stole his heart, bore his child, left their baby behind, and took off for points unknown, according to Aunt Caroline. Della Olympia wasn't an all-purpose name, but she loved to say it out loud in bed at night, when no one cared what she did or thought.

"Olympia," she said, then turned back to "Venice the Beautiful," satisfied.

Della hadn't meant for her escape from the Anders to turn into bona fide rebellion, but once the stationmaster assured her that her luggage was safe at the depot in Provo, she had no burdens beyond a handbag and a box of fox. The August air was fragrant enough from petunias, zinnias, and asters to turn her generally purposeful stride into a saunter. She decided to enjoy the day and the knowledge that her time was her own, at least for another week, until school started.

She had been to Jesse and Amanda Knight's quirky home several times, but it was noontime and she doubted even as friendly a soul as Amanda, Aunt Caroline's distant cousin, would relish an unexpected luncheon guest. Besides, how many times had she walked down Center Street and wanted to stop at the Palace Drug Store lunch counter?

They had been there once when she was thirteen. She

had longed to sit at the counter and watch the man behind the counter pour fizz into brown syrup and see the foam. Aunt Caroline wouldn't hear of it.

Della sat at the counter, eyed the menu, and took her time. Tomato soup for a nickel came with lots of oyster crackers, the better to fill her with, so she asked for that and a sarsaparilla. She watched, fascinated, as the soda jerk let the brown syrup slither down the side of the glass. He poised the glass under the soda fountain handle, savoring the drama, from the look on his face.

"A little or a lot, miss?"

"A lot."

He filled the glass with carbonation, stirring it with a long-handled spoon and presenting it with a flourish that Aunt Caroline would have called vulgar. Della smiled when the fizz tickled her nose.

The tomato soup came with so many crackers that she wanted to stash some in her handbag. Della refrained, remembering her first meal at the Anderses', when she had filled her pockets with croutons because she wasn't entirely sure when her next meal would materialize. If her pocket hadn't had a hole in it, she could probably have reached her bedroom, her secret safe.

Satisfied for fifteen cents, Della continued her amble up Center Street. She could come back later and secure a room for the night at the Young Women's Christian Association boardinghouse, which she had noticed on an earlier trip. At a quarter a night, plus an earnest sermon from the matron, the price was right. She could catch an early-morning train to Scofield and be in her own house that evening for the first time in her life.

She couldn't help but smile as she walked up to the front door of the Knights' home, newly built with a cupola and Moorish arches, a house for Ali Baba. She pulled the doorbell, impressed with the gong-like sound totally suitable for a house that should have a flying carpet.

The maid curtseyed, and Della held out the pasteboard box with the foxes. "Please give this to Mrs. Knight," she said. "It's from her cousin Caroline Anders."

Duty done, Della turned away and started down the walk.

"Don't you take one more step, Della Anders!"

She turned around in surprise to see Amanda Knight coming after her. Della stopped, amused. "Not one more step, Sister Knight?"

The woman took her arm. "Really, my dear, what is the idea of dropping off a fox and running away? This isn't May Day."

By now, Amanda had wreathed her arm through Della's and was gently tugging Della back to the wonderful house. "You'll stay with us tonight, and I won't hear otherwise."

"Oh, but . . ." It never occurred to Della that Amanda Knight might want to see her, since she didn't come meekly in tow with her cousins and aunt. "Are . . . are you certain?"

"Positive," Amanda said crisply, not loosening her grip. "You and I will go inside, and you can tell me your side of what Caroline has just written me." She stopped. "No. We will wait until Jesse comes home, and you can tell us both." She looked around. "You don't have any luggage."

"I left it at the depot. I was planning to get a room at the YWCA tonight."

Amanda gave Della's arm a tug. "If you weren't so charming, I'd give you a swat!"

Della laughed out loud. "Charming? *Me*?"

"Far more than your cousins, but don't tell them I said that. Think how awkward family visits would become."

She let herself be led inside, breathing the sharp odor of new paint, happy to sit at the kitchen table and peel pota-toes. Amanda set two glasses of lemonade on the table, then ͭt to the door.

"ʼll be back to help," she said. "I'm going to send

my yardman to the depot to fetch your luggage *and* my husband."

Della peeled potatoes, feeling more care slide away. Trust Sister Knight to call him the yardman, when Aunt Caroline would have called him the chauffeur and given him a uniform.

The potatoes were bubbling on the cooking range when the yardman returned with her luggage and Jesse Knight, who made his way to the side porch, where Della and his wife sat. He planted a whacking kiss on Amanda's cheek and accepted a glass of lemonade from her. He looked at Della next, then clinked his glass to hers.

"Della, Della, pretty Della," he said with that gusto she remembered and which had always made him the most interesting of men. "So you're going to a mining camp?"

Della listened for some admonition in his voice, but there was none. He sounded as relaxed, calm, and interested in her as always, which never failed to surprise her. Jesse Knight was one of Utah's richest men, but she doubted he had a pretentious bone anywhere in his body.

"Aunt Caroline thinks I have taken leave of my senses."

"Have you?" he asked gently.

"No. I just feel a great need for something different."

She knew there was more, and looking at Uncle Jesse, as he liked her to call him, she knew he knew. "I remember the mining camp in Colorado. I wasn't ready to leave there, but I had no choice." She looked at a boy across Center Street who was mowing the lawn. "Aunt Caroline never had a good word to say about my father, but he's dead." She returned her attention to the man seated beside her. He had unbuttoned his collar in the August heat. "Did you know him?"

He nodded. "We all came across the plains together. He never cared much for church and had an itchy foot. I guess he just kept going. He loved you, though."

"I know," she said softly, thinking of the nights he'd come out of the mine, clean up, cook for dinner whatever

9

they happened to have in the shack—sometimes a lot, sometimes a little—then read to her. Sometimes the reading had to substitute for food. "We never had much. Uncle Karl called him a dreamer."

It irked her that the memories were fading. Frederick Anders was growing more indistinct with each year. "I wanted to be blonde and blue-eyed like my father. And then when I went to Salt Lake, I wanted to be blonde and blue-eyed like my cousins." *Anything to fit in*, she thought.

"Then you'd look like three-quarters of Utah." Uncle Jesse took a long gulp of the lemonade and set down the glass with an "ahh."

"I'd fit in better." Funny how sitting on the side porch with the Knights limbered her tongue. She'd never said that out loud before. She glanced at Amanda. "Once I asked my father what my mother looked like. He just picked up a mirror and held it to my face."

"And what a pretty face." Uncle Jesse turned to his wife, his voice not even half serious. "Amanda, I ask you, why on earth hasn't this . . . let's see . . . this shirttail relation of ours . . . found some lovesick swain to lead around on a leash?"

"I can't imagine," Amanda said, her eyes lively.

"I can tell you," Della said. "Aunt Caroline made sure everyone knew my father had never married my mother. Could it be she wanted people to see how noble she was to take me in?"

This was turning into a day of surprises, this first day of her independence. Della had never admitted that out loud, and here she was blurting out family skeletons. Maybe it was the wrong thing to say.

"I spoke out of turn," Della said, fearful of distressing these kind people. "I thought you knew."

"We did know, and from that same source," Amanda said finally, and there was no avoiding the hard sound to her voice. She turned back, and her eyes were filled with tears. "How could Caroline *do* that?"

"She thought it best to warn people." Della took a deep breath, relieved. "I want to go someplace where no one knows me and no one will judge me for something that I had nothing to do with. My students in Winter Quarters won't care."

Jesse was silent a long while. Della's dread turned to hope because there was nothing in his face—in either of their faces—of condemnation.

"Maybe I'm just trying to figure out who I am," Della explained.

"You could have picked an easier place than Winter Quarters," Jesse chided gently.

"I could have. That's what my bishop said too." She looked at her hands, the soft olive of her skin more pronounced in summer. "I think I want to pick up where I left off in Colorado, at the Molly Bee."

"I'm not sure you can do that. It's hard to go back."

"I can try."

Chapter 2

꧁☙꧂

To Della's infinite pleasure, Amanda Knight let her sleep in the turret-shaped room with the Moorish cupola, even though it was her sewing room. The sofa made nicely into a pull-out bed. They both laughed over the Persian carpet, Amanda telling Della not to stand on it too long, and certainly not to make a wish, or she would be flying low over Provo.

Breakfast was another pleasure, when Uncle Jesse insisted on taking her to Spanish Fork in his private railroad car. "I'm heading south on business, so why not?"

"I won't argue. Tell me something about the miners at Winter Quarters," she asked over bacon and eggs.

"You can walk from one end of that narrow canyon to the other and not hear a single American accent," he told her. "The Welshmen are the little dark ones, and every sentence sounds like a question. The Scots think they own the world, the English run it, and the Finns like to roll naked in the snow when no one's watching."

Della laughed, thinking about the Finns. "Just assure me that the miners are concerned about their children's education."

He looked at her seriously, all joking gone. "You'll find a hard-eyed bunch of realists in that canyon. They're immigrants and staking everything on their children's success in this new land. They are in deadly earnest."

She thought about that as she went upstairs again to dress, looking in the mirror to see herself as she was, all wishing aside: young, olive-skinned, and Greek of face with a head of unruly black curls and a nose charitably called aquiline. *I am young, but please let them take me seriously,* she thought. *I can do this.*

"Here's another good thing to know," Uncle Jesse told her, as the train pulled away from the depot with a hiss and a jolt. "Winter Quarters mines are called family mines."

"Why?"

"They're considered so safe—not gassy with methane, like some mines—that men with families have gravitated there. The camp doesn't look like much, so don't be imagining a thing of beauty and a joy forever. I hear it's a cheerful canyon."

She nodded and looked out the window when he picked up his newspaper.

He put the paper down and looked at her with the familiar twinkle in his eyes. "Della, did you sing in your ward choir?"

"I did. Contralto."

"Are you pretty good?"

"Well, I don't wait for a summons from the Tabernacle Choir, but I think so. Should I join the ward choir in Winter Quarters?"

"Oh, yes."

"Most choirs need altos," she said. "Have you been to church there? Does the choir need some help?"

He laughed. "You'll find out! I'm not even sure they have a piano. For sure no organ."

"Heavens. That tells me a lot."

Well, why not, she told herself as Provo turned into Springville. *I've been in plenty of so-so choirs. One more won't hurt.* She glanced east to the mountains, seeking out the canyon where the Denver & Rio Grande Western Railway would take her. By tonight she would be in her own place.

She felt a pang, saying good-bye to Uncle Jesse at the

13

depot. Through the years, she had visited the Knights with her Anders relatives, but this had been her first trip by herself to see them. She had been too shy before to see their kindness.

He kissed the top of her head. "Della, you're a fine specimen. I never noticed before," he said, so maybe she hadn't been alone in her shyness. He motioned for the porter to take her luggage. "Now I'm off to my own mines at Tintic. Come see us at Thanksgiving."

"I just might," she said, after the conductor assisted her down the steps, solicitous as only a man can be who is helping someone down from a private car. *I could like this*, she thought.

Uncle Jesse handed her a folded piece of paper through his open window. "I found this somewhere. It'll give you a chuckle."

She took it and blew him a kiss, sorry to see him go.

"Miss?"

Della turned around to see the stationmaster. "Yes, sir?"

"We are holding the D&RGW for you on that track over there," he said, gesturing toward the much longer train. "Mr. Knight had telegraphed us to do that."

She stared at him. "Mercy! I'll hurry." She grabbed her carpetbag, picked up her skirts, and ran.

Della sank into the nearest seat. She hadn't the nerve to look around the car, fully aware that every man on board—and there seemed to be no one but men—had ample opportunity to gaze at her ankles as she dashed along the platform. The only satisfaction she could own was the knowledge that at least she wore matching stockings and her petticoat was clean. Aunt Caroline did have her uses.

Maybe she could just stare out the window until the train reached Colton, the stop where she would change again for the ride to Scofield. She looked at the man seated across the aisle from her, regarding her with a smile.

He tipped his bowler hat to her. "I know this is

forward, miss, but are you the new schoolteacher for Winter Quarters?" he asked, leaning across the aisle. "Mr. Bowman—he teaches grades four through six—mentioned a teacher was due any time now. I'm on the school board."

"Yes, sir. I'm Miss Anders," she said, leaning toward him to hold out her hand.

"Emil Isgreen." He shook her hand. "Do you mind?" he asked, indicating the seat across from her.

I'd better not mind; you're on the school board, she thought as she gave him her sunniest smile.

He joined her, taking off his bowler and setting his black bag at his feet. She looked at the bag, which had the initials E.I., and looked like a physician's satchel. His eyes followed the direction of her gaze.

"I'm the Winter Quarters surgeon," he explained. "I've been visiting my folks in Tooele."

"Pleased to meet you," she said. She couldn't help notice that his own accent had a lilt to it, which made her suspect he was one of the many in Winter Quarters that Uncle Jesse said were at least some part foreign. "Are there many physicians in Winter Quarters?"

"I'm the only one," he told her. "I work for the Pleasant Valley Coal Company." His expression turned wry. "And probably will for a few more years until my loans have been whittled down. Doctor Bascom works in Scofield, so there are two of us."

"Is there a hospital?" she asked, interested.

"There is. It's right at the mouth of Winter Quarters Canyon."

"How many children do you have in the school?"

"I worked my way through medical school and couldn't find a wealthy woman to support me," he joked. "No wife, no children. Bishop Parmley wanted me on the school board because I do twice yearly health visits to the school."

"Parmley. Parmley. Uncle Jesse mentioned him," she said.

"He's the Winter Quarters mine superintendent *and* the bishop. Are you . . . ? Do you go to . . . ?"

"Yes, I'm a Mormon," she told him, recognizing all the hints.

"Same here. My parents joined the church in Scandinavia and met in a handcart company."

Uncle Jesse is proving his case, she thought. *I doubt the good doctor's first language was English.* "What about I. W. Bowman, the upper grades teacher?" she asked. "I took this job on such a whim and know so little about Winter Quarters."

"Israel? You'll like him. He's from Ohio and one of the few bona fide Yankee Doodles in the camp. I suspect he has a sweetheart in Provo. He spends all available weekends there, at any rate." The doctor interpreted her expression correctly. "Miss Anders, everyone knows everyone's business, so if you have any deep, dark secrets . . ."

". . . I'll never reveal that I'm Russian nobility, coming to teach miners' children to make good a bet," she finished.

He smiled at that. "I'd have thought Helen of Troy, or maybe the Winged Victory of Samothrace."

"This face hasn't launched even one ship yet," she said, pleased that he knew his mythology. "My mother was Greek, though." She thought of the times Aunt Caroline ordered her never to mention her mother or her father, and she felt a certain comfort in telling this inquisitive man even as little as that.

"In Winter Quarters, we all come from somewhere else," Dr. Isgreen replied. "That's the nature of mining camps."

She nodded, remembering the Molly Bee and Pa's determination to make his fortune in silver. Poor Pa—the only silver he ever ended up with was his silver-finished coffin plate.

"You will like this about the school—two years ago the school district replaced the log building with a frame one. It has one story so far, and a gymnasium in the basement. Your classroom will be on the main floor. You'll probably have at least thirty students."

"So many?"

He shrugged. "Lots of Mormons. Lots of children." He looked at her closely, trained by his profession to observe, or maybe inclined that way. "Miss Anders, your task will be a little easier, because I think all your boys will be in love with you."

"Dr. Isgreen," she murmured.

"It's just an observation," he said, then retreated behind his newspaper. "*Min nåds Gud*, it says here that there has been considerable hurricane damage in Porto Rico. Miss Anders, I am subtly changing the subject."

Della had to laugh. Aunt Caroline would have been scandalized by Dr. Isgreen, but Aunt Caroline wasn't there. She glanced down at the paper Uncle Jesse had given her. *Rules for Teachers, 1900*, she read silently. *Rule No. 1. You will not marry during the term of your contract.*

Her amusement increased as she scanned the document. Hard on the heels of Rule Number One was Rule Number Two: *You are not to keep company with men.*

"Oh, dear," she said out loud, looking at Rules Ten and Eleven: *You must wear at least two petticoats* and *Your dress must not be any shorter than two inches above the ankle.*

The newspaper rustled. "You know I have to ask. Your 'oh, dear' compels me."

She handed him the Rules for Teachers, and he scanned it, his smile widening with each entry. He handed it back to her. "You can't loiter downtown in ice cream stores because we have none in either Scofield or Winter Quarters."

"What a relief," she murmured. "And all the other felonies?"

He gave her a measuring look. "Might not be a bad idea to commit this list to memory," he suggested at last. "I haven't mentioned our principal, Miss Clayson. She's also the seventh and eighth grade teacher. Excellent educator, but a bit of a gorgon."

She took back the sheet. "I can already assure Miss Clayson that I don't smoke cigarettes and will never dye my hair."

"Good! Can you do something about your curls? I doubt Miss Clayson will approve."

"I'll try, I'll try," she joked. "Does she have a first name?"

"I rather doubt it," he told her. He elaborately shook out his newspaper again. "I'll behave myself now, Miss Anders," he said.

They stopped briefly in Thistle to take on travelers. The climb continued, the grade steep enough to make Della look anywhere but out the window. Staring at the swaying lamps in the car did nothing to calm her because even they seemed to be struggling.

"You'll get used to it," the physician said, correctly interpreting her gaze. "I tease Israel about going home to Provo so often. Takes a man in love to willingly ride the train through Spanish Fork Canyon as often as he does!"

She couldn't help but draw in her breath when the slowly moving train edged off the main track and onto a siding. Only seconds later a train loaded with coal raced by on the downward slope.

"You'll get used to that too," Dr. Isgreen said. "At least two trains a day leave the tipple and head north. Mining's a little slow right now, but with winter coming, it'll pick up."

"What do the men do when they don't mine?" she asked. The coal train rumbling by made talking difficult, but she was so nervous she had to distract herself. "It must be hard to make ends meet. My goodness, that coal train *does* make this train shake."

"Some of them work for the farmers in the valley. Nearly every miner ends up owing more to the company store, though, and it's hard to pay it back." He gave her another professional appraisal. "Breathe in and out, Miss Anders! I don't think the D&RGW has ever lost a passenger in a coal train draft."

"That's a load off my mind," Della said, relieved when the coal train shot by and the passenger train quit rocking. "So everyone stays in debt to the company store? That's harsh."

"That's mining."

They left the train at Colton, a small town built on a slant with hotels and saloons. Although the day was warm, they were so high in altitude that the breeze was cooler than she would have reckoned. She looked around the high valley, wondering how bitter it would get when the winter winds roared.

Dr. Isgreen went into the Western Union office while Della waited by her luggage, wondering what came next.

"I just sent a telegram to Israel Bowman," he said when he came out. "He'll meet you in Scofield and see that you get to Winter Quarters.

"Thanks for doing that," she said, still not used to anyone's solicitude.

"We're glad to have a teacher."

Della watched while Dr. Isgreen had her trunk removed from the baggage car, corralling two blond, impossibly handsome men to wrangle it. The men spoke a language that she did not know, and she looked at the physician, a question in her eyes.

"It's Finnish," he said. "Some of them mine at Clear Creek, but the rest are at Winter Quarters. A big family of Luomas. I think ten of them work in Number Four and Number One."

"*This* is the promised land?" she asked, only half serious.

"Yes, if you're used to hard work and don't mind the cold. Heikki and Juho here tell me they've done so well that they're sending for their parents next spring." He took her worn out carpetbag over her objections. "Bit by bit, Miss Anders. That's how most people make it in this world." His eyes were merry. "Maybe even the exalted Anderses had to struggle once."

"They did," she said, thinking of her father, even though the memory of him coming home so dirty and tired from the Molly Bee was starting to fade. She looked at the Luoma men with respect, understanding them perfectly.

She stood on the platform, hesitating.

The physician seemed to understand. "I'm on the school board, and I forbid second thoughts. All aboard, Miss Anders?"

They arrived in Scofield an hour later, topping out at nearly eight thousand feet, according to the doctor, who seemed to have a wealth of facts at hand. "They've been mining coal here for twenty-five years," he told her as the train entered an enormous valley with a stream flowing through it, rimmed by even taller mountains.

She looked with interest to see haying machines in the meadow and in the distance a town. The meadow was broad and tawny in late August.

"See that little gap to the south of the town? That's Winter Quarters Canyon. I'll warn you: it's not pretty there until you hike up the canyon and get away from the mines, machinery, and buildings."

I know, she thought, remembering the Molly Bee, even higher than this in the Sangre de Cristos Mountains. *Mines are ugly.* "I don't mind."

She hadn't meant to sound wistful, but she must have, because he looked at her thoughtfully then.

"I . . . I've seen mines before," she said, unwilling to say more, surprised at the flood of feeling that washed over her. She was usually better at training her thoughts; maybe it was the altitude.

"I suppose the Anderses own mines, don't they? I know Mr. Knight does. Lots of them."

"My Uncle Karl has some shares in them, I believe," she said. "He's a railroad lawyer."

"You're too modest. He's *the* railroad lawyer," Dr.

Isgreen said. "We all read about the verdict in Union Pacific versus Duncan." He whistled. "Impressive."

"Yes. Malcolm Duncan and his syndicate had no idea they were sending my aunt and cousins on a three-month trip to Europe this fall!"

"Nice of Duncan."

With a hiss and grind, the train stopped, then seemed to wheeze and pant, worn out with the altitude. Della let Dr. Isgreen hand her down to the depot platform. She took a deep breath, breathing in the fragrance of newly mown hay. Only four hours away and four thousand feet lower, it was a hot August afternoon. She couldn't fail to notice the slight chill of autumn.

The same two Finnish miners took her trunk from the baggage car and brought it to her, smiling.

"I have to tell you, Miss Anders: Israel Bowman and Bishop Parmley did some speculating as to why you're here in the first place. Not everyone would turn down a Grand Tour through Europe for Winter Quarters," the doctor said.

Not everyone was invited on that trip, she thought. She was spared the necessity of reply when a man not much older than her, hat in hand, came toward her. He held out his hand.

"Miss Anders? I'm Israel Bowman, grades four through six. Pleased to meet you."

She shook his hand, pleased with the firm grip and the welcome on his face.

"I wasn't relishing the idea of adding grades one through three to my classroom. You're a welcome sight. Emil, thanks for keeping her from bolting when she saw that grade up to Scofield and the way the rail seems to sort of lean out over the canyon."

"Surely no one . . ." she started.

The men looked at each other and laughed. "You'd be amazed how quickly some teachers have arrived here and

21

turned right around," Israel said. "Miss Anders, I hate to be the bearer of bad tidings, but you know that little house we promised you?"

"I am looking forward to it."

"It burned down two nights ago."

Chapter 3

"Well, dirty bird," Della said. "What happened?"

"That's a new one," Israel said. "I could like it."

She glared at him, which made Emil grin.

"I've heard a bunch of stories already," Israel said. "You'd be amazed how fast news travels up and down the canyon. The place had been uninhabited for several years, and winters up here are rough on empty buildings. And summers aren't so warm! The school custodian claims he lit a fire in the kitchen range to warm it up a bit while he swept. He left for lunch, and apparently the stovepipe was clogged with birds' nests, or maybe old miners. The heat gathered around that spot where the pipe leaves the roof, and it was too much. At least that's the story he's sticking to."

Della couldn't see any point in mourning the loss of not much. "Mr. Bowman, the district office sent a letter which mentioned that you live in a boardinghouse . . ."

". . . which I wouldn't recommend to any woman younger than eighty-nine," he said, his voice firm. "A miners' boardinghouse is no place for a lady."

"What do you recommend?"

Della wondered how successful Mr. Bowman was at keeping order in his class, because his eyes were so kind. "First, I recommend that you call me Israel. Then I recommend . . ." He paused. "Um, are you, do you go to . . . ?"

"I recently had this awkward conversation with Dr. Isgreen," Della joked. "Yes, I'm a Mormon. See? I know the code words."

"Then you know where I'm going to take you."

"The bishop."

"None other."

After the short line railroad pulled away to a siding, Heikki and Juho Luoma took her trunk to the track that branched south. Emil Isgreen kept his grip on her carpetbag, and Israel offered her his arm to help her across the track.

Della looked back at the depot. "We don't need a ticket?"

"Mercy, no. See that little engine and flatbed?"

She nodded and took a tighter grip on her hat. "I have a feeling . . ."

"There's always a miner's coach in the winter, but sometimes it's casual in the summer." He waited while the Finns hefted her trunk onto the flatbed, then came toward her, full of good cheer. "Hang onto your hat and keep smiling."

Della couldn't help her shriek as Juho picked her up and held her up to Heikki, already on the flatbed. He caught her as though she weighed nothing and escorted her to the center of the flatbed.

"Sit, professor," he said, with a courtly bow.

Della did as he said. She thought about the Rules for Teachers and the rule not to ride in a carriage or automobile with any man unless he was a relative. There wasn't anything about a flatbed car, so she felt inclined to overlook the matter. Della glanced at her dress hem, which modestly brushed her shoe tops. Of course, when Juho tossed her up to the flatbed, her ankles were probably exposed, along with both those petticoats the list said she should wear.

If I had a canary—maybe there's one in the mine nearing retirement age—I would line his cage with the Rules for Teachers, she thought. She smiled at the doctor, who seated himself beside her, and then at Israel, her fellow educationist, already allies.

"You look surprisingly calm about this," Israel

commented. "You should have seen the teacher who came here in July for a look around." He shook his head. "No spirit of adventure."

The train chugged through Scofield, stopping twice to let on miners, who looked her over and talked among themselves. For the most part they were dressed in black overalls, fragrant with the odor of sulfur and coal. Each man carried a round tin lunch box.

"Afternoon shift starts in half an hour," the doctor said. "I'd say not quite half of the mine crew lives in Scofield. They can buy their own homes there."

"But not in Winter Quarters?" she asked, hanging onto her hat again as they started up the slight grade toward the canyon mouth.

"Nope. That's Pleasant Valley Coal Company property," Israel chimed in. "You can build your own shack there, but it's on company land and not yours."

Della smiled when one of the miners started to sing, and the others joined in. The tune was familiar, but the language was not. She looked back toward Scofield, impressed with the sweep of the valley that stretched toward the lower rim of softly rounded hills, first in a series of mountains that made her wonder if this was what the top of the world looked like. She remembered the sheltering valley of the Molly Bee, where her father died. The thought made her swallow, but that could have been the effects of altitude.

"Papa," she murmured, her voice too low to be heard over the engine and the sweet singing, her lips barely moving. "I think I could be home."

The train slowed and stopped at the canyon mouth, close to a frame building.

"My hospital and posh digs," Dr. Isgreen announced. "Miss Anders, if you need anything, I am a mere house call away." Two of the miners helped him down.

They continued the climb into the canyon, which

narrowed almost immediately. Israel moved in front of her. "I'm not being forward," he told her, "but the grade gets steep and we'd be sadly disappointed if you sailed off the back end. I'd probably never forgive myself. Hang onto me."

Della gripped his shoulder as the truth of his words came home quickly. It touched her that at least half of the miners moved in front of her too, bracing themselves against the lip of the flatcar so there was no way she could slide off.

"I guess they want a teacher for their children," she said.

"Miss Anders, you can't fathom how much they want us here," Israel told her. "It's all about their children."

Emil was right; Winter Quarters Canyon was tight and ugly, with two- and three-room shacks marching up the canyon's inclines with no rhyme or reason to roads. The rails ran parallel to a dirt road, which edged near a stream. Any trees had been cut down long ago.

She looked around at the disorder and the ugliness, her face thoughtful. She glanced at the miners bracing themselves in front of her and realized with a jolt that they were watching her expression, wary and careful. *They're hoping I like it here. They want me to like their canyon*, she thought. The enormity of what she was about to do this school year grabbed her heart and she felt tears welling in her eyes.

Horrified, she glanced at the miner seated closest to her, who surely could see her tears. *Please, please don't let him think for one second that I don't want to be here*, she prayed in her heart.

Without a word, he handed her a handkerchief. It was snowy white, and she thought of her father, who made sure he always carried a clean handkerchief into the mine. "No telling when I might need it," he had told her. His handkerchiefs were always black with rock dust when he came out. She took the handkerchief, smiled her thanks, and dabbed at her eyes.

"Cinders, miss?" the man asked. His voice had a delightful lilt.

She nodded, hesitated, then handed back the slightly damp handkerchief. "I should probably launder it for you first," she said.

The miner shook his head. "I'm now the envy of nations," he told her, and the lilt in his voice made the statement a question. Della told herself this must be one of the Welshmen Uncle Jesse had mentioned.

The grade steepened and the little engine slowed. Della felt more at ease as the grade leveled out a little.

Israel Bowman appointed himself her tour guide, gesturing toward a building in a row of shacks pointed this way and that. "The saloon. You'll hear any number of sermons against it."

"You said this was coal company land."

"It is. The Pleasant Valley Coal Company can shut it down anytime it wants." He chuckled. "Of course, all the Finns, the Poles, and most of the Austrian miners would leave. Maybe some of the Mormons."

The train slowed even more as they passed two long, two-story buildings. With what looked like practiced ease, several miners standing by the track held out their hands and other miners on the flatbed pulled them aboard.

"That's the bunk house and one of the boarding houses," her colleague said.

The newcomers gave her the same swift once over, then seated themselves close by, everyone apparently determined that she not slide off the flatbed.

Her colleague nudged her. "That's the LDS meeting-house," he said as they passed a frame, single story building. "Sunday School at 10:00 a.m. Sacrament meeting at 2:00."

She nodded. "And that?" she asked, pointing to a stone building close to the tracks.

"Our destination. It's the Wasatch Store—company store and office for the coal company." He tapped the man next to him, the one whose handkerchief she had used. "Would you pass the word to the engineer to come to a full stop here? I'd hate to lose a certified teacher."

"Especially a pretty one," the miner said, with a wink that made Della blush.

Sure-footed, he stood up and walked toward the engine. In another minute, the train came to a stop by the loading dock, which looked so far below.

Eyes wide, Della watched as one of the miners tossed her carpetbag to someone on the dock, and the Luoma brothers handed off her trunk. Israel stood up and held out his hand for her.

"Hmm," he said, eyeing the distance from the flatbed to the loading dock. He looked at her. "Are you game?"

"I'm here," she reminded him, calculating the distance.

"Hand me your hat," Israel said. "It'll never survive this on your head."

She did as he said. He sailed it across the space and into the hands of a young man in shirtsleeves who didn't look like a miner.

"Stand right here," the teacher said. He pantomimed to a sturdy-looking miner on the dock, who took a stance and held out his hands.

"Oh, no!" Della exclaimed, as Juho Luoma picked her up and carried her to the edge of the flatbed. "This isn't a good—"

She could have saved her breath. Della closed her eyes as Juho tossed her down to the dock and the miner caught her. She grabbed him around the neck, and he made strangling noises, which made all the men on the flatbed laugh.

"Miss, I'd never drop you," he told her, setting her down as carefully as if she were her aunt's Limoges china. "If I did, Bishop Parmley would make me draw my time. Welcome to Winter Quarters."

Della took a deep breath as Israel nimbly scrambled down the flatbed to the dock. "Nothing to it," he told her.

She nodded her thanks to the miner, who took her by the elbow and moved her farther away from the edge of the loading dock. Della pointed to a frame building close to the Wasatch Store. "That's the school?"

"It is."

"Here's your hat, miss."

Della turned around to accept her hat from a young man with curly hair, a southern accent, and a shy smile.

"Clarence Nix, ma'am. I clerk here."

She held out her hand to him. "I think I teach here." Now that everyone on the loading dock had seen more than two inches above her ankles and both of her petticoats, she mentally discarded the Rules for Teachers. After stuffing in a few hairpins jarred loose, Della set her hat on her head again. Israel indicated the wooden steps up to the store and then a set of covered steps up the back of the building.

"Mr. Parmley might be here, or he might be in a mine," he said, leading the way.

Parmley's secretary, an older lady with a dignified air, smiled at her. "You're the first teacher that ever came on the flatbed," she said. "It's too late to tell you never to listen to anything Mr. Bowman suggests." She stared down Della's colleague over the top of her spectacles. "Israel Whitaker Bowman, your mother should horsewhip you."

"I'm safe. She lives in Provo," he said, not at all perturbed. "Is the bishop here?"

She gave him another look. "And where would he be at shift change? And you are *not* to take this nice young lady to the portal!"

"I've . . . I've been to portals before," Della said. "My father was a miner in Colorado."

She said it softly, as if testing the waters, remembering all the times her aunt had told her never to mention her father. "We will not talk about him," Aunt Caroline had told her when she had arrived, twelve and sad.

"I had no idea. Want to walk to the portal? I'll be careful with her, Mrs. Perkins," Israel said, as though she had suddenly turned into an even more precious commodity.

Mrs. Perkins ruffled through the paperwork on her desk and held up a telegram. "*The* Mr. Jesse Knight sent a telegram to Mr. Parmley about you," she said to Della. "You have distinguished relatives."

"Uncle Jesse is a shirttail relative, to be sure," Della explained, feeling her heart sink. "He's more my aunt's relative than mine."

"Shirttail or not, Mr. Parmley raised his eyes at that one!" the secretary exclaimed, and there was no mistaking the deference in her voice.

"Jesse Knight," Bowman said as they walked down the outside stairs. "And Karl Anders the railroad lawyer is your uncle? Miss Anders, why on earth are you *here*?"

"I want to be here," she said simply. "That's all."

Her trunk with her shabby carpetbag perched on top had been moved next to the outside wall of the building and had a sign on it: "Hands off! This is our teacher's duffle" that was written in ink but smudged with black fingerprints.

"'Our teacher?' Looks like the miners are already taking care of you," Israel said with a grin.

"I'm grateful." *Our teacher.* She had come to teach their children. She felt the magnificence of her profession settle around her. *I've learned a lot today*, Della thought as she walked with Israel and tried not to puff as the road steepened.

He must have noticed that her face was red, because he slowed down. "I forget about the altitude," he said. "Remind me or just wheeze and clutch your throat."

Della gestured to the school. "Where's my room?"

"The one on the right. I'm across the hall from you and Miss Clayson is further back," he said. "I'll take you inside tomorrow to meet her."

"Where does she live?" Della asked, trying not to wheeze as they walked steadily.

"In the basement. There's a gymnasium too and a small

kitchen for home economics, a new course for the upper-grade girls."

She wanted to comment, but she was finding it harder and harder to breathe.

Israel gave her a thoughtful look. "Della, am I pushing you too hard?"

She stopped and caught her breath, embarrassed as more miners passed them, carrying boxes of what looked like blasting powder, picks, shovels, and lunch pails and talking too. And here she was, barely breathing.

"No," she gasped. "Well, yes."

Israel stopped. "We'll wait here." He scratched his head. "Come to think of it, I doubt you'd want to take the trestle up the incline. It's a true mantrip, with miners sitting knee to knee."

"Let's not," she said. Her colleague sat her on a tree stump.

He started to say something, but a sudden roar filled the canyon. Della looked up, startled, then relaxed. She pointed up the canyon again. "The tipple?" she shouted.

Israel nodded.

She wanted to be closer, wanted to see the coal drop into the railroad cars that she could see were backed up much farther into the canyon.

"It's still slow because it's summer," Israel said, crouching down and practically talking into her ear. "In the winter, engines pulling fifty cars or more are typical."

Della nodded, her eyes on the coal dust that rose in the distance.

"Miners only work two or three days a week in summer," Israel told her. "Winter's coming. It'll be six days soon."

What on earth do they live on in the summer? Della wondered. She remembered tight times at the Molly Bee, when Papa used to cook Lumpy Dick for breakfast and supper. Early in her stay in Salt Lake City, she had tried to explain Lumpy Dick—flour, boiling milk, and raisins—to her cousins, and they only stared at her with a look of faint disgust. They would never have believed her if she had told them that sometimes it was water instead of milk, when times were really hard.

Black with coal but their teeth shining white, the miners on the early shift were making their way down the incline. Her ears hummed when the tipple's roar stopped, as though the sound had sucked all the air from the canyon. The train started inching toward them as the engine pulled forward to position another car under the tipple.

"Should we just wait for the bishop in his office?" Della asked.

The teacher's eyes were on a round little man coming toward them, carrying a black clipboard. "No need. Here he is."

Della stood up. Bishop Parmley looked cleaner than the men sauntering along on either side of him, with a watch fob stretched tight across his vest. He looked at her, a smile on his face. In another moment his hand was outstretched, enveloping hers, before he realized how dark it was with coal dust.

"I forget," he said, by way of greeting. "You're probably the tidiest thing near the trestle. Certainly the prettiest. Sister Parmley will have my hide! Sister Anders, is it?"

Della nodded, suddenly shy but wanting him to speak again, because his English accent was as delightful as his smile. "Yes, sir. I'm teaching the lower grades this year."

The bishop looked at the man next to him, who was balancing a hand-hewn stake on his shoulder taller than he was. He had obviously been in the mine, but his face was clean. "Owen, your daughter will be in her class, eh?"

"Aye, bishop. Angharad is six," he said, his voice rising on the end of the sentence, in the way that would set him off forever as a son of Wales. "She can read already, miss."

"Then she'll be ahead, Mr. . . . ."

"Owen Davis," he said, extending his hand too, after

looking at it in such a wry way that Della had to smile.

"I don't mind," she said as they shook hands. His hand-shake was as firm as his features.

"You're busy, and I'm interrupting," she said to Bishop Parmley. "Mr. Bowman wanted me to meet you."

The bishop looked at her colleague with an expression similar to Mrs. Perkins's expression in the mine office. "Mr. Bowman, the men coming on shift told me you brought this sweet person up here on the flatbed! We should have warned her about you."

Della decided that nothing perturbed Israel, not even the bishop. "Guilty as charged," he said, the picture of good cheer. He leaned closer. "Personally, I thought I'd give Miss Anders the trial by fire first, rather than wait until she got here, looked around, and turned us down. She's still here."

Israel seemed to know how to work over Bishop Parmley, because the mine superintendent started to laugh.

"And you're still a rascal," the bishop said.

"I know." Israel said it with such complaisance that Della had to look away too, amused. Maybe everyone loved a rascal.

"*Are* you staying, Miss Anders?"

Della regarded Owen Davis. She had never been one to look men of no acquaintance right in the eye, but she did because he was about her height. She saw the intense expression of the miners on the flatbed mirrored in his brown eyes. He wanted her to succeed for his daughter's sake, and she didn't even know him.

"I'm staying, Mr. Davis, provided someone can find me a place to live." *I would stay anyway,* she thought, *but you and the bishop don't need to know that.*

"Owen and I have been talking about that very subject," Bishop Parmley said. "He's my elders quorum president."

"Oh?"

"Aye, miss. I suggested to the bishop that we put the

question to the Sunday School and see what turns up," Owen Davis said. "That is, if you're not too particular."

There it was again. *Has everyone heard I am related to Utah's sharpest attorney and actually think it matters?* she asked herself, surprised. "I'm not particular."

"Then we'll manage, miss—aye, we will."

Chapter 4

Imagine that, Della thought, diverted.

"You'll be auctioned off on Sunday," Israel teased.

"Mr. Bowman, that's enough," Owen Davis said.

Della looked at him in surprise. She had a champion ready to defend her, and she didn't even know anything beyond his name and that he had a daughter who could read. She knew that Israel hadn't been fazed by Mrs. Perkins or even Bishop Parmley. There was something in the way Owen Davis bit off the words that brought him up sharp.

"Yes, sir," the teacher said, serious now, the teasing gone.

What just happened? Della wanted to ask. There wasn't any tension in the air, just the firm assertion of a man of middling height in dusty coveralls and cap with a miner's lamp. Maybe Owen Davis wasn't as fond of rascals as everyone else, or maybe he was just a man who didn't joke about women.

The storm, if there was one, blew over as quickly as it came. If Bishop Parmley was startled, he recovered quickly. Of course, maybe he knew his miners better than he knew the teachers.

"Mr. Bowman, how about you round up a carter at the store to take Sister Anders's luggage to my house." The bishop turned to her with a little bow she found as incongruous there in the middle of a dirt road as it was endearing. "My dear, you'll stay with us Parmleys tonight, for sure." He smiled at her. "We're a bit crowded, but you don't take up much space, I vow."

"Bishop, I could just as easily stay at a hotel in Scofield," she began.

Maybe he could tease too. "And risk the danger of you getting on the short line back to Colton?"

Israel tipped his hat to them all and started down the incline, hands in his pockets, strolling along, apparently unruffled by Owen Davis.

"I should apologize, Sister Anders," Owen said, when Israel was out of earshot. "I didn't mean to be sharp with him, but I don't talk about ladies that way."

She wanted him to say it all again, because Owen's lilting, rollicking pattern of speech delighted her. "Surely he meant no harm. I think he's just a bit casual."

"I'm not."

It was simply said and touched Della more than an ocean of explanation. "Owen, show her to my house, please," Parmley said. He looked at his clipboard. "Time is money. Sister Anders, we'll make it all right on Sunday."

"I hope Sister Parmley doesn't mind," she said, making one last attempt.

"After all these years, she's used to me," the bishop said simply. "Besides, we discussed the matter at breakfast." He chuckled. "We discussed the matter the day your wee house burned down!"

With a wave, he left them. Owen Davis picked up the pole as casually as if it weighed nothing and shouldered it again.

"It wasn't much of a house," he said. "I'm sure you're used to better."

"I didn't plan to become attached to it. I only signed a one-year contract."

"I was only going to work here a year and then try the mine lower down in Castle Gate. Plans change."

As they walked, she found herself laboring to keep up because she was having trouble breathing again. Owen must have noticed, because he slowed down. It embarrassed her to make him walk slower, since he carried such a heavy pole, but she already knew he wasn't a man who would leave her to find her way alone.

After a few more minutes, he stopped outside a three-sided building with other poles in it. He stashed the one he carried and took off the tool belt he wore, putting it in a lock box and securing it with a key he pulled from a chain around his neck.

When he finished, he indicated a bench. "Let's sit a minute."

She could tease too. "Did that pole wear you out? I'm glad, because I'm exhausted!"

He just smiled and leaned back against the logs. "You'll get used to the altitude. We're at about eight thousand feet here. It'll give you a headache, and you'll want to go to bed with the chickens. Give yourself a week."

She nodded. She sat in silence, then gathered that the polite man beside her was waiting for her to talk first. All she had were questions.

"Are you a miner?"

"Aye, miss."

"Then why . . ."

". . . do I carry around heavy poles? Summer is a slack time in the mines. Bishop Parmley asked me to check the timbers on all raises and levels."

"Why you?"

"I like wood almost as much as I like coal," he replied with some relish. "I replace timbers if need be, if the mine is starting to talk." Maybe he thought it was his turn for a question. "Did your da's mine talk? I'm not a hard rock miner; I wouldn't know."

"I don't think so," she said, uncertain, realizing how little she knew about the Molly Bee. "Talk?"

"I listen to wood pillars. They started to creak and groan when the ceiling shifts—the mine is talking. Back home in the colliery, we called them *bwca*, those evil spirits that tease miners, or sometimes warn miners before a collapse." He shrugged. "Most of us leave a bit of lunch behind for the *bwca*, so they'll keep talking."

"Booca?" she asked.

"Sprites or brownies or evil genies, whatever you will."

He must have noticed her skepticism. "You don't believe me, Sister Anders? Wise of you! Up you get. We'll go slow, and I want to stop for Angharad at the Evanses' house."

They walked slowly. The coal from the tipple was filling another railcar, so conversation was out of the question. She looked at the tiny shacks, almost random in their location, that clung to steep canyon sides.

Worn out even with slow walking, Della could have dropped down in relief when they stopped before a slightly larger shack, dark gray with coal dust like all the others. Stunted by a combination of altitude, poor soil, and short growing seasons, the zinnias by the door looked as exhausted as she felt.

Timbered steps were cut in the slope, which Owen went up quickly. He held out his hand to her. Della shook her head. "Go on and save yourself," she joked. He continued up the slope without apparently drawing a difficult breath. He wasn't a big man, but he was a strong one.

He came out a few minutes later with his daughter, who wore a simple dress and checked pinafore, her hair in neat braids. *Sister Davis is not one for frills*, Della thought as she watched Owen, his hand on the child's shoulder. *I wonder which one of them taught her to read.*

The steps were steep, so he picked his daughter up and carried her down. Della smiled to see the way her arms seemed to go around his neck so naturally.

"Angharad, this is your teacher, Miss Anders," he said as he set his daughter on her feet. "Give a wee curtsy?"

To Della's delight, Angharad did, dimpling up and then putting both hands in Della's one hand. She spoke to her father in Welsh, and the wrinkles around his eyes crinkled in good humor.

"In English, my dearest," he advised, nothing in his voice of criticism. "Remember now. In school it's English."

"Pleased to meet you," Angharad said, her accent as pleasant as her father's. She looked back at him. "Is that right, Da?"

He nodded.

"I'm pleased to meet you," Della said in turn. "Your father tells me you can read."

Shy then, Angharad nodded and leaned against her father's leg.

Charmed, Della could almost see the gears turning in the girl's head and knew she wanted to speak Welsh. Manners warred with curiosity, and curiosity appeared to win because she gestured her father to lean down and she whispered to him.

"I don't know, dearest," he said in English. "Shall I ask?"

Angharad nodded.

It was Owen's turn to hesitate.

"It can't be anything I couldn't answer," Della prompted. "I *do* know six-year-olds."

He took a deep breath, and she was reminded again of what a gentleman stood before her, even if he was in coveralls and that miner's cap. "She's never seen someone who looks quite like you. She wants to know, are you a *tywysoges*, a princess?"

Della laughed and clapped her hands, which sent Angharad retreating halfway behind her father. "Oh, my dear, you have more than made up for the fact that my house burned down and I can barely breathe!" she said, then slowly held out her hand for the child, who came forward again, cautious but interested. "I'm no princess, but my mother was Greek, and ladies from Greece have black, curly hair and lots of it, and noses that I choose to call elegant. I'm nobody special, Angharad. Just your teacher."

And at this moment, I wouldn't be anything else, she thought, moved in a way she hadn't imagined, when she

39

set out that morning to teach school in Winter Quarters.

"Is it hard to brush?"

You are so practical, Della thought, charmed. "Yes! My father said I used to cry when he tried to brush it. I'll tell you a secret. I put a little olive oil on it after I wash my hair and that helps with tangles. Only a little, though." She laughed. "Too much, and I might slide right off my pillow onto the floor!"

Angharad's eyes got wide, and she laughed. "That's silly."

"Only a little silly. Be grateful for straight hair, Angharad."

"I know I am," Owen said to his daughter. "We'd be hours working over your hair, and I'd be late to the pit."

Angharad nodded, apparently satisfied. She took her father's hand and walked between them.

"Which of you taught her to read English?" Della asked Owen.

"Which of us?"

"You or your wife?"

"I did. Gwyna died when Angharad was born. She was our only child." He said it in a matter-of-fact way that asked for no pity. "As I said, plans change."

"I'm sorry," she said quietly. "Does Angharad stay with the Evans family while you work?"

He nodded. "Richard and Martha Evans. It works out well enough." He gestured toward his daughter. "I'm talented enough for braids. If Angharad had curls like yours, I'd probably be committed to an asylum."

Della laughed out loud, then found herself stopping for a breath. "Don't be so funny," she said, when she could speak. "I can't breathe!"

"I'm surprising myself," he said in turn.

They walked along slowly. The train moved farther toward the valley below as more coal rumbled into the cars.

"What's for supper, Da?" Angharad asked.

"Probably oats in some form or other," he replied, coloring a little. "Sister Anders, we're at the end of a summer, and miners don't have much work in the summer. So it's oats."

"Believe it or not, I remember lean days in the mines," Della said, thinking of endless Lumpy Dick.

She could tell by his expression that he didn't believe her. She began to wonder how quickly news of that telegram from Jesse Knight had traveled up and down the canyon. *Wait*, she wanted to tell him. *You're getting the wrong idea.*

"At least you can work with the timber for the mine."

"I don't get paid for timber work."

"Really? I would think . . . well, I don't know what I would think," Della confessed.

"We don't *work* for Pleasant Valley Coal Company," Owen explained. "We're independent contractors. We supply so many tons of coal a day and that's all we're paid for. I don't mind timber work. When the mine talks, I listen, and the men I work with are happy about that."

"I would be too," she said. She opened her mouth to speak, then closed it again. She was asking too many questions.

He was watching her, though, which she found surprisingly flattering. In all her years at the Anders house, no one had paid her much attention.

"Are you wondering how we stay alive during the summer?" he asked, the humor evident in his voice, as though he could turn it into a pleasant topic.

"A little."

"The company store keeps a tab on miner expenses, and mostly we pay it off in the winter." He stopped and faced her. "Understand one thing: We don't feel sorry for ourselves and require no pity."

He said it in that same tone of voice he had used on Israel Bowman, firm and matter-of-fact but in no way aggressive. That kind of honesty required the same in return.

"Brother Davis, I could never feel sorry for someone lucky enough to have Angharad for a daughter."

His eyes softened at her words, and he started walking again. "Gwyna named her before she died. *Angharad* means 'much beloved one.' And so she is."

He had changed the subject so adroitly that Della didn't have a moment to feel embarrassed. She wanted to tell him she felt no pity because it was becoming obvious to her, the longer she walked beside the Davis family, that they were far luckier in each other than she had ever been in her relatives.

"I do work with wood in a more refined manner than just propping up a mine ceiling," Owen said. "And now you're supposed to ask, 'What is it you do, Brother Davis?'"

Della laughed out loud. "Very well, sir! What *do* you do, when summer is lean?"

Owen looked at his daughter and gave her hand a tug so she stopped. "Angharad, should we show your teacher what else I do to put jam on our oatcakes?" He whispered something in her ear. "Show her. I'll wait."

Della looked at him, a question in her eyes, but the child was tugging Della toward another of the many small shacks around them. "Where are we . . . ?"

There weren't any zinnias, weary or otherwise, in front of this house, but there was an elaborately carved name over the ordinary door. "'D-a-v-y-s,'" she said. "Lovely."

Angharad opened the door. Della looked back, uncertain, but Owen gestured her inside from where he stood on the road. She was struck again with what a gentleman he was, not coming into his own home because she was a single woman.

She found herself in the front room with a simple settee, table, and two chairs, surely made by the man who stood in the road. On the table were two hinged boxes, one elaborately carved with fantastic creatures and the other partly done, the carving knife close by.

"My goodness," Della said. "Your father is a master."

The child nodded. "Come in my room."

Della followed her, then backed away. The other room was obviously Owen Davis's, with a bed, gorgeous carved chest, and a Book of Mormon lying open on the pillow. "I shouldn't," she said, but Angharad had her hand and tugged her beyond the small room to another even smaller room that might have been a storeroom at one time.

Owen Davis had made it into his daughter's bedroom, with a carved bed, smaller chest, and the most beautiful dollhouse Della had ever seen. She couldn't help herself. She knelt and gazed in admiration at the wonder before her. This was a dollhouse for a . . . she couldn't remember the Welsh word for princess, much less pronounce it, but it belonged to a princess.

"Angharad, I have never seen anything so lovely in my life," she said. "Do all the little girls in Winter Quarters want to play here?"

She nodded. "Da tells me I am worth one hundred of these."

It was said quietly and with love. Della got up, surprising herself with her reluctance to leave the room. *I am twenty-four, and I want to play.*

Della let Angharad lead her out of the house and back to the road, where Owen still waited. "My goodness," was all she could say.

"I have a market for the carved boxes," he said. "We don't always eat oatcakes. We have a miner in Number Four here from Tennessee, and he told me about sorghum molasses. I traded a box for five gallons of molasses."

"That dollhouse!" she exclaimed. "I wanted to play."

"Well, I probably can't invite you over," he said, which made her smile. "I will say—when you go to your classroom, you'll see a lot of carved letters. I made those last year because I knew Angharad would be in school this year. You can make all kinds of words. If you need more, just let me know." He gestured down the road. "Time's passing. Angharad, take us to the bishop's house."

The child darted ahead. "I hope I can run like that again," Della said. "You say it takes about a week to get adjusted to the altitude?"

"About."

They passed the school. Della looked at the building. "Mr. Bowman said my classroom is the one on the right," she said. She looked at the classroom on the left, where a woman stood. "Is that Miss Clayson?"

"Aye," he said. "Want to go in?" The building looked new, with a stone foundation and wood siding. She turned the handle, but the door was locked. She knocked on the double door. She waited for someone to open the door, but no one did. She knocked again, then looked back at Owen Davis, a question in her eyes.

"I think she is a complicated woman," he said, after some thought.

"But she's my principal." She looked up again. No one was there. "Maybe I'll see her at church."

He shook his head. "I've never seen her there, and no one calls her Sister Clayson." He pointed to the two-story house behind the church. "The Parmleys."

And you have changed the subject again, she thought, as she followed his lead.

"You are slow," Angharad told her father. "I have been waiting *so* long to ring the doorbell."

"It's the only doorbell in town," Owen whispered to Della. "By all means. Ring that doorbell."

Della smiled to hear a thunder of feet coming toward the door. "Sounds like a houseful."

"Aye. From Maria to William, it is that, but William isn't walking yet. Stand back a little. That's safer."

Her eyes lively, a girl opened the door, clapped her hands and pulled in Angharad. "Brother Davis, let her stay because she is *essential* to our plans."

"Mary is the dramatic one," Owen said as the girl tugged his daughter toward the stairs. "Ten minutes only, now."

"A Mary and a Maria?" Della asked.

"Winter Quarters is full of Marys and Marias, and Margarads and Marians. And here is She Who Remains Calm. Sister Parmley, let me introduce our homeless teacher, Miss Anders."

Della found both of her hands in Sister Parmley's grasp, no mean feat, because the woman was carrying someone who must be William, tucked against her hip.

"Sister Anders, you're a welcome sight!" Sister Parmley said, pulling Della into the house in much the way her daughter had tugged Angharad upstairs.

"I hate to trouble you," Della began, but Sister Parmley interrupted her with a laugh.

"What's one more person in this menagerie?" she asked. "Thank you for steering her here, Owen. Her luggage is already upstairs."

"Well, then, I believe I will leave you ladies. Just send Angharad home in ten minutes, even if Mary, the dramatic one, droops and dies on the doorstep."

"Oh, you! I will."

Owen started to close the door, but Della opened it again, following him onto the porch.

"Thank you, Brother Davis," she said. "You've been a help. I'm interested in seeing your carved alphabet tomorrow, provided Mrs. Clayson lets me in."

She couldn't have said why, precisely, but Della didn't want him to go. "One more thing, sir: my Uncle Jesse told me I might want to join the ward choir. He said every choir needs contraltos, maybe even the one here."

"You'll be welcome, I'm sure. Richard Evans—where my daughter stays—is the conductor."

"Will I . . . will I see you tomorrow?"

"Not likely. I'm in Number Four tomorrow. See you Sunday. You can tell me what you think of the choir."

Chapter 5

If Della was prepared to feel shy around the Parmleys, the feeling lasted only as long as it took for Sister Parmley to sit her down in the kitchen and put a bowl of beans in front of her to string and snap.

"I'm certain you never did this in the Anders house, but I could use the help," the bishop's wife said.

"I've snapped many a bean," Della said. "I spent one summer after school was out, cooking in a camp where the men were laying telephone lines. Mostly I washed dishes."

There was no disguising Sister Parmley's amazement. "But your uncle . . . and word has got around about a telegram from Jesse Knight himself! Why would you be a kitchen flunky?"

Della paused mid-snap. "Word travels pretty rapidly here."

"It's a small canyon," Sister Parmley said. "I believe Mrs. Perkins in my husband's office has some sort of *bwca* of her own to speed news around." She touched Della's hand. "Even the wealthiest of men are wise, who keep their dear ones grounded in honest toil."

If you only knew, Della thought. "I do hope people don't think I am something I am not. All I want to do is teach here this year."

"That is all that matters," Sister Parmley said. She set William in his highchair and turned her attention to the stew on the range top. "Mrs. Perkins was right about one thing. May I call you Della?"

"Certainly."

"She said she'd never seen anyone here who looks like you."

Della laughed out loud. "I intend to take that news however I want!"

"She came here, her eyes wide, and told me, 'The new teacher is *exotic*.'" Sister Parmley put a handful of the raw beans on the highchair tray, and William chortled.

Della tickled him, and he laughed some more. "I don't look like a single Anders because my mother was Greek." She decided to take a page from Owen Davis's book and turn the subject. "Tell me, what nationalities are in this canyon? I've met the Welsh. You and your husband sound quite English, and someone named Heikki Luoma and his brother Juho tossed my trunk around like it was a bandbox. What handsome men."

Sister Parmley started on the beans too. "Thomas and I are both English, but we met here. His brother William and Mary—she's Welsh—live next door with their brood. William is foreman in Number Four. It's our newest mine and the best one. Andrew Hood is close by with his own menagerie. He is from Scotland, and Rachel is from Wales. The Muhlsteins are Swiss, I believe. There's a Frenchman or two. No Greeks yet. South in the canyon is Finn Town. I can't pronounce their names, but their wives make the best Christmas cookies."

"Are they all church members?"

"Mostly the English, Scots, and Welsh are. You'll find this interesting: Everyone attends our church parties. That's how I know about the Finns' Christmas cookies." Della saw the quiet pride in her eyes. "We're a family here. We rejoice in each other's successes and cry at everyone's sorrows. My Thomas works hard to make it so."

Della nodded and worked in silence, thinking of the Molly Bee and the generous women there who raised her when her father was in the mine. *We all ate Lumpy Dick when times were lean and oyster stew from cans when times were better*, she reminded herself. She stopped snapping, struck again by her similarity to Angharad.

"Brother Davis is raising Angharad by himself?" she asked.

"He is. You might want to call him Brother Owen; we do. There are so many Davises here," Sister Parmley said. "Gwyna died when Angharad was born." Her eyes filled with tears at the memory. "'Tis sad to see a man stand at an open grave, holding a wee infant in his arms. He's a good father, though."

"Angharad showed me her dollhouse, and I saw carved boxes on their table," Della said. "Why doesn't he just come out of the pit and work with wood? It has to be better than mining coal."

The other woman put her hand over Della's, pressing down, and her voice was firm. "Sister Anders, learn something that will keep you out of trouble in Winter Quarters: coal mining is not something a man does when he can do nothing else."

"I didn't mean to imply . . . "

The pressure increased. "These men are proud that they daily face the challenge of the pits. Please *never* pity them or us and you will do well here."

Della absorbed the gentle rebuke. "I'm sorry," she murmured, her eyes on the bowl of beans. "It's hard here, isn't it?"

"Very." The word was softly spoken. Sister Parmley touched Della's chin and lifted it so they were eye to eye again. "I never met better people; neither will you. Lesson learned?"

"Yes."

Sister Parley got up. "Good. When you finished those beans, there's a pan on the stove for them. William is drooping. If I put him down for a nap right now—I'll rue it later when he's up all hours tonight—we might have a fighting chance to get supper on the table when my Thomas comes home."

My Thomas. The words were almost a caress. Della continued snapping beans. She tried to think of a single time she had heard Aunt Caroline say Uncle Karl's name that way and came up dry.

Dinner was on time. Everyone sat cheek to jowl around the table, the talk lively. William, resuscitated now, banged on his highchair tray with his spoon, reminding his oldest sister to supply more bread. Without being asked, Della took her turn refilling the bowl of potatoes and beans. Shy at first, but with growing confidence, she told the Parmleys about her two years teaching on Salt Lake's west side, and her own experience with children of immigrants.

"Sister Anders, you might be asked to take some of the Finnish women into your classroom," the bishop said.

"What do these Finnish ladies do in the classroom?" Della asked.

"I believe they mostly listen and absorb what they can of English and the rudiments of writing."

"Mrs. Clayson allows that?"

He nodded. "She leaves it up to the teacher. I hope you are willing."

"I am. I expect they are also useful in keeping order."

"You'll have no trouble with order. I'll guarantee that one or two words to a father or mother will result in cherubs in the classroom. No one here jokes about education."

She told them about sitting on the flatbed that afternoon and watching the faces of the miners when Israel Bowman announced she was a teacher.

"*You* got to ride the flatbed?" Joseph, one of the sons, asked, obviously hearing only that part of her narrative. His eyes widened in amazement.

"I did. Was I privileged?" Della teased in turn. "Mostly I didn't have a choice."

Joseph glanced at his parents with a wounded look. "I

tried to ride the flatbed and it was bread and water in my room for one whole day. I nearly starved."

Della turned away to cover her smile with her napkin. "Joseph, two Finnish men even tossed me onto the flatbed! I suppose I should have bread and water in my room too."

Everyone laughed, even William, who looked around at his family, pleased to be in on the joke.

"No. You're way too old for bread and water," Joseph replied when the laughter died down, only to cause it to rise again. Sister Parmley laughed so hard she had to dab at her eyes.

"Children! She'll abandon us if we keep this up," the bishop's wife said. "Thomas, what plans have you for Sister Anders that don't involve bread and water?"

After a lingering look at the roast beef, the bishop pushed away from the table. "I'll make an announcement in church, inviting someone to take her in. Sister Anders, you would agree to pay room and board somewhere?"

"Most certainly."

"I've already made some inquiries among my flock. We'll find you a suitable place." He looked around the table, satisfaction large on his face. "I fear you'll be coming down a peg or two in the world, no matter what we find, but if the Finns and the flatbed didn't frighten you away, you'll rub along pretty well here."

"Bishop, I'm not coming down a peg," she assured him. She could tell by the look in his eyes that he didn't believe her, but everyone was up then and clearing away the dishes. Maybe there would be time later to acquaint him with her actual circumstances.

"Be sure of one thing, Sister Anders," he said, taking her hand. "You're welcome in Winter Quarters. It's a narrow canyon, but there is room for all."

She carried that thought with her through kitchen cleanup with Maria and Mary, shy at first, but laughing and telling her about the school by the time the last dish was put away and the dish towels draped on chairs to dry. By the time they finished, Della was so tired that she wanted to put her head on her arms and just rest at the kitchen table.

Maria and Mary wouldn't hear of it, so she spent the evening with them in the parlor, playing Chinese checkers while the bishop read the newspaper and Sister Parmley rocked William to sleep. Della wanted nothing more than to crawl into bed, but she had no idea where she was to sleep.

Bishop Parmley finally laid down his newspaper and took a good look at her.

"Mary Ann, we're remiss," he said. "Our guest probably rose with the chickens this morning to get here. She's about to dive face-first into the marbles."

Della laughed but did not disagree. "Brother Davis—Brother Owen—said the altitude would get me for a while."

"He's right," Parmley said. He held up his hand. "Let's let Mama get William down, and then we'll have family prayer. Join us, Sister Anders?"

"Certainly," she said, trying to remember the last time the Anderses had gathered together for family prayer. Her uncle had remarked to her once that family prayer was something he always intended to do.

Sister Parmley was back in a few minutes. "We kneel together," she told Della, as her husband helped her down.

Della joined the girls and their brother Joseph. The bishop prayed for his family, his congregation, and the mines, mentioning people by name—people she didn't know yet but probably would as they took on form and became part of her life.

"And bless us to find a good situation for Sister Anders, who has come to teach," he concluded. "Touch some family to open their home to her."

Della added her whispered amen when he finished. He put on his coat again and took the lantern Sister Parmley handed him. He gestured to Della. "Come outside a moment, if you will."

Della followed him onto the porch, where he stood watching the glimmering lights up and down the canyon.

"I hold their lives and spirits in my hands," he said. There was nothing of pride in the statement. All she heard was a certain wonder that humbled her. "I've been superintendent here since 1885, and bishop since 1889. I'm your bishop now. If you need me, I am here."

He spoke so simply. *All the people in this canyon are his responsibility, one way or another,* Della thought, wondering that one man could be both and so calm. "I appreciate that," she said. "I'll do my best."

"I thought you would. Sister Anders, my father died when I was six years old, and I went into the colliery in England when I was ten. I know my business, and I only contract men to work here who know their business too. No fears now. Good night."

He shook her hand again, then went down the steps slowly. Della watched as he walked toward the Wasatch Store. Soon all she could see was the winking light. The door opened, and Sister Parmley came onto the porch.

"What is he doing?" Della asked.

"Summer and winter, he walks the canyon with his lantern. Sometimes members ask him in for a prayer or a word of advice. Sometimes he checks on the horses in the barn. He even visits the Finns, although none of them are members." Sister Parmley's voice was soft, her love powerfully evident. She put her hand on Della's shoulder. "I asked him once how he bears such responsibility. He just kissed my cheek."

She gave Della a little shake. "If you don't get to bed soon, you'll drop in your tracks!"

"I'm tougher than that," Della told her, thinking how puny she was to feel so exhausted, when everyone in this canyon probably worked harder than she ever would.

"You'll have to share a bed with Mary, but she's small, so it won't be a tight squeeze," Sister Parmley said, all business again as she crooked her arm through Della's and led her into the house again. It touched Della to see her linger a moment at the door, looking out. *The bishop is short, overweight, and smells of coal, and she loves him*, Della thought, as though the warmth of Sister Parmley's love sheltered her too.

She took Della upstairs, regarding her as though she wanted to say something. "It's nothing, really. I've just never seen Brother Davis smile like that, when he ushered you inside the house. Good night now."

Della slept until the sunlight glanced across her pillow. As she listened, she heard the rumble of coal into railcars. She thought of the small shacks closer to the tipple and wondered if it were possible to blank out the sound. She thought of her first year in the elementary school on the west side of Salt Lake, so close to the rail yards and the smelters, where housing was cheap and immigrants settled. By the time school was out for the summer, she paid the noise no mind. By the time May came here, she doubted she would give the tipple a second thought.

Mentally she reviewed the contents of her trunk, taking an inventory of her shirtwaists and skirts and long underwear. Her cousins had snickered to see her practical clothing as they packed their own trunks for Europe. She hoped her winter coat would be warm enough, considering the chill in the room. Maybe next year, if she felt adventurous enough, she could find a school in southern Arizona that needed a teacher.

She dressed at her leisure, wishing she hadn't been too tired last night to tame her hair into braids. As it was, she could barely drag her big-toothed comb through her curls. "My hair is the curse of the earth," she muttered, not for the first time.

She remembered the little tintype of her mother that Papa used to put up in every shack they lived in. Aunt Caroline had been aghast when she put it up in her room in the Anderses' house. "That must go," Aunt Caroline had said. Dutiful, Della had tucked it away, hiding it in the lining of her shabby carpetbag.

There it had remained for twelve years. Della took it out now and held it up to the daylight. She looked at Olympia's high arched nose, her full lips, and the way her deep-set eyes and heavy lids gave her a sleepy look. Della looked closer at Olympia's ever-so-slightly tilted eyes, a reminder that Greece wasn't all that far from Turkey. She held the tintype up to the mirror, looking at herself and her mother, as close as they would ever be.

But this was not getting her dressed and downstairs. She put away the tintype and hurried into her clothes. She was downstairs five minutes later, sniffing the fragrance of pancakes and molasses.

"Saturday is pancakes," Sister Parmley said, as she presided over the griddle on the range top. She handed Della the pancake turner. "You're in charge. I'll round up the Parmleys."

"The bishop too?"

"He never misses pancakes." Sister Parmley laughed. "Even though maybe he should!"

Everyone was seated and eating when the bishop came into the dining room, smelling of coal. He rubbed his hands together. "Mary Ann, you are a continual wonder!" he exclaimed, loud enough for his wife to hear him from the kitchen.

"He says that every Saturday," Maria whispered to Della and giggled.

"I stopped by the schoolhouse on my way back," the bishop said after prayers as the pancakes went around. "Mrs. Clayson said you may come over anytime." He reached in his pocket. "Here is a key to the school."

She accepted it. "I've never had a key to a school before. I guess my principal on the west side never trusted us enough. Do I need one?"

"She thinks you might." The bishop buttered his pancakes and gestured for the syrup. "Joseph, you're drowning those!" He poured his own syrup and handed it to Della. "The miners are calling you Helen of Troy."

"Oh, heavens!"

"Apparently the miners on the flatbed overheard that scamp Israel Bowman call you that yesterday," Parmley said. "It may become your cross to bear. At least, that's what Owen Davis told me this morning when he went into the pit." He shoveled up a forkful of pancake and eyed it. "Sister Anders, there's not a secret anywhere in Winter Quarters. Get used to it."

Maria and Mary were her willing escorts to the schoolhouse after breakfast and dishes. Each one carried a sack of supplies and bulletin board trim as they walked past the Wasatch Store, escorted by the bishop, and then to the school just beyond.

"I've never been in here when school wasn't on," Mary said as they climbed the steps and Della took out her key. She leaned close and lowered her voice. "When I was a little girl, I thought all the teachers lived here and slept in the basement."

"You're *still* a little girl," her twelve-year-old sister said, her voice no louder. "Only Miss Clayson lives in the basement."

"It's haunted," Mary said.

"Silly, it's only three years old," the more practical Maria replied, her tone weary in that way of big sisters explaining the world to little sisters. "A building has to be at least . . . at least twenty years old to be haunted. Isn't that right, Sister Anders?"

"I'm not sure any buildings are haunted," Della said, amused. "And look, the door is open today. Shall we?"

They went inside, and Della breathed deep of the chalk dust and scent of oiled floors that seemed to shout "school."

"Isra . . . I mean, Mr. Bowman said my room was the one on the right."

"No children in the building until September!"

Della stopped, her hand on the doorknob to her classroom. Mary and Maria crowded close to her. She blinked her eyes to accustom them to the gloom. Miss Clayson stood there, silhouetted against the light, her features not visible. Mary whimpered and crowded closer. Della patted her shoulder.

"Miss Clayson? I'm Della Anders, your new teacher," she said, holding out her hand.

"These children must go."

Do you want to frighten them off school before it even starts? Della wanted to ask, but had the good sense not to. "I enlisted them to help me carry school supplies, Miss Clayson. Thank you, girls. You may go now."

Without a word, Mary and Maria piled her bag and parcels by her classroom door and fled the building. Della resisted the urge to follow.

"September fifth and not a day sooner!" Miss Clayson called after them. When the outside door closed, she turned to Della. "You are Miss Anders only. No need for the children to know your other name."

"It was unavoidable," Della told her. "I'm staying with the Parmleys right now and . . ." She stopped. "Yes, ma'am."

"That's better. Let me help you." Miss Clayson opened the door while Della picked up her parcels. The principal stalked into the room, looking from side to side, almost as though she expected to see some leftover children from May, when school adjourned.

Della set the parcels down on what must be her desk at the head of the room, conscious of the woman's eyes on her, looking her up and down.

"That simply will not do," she said at last.

"Wh . . . what won't do?" Della asked, when she found her tongue again, the one the cat had snatched.

"Your hair is an absolute disgrace."

Della stared at her. She touched her hair, which she had subdued into what she thought was a tidy bun, at least, tidy for her hair. "I don't know what I can do about it, Miss Clayson. It's my hair!"

"Think of something."

Chapter 6

❧

*D*ella gulped, hoping the sound wasn't audible.

"And while you're thinking of something, Miss Anders, tell me what on earth possessed you to ride the flatbed into Winter Quarters yesterday?"

"Israel Bow . . ."

". . . is a scoundrel. I have no idea why the school district, in its infinite wisdom, afflicts me with teachers like Mr. Bowman. And now you." She pointed her finger at Della. "If I ever hear of you riding the flatbed again . . ." She paused. Her eyes narrowed. "That dress will never do."

Dismayed, Della looked down at her dress. It had seemed like a good idea to put on one of the two old dresses she brought along, because she knew she probably would be cleaning and sweeping today. She opened her mouth to say that, then closed it again. She felt that familiar feeling in the pit of her stomach, the one she had endured for twelve years, living in the same house with her Aunt Caroline. *Nothing I say will make any difference*, she thought, wondering how soon she could leave Winter Quarters.

Miss Clayson was saying something else, but it wasn't registering because suddenly Della remembered the look in the miners' eyes when they knew she was going to teach their children. She thought of Owen Davis and all the letters he had carved. Heaven knows how long it had taken him, and she was going to surrender so soon?

No, I'm not, she thought. *I wouldn't dare and call myself a miner's daughter, because that is what I am.* For the first time in her life, that thought gave her strength instead of shame.

"Miss Clayson, I wore this old dress because I plan to clean my classroom today," Della said, riding over the principal's ongoing critique, even as she cringed to be so rude. "I have shirtwaists and dark skirts that all end about two inches above the floor. My hair is my hair and I do my best. Excuse me now; I have work to do."

Silence seemed to hum in the air. Della heard the tipple roar in the distance. *I'm doing this for you, Papa*, she told herself as she looked Miss Clayson in the eye. "Let us begin again," she said, her voice firm. "I am Miss Anders from Salt Lake City, and I have been hired by the district to teach the younger grades in the Winter Quarters School. I have two years' experience, and I am a good teacher."

"We shall see about that," Miss Clayson said, but the bluster was gone. "You'll find a mop and broom in the hall closet. Good day now." She turned on her heel and left the room.

Before she closed the door, Miss Clayson turned back, drawing herself up tall. "Do bear this in mind, Miss Anders—there will be no fancy airs in my school. I do not care who your uncle is." She closed the door with a decisive click.

Della dug her toes into the soles of her shoes to keep from running to the door to see if she was locked in. *I am being absurd*, she told herself.

Della sank into the nearest chair. She had never spoken like that to anyone in her life. And there it was again, coming to haunt her. She rested her elbows on the desk, chin in hand. "It appears I am never going to be free of you, Uncle Karl, no matter how hard I try," she murmured into her hands. "I just want to be Della Anders."

She sat in silence, wondering what had just happened, and wondering if the woman had a good side. *Was there something I was supposed to say and do, and I didn't?* she asked herself, bewildered. She would have to ask Israel Bowman.

Della took a deep breath and looked around her class-room. Gradually, the calm and order in the empty room crowded out the distress of her first encounter with her principal. She looked toward the front of the room with its blackboard and the usual portrait of George Washington above it. There was an American flag in the corner and a Regulator clock ticking next to George. If Owen Davis was right, somewhere in the room were hand-carved alphabet letters. She stood up, straightened her dress, and walked to the front of the class, counting the desks—twenty-five desks, five to a row. In another week there would be pupils in here, some of them eager, some of them reluctant, and maybe some knowing no English. It would be a class much like the one she had taught on Salt Lake's west side.

She glanced out the windows. Three windows. She had enough construction paper to make autumn leaves for the windows. She would make a few and her students would make more, following her lead because she was their teacher and meant to give them her knowledge, her skill, and her heart. So what if there was a gargoyle living in the basement? Della had signed her contract and she would teach.

Decisive now, she went to the cabinets on the inte-rior wall, opening one after the other to see books in neat rows. Her heart slowed to its normal rhythm as she read the familiar spines and felt her confidence returning—*American Speller*; *McGuffey's Eclectic Reader Grades One through Three*; *Our Amazing World*; *Arithmetic for Elementary Grades*. She reached further into the cabinet and pulled out a poster that made her eyes widen. "'Black powder and blasting caps are dangerous! Do not touch!'" she murmured out loud. An attached note read, "Display in all classrooms in Carbon County, by order of Gomer Thomas, Utah Inspector of Mines."

Very well, she told herself. *These will be the first words we learn.*

She looked in the top drawer of her desk, found a thumbtack, and tacked the poster to the cork board next to the blackboard. "Miss Clayson is dangerous!" she whispered and chuckled. "Avoid at all costs!"

She opened another cabinet and sighed out loud. "My stars, you are a wonder, Brother Davis," she said. He must have built the boxes too. A smile on her face, Della lifted out seven wooden boxes, each with four compartments, and set them on an empty table by the cabinets. Each compartment was divided in half, with lowercase and uppercase letters carved simply. She held one up. It would be easy to see from any place in the room.

She looked closer, enchanted to see a tiny carved lion on each piece. She had noticed the lion on the carving over his door, along with flowers. *Who has this kind of patience?* she asked herself as she touched the letters.

Della looked in the cabinet again and pulled out a flat board, sanded and painted white, with wooden pegs in even rows. "You thought of everything, Owen Davis," she said as she propped the board on the blackboard trough. It would be an easy matter to put up the alphabet for learning, and then simple sentences and more complex ones later on. This was an elementary teacher's dream come true, all from a Welsh coal miner who loved wood.

She had come into the school with a light heart, until Miss Clayson scared away her helpers and bruised her ego. As she looked at the letters, the bruise faded. Humming to herself, Della found the letters for her name and attached them to the board: Della Anders. She started to go to the back of the room to see the effect, then stopped, returning to the board and moving her last name down several pegs. She found the letters for Olympia and attached them underneath Della, then went to the back of the room.

Perfect. "Della Olympia Anders," she said.

She left the letters on the board and went in search of the broom and mop. There was a pump out back, so she filled the pail in the closet and carried it inside, pouring in some of the industrial powders that every schoolhouse in Utah probably had in its custodial closet. The familiar scent soothed her heart even more. By the time the floor was mopped, her heart was entirely right again.

Chin in hand, she perched herself on a desk in the back row while the floor dried. The room was warm with sunshine. She could clean the windows on Monday and maybe give the books a good dusting. There would be bulletin boards to do, lessons to plan. Maybe if she worked up her nerve, she could ask Miss Clayson if there was a roster of her students, so she could visit them. Probably Sister Parmley and the bishop would know everyone; it might be safer to ask them.

She went to the front of the room again and pulled down the maps, one by one, looking out the window to see miners moving along the one road through Winter Quarters. Maybe it was shift change. She listened for the roar of coal in the tipple and wondered how distracting that would be for her students.

Della returned her attention to the maps, looking at Europe the longest. Aunt Caroline had said they would sail to Southampton and then spend a week in London, followed by a night crossing from Dover to Calais. Paris in late summer was next, followed by the Cote d'Azur, Monte Carlo, and then Rome and Florence. Her hand went to the islands of Greece. She wondered just where it was her mother had come from.

She heard the door open and froze, hoping it wasn't Miss Clayson come to ruin her daydream.

"I couldn't figure out how to attach periods and commas. They were too small for my drill bit and pegs."

Della turned around with a smile. Owen Davis stood in the doorway, his hands clean but every other part of him black with coal. He set down his round lunch box and moved down the aisle, appraising the letters on the board.

"Olympia. What a magnificent name," he said. "Olympia. That's a name to dust off and use, every chance you get. Even better than Helen of Troy. Olympia. A name fit for the gods. And goddesses."

"My father called me Oly, now and then," Della said, suddenly shy. She blushed and changed the subject. "If you could carve some commas and periods, I think I could glue them to thumbtacks."

Owen smacked his head and the coal dust flew. "Of course! Consider it done."

"You're a patient man," she said. "It must have taken forever to carve all those tiny lions."

"Dragons," he corrected. "*Y Draig Goch.* On my national flag—at least, when the English aren't looking."

"Of course," she said, smiling. "I have a lot to learn. You did this for Angharad, didn't you?"

"Of course," he echoed. "She told me last year that she might be afraid going to school and not being with me or with Richard and Martha Evans. We are all she knows. I want her to look at these letters when I am not with her and realize she is not alone." It was his turn to look shy now. She could see it through all the coal dust, and it touched her.

"I beg your pardon!"

Startled, Della turned around to see Miss Clayson. What happened next surprised her even more. Owen took a step and stood between her and the principal. With desks on either side of him, there was no way Miss Clayson could reach her, even though Della knew that was not her intent. He had acted out of instinct, and it warmed Della's heart.

"You're making a mess in this classroom. I insist you leave at once. Now!"

Secure behind Owen, Della listened for some hesitancy from the principal, and there it was. Miss Clayson must have felt Owen Davis's instinctive protection too.

"I just wanted to see how Sister Anders was doing,"

Owen said, moving aside and toward the door, which made Miss Clayson back up.

Maybe he didn't say it with enough deference. "What is your name?" the principal demanded, even as she backed up. "Mr. Parmley will hear from me!"

"Lloyd Llewellen," Owen said promptly, which made Della turn around and dig deep to keep from laughing out loud. "Good day, ladies."

Miss Clayson glared at her. "You would do well to stay away from the miners," she said.

"Yes, ma'am," Della replied, not daring to look out the window, in case Owen was standing there. She went to the broom she had leaned against the back all and started sweeping again. When she looked up, Miss Clayson had gone.

Laughing to herself, Della started to take her name off the peg board, but she changed her mind. It could stay there through Sunday and greet her on Monday, when she came back to get ready for school and figure out how to sweeten up the dragon that *wasn't* on the Welsh national flag.

She closed her classroom door and went outside, standing on the steps a moment and looking up the canyon toward the tipple. The day crew must have been busy, because the train was already moving down the slope.

"Is it safe?"

Della looked around to see Owen sitting across the road by the storehouse. She put both hands to her mouth and laughed into them, on the odd chance that Miss Clayson was looking out the upstairs window. She wasn't about to turn around and look.

"Coast is clear," he said, looking up at the school. "The dragon has returned to her lair."

"You're going to get someone named Lloyd Llewellen in real trouble, if she complains to Bishop Parmley!"

"Not a chance. Lloyd mines down in Castle Gate."

"Yes, but when you bring Angharad to school, what will she *think*?" Della asked, when she stopped laughing.

"Still not a chance. When our faces are black, we look all the same to people who don't mine." He appraised her. "But you knew it was I."

"Of course," she said, wondering if all men were so dense. "I know the sound of your voice! I'm good that way."

He seemed to think about that, then looked over her shoulder at the school. "I wonder why she's so sour. She could make your year here a trial indeed."

"She already wants me to do something about my hair."

"Shave your head?" he suggested, and she laughed.

"You're hopeless, and I am going back to the bishop's house."

He just smiled and tipped his hat again. "And I'm off to collect my lovely daughter. See you in Sunday School tomorrow?"

After the Parmley children were in bed that night and the bishop and Mary Ann Parmley were seated in the parlor, Della told them what had happened in the school between her and Miss Clayson. "I don't know what I did to set her off. I thought she would want another teacher."

Bishop Parmley put down the newspaper and frowned. "Miss Clayson is an excellent teacher, and a firm disciplinarian, but I never have found her unreasonable," he said, after some thought. "It may have something to do with what happened to the teacher you are replacing."

"Did she run off with a coal miner?" Della asked, only half serious.

"As a matter of fact, it was a mining engineer," Parmley said. "He came here from Grand Junction to draw up plans to install another fanway for Number Four. When he left, he took the teacher with him. Rumor has it that she just slid a note under Miss Clayson's door and took off."

"I'm not sure I can blame her," Della said. "I wanted to take off running myself!"

"Thanks to that elopement, Miss Clayson spent most

of last school year with substitutes from Spanish Fork and Springville, none of whom wanted to be here." He rustled the newspaper and exchanged a look with his wife. "Sister Anders, you're probably not homely enough for her! Maybe I should assure Miss Clayson that no mining engineers are expected this year."

"That is no answer, Thomas," Mary Ann said crisply.

"Maybe not. We already know she doesn't care much for Mormons." He seemed to fish for the right thing to say. "I'll admit some of us are wondering why an Anders chose to come here. Maybe she is too."

"Bishop, I wanted to be here, and it really doesn't involve my uncle," she told him. *Tell him what he's too polite to ask*, she thought. She opened her mouth to confess, then one of the Parmley children came downstairs to complain about the baby's crying, and the moment was gone.

Mary was already asleep and curled up into a tidy package when Della said her prayers and slipped between the sheets. The sound of the child's gentle breath soothed her as she lay awake, wondering about Miss Clayson. Mentally, she ticked off her list: *I won't run off with a mining engineer; I'm far from being too pretty for Winter Quarters school; I can't help being a Mormon; and yes, I am an Anders, but that's only on sufferance, even though none of you know it yet.*

She sighed and made herself comfortable, moving a little closer to Mary because the child was warm and the nip of autumn was already in the night air. Maybe southern Arizona next year would be a good idea, after all. Maybe it was far enough from the Anders name.

She had learned long ago to make herself think of one good thing before she closed her eyes. Papa had told her once if she did that, it would be her first cheerful thought in the morning. The little game had carried her through a multitude of slights and bruises, starting with the shock of his death in the Molly Bee, and her solitary train ride from Colorado, with the Anderses' address pinned to her cutdown black coat. Maybe it was too early to abandon that little custom.

Mentally she rehearsed her delight at seeing all those hand-carved letters and the pegged board with *Della Olympia Anders*, which would be waiting for her on Monday morning when she opened the door to her classroom. Her smile widened. Owen Davis had called Olympia a name for a goddess. A Welsh coal miner black from hard work had defended her from a gargoyle, and he had made her laugh. She had forgotten what it was like to know someone who protected her.

Chapter 7

$\mathcal{S}$unday began the way Della thought real Sundays should be—chaotic with some fun mixed in. Aunt Caroline would never have agreed.

After Mary Ann Parmley, her hair still in rags, ushered her brood downstairs, Della dressed in peace, listening to the tumult below in the dining room. *This is what a family ought to sound like, Aunt Caroline,* she thought as she tightened her corset.

Mary, the dramatic one, clasped both hands to her heart when Della made her dining room appearance. "Mama, I will be utterly *devastated* if I do not have a dress that color some day," she declared, which earned her a stare down the nose from her mother.

"I expect you'll have a prettier one," Della said, pleased. She held out her arms for three-year-old Florence, she of the mutinous expression and with one shoe on. Sitting Florence on her lap, Della pulled on the other shoe, which had somehow ended up next to the pitcher of milk.

The bishop left for priesthood meeting while Della brushed Florence's hair. Della looked out the window to see a whole troop of soberly dressed men in suits and hats, walking toward the meetinghouse.

"They clean up' well, don't they?" Mary Ann asked as she handed Della a brooch to center on the lace fall on the front of her dress. "Of course, the first time *I* saw the bishop, he was black from the pit, so I suppose it doesn't matter."

The two women laughed together, Della flattered to be

68

included in such a candid observation.

With her curls as subdued as she could manage, Della took Florence by the hand and followed the older children to the meetinghouse. Sister Parmley brought up the rear with William in her arms.

Although there was the usual nervous I'm-the-stranger feeling in the pit of her stomach, Della felt herself relax as she went inside the meetinghouse. The little glances in her direction were kind, and she thanked the Parmleys in her heart for sharing their home with her. If the glances her way were any indication, the Parmleys' wholehearted endorsement of her communicated itself to everyone in Winter Quarters, with Miss Clayson being the possible exception.

She wasn't entirely without acquaintances in the congregation. Dr. Emil Isgreen smiled at her from the stand, so he must be a member of the Sunday School superintendency. Della spotted Owen Davis and Angharad sitting near the front, close to what looked like a family of stair-step children. To her pleasure, Angharad turned around and gave her a little wave. Della sat down with the Parmleys, Florence on her lap.

Della looked around, not surprised at the lack of an organ; only the wealthiest wards in Salt Lake City were so blessed. It would probably take a modest little ward like the Pleasant Valley Ward right up to the Millennium to hold enough bake sales to buy one. She noticed the piano was closed and no one sat on the bench.

Sister Parmley must have caught the trajectory of Della's gaze. She leaned over Joseph and whispered, "It needs a piano tuner in the worst way, and they're hard to come by here."

"That must make singing difficult," Della whispered. *This should be interesting*, she thought, wondering if everyone in the congregation was just going to pick a random note to start on. She decided Uncle Jesse had been teasing her about joining the Winter Quarters choir, which, with no piano, must need more help than even one reasonably competent contralto could furnish. She clasped her hands around Florence's middle and waited for the superintendent, probably that stern-looking man, to rise and begin.

The stern look vanished as he rose. "'Tis the hour, my dears," he began, in the loveliest Scottish brogue this side of the Atlantic Ocean. He gestured to the congregation. "Give us a good round note, Brother Evans."

This will be catastrophe, Della thought, amused.

She had seldom been so wrong. A pure tenor note sounded from what seemed to be the row the Davises were sitting on, to be followed by an equally lovely soprano, then alto and bass from other corners of the room. After the four notes resonated, the music director pointed to a small boy seated behind the row of deacons and gave the downbeat.

Della held her breath as the sweetest sound filled the small chapel, the sound of one child singing: "'Never be late to the Sunday School class, come with your bright sunny faces; cheering your teachers and pleasing your God— Always be found in your places.'"

Her jaw dropped when only the adults sang the chorus in perfect harmony, singing to their children grouped around them: "'Never be late, never be late; children, remember the warning: Try to be there, always be there, promptly at ten in the morning.'"

"My word," Della murmured, enchanted. Owen Davis had turned slightly to face his little daughter, as though he sang the chorus only to her. He kissed her forehead when he finished, and Della felt her heart turn over.

As she listened, delighted, the next verse was sung by the little boy and a girl slightly older harmonizing, with the adults on the chorus again. Everyone sang the last two verses and the chorus, ending as perfectly on tune as when they started. Della had been too amazed to sing.

These people don't need an organ or a piano, she thought.

"Don't you know the words?" Joseph whispered to her.

"I just forgot to sing."

She nearly laughed out loud at the wry look the boy gave her. "I'll do better on the next song," she promised him.

After the prayer, Della glanced at Mary Ann Parmley, who was looking at her with a smile. "Do they need a piano?" the bishop's wife whispered. Della shook her head.

The usual business of Sunday School followed—the roll call of teachers, and then the reading of the minutes. The short talks mirrored the ones in her Salt Lake City ward: one terrified child, followed by an only slightly braver boy who came up from the deacons' row. When he finished, the Sunday School superintendent said simply, "The sacrament, my dears."

Della closed her eyes as the elder at the sacrament table prayed. She decided he must be Welsh, because each sentence became a question, in that lilting way she was coming to savor. When both men handed the trays of sacramental bread to the deacons, she watched as Owen Davis and the man seated next to him rose and walked to the front. *Now what is this*, she thought, interested, as the boys began to pass the bread down the rows.

With no evidence of either man sounding a starting note, they began to sing softly in harmony, "Come Unto Jesus."

Good heavens, Della thought, stunned by the beauty of their voices. She had never heard anything so lovely in her life. As she listened, amazed, Joseph had to bump her arm to remind her to take the bread and pass it on.

As he sang, Owen Davis suddenly looked at her and grinned so broadly that some on the front row turned around to see who he was targeting. Della slowly slid lower in the pew, her face red. She couldn't think of a time she had been so neatly trussed up by a practical joke. And he had thought to warn her about the choir! She felt her shoulders start to shake as she clamped her lips tight together and tried to remember this was the sacrament and she ought to think of Jesus.

When they finished singing, the deacons walked to the sacrament table again and the other elder, his hands raised, prayed over the goblets of water. Della listened as the two men softly sang in perfect harmony. This time, she let the beauty of the hymn carry her into that peaceful place where her mind and heart were on the Savior and not on the joke Owen Davis had played on her. She closed her eyes in contentment.

When she opened her eyes, the song was over and the men returned to their seats, the taller man's hand on Owen's shoulder. Della looked around. No one else in the congregation seemed to realize what magnificent singing they had just heard. *I'm the fool*, she told herself. *They're used to this every Sunday.*

The superintendent rose again, then looked at Bishop Parmley. "Our dear bishop has some business before we adjourn to class," he said.

Bishop Parmley gazed at his congregation, his eyes warm. He looked at Della and gestured to her.

"Stand up, Sister Anders. Let us see you."

She did as he said, too shy to look around now, then sat down again, Florence still clutched in her arms.

"This kind lady has come to teach your children," Bishop Parmley said. He sighed, which made Della think that maybe Mary had inherited her dramatic flair from her father. "And you all know what happened to the wee house promised to her. Whoosh! Up in smoke."

People nodded and murmured.

"We can't have her showing us a clean pair of heels because there's no place for her to live." He looked over his people again. "Please consider your own homes and ask yourself if you have room for one medium-sized teacher. I can already testify that she is good with children, and she's a willing kitchen helper." He leaned on the pulpit. "She even told my wee ones a bedtime story last night that made me stop and listen too!"

Laughter and more murmuring. "Just think about it, my dears. From September to May, you could help us keep a good teacher in Winter Quarters." He nodded to the superintendent again. "That's all I have, Brother Hood. Let's send this lot to class."

Knowing her place in the greater scheme of Sunday School, Florence hopped off Della's lap and followed her teacher. Mary Ann Parmley shouldered a sleeping William and gestured toward the smallest children, who followed her. Della sat alone on the row now, not sure where to go.

Owen Davis stood up and came back to her pew. "Theology meets in the basement, Sister Anders, perhaps because we're all such sinners," he said, his eyes merry. "I owe you an explanation."

"You are a dirty bird, Brother Davis," she said softly.

Maybe he forgot it was Sunday. Owen threw back his head and laughed the kind of belly laugh that only a stone gargoyle could have resisted. Della glanced around as others started to laugh. More were staring in surprise, which puzzled her. Didn't his own ward friends know what a terrible tease he was?

"Well, you are! After what you said yesterday, I was quite resigned for the worst," she told him as she followed him downstairs to the classroom.

"I couldn't resist."

"You didn't even try!"

"Guilty," he said cheerfully. "May I sit by you, or would you rather slap me silly and make me stand in the corner?"

"Oh, sit down," she said, laughing. "I have to know: which of you gave the other the note to start off the sacrament hymn?"

"Neither of us," he whispered back, his eye on the Sunday School teacher, who had finished writing the twelve sons of Jacob on the board.

"You just started singing? Do you mean to tell me that both of you have perfect pitch?" she asked, amazed.

It was Owen's turn to look puzzled. "Doesn't everyone?"

"Double dirty bird," she said under her breath.

He was sitting close enough on the bench for Della to feel his shoulders shaking. She took a deep breath and resolved not to look at him until the lesson was over.

She tried to turn her attention to the lesson on the sons of Jacob, but all she could do was wonder where she had found the courage to speak to a man that way. Too many years with Aunt Caroline had conditioned her to silence, on the notion that if she never said anything, no one would notice she was there.

Deep in her own thoughts, Della jumped when someone tapped her shoulder. She turned around to see the bishop, who motioned for her to follow him.

"We have a ward member willing to offer you room and board," he said. "Come into what I laughingly call my office."

He opened the door for her and she found herself crowded into a small space taken up mostly with a desk probably meant for greater things but now hiding its light under a bushel in the Winter Quarters meetinghouse.

A small woman dressed in black rose when Della came in and held out her hand in a gesture as friendly as her smile. "I'm Mabli Reese, and I believe I have just the place for you," the woman said. "You'll need to be a bit adventurous."

They shook hands. "I never thought I was adventurous before I rode the flatbed into the canyon," Della said.

"That story will make the rounds for a long time," Mabli Reese said.

"Tell me why I need to be adventurous to board at your house, Sister Reese?"

"I cook at Mr. Edward's boardinghouse, which is hard by the Number One mine portal. I have a four-room house next to the boardinghouse and an extra room which I am offering you."

"Dr. Isgreen told me to stay away from boarding

houses," Della said, giving the lady a regretful look.

"You will never be bothered, because not a single man in that boardinghouse wants to face the wrath of fathers with children in your class," Mabli told her. "I'll charge you six dollars a month for the room. Board will be free, if you'd like to help me prepare breakfast in the kitchen."

Della considered the offer. "What do you think, bishop?"

"It's a good offer from a lady I admire," he told her. "There have been other offers, it is true, but no one except Mabli has an unoccupied room."

"I'll do it," Della said to Sister Reese. "I'm an early riser and I'll be happy to help cook for armies. For two summers, I was a kitchen flunky for a crew laying telephone lines in Cottonwood Canyon. I had to scare away a bear once."

The bishop looked at her in frank surprise. "I'm amazed that your uncle would ever permit you to do such a thing."

You'd be surprised the lengths my relatives went to, to get me out of sight and mind, she thought, as her uneasiness returned. "He wanted me to be self-sufficient," she said, wincing inside at how lame it sounded.

The bishop looked from Della to Mabli Reese. "Are we agreed?"

Della nodded.

"Aye," Mabli said. "I'll need to rearrange a few things, but I'll be ready tomorrow."

"Excellent," he said, standing up. He ushered them out of his office and into the chapel, which was filling up with teachers and students.

"I hope the kitchen help is agreeable," Mabli whispered. "I had a chore girl, but she married a miner in Castle Gate. Let's sit here."

Mabli slid into the pew next to the man who had sung with Owen Davis. Della followed, her eyes lighting up when Angharad sat next to her, followed by her father, looking not even slightly repentant for his joke.

From his seat on the stand, the bishop leaned over and spoke to the superintendent, who nodded and stood up. "Good news. Sister Anders has agreed to board with Sister Mabli Reese, so there will be peace and the ABCs in the canyon."

After a reminder from the bishop about sacrament meeting in two hours, the closing prayer came with French accent this time.

"Will you be at sacrament meeting?" Mabli asked.

"Of course."

"Afterword, would you like to walk up the canyon with me to see my house?"

"I would. Thank you, Sister Reese. I promise to be a good tenant."

"Sister Anders, if you're still speaking to me, would you care to join us Tuesday evening for choir practice?" Owen Davis asked, as he nudged his daughter along the row.

Della shook her head. "The last thing *this* ward choir needs is another alto."

"Could I find a way to make you change your mind?" he asked. Angharad had him by the hand and was towing him from the building.

"I sincerely doubt it," Della replied, picking up Florence.

Owen smiled at her over his shoulder as Angharad led the way. "I'm not through trying."

Oh, yes you are, she thought, amused at his persistence, when the choir obviously far outran her puny talents.

Dinner was sandwiches and soup, with William nodding to sleep from his high chair. Mary Ann took him away while Della helped Florence, who was tugging at her eyelids and yawning.

"I could use a nap," the bishop said. "Haven't had one in years. What do you think of us, Sister Anders?"

"Outside of a few teases and scoundrels, I think you have a fine ward," she joked.

He laughed at that. "I wondered if maybe Brother Davis had told you a stretcher about the quality of singing in our chapel. I was watching you when they started to sing. You looked fair gobsmacked."

"I can't blame Brother Davis totally," Della said. "Before I left Provo, my Uncle Jesse told me I should join the choir and gave me to believe they actually *needed* singers. He will hear from me! Owen . . . Brother Davis just compounded the felony." She leaned her elbows on the table, since the bishop was doing the same thing. "But tell me: everyone looked so startled when he laughed so loud. Why is that?"

The bishop's expression grew wistful. "I doubt anyone has heard him laugh like that since Gwyna died. I honestly never thought to hear him laugh like that again. Maybe you're a tonic, Sister Anders."

"Maybe I'm a good foil for a tease," she retorted, pleased in spite of herself. "Now tell me something about Mabli Reese, if you have time, sir."

"She's a widow from Glamorganshire, Wales, where a good number of my miners come from. Her husband died in a cave-in three years back, and she stayed on as a cook. The Reeses had no children, so she's alone." He leaned back in his chair, appraising her in that way of bishops. "Mabli is a quiet lady who keeps to herself. I was a little surprised she offered her extra room to you."

"It's much appreciated," Della assured him.

"Maybe you're going to bring out the best in us."

I rather think you people are going to bring out the best in me, Della thought, as she got up to clear the table.

The bishop left a few minutes later to return to church. Della started the dishes while Mary Ann carried a sleeping Florence to her bed and admonished her older children to occupy themselves in a Sabbath manner.

"Whether they do so always remains to be seen, but I do enjoy a peaceful sacrament meeting," she said as they started for the meetinghouse again.

There were few children in sacrament meeting. As Della looked around, she knew she would see Angharad there, seated by herself because the choir was on the stand this time.

"Would you mind?" Della whispered to Mary Ann, who nodded, seeing her intention.

She called to the little girl quietly, who saw her, then looked up at her father, who nodded. Angharad sat next to Della.

"My father sings second tenor," she whispered to Della.

"You'll be up there in a few years."

"I expect I will," Angharad replied, completely assured in a way Della found endearing.

"I have much to learn," she murmured.

"You're a teacher," the child whispered. "You already know everything."

You'd be amazed how little I know, Della thought. Angharad settled in next to her. By the time to bless the sacrament, Angharad was leaning against her arm. *I hope her father doesn't think I am forward,* Della thought, as she eased her arm around the child, who sighed and nestled closer.

She was prepared for singing during the sacrament now, but this time it was a solo soprano voice, singing "Nearer, Dear Savior, to Thee," so lovely and with such longing that Della felt tears in her eyes.

"Oh, my," she breathed, as an alto joined the soprano on the chorus: "'Take, oh take and cherish me, nearer, dear Savior to thee.'"

Cherish me. Della tightened her grip on Angharad, remembering herself sitting so straight beside Aunt Caroline, who never in a million years would have thought to put her arm around her desperately lonely niece. She glanced down at Angharad, then looked up to see Owen Davis watching her. *No, I won't sing in your choir,* she thought, *but I am growing fond of your daughter.*

Chapter 8

*D*ella walked with Mabli Reese after sacrament meeting, breathing deep of the late afternoon air, cooler now in the canyon because there was only so much the sun could touch in such a narrow place. Everything smelled slightly sulfurous, but she heard the stream below the tracks because the tipple was silent. By the edge of the wagon road—maybe they had escaped—were thistles, deep purple and feathery. She remembered thistles like that by the Molly Bee.

"It must have been lovely here before all the trees were cut down for lumber," she said to her new landlady, and then looked up toward a higher wagon road. She figured a hike was in her future, as soon as she could breathe without gasping.

"Passing on the left," Della heard behind her.

"Walk with us, Owen," Mabli said, putting out her elbow so he could conveniently crook his arm through hers.

"Anytime, Mabli," he said. He hesitated a moment, then crooked out his other arm.

Della didn't hesitate. She put her arm through his. "That's the best choir I ever heard in my life! I looked around and everyone just sang along as though it was an ... an everyday occurrence!"

Mabli and Owen looked at each other. "It is," Mabli said.

The Davises walked with them past their own house. "We have to make sure you get to Mabli's," he told her.

"Haven't you heard of Butch Cassidy and other road agents?"

"We have to make sure she doesn't back out," Mabli added. "I live close to the tipple, but you'll get used to the noise."

I wonder, Della thought, doubtful, as she stood outside the little house, built into the hillside like most of the houses in Winter Quarters. She imagined the racket when the coal ran through the tipple.

"Is this the only tipple?" she asked Owen. "Why isn't there one by your mine?"

"Because of the levels and raises in Number Four, it's easier to get the coal out through Number One," he said. "They connect."

Mabli opened her door and they all went inside. The house was small, to be sure, but Della saw order everywhere. Her eyes went first to what must have been a wedding photograph of Mabli and her husband.

"Salt Lake Temple," Mabli said proudly. "Wasn't he the handsome one? Dafydd. I miss him with every fiber of my heart."

"Da, I am starving," Angharad said. "And it had better not be just oatcakes at home!"

Her good-natured complaint cut through the mood. "My dearest, you know there will be oatcakes a little longer."

Mabli went into the lean-to kitchen, coming back with cookies. "This will help take away the pain of oatcakes," she said. "Come by tomorrow after breakfast, Angharad. I can almost guarantee an apple turnover."

"You'll spoil her," Owen said.

"Good." She gave him a little shove. "Go on now." When the door closed, she laughed. "You're wondering why I am so familiar with that good man?"

"Well, I . . . It's not my business," Della said.

"His wife Gwyna was my little sister. Angharad is my niece." She handed Della a cookie. "We're all related here in the canyon. Let me show you your room."

To call the room Spartan would have been to engage in real prevarication, Della decided. There was a mattress but no bedstead, and boxes everywhere. The only window was small and bare of curtains. "Hmm."

"It will look better tomorrow. In exchange for a week of meals in the boardinghouse, Owen has agreed to make you a bedstead. If you walk up here slowly tomorrow, it'll be done by early afternoon. I can find some curtains too—thick ones." Mabli peered out the window. "Your view is the boardinghouse privy, and you don't need that much education, even if you are a teacher. Sometimes they forget to close the door. Men."

After paying her six dollars for September, Della left a few minutes later. She paused outside the door. It was going to be a long walk in winter, but her shoes were sturdy.

Della walked down the canyon by herself now and perfectly at liberty to pause whenever she wanted. Halfway back to the Parmley's house, she sat by the timber shed, where she had stopped with Owen. Her head ached from the altitude, but she allowed herself the privilege of remembering the Molly Bee and her father. As she sat there, she felt one more tie to the Anderses snap like a flimsy cotton thread. She had deliberately stepped back into the life that her aunt and uncle probably felt they had saved her from. No wonder the Anders were confused; she didn't understand why either.

After lunch the next day, two miners knocked on the door to retrieve Della's trunk. "We'll put it on the flatbed and take it directly to Mabli Reese's house," the braver of the two said, as the other man twisted his cap. "She promised us apple turnovers."

"This is really a hard time for them, isn't it?" Della asked as she watched the men head to the tracks with her luggage and a bag of sandwiches from Sister Parmley.

"Coal orders are down in the summer," she said. "I remember hard times too." She touched Della's cheek. "You

81

wouldn't know about hard times in the mines, but there is real want."

"Actually, I . . ."

She stopped. Sister Parmley had turned away because Florence was tugging on her skirts and demanding attention. She knelt by her daughter, solved her small problem, then turned back to Della. "I'm sorry. You were saying . . ."

"It's nothing. Maybe I'd better hurry after my belongings," Della said. *I'm not who you think I am*, she thought, *but if you were to ask me who I am, I am not sure I could tell you.* "I should leave now. I plan to spend some time in my classroom," she said, holding out her hand to Sister Parmley. "Thank you so much for your hospitality."

Too bad Mabli Reese's house wasn't as close to school as the Parmleys' was to church, Della decided as she walked by. She looked up, hoping Miss Clayson wouldn't be staring down, then scolded herself for being a gutless wonder. She tried the front door, which wasn't locked.

The hall was empty. "Miss Clayson?"

"I'm here, Miss Anders," Della heard from the steps leading to the basement. "You're not my first visitor." It sounded like second cousin to an accusation. Della sighed.

In another moment, the principal turned the corner on the landing, still dressed in unrelieved black.

"I don't want to think of myself as a *visitor*," Della said, prepared to be cheerful, no matter what. "How are you this lovely morning?"

"I'm here," Miss Clayson said precisely, obviously not a woman for small talk.

Doesn't like idle chat. Doesn't care for miners. Doesn't like curly hair. Della mentally ticked off a list of misdemeanors, all of which she was already guilty of in the principal's eyes. *I wonder how she feels about President McKinley and tariff reform? At least my skirt is no higher than two inches from the floor. Show no fear.*

"I wanted to work in my classroom a little this

afternoon," Della said. "Will we . . . will we be meeting together this week before classes start?"

"We will, indeed, as soon as Mr. Bowman returns from Provo. He has a sweetheart," the principal said with as much distaste as if Israel Bowman carried typhoid from county to county. "I do hope you have no romantic inclinations, Miss Anders. I had enough trouble with the last lower grades teacher."

"None whatsoever," Della said cheerfully. "I don't know a single mining engineer."

"Neither did Miss Forsyth, until one showed up," the principal said. "That resolution had better last you through May."

"It will."

To Della's surprise, her lips moved upward in faint approximation of a smile. "One thing: That nice Mr. Davis brought you a handful of periods, commas, and question marks for the peg board. He left a few exclamation points too, although I told him we didn't encourage exaggeration in *this* district school."

"Well, you never know when excitement might strike," Della joked, then sobered immediately, because Miss Clayson's frosty look dictated otherwise.

"Watch the levity, Miss Anders," she warned, then softened slightly like a glacier in late August. "I must say, it *was* nice of him to make all those letters. I let him in to deposit them on your desk. Good day."

Della stifled her laughter until Miss Clayson was down the stairs. Owen Davis was right. Miss Clayson hadn't recognized him as Saturday's coal-black miner. Della could barely wait to tell him. She opened the door to her classroom and stood there in surprise.

Someone—imagine who—had taken her name off the peg board and substituted *Choir practice is Tuesday night at six thirty See you there* all run together because the punctuation marks were still piled on her desk, along with a new box to keep them.

"I distinctly told you I would not sing in your magnificent choir, Brother Davis," she said out loud. "Don't you listen?" Still, it was flattering. A smile on her face, Della put the letters in the compartmented box and sat down with glue and thumbtacks. She spent the next hour gluing, an occupation dear to the heart of any lower grades teacher.

"Miss?"

Della looked up, surprised. She hadn't heard anyone open the door and here were two people. She recognized Heikki Luoma. Standing close, her eyes so shy, was a lovely blonde woman who just seemed to fit next to him. Della knew she could search for years and never meet a handsomer couple.

"I know you," she said to the man. "Do come in." She stood up as they came down the aisle toward her, the beautiful lady hanging back, but her husband—he had to be her husband—putting his arm around her waist to nudge her on.

Della looked at the woman beside him. She didn't think it was possible for a human to have such crystal blue eyes. "And you are . . . ?"

The woman smiled, too shy to say anything.

"Her is Mari Elvena Luoma. My wife," Heikki said.

Something about the way he said it, as though he were testing the word, told Della all she needed to know about the length of their marriage. She held out her hand. "I am pleased to meet you, Mrs. Luoma."

Mari Elvena turned her face into her husband's sleeve, but he spoke to her softly in Finnish. She touched Della's hand. "Thank you and good night."

That's good enough for now, Della thought, enchanted. "What can I do for you?"

Heikki thought a moment, the expression on his face telling Della worlds about his own grasp of English. "I want Mari to learn to speak, professor," he said.

Israel Bowman had told her this might happen.

"English? I will be happy to help," she replied. "And I'm just Miss Anders."

"Thank you, just Miss Anders," he said. "She will be good and quiet and learn lots."

"I believe she will," Della said. She looked at Mari Elvena. "We will begin at eight thirty next Monday morning."

Heikki translated, and Mari Elvena touched her hand again then added a curtsy.

Heikki bowed. "You will be happy with her," he said. "Good night now."

"I'm happy already," Della said softly as they left her classroom as quietly as they had entered.

She took off her apron and hung it on one of the hooks lining the inside wall, probably for coats in winter. Miss Clayson knocked on her door and came in.

"I just agreed to add a Finnish woman to my class," Della said.

"You should have told me."

Della looked her in the eye, digging up courage from some back room where it must have languished for years. "That's what I am doing right now. Miss Clayson, I'm going to do my best here." She drew herself up. "I am a certified teacher and I came with excellent references."

Miss Clayson just looked at her, a frown on her face. She glanced away first, which gave Della a tiny feeling of success.

"I'll have the custodian bring up a larger desk." The principal turned on her heel and left the classroom.

Della wiped her sweating palms on her dress and let out the breath she had been holding. Before she left her room, she closed the windows and took one last look at the commas and periods drying on her desk.

She stood for a while on the school steps, looking down on the wagon road and then across the road to the canyon. A rank of trees still held its own along the ridge, although so many trees must have been cut down. Winter Quarters was a raw mining camp, destined to last only as long as the coal. She thought of the Molly Bee and wondered if anyone still grubbed about there, hunting for silver. Maybe some entrepreneur had reopened the caved-in section where her father and two other miners had died. "Papa, I will do well here," she murmured.

She walked the short distance back to the Wasatch Store, feeling as shy as Heikki Luoma's wife but curious. Sister Parmley had sent Maria to the store on Saturday for some forgotten Sunday dinner ingredient. She knew there was food somewhere in the building and she was hungry.

The matter resolved itself quickly. As she approached the store, she saw two women going in with baskets on their arms. They turned around as she approached, smiling at her.

"I need to buy some food and wondered where it was," she asked the one who looked vaguely familiar.

"Right here," the woman said, holding open the door. "I'm Sister Annie Jones, and I'm in the choir."

Of course. She was the soprano who sang half of the sacrament duet yesterday afternoon. "I'm pleased to meet you officially," Della said.

"You'll have two of my children in your class." She leaned closer. "They've been told to mind, and they will."

The Wasatch Store took up most of the main floor in the stone building. "You'll need to bring a basket next time," Annie whispered. "I have an extra one I can leave at Mabli's for you."

"Thank you. I just want enough to tide me over," Della whispered back, wondering why they were whispering.

She looked around and figured out why. Seated behind the counter, his head on his chest, was an older gentleman, sound asleep.

"Bishop Parmley made Mr. Nix put David Lloyd in the store to wait on us, because he had nowhere to go once his lungs went bad," Annie whispered. "We're as quiet as church mice until we need his help."

Della nodded and tiptoed through the rows of shelves, all neat and well-arranged. The prices looked higher than similar goods sold in Salt Lake City. Maybe the Pleasant Valley Coal Company added the price of haulage to their goods. *No wonder Angharad eats a lot of oatcakes*, Della thought. It wouldn't take long for a miner to rack up a bill he'd spend all winter working off.

Annie Jones needed something from the butcher shop, so she tiptoed to the sleeping man and touched his shoulder, speaking to him softly in Welsh. He woke up and went behind the meat counter to help her.

"Miss Anders? Can I be of service?"

She turned around to see the man who had caught her hat so handily when Israel Bowman flung it off the flatbed. "Let's see . . ."

"Clarence Nix," he reminded her. "I'm the store manager. I'm in charge of the coupon books the miners use. I could set you up with one too, if you'd rather pay monthly."

"I think not," she said. "I'm just going to get some cheese, bread, and meat, and . . . and any apples, if you have them."

"We do. Let me help you."

The salami looked good, so she asked for a pound of that and a pound of cheese. She glanced over at Annie Jones's basket. She noticed Annie's much smaller parcel of cheese and no meat, and she was probably feeding a family. *I hope we have a long, cold winter with snow to the rafters, so everyone in Utah needs a lot of coal*, Della thought. She walked to another shelf where she thought she saw some bread and stood there, eyeing the less-than-promising selection.

"I baked oat bread this morning," Annie said. "Let me give you a loaf of that. This stuff tastes like sawdust."

"I couldn't possibly do that. You have a family to feed," Della said quickly. To her dismay, Annie's face fell. *I just made her feel poor*, Della thought. *Now what? Oh, please, Lord.*

It was the simplest prayer and it was answered quickly. Maybe Heavenly Father liked that Sunday singing as much as she did, because she knew what to do.

"Let's do this, Sister Jones. I'm getting some apples. I'll trade you some of those for a loaf of bread. Is it a deal?"

Aunt Caroline would cringe at such slang, but Della didn't care. Annie Jones's pride was on the line.

The woman's eyes brightened. "It's a deal, as you say. Come home with me."

She walked with Annie Jones up the canyon, only asking to stop once while she gathered her breath. "Please tell me I'll get used to this soon," she gasped. Annie wasn't even breathing heavily.

"You will! We all went through this."

The house was a repeat of all the shacks she had seen, but Della stopped and looked over the door frame, recognizing the elaborately carved name.

"Does Brother Davis carve everyone's name over doorways?" she asked as Annie opened the door.

"If we want him to," the woman replied. "He'll probably carve your name if you ask."

She followed her hostess inside to another tiny room just as neat as Mabli Reese's and through to the kitchen, where two girls were washing bread pans. Della breathed deep of the fragrance of freshly baked bread, counting eight loaves on the table.

"It's my week's baking," Annie said, and there was no mistaking the pride in her voice.

"If I take a loaf, will you come up short?" Della asked.

"We never come up short. Every woman in this canyon makes an extra loaf," Annie said. "You never know when a friend will drop by. It's the Welsh way."

It was simply said, so proud and kind. One more flimsy thread binding Della to her own relatives tore away.

Annie took a loaf and wrapped it in waxed paper, and Della took six apples from her stash, noticing how the little girls' eyes lighted up. She added another apple. "For a friend who drops by," Della murmured and accepted the bread in exchange. It was still warm.

"One moment." Annie turned to her cupboard and took out a small box, pouring a handful of salt into a square of waxed paper. She twisted it tight and handed it to the younger of the two girls. She put her hand on the child's shoulder and whispered to her.

"This is Myfanwy. She is just turned six, so you will be her teacher. There now," Annie said and gave her daughter a gentle push.

Too shy to look up, Myfanwy handed Della the salt, dipped a little curtsy, and said something in Welsh. She stepped back and turned her face into her mother's apron.

"She bids you welcome to the canyon. Bread and salt."

"Thank you, Myfanwy. I'll sprinkle a little salt on my apples," Della said, managing to talk around the boulder in her throat. "Thank you, Sister Jones. I know I got the better deal."

"Oh, no," Annie gently contradicted. "We did, the day you decided to teach here."

"You don't even know me."

"I believe we do. God bless you today and all days."

Chapter 9

*T*hese *people are going to amaze me every day I live here*, Della thought as she left the Joneses' house.

She was passing the powerhouse when someone called her name. She turned around to see Clarence Nix waving at her, so she waited, glad enough to have an excuse to stop for a breath.

Incongruous in his white shirt and bow tie, he passed a group of miners, dusty black, who waved to him. He glanced her way but stopped to chat for a moment, obviously in tune with the friendliness of the miners.

He joined her a moment later, ready to apologize; she could tell by the look on his face. She put out her hand to stop him.

"I'm already learning to slow down and chat," she told him, which made him nod. "And if they aren't all related, they at least know each other!"

"You're definitely getting it," he replied with a laugh. "Let me be a company man—time is money to Americans— and tell you straight up what I want."

They were passing the timber yard, so he gestured for her to sit on the bench so warm in the sun. "It's this, Miss Anders," he said when she was seated. "Mr. Parmley suggested it, and I agree. We have a small library upstairs at the Wasatch Store. It's nothing grand—just books for adults, some for children, and newspapers from foreign places."

"That's nice to know," Della said. "Do you let people check out the books?"

"We do. This little canyon has an amazing number of avid readers."

Just because they are miners doesn't mean they are stupid, Della thought but had the wisdom not to say it. One of her happiest memories of her father was sitting on his lap while he read out loud to her. Sometimes it was the newspaper, sometimes a mine report or even a ladies' magazine—whatever was handy. "I understand that," she said.

"The library is open from seven to nine, Monday, Wednesday, and Friday. Or at least, it should be."

"What do you mean?"

Clarence gave her an appraising look, as if wondering how to broach the subject. "It's like this, Miss Anders: The lower grade elementary teacher took on the task, and that's where . . ." He looked over his shoulder, as if expecting Miss Clayson in all her fury to materialize. ". . . where she met the mining engineer."

"Oh, dear," Della said, amused.

"Miss Clayson took over the library when Miss Forsyth eloped, and by the end of the school year, not a single miner came to the library."

Della leaned closer. "She frightened them way?"

"She put up signs everywhere, warning them to wash their hands so they wouldn't get the books dirty."

"That's not unreasonable," Della pointed out.

"Not at all, but then she made them wash up in a basin by the door while she watched, and then show her their hands." Clarence sighed. "Miss Anders, these are grown men, not children! I thought their hands were plenty clean, but not Miss Clayson."

He looked down at his own hands, which had ink spots. "She probably would have thrown *me* out. She humiliated them," he said simply.

"Sad. Do you want me to keep the library open on those evenings?"

"I really do. The store will pay you fifty cents for each

night you are there." He shrugged. "I know that's awfully small potatoes to an Anders—maybe it's even a joke—but that's the offer."

There it was again. *They think I'm someone I'm not, and I don't want to fool these good people*, she thought, dismayed. Maybe she could change the subject or drop it entirely. "I'd enjoy doing this, Mr. . . . Clarence. I wanted to take a librarian's course at the University of Utah, but tuition for a teaching certificate fit my budget better." The moment the words were out of her mouth, she knew should never have said that.

Clarence stared at her. "But you're an Anders! *Aren't* you?"

Della nodded, even more dissatisfied with herself, because she really wanted to say "sort of," and that would never do. "I . . . I had to economize." She tried to turn the matter into a joke. "That's how rich people hang onto their money, or . . . or so my uncle says." She could have cringed at the mystified look in Clarence Nix's eyes as she made a total hash of the matter. Better just to stand up and end it. "I'd be happy to take the library," she told him. She leaped to her feet and glanced down at the watch pinned to her shirtwaist. "Oh, the time! I must get to Mabli Reese's house. Good day, Clarence. I'll be at the library Wednesday night," she finished in a rush.

"That's all I want," he said, and there was no denying the bewilderment in his voice, mixed with what she hoped wasn't frost, but probably was.

Stupid, stupid, stupid, she berated herself as walked. *He thinks I'm a snob and too good for Winter Quarters. Please, please don't let him say anything to Mrs. Perkins! Everyone in Pleasant Valley will know.*

Her vision blurred as she hurried up the wagon road where it branched away from the tracks. Clarence Nix had no idea that an extra six dollars a month was a real windfall. Since the room was only six dollars a month and there probably wasn't much place to spend her salary up here, she could save most of it and plan for a warmer climate next year. Maybe Indonesia would be far enough.

Agitated, she stopped to breathe. As she stood there looking toward the tipple and the coal in the chute, she felt her common sense return from wherever it had fled. "All anyone wants is a good teacher, Della, you nitwit," she murmured. "Why does it matter?"

She started walking slowly as she realized it mattered very much because she was already coming to like these people. *I wish I knew what to do*, she thought.

She paused outside Mabli Reese's door for only a moment, because the woman had left her a note. *Next door in the boardinghouse. Come see me and use the side door,* she read.

The side door opened directly into the kitchen, and there was her landlady, rolling out piecrust, from the look of the table where finished pies waited their turn in the oven. The room was hot and smelled of cinnamon.

"Apple pie?" Della asked, happy to not think of the skepticism on Clarence Nix's face.

Mabli stopped her practiced strokes and pointed with the rolling pin. "Apple, peach, and pumpkin. Want a piece?"

"You know I do," Della said. She held out her package. "I bought myself some salami, cheese and apples, and Sister Jones—"

"Which Jones?"

"Oh, dear, there are so many, aren't there?" Della asked. She thought a moment. "She has a daughter named Myfanwy."

"That narrows it to three or four," Mabli said with a laugh. She sliced a healthy hunk of pie from the ones cooling on a side table.

"*This* Sister Jones sang half of the duet during sacrament meeting."

"Mrs. Levi Jones! Elizabeth Ann. Here." Mabli held out the pie.

"She gave me a wonderful loaf of oat bread, for which I bartered apples. May I keep food in your kitchen or this one? Oh, this is delicious."

"My kitchen. I don't trust a single man here, and you mustn't, either," Mabli said in good humor. "Do walk in. The door's unlocked, and you'll want to unpack." She picked up her rolling pin. "And try out a beautiful bed."

"Did he really make me a bed?" Della asked. "This is better than Christmas."

"Wait until you see it," Mabli said, stretching the pie dough round across the top of another apple pie. "My rascal of a brother-in-law and I made a discreet wager. I had to overcome his natural disinclination to wager on a lady."

"Such nicety! I'm almost afraid to ask."

"I told him you would cry. He said no, that you were too practical. Then we had an argument when I told him he was forgetting what women are like."

"I've never cried over a bed before." Della ran her finger around her empty pie plate and stuck her finger in her mouth, not willing to let even the smallest goodness escape. *Good thing you're not here, Aunt Caroline*, she told herself, feeling more wicked than worried. "What is the wager, or dare I ask?"

"If I win, he makes me a new rolling pin. If he wins, I make him and Angharad pie for a week."

Della thought about that. "This is premeditated, Mabli. I'll try not to cry, because I'd rather he and Angharad had pie, since it will probably be as good as this one."

"Don't worry! Cry if you choose. I'll see that he gets pie too, one way or other."

Della went next door, going first to the kitchen with her food. She opened the door to her room cautiously, not sure what to expect. She gasped, then dabbed at sudden tears. Mabli won the bet.

She knew nothing about wood except that it was a soft honey color, all simple lines. The glory was the headboard.

He had carved *Olympia* in the center, surrounding it with daffodils and something else she didn't recognize. "I am Olympia," she whispered, tracing the careful strokes.

She sat down on the bed, staring at the beauty before her, then looked closer and swallowed. He had carved a profile of her face on one side of the headboard, getting her aquiline nose precisely right.

Someone knocked on the outside door. "Come in," she called, digging in her pocket for a handkerchief.

"I didn't know what to carve on the opposite side, so it doesn't balance. When you think of something, let me know. I can add it when you're gone for Thanksgiving or Christmas holiday."

Owen Davis stood in the door, wearing his coveralls, his tin pot lamp in his hand. When she blew her nose, he chuckled. "Looks like I lost my wager."

Della dabbed at her eyes next. "You shouldn't bet—not because I'm a lady, but because you're not very good at it."

"It's oak," he said, still standing in the doorway, obviously not going to take another step unless she invited him into her bedroom. "Did I spell Olympia right?"

Della nodded. "And you get an A plus for even remembering I *have* a middle name!"

"A man—this man—doesn't forget a name like Olympia."

"Come in," she said, and he did. "I recognize daffodils, of course, but what are these?"

"Leeks. Daffodils and leeks—every Welshman knows them. Look at the inside of the footboard."

She did, charmed to see what she now knew were dragons. Daubed with red paint, two small rearing dragons, simply carved, faced the center of the footboard, where she could see them from bed. "I'll see these first thing every morning," she said.

"They'll bring you luck. Angharad carved them."

She heard the quiet pride in his voice. "They're

wonderful. You're teaching her to be a woodcarver?"

"Aye. I have no son, but I have a clever daughter. A machinist made small tools to my specifications, and she carves my dragons now. I put them on every piece I carve, or rather, she does."

"Pine would have done for a bed," Della said. "I'll only be here through the school year."

He shook his head. "I build things to last and I happened to have some oak."

"No one just *happens* to have oak," she chided, touched that he went to all this work. "I hate to think how little sleep you got last night."

"When my shift's over and the moon is going down, I'll sleep well tonight." He stood up and ran a practiced hand over the headboard, flicking off imaginary dust. "And so will you, teacher of my daughter. Good day now."

Humming to herself, Della opened her trunk and shook out her clothes. True to her word, Mabli had tacked up thick curtains. Della peeked through a gap in the curtains and put her hand over her mouth. There was the boardinghouse privy, and sure enough, the men weren't too concerned about who saw what. She closed the curtains and found a hat pin to secure them.

Across the end of the narrow room, Mabli had strung a long curtain on a dowel, creating a closet, with a small bureau inside it. She carried her underclothes to the bureau and opened the top drawer. A small carved box nestled inside. "My stars," she murmured, putting in the clothing and taking out the delicately carved little box, one made to hold treasures that schoolteachers probably never accumulated. She turned it upside down, and there was Angharad's red dragon.

She opened the box and laughed out loud. Owen had left a note: *Choir practice at 6:30 p.m. Tuesday.*

Mabli laughed over the note too, an hour later, when she returned to her house and Della showed it to her. "He's not one to take no for an answer, is little Owen," she said. "You should have seen how persistently he courted my sister!"

"I have no plans to go to choir practice *ever*," Della said, "not in this ward of singers!"

"Is that so now?" Mabli asked, trying to sound innocent and failing. Mabli took her arm. "Tell me: do I get a rolling pin?"

"You know you do! I took one look at the bed and started to cry."

"I knew you would," Mabli said, satisfied. "Sit a moment and let me explain my house rules for boarders. Pay close attention. Last one in locks the door."

"That's it?" Della asked. After Mabli nodded, Della handed her the Rules for Teachers. Her eyes wide, she read the list. "I don't mind if you have gentleman callers," she said finally.

"I already promised Miss Clayson there would be no mining engineers. I don't smoke cigarettes, and I have no plans to dye my hair. Straighten it maybe, if I could, but not dye it!"

Della spent the late afternoon and early evening in the kitchen, glad to be busy. She had no trouble keeping up with Mabli because she had worked this way for several summers, saving every penny for tuition during her single year at the university. No one here would believe her if she told them that arranging her summer jobs was the only thing her Uncle Karl ever did for her.

The sound of men eating and laughing in the other room, the scrape of chairs, and the clink of china tugged at her heart. Before her father's death, she had worked in a Molly Bee boardinghouse, scraping plates and washing dishes for her dinner, when times were lean. Because times always seemed to be lean, she grew up with hard work. She almost said something about that to Mabli but stopped herself in time. Mabli would probably just wonder why on earth an Anders had to work so hard. *We'll let her think I'm a fast learner*, Della thought.

One of the boarders must have seen her when Mabli hurried in and out of the swinging door, carrying more bowls of food. By the time the soup tureens had been removed and the bread platter resupplied, the bolder men were looking into the kitchen, then going to the kitchen to ogle—Mabli was right—and ask her for more ketchup and jam, or whatever they thought they could get away with. German accents, French accents, an Italian or two—Della began to wonder where Bishop Parmley found his miners. Maybe Mabli shouldn't have worried: they were all polite to her.

When the congestion got thick in the kitchen, Mabli waded into the boarders with her wooden spoon, telling them what she thought and earning good-humored protests when she cracked the spoon on heads and shoulders. The more brazen miners offered to help with the dishes, which Della found flattering.

Finally the dining room emptied. Mabli looked at the clock and sat down with a yawn, pulling up her skirt around her knees.

"Should I start clearing the tables?" Della asked.

"No. I have a cleaning crew," her landlady said. "You'll see."

Della sat down beside her, watching with interest and dawning admiration of Mabli Reese when a little army of girls came into the kitchen through the side door. With shy smiles at her—Della recognized Annie Jones's daughters—some gathered dishes from the dining room while others started washing the plates Della had scraped and stacked.

"When they're done, I divide up the extra food," Mabli said quietly. "It's not so important in the winter when their fathers are working full shifts, but someone always needs this food in late summer."

"Mabli, you're a good woman," Della whispered. "I was wondering why you seemed to have cooked so much extra. Our secret?"

"Not really," she replied. "Mr. Edwards gives me a certain amount each month to buy food. Beyond that, he's not concerned, and no one can contrive like a Welshwoman. He never loses money."

Della watched the girls with real respect as they worked quickly, chatting and sometimes singing. "How do you divide the food?" she asked Mabli.

"The girls take it to Annie Jones. She's first counselor in the Relief Society," Mabli explained. "She knows who needs what. The girls are in the Young Ladies Mutual Improvement Association. This is their summer project."

"I am impressed," Della said. "All we ever did in YL was learn to embroider and paint on china."

"We do that too, but right now, this is more important." Mabli looked at her crew, her fondness unmistakable.

So you have no children of your own? Della asked herself. *I beg to differ.*

When everyone finished, Mabli brought over two pies and divided them. The girls clustered around, taking a slice apiece and holding it carefully, not dirtying another plate or fork. Mabli quickly packed the leftovers into tins. Each girl took one, plus cookies Mabli found somewhere to stave off starvation between the boardinghouse and their homes. They left as quietly as they came. Della looked out the door, pleased to see that older brothers and fathers were waiting to escort them home safely. She smiled to see the girls give their cookies to their escorts.

"How does Annie know . . . ?"

"Who needs what? My dear, this is the Relief Society," Mabli said. "I never question it."

Her landlady sat still another few minutes, as if gathering her energy, then directed Della to setting bread dough to rise. Soon the fragrance of cinnamon was replaced by the tang of yeast. By the time she finished kneading the dough, Della was pleasantly tired.

She stood in the doorway while Mabli took a last look around her kitchen, where all was swept and tidied, dish towels dry now and folded, dough covered to rise until before dawn, when Mabli's day would begin again.

"Have you ever thought about going to Spanish Fork or Provo and managing a restaurant?" Della asked. "It might be easier."

"Dafydd is buried in Scofield. I'd be too far away," she said simply. "Let's go home."

Maybe it was home already. She had a bed made especially for her. Soon enough Mabli would probably have a new rolling pin, and Owen and Angharad would have pie too. Mr. Edwards still made money on his boardinghouse, hungry families had more than oatcakes, and the coal roared into the tipple. She hadn't been in Winter Quarters a week, and Della could already see the intricate web that bound them together.

Tired, she changed into nightgown and robe and washed her face in a basin in the kitchen.

"The tin tub hangs just outside the back door," Mabli told her. "You're welcome to all the hot water you need, of course, and my curtains in here are very thick!"

Della yawned. "Owen . . . Brother Davis . . . said I'd be tired for awhile, until I get used to the altitude."

"So you shall."

She rested her head on her arms, comfortable at Mabli's kitchen table, trying to remember that last time she had sat with anyone while in nightgown and robe. Aunt Caroline never approved of such unseemliness. She knew she should go to bed, but she was struck with the realization of how much of her home life in Salt Lake had been spent in solitude. The Anderses all kept to themselves, and she had never been invited into their circle. And here she sat with a kind woman she barely knew, content.

She rested her chin on her hands. "Mabli, Brother Davis told me that Angharad stays with the Evans family while he works. What about the late shift?"

"We call it the afternoon shift. He'll go in their pitch-dark house—miners aren't troubled much by darkness—and come out with his sleeping daughter. He always takes her home, no matter how late."

"It's hard for him, isn't it?" Della asked.

"It would be harder if Angharad had died too, when her mother died," Mabli said, not even trying to hide her own pain.

Impulsively, Della covered her landlady's hand with her own. "Maybe I understand better why you stay here."

"I thought you might. Good night, my dear."

As tired as she was, Della lay awake a long time in her beautiful bed, trying to remember the last time anyone had called her "my dear." She reached her hand behind her to outline one of the daffodils, tracing it over and over until she grew drowsy, acquainting herself with the smooth strokes of the master carver. She closed her eyes, knowing that when she woke up, there would be little rearing dragons at the foot of her bed.

Chapter 10

*D*ella helped Mabli in the boardinghouse kitchen in the morning, turning pancakes until she wondered just how many of them hungry men could eat. When Mabli decreed the mound sufficient, Della fried eggs until she had another mound.

"You realize we could bury medium-sized animals in these two stacks," she said. Mabli laughed and told her to keep cracking eggs.

"What do they do about lunch in the mine?" Della asked when all the food was on the tables and Mabli had time to sit down in the kitchen.

"I put bread, meat, cheese, and cookies on a table, and they choose. Cake, sometimes, if the mood is on me. Apples."

"If they're not in the mines?"

"They'll come in for sandwiches, and I'll have stew."

Della wiped the sweat from her forehead. "Mabli, you should take the one-year teaching certification course at the university. I did, and I don't work nearly as hard as you do."

"Dafydd taught me to read. I don't think I am university material." She took Della's hand and lowered her voice. "That's why *I'm* glad you're here. If you can give the boys enough learning, they can be checkers and weighers, and not go in the pit." She looked away, as though someone had moved the back wall of the kitchen and she was seeing much farther. "They don't need to be in the pit."

Della thought about what Mabli said, and with such

intensity, as she worked in her classroom that day. Even in her fervent plea for Della to teach the boys, Mabli couldn't see beyond the mines. Checkers and weighers meant they would be aboveground, but they would still be here. *I want them to be teachers and shop owners*, Della thought. *Maybe even lawyers. Doctors, someday, and scientists.*

As she planned her first month of lessons, Della's mind kept returning to Mabli's words. When Miss Clayson came into her room, her expression militant, Della decided to have the first word, even if she knew her principal would have the last one.

"Miss Clayson, what are we educating these children for?"

Della cringed inside to see Miss Clayson's expression turn from militant to disbelieving. She would have gladly taken back her impulsive question, except Miss Clayson's expression didn't stop at disbelief. It moved on to what Della thought might be a close cousin to concern and softened, making the woman in black look surprisingly close to human.

"That is an impertinent question from a teacher," she began, and Della felt her heart sink. Perhaps she had misread Miss Clayson's expression. Perhaps not. The principal sighed, and Della saw uncertainty for the first time.

"I asked myself that when I started here ten years ago," she said finally, and there was no mistaking her uncertainty. "We educate them here through the eighth grade. By then they are fourteen. Some have already started going to the pit with their fathers to pick rock out of the coal before it's weighed, or they open and close mine doors. That way they can take home a bigger paycheck. Some of *your* students will even do that on Saturdays."

"But they're only six or seven!"

"They're old enough to know rock from coal and open doors."

Della thought of the young girls helping Mabli last

night, everyone working hard to feed their families or others even more in need. "And the girls?"

Her principal shrugged. "They can read, write, and cipher, and they marry miners." Her expression hardened. "And when something happens in the mine, they rush to the portals and watch to see who comes out alive." She shuddered. "Wait until you hear their wailing and keening at the portal. You'll never forget the sound."

"There should be more to life than that," Della said.

Maybe she said the wrong thing. Miss Clayson's eyes lost their half-wistful, half-worried look, narrowing into an expression that made Della's stomach start to hurt.

"You think I don't know that!" she stormed. "You're coming here all benevolent and superior to tell *me* that! Miss Anders, remember yourself!"

"Oh, I . . ."

She was speaking to empty air. Miss Clayson left the room with an angry twitch of her skirts. Della put her face in her hands, the day ruined. She thought of her father, dead in a mine, and her own tears when the mine owner told her, then offered her one-way passage to somewhere she had relatives.

"I do know what it feels like to lose someone in the mine, Miss Clayson," she said into her hands. "Do you?"

Her walk home was thoughtful and slow, no buoyancy in her steps this time. *What do these children need to know?* she asked herself. *Am I the one to teach them?*

The shift was changing. She stood still to catch her breath by the Number Four incline, a system of tracks that carried miners and equipment up the steep trail to the portal, located out of sight in an even smaller canyon. Through the day she had heard the distant rumble of what she thought was thunder at first but which she realized were explosives in the mine, since the sky had not a cloud in it.

She had no doubt the men inside knew their work. As she looked toward the portal she could not see, she wondered why they felt such danger was worth it. She had wanted to ask her father that. Since his death, she had asked it over and over. How dare Miss Clayson dismiss her? A moment's reflection gave her the answer: *How is she to know otherwise if you never tell anyone?* Della asked herself.

She walked past a group of miners as black as the coal they blasted and dug. One of them reached out his hand but did not touch her, so she stopped.

"Sister Anders, what do you think of my Annie's oatbread?"

It was Levi Jones, maybe unidentifiable to Miss Clayson, who couldn't tell one miner from another. To Della, Levi was the husband of the Relief Society first counselor and father to Myfanwy, who would be her student soon.

"Brother Jones, that's the best bread I ever ate," she said, and meant every word.

The contrast of his white teeth against his black face took her out of her own misery. "To tell the truth, I don't care much for oats, so you know it was good if I liked it."

Levi Jones laughed. "You'd be a sorely tried Welshwoman!"

"An utter failure," she agreed. "Not only was it good bread, it was kindly given."

"That's our way," he told her. "Now *you* be charitable if a certain persistent second tenor asks about choir."

Della sighed. "I am *not* the caliber of singer you want in the choir!"

"You could let us be the judge of that," was his mild comment.

Della opened her mouth to reply, then closed it, shook her head, and walked on, only to realize a moment later that she had nearly walked into that second tenor. He took a side step so she wouldn't plow into him and get dirty, but he slowed his steps to match hers.

Better to beat him at his own game. "Brother Davis, I know you mean well, but I am not the singer for you."

She expected an argument but got none, which surprised her.

"I can be philosophical."

Della realized it was a subject needing to be changed. "I do have some news for you from Clarence Nix," Della said. "He asked me be the Wasatch Store librarian on Mondays, Wednesdays, and Fridays. I'll be in the library from seven to nine on those evenings. Maybe you could pass the word."

If he thought her crass to ask a favor after turning him down, Owen did not indicate it. "I can. I'll tack up a note at both portals." He stopped, so she stopped, as other miners grinned and walked around them, heading home. "I'll tell you, though—no man takes kindly to being scolded like a child for dirty hands."

"I have a better idea," Della assured him. "I expect clean hands. Pure hearts would be nice too, but I'm a realist."

He laughed at her joke, waved a dirty hand, and continued up the slope with his friends. She took a more thoughtful pace, part of her relieved that he didn't seem disappointed with her rejection of choir, the other part of her wishing he had protested a bit more. *You can't have it both ways, Della*, she told herself.

She walked to school by herself the next morning, until she passed one of the small boarding houses close to the Number Four incline and Israel Bowman waved for her to wait.

"So you've wandered back from Utah Valley?" she asked, when he joined her.

"You may congratulate me," he told her, making no attempt to hide the pleasure on his face. "I am now engaged to Miss Blanche Bent of Provo. No applause necessary; just send a wedding present next summer."

"I'll embroider days of the week dishcloths. Ten months should be enough time for someone with as little talent as I have. I'm happy for you."

They walked together to the school. When she slowed down, Israel stopped her. "Miss Anders—Della—why do I get the feeling that you're reluctant to face Miss Clayson? If you walk any slower, vines are going to grow over you."

"She can't think of anything nice to say to me," Della said. "I know she resents that I'm an Anders, but I can't help that. Why is she so bitter?"

"It's a mystery to me," he replied with a shrug. "It's probably not personal. She doesn't think I can teach either, so you're not alone." He scratched his head. "This will be my last year, because I know Blanche doesn't want to live in Winter Quarters."

"Will you miss it?"

"Yeah, I will," he said simply. "I like the children and the parents."

The main floor of the school was empty. Della glanced in her classroom, half hoping to see a new note for her on the alphabet peg board, but there was nothing. Miss Clayson had tacked a one-word message to the newel post: "Downstairs." They obeyed, Israel leading her into the gymnasium where Miss Clayson waited, tapping a sheaf of papers against her arm, her lips in a tight line.

"I'm relieved you could tear yourself away from Provo, Mr. Bowman," she said by way of a greeting.

"Wasn't easy, ma'am," he replied cheerfully. "I am now engaged to Blanche Bent."

"I suppose this means we'll have even less of your attention this school year."

"Not at all, Miss Clayson," Israel replied. "I know my job." He said it with just enough crispness in his words to make Della look at him anxiously, hoping Miss Clayson wouldn't pounce.

She didn't, to Della's surprise. She made a mental note: *Learn to stand up to bullies.*

After a long and deliberate stare at Israel Bowman, Miss Clayson turned to Della, cleared her throat, and began. "We begin school at eight thirty every morning, Miss Anders, and conclude at three o'clock. I will remind you both that children are to eat their lunch here in the gymnasium. No mess will be tolerated. Many go home for lunch, but the students most distant from school—mostly the Finnish children—will eat here. You will supervise them, of course. During bad weather they may play in the basement. Everyone is outside during good weather, of which there is precious little in the winter."

She handed Della and Israel the papers in her hands. "Here are the tentative student rosters. Mr. Bowman, we will go through your roll first."

Della looked at her own roll while Miss Clayson took her colleague through every student from the fourth to sixth grades, discussing more felonies and misdemeanors, to her ears, than successes. Israel Bowman's face was a study in impassive blandness. She wondered if he was even listening. Then Miss Clayson cleared her throat and glared at Della.

"Miss Anders, you will pay close attention to what I tell you about your second and third grade students. Your first graders are, of course, a clean slate because they are new to us. It will be up to you to mold them into good students and American citizens."

Her words sounded like grim duty. Miss Clayson looked down the list, frowning, then jabbed her finger at the paper, her eyes ever narrower. "Billy Evans! You will find him exasperating because he refuses to read. Miss Forsyth had no success. After she . . . left us, I tried, and then a host of district substitutes."

"Does he need spectacles?"

Miss Clayson sighed, and Della could tell she was frustrated. *You do care,* she thought.

"No, his eyes and hearing are excellent. He's a smart child." She tapped the paper again. "I expect him to read this year, make no mistake."

And so it went, twenty-five boys and girls in her

classroom, and one Finnish bride. Tomorrow she would find out what they already knew and build her lessons. There would be successes and failures, but that was education. Some students would learn better than others. If this class bore any resemblance to her Westside School classes, she would learn from them too.

Della wasn't sure what she would learn from the library that evening, or if anyone would even show up. She rushed through supper preparation with Mabli, then worked up her nerve to stand in front of the men at the long tables and announce that the library would be open that evening from seven to nine. She laughed when they applauded.

When she arrived early at the Wasatch Store that evening, Clarence Nix was waiting. He led her to the top floor and opened the library. She sniffed. No one had used the library in months, if the stale air was any indication. At least she smelled no mildew. Clarence showed her what to do and said he'd be downstairs in the store if she needed him.

When he left, Della opened the windows and lighted all the kerosene lamps. She took down the big signs that Miss Clayson must have put up, more threats than mere admonitions that the patrons wash their hands. Della only had one sign, and she put it over the space above the entrance.

"'Through *this* portal pass readers,'" she read out loud. *No more threats*, she thought.

She arranged newspapers that had been accumulating since Miss Clayson drove away the patrons and sat in an empty library filled with clean books but no readers. The old newspapers went in a stack by the door with another sign: "Take these for your own use." The most recent ones were given pride of place on the narrow table that ran half the length of the room. There were German papers, *The Scotsman* from Edinburgh; newspapers that must have been Welsh, because she recognized Cardiff and Merthyr Tydfil; papers from Belgium, Paris, Rome, and England.

She went around the room, impressed with the shelved books. Someone must have been especially fond of Charles Dickens and Robert Louis Stevenson because they were well-represented. She ran her fingers along the titles and pulled out *Treasure Island*, remembering how she had begun reading it at the Molly Bee that month before Papa died. She took the book back her desk and sat down, ready to begin again.

Seven o'clock came, and she sighed with relief to hear people climbing the stairs. She recognized two of the men from the boardinghouse, all cleaned up and looking surprisingly shy for men who seemed so rough when they came into the dining room. They both laughed when they read her sign over the door, came in, and went immediately to the newspapers, one to a German paper, the other to a French one.

By eight o'clock, the room was pleasantly full, men sitting at the table with the newspapers and others browsing the bookshelves and checking out volumes to take home. If there had been more comfortable chairs, she thought some would have stayed to read.

Some wives came with their husbands. They introduced themselves to her and mentioned their children, whose names she had seen on her roll that morning. They gravitated toward the women's magazines, heads together, pointing out the fashions. Della dug out old copies of *Ladies' Home Journal* and *McCall's Magazine,* wishing there were more. Tomorrow, if she had time, she would renew subscriptions with her own money.

Shortly after eight, Owen and Angharad arrived. The child brightened to see her, to Della's delight, and let go of her father's hand. Della knelt with her by the low shelf that held the few children's books.

"Da likes to read the newspaper," Angharad whispered. "Is this my library voice? Da told me."

"Your library voice is excellent," Della whispered back.

In a moment, Angharad had a picture book and was sitting on her father's lap while he read the Merthyr Tydfil newspaper.

Della sat back, satisfied, watching the patrons and listening to the rustle of newspaper. She decided that with her six dollars a month from running the library, she could easily subscribe to more magazines and newspapers. There should be more children's books too.

"Sister Anders, you're woolgathering. I was about to set myself on fire to get your attention."

She looked up in surprise to see Dr. Isgreen standing before her desk.

"I suppose I am," she whispered, clasping her hands on the desk. "No matches, please. Check out a book; check out two!"

He sat down in the chair beside the desk. "My principal aim this evening is to invite you to dinner Saturday night at one of Scofield's finest restaurants."

"I didn't know there were any," she whispered back.

"There are if your expectations are low. Interested?"

She was and told him so, then wagged her finger at him. "Only if I don't have to ride the flatbed."

The doctor put his hand to his chest as if she had struck him a mortal blow. "I blame Israel for that one."

"You would!"

Eyes lively, he put his finger to his lips. "Softly! No flatbed. Wear sturdy shoes and we'll walk. Six o'clock all right, barring any emergencies that trump everything?" He leaned closer. "That's always the caveat about physicians."

She nodded. "Barring any emergencies. I could walk to the hospital and save you a long haul up the canyon."

He agreed. "That's not too gentlemanly of me, but it will be a time-saver. I *will* walk you all the way home."

"You'd better," she said, wondering where her courage came from to be so flippant. She couldn't remember her last invitation from a gentleman.

He bowed, and she hoped the other patrons were busy reading. "I am reassured. At least you didn't call me a dirty bird, like poor old Owen over there," he whispered. "He's still laughing about that." He gave her a wink. "See you Saturday at six."

Della bit her lip to keep from laughing out loud again. She turned her attention to her actual patrons as Dr. Isgreen made his genial way from the library, stopping to chat with friends. When she looked up again it was after nine o'clock. The women and children had left, and Owen was folding the newspaper. As she watched, Angharad whispered in her father's ear, and he nodded. She came to Della's desk.

"Please, could you pick out a book? Da said he'll read it to me. I can just read small words."

"I will be happy to, Angharad," Della replied. "I think I know just the book."

She looked under Kipling, found *The Jungle Book*, and handed it to the little girl. "This is one of my favorites. You can get your father to read you a story every night."

Angharad looked through the book and nodded, handing it back for a stamped due date. "Any scary stories?" Owen asked.

"A tiger named Shere Khan, and a boy raised by wolves," Della told him, relieved to see the twinkle back in his eyes. Maybe he wasn't so bothered about her refusal to join the choir.

"Usually scary stories mean Angharad has to share my bed."

"Da! You're the one who gets scared!" Angharad teased.

"Then why are you the one who wants to sleep with me?"

"To keep you safe," she said with a perfectly straight face.

Della held her breath with the loveliness of their familiar banter, remembering her own father. "My father used to read to me too."

"You didn't have a mother?" Angharad asked. "I've heard that mothers read to children too."

"So have I," she replied, not looking at Owen. "I didn't have a mother either."

"It's not fair," she said as Della handed her the book.

"Probably not, but you have a good father, even if he is persistent."

"Is that a good thing?" the child asked as Owen turned away to laugh.

"Sometimes," Della said. "I'll see you Sunday."

Owen ushered his daughter toward the door, then turned around to look at Della. He tipped an imaginary hat to her. Satisfied, Della circled the room, straightening books and arranging newspapers, newest first. The other readers took the hint and left. She had extinguished most of the lamps when Clarence Nix came into the library. He looked around, approval in his eyes.

"I counted them," he told her. "Don't laugh; it's what clerks do. Thirty-five people this evening, and it's just the first night. Good job, Miss Anders. Any horrible black fingerprints?"

"None that I can see, except on the newspapers, and that might be newsprint. Clarence, if I give you money, could you subscribe to more ladies' magazines and the *Saturday Evening Post*?"

"I think the company is good for a few subscriptions. Save your spondulicks, even if you Anderses are plush."

There it was again. Best to ignore it. She handed him her list. "Thanks, Clarence."

Della went down the stairs and out into a cool night. Two men stood in the shadows, and she stopped, wary. Maybe Clarence wouldn't mind escorting her, if she waited.

She held her breath when both men stepped toward her, then let it out in relief. They were the two men from the boardinghouse who had been her first library patrons.

One of them tipped a real hat. "*Mademoiselle* Anders, you probably shouldn't walk alone. The saloon's closing soon, and we can't vouch for *them*."

One on each side of her, the Frenchman and the German walked her home, carrying on respectable conversation, unlike what she sometimes heard in the dining hall. She doubted her cousins touring Europe had half such gallant escorts.

Later, her scriptures read, she lay peacefully in bed, thinking of more books Clarence might be cajoled into ordering. She closed her eyes finally, thinking that Owen Davis needed a haircut, even if winter was coming.

Chapter 11

*D*ella changed her mind three times before settling on a simple green, polished cotton dress for her dinner with Dr. Isgreen. Mabli had thought the black bombazine too stern, and the voile better tucked away for summer next year.

"Green is just enough for dinner with Dr. Isgreen," Mabli said. "I have an ivory brooch that will be perfect."

Maybe she should call him Emil, instead of Dr. Isgreen. He had stopped in on Friday to the school, claiming to need to speak with Miss Clayson about students' physical examinations, even though he spent most of the time sitting at a too-small desk, chatting and printing names on heavy cardboard.

"Dr. Isgreen, your printing is not very good," Della said, looking over his shoulder.

He merely shrugged. "Free labor—it's worth what you pay for. Do call me Emil, because then I can call you Della." He frowned at his own printing. "You could be right, Della. Tell you what: I'll cut out the place names and *you* do the lettering."

When he finished, he gave Della a cheerful salute. "See you Saturday," he told her and left. She watched him out the window, hands deep in his pockets, nodding to friends and making his amiable way down to the canyon's mouth. "My goodness, someone asked me out," she murmured, her eyes on the doctor. She could count on one hand the times any man had asked her out, which invariably reminded her of Aunt Caroline's admonition about accepting such invitations. It occurred to her that he didn't have to know everything.

She walked home slowly that afternoon, relishing the balm of late summer, when the balance seemed to be tipping toward cooler, longer nights. She walked slowly on purpose, doing her best to get used to the higher elevation that still made her gasp for breath as if she were an old woman.

As she paused, she noticed a higher wagon road that wound up the canyon toward the ridge. Maybe she would take that road in a few weeks. She remembered Papa's never-flagging curiosity about such roads that meandered into the distance. "Oly, there might be something stupendous on the other side," he had told her. "You'll never know until you look."

Mostly she believed him, because she had never hesitated to walk with him to that ridge or high point. Generally, the view was more of the same, but Frederick Anders always had to look, just to make sure. She realized now that until his death in the Molly Bee, the two of them, odd adventurers, had followed many such trails, always looking for treasure on the other side.

You never were content to stay in one place, Papa, she thought, her eyes on the road as it angled toward the ridge. *There was always going to be a silver strike like the Comstock Lode just ahead or some Lost Dutchman Mine waiting for you.* When his death forced her to go to Salt Lake, she had resented his wanderlust. She didn't now; that was just Papa, imperfect like most people.

By Saturday afternoon, everything was ready for Monday's first day of school. She had spelled "Welcome, scholars" on the pegged board, using Owen's wonderful letters. She had titled one bulletin board, "Nuts and Bolts," which made Miss Clayson frown. Della just smiled, determined not to fall victim to the principal's pessimism.

"This is where I will post grades, and permission slips, should we need them, and notes that must go home—odds and ends, nuts and bolts," she explained. She pointed to the other board titled, "Autumn Leaves," with its bare-branched tree made of brown construction paper. "We'll add leaves with spelling words on them, some on the tree, and some in piles."

No comment. Miss Clayson walked around Della's classroom, looking at the place names on her desk, running her finger along the chalk trough, and blowing imaginary dust off the row of books. "Be here early Monday morning," was all she said as she left the room.

Della made a face at the principal's back, remembering all of the slights and criticism from Aunt Caroline. *You're too late to flummox me, Miss Clayson. I trained with Caroline Anders*, she thought.

After helping Mabli Reese in the boardinghouse kitchen, Della went back to Mabli's house. She pulled the tin tub into the kitchen, closed the shutters, and filled the tub from the cooking range's ample reservoir. When the water was just right, she took a change of clothing into the kitchen and closed the door.

The water was on the warm side, so she settled in slowly, happy the tub was large enough, or she was small enough to allow a welcome soak. Della figured Dr. Isgreen was worth her lily of the valley soap. She applied it generously, humming at first and then singing selections from Gilbert and Sullivan louder than she would have ordinarily, because coal was flowing down the tipple and she could hardly hear herself.

The coal quit roaring by the time she finished giving ". . . three cheers and one cheer more for the mighty captain of the Pinafore," when someone knocked on the kitchen door. She gasped.

"That's lovely, Sister Anders," she heard, as she stopped in mid-wash. "I need you in the choir."

"You're a dead man if you open that door," she threatened.

"'What never? No never,'" she heard, sung in a magnificent baritone, which made her laugh, even as she slid down lower in the water and listened to him finish with, "'What never? Well . . . hardly ever.' I'm not really a dirty bird."

She laughed in spite of her embarrassment. "This kind of subterfuge is *not* designed to get me into your choir."

"I would never stoop so low," Owen said. "Well, hardly ever . . . Didn't Mabli warn you?"

"That you're a rascal? No!"

"I told her I was going to put up shutters in your room. They'll help keep out the cold. Just finished them. May I go in your room?"

She thought a moment, remembering that her silk stockings were draped over the footboard and she couldn't recall where her corset was. She had left her bedroom door wide open too. Hopefully he was blind in one eye and couldn't see out of the other. "Um, could it wait?"

"Aye. I'll come back later. G'day, now. Do you know Yum Yum's solo from the first act of *The Mikado*?"

"I can only hit notes that high when the bath water is colder. Go away!"

She heard him set down shutters, if she could believe a man who recruited for the choir when she was sitting in bathwater. "I'm gone," she heard, then footsteps, then, "Nice stockings."

"You *are* a dirty bird!"

The house was quiet again. Della sighed and did sing Yum Yum's solo, but softer this time, since the coal was not competing.

She decided Dr. Isgreen was worth a French braid, and it turned out quite elegant, with Mabli offering comments and tucking in her curls here and there.

"Seems a crime to set a hat on it," the woman said, as

she handed Della her smaller hat. "Just this little one, and tip it forward."

As she walked toward the hospital, Della was joined by the Parmley girls coming from the store, if the striped bag Maria clutched was any indication. "Mama gave us three cents each for candy," Mary said. "Are you going somewhere with Brother Isgreen?"

"There's not a single secret in this canyon, is there?" Della asked. "He invited me to dinner. Is there really a restaurant in Scofield?"

"Two," Maria chimed in. "Papa says only a starving man would eat at one of them; I can't remember which one that is." She handed a spare Good & Plenty to Della. "Do you like Brother Isgreen? Your hair is so pretty."

Mary glared at her little sister. "Maria! Mama says ladies like their privacy."

Maria opened her mouth again, but Mary shook her finger at her. "I'm going to tell Mama you are prying!" She dropped a playful curtsy to Della. "I hope you have a lovely time, but don't stay out too late."

"I promise I won't. Cross my heart," Della said. "Thanks for the Good & Plenty, Maria."

Dr. Isgreen waited for her on the porch of the hospital, walking out to meet her in the road. She told him about the Parmley girls, and he just shrugged. "I don't think I mentioned to anyone that I was taking you to dinner."

"According to Maria, only one of Scofield's two restaurants is safe to eat in," she said. "I trust you know which is which."

"Heavens, so do I," he said. He stuck out his elbow, and she crooked her arm through his. "Ground's a bit uneven." He looked around. "This is far removed from the *glamour* of Salt Lake City, but I can't argue with the view here."

She couldn't either. The broad expanse of Pleasant Valley spread before them, a marked contrast to the tight canyon they had just left, and the narrow canyons she remembered from Colorado. "It looks like the top of the world."

"It really will in winter, when all you see is snow."

"As for glamorous Salt Lake, I was a hardworking teacher there," she said, after they were seated in the restaurant. She glanced around. After the waiter took their orders, she leaned across the table. "Dr. Isgreen . . ."

". . . Emil . . ."

"Emil, kindly tell me what rumors are circulating about me." She lowered her voice. "I'm a nine-day wonder, and I'm not sure why."

His expression turned thoughtful as though he weighed each rumor and found it wanting in some way. "You really want to know what I've heard?"

"I do. I fear my Anders name has preceded me."

"It has."

Della sighed. "Don't stop there."

"Well, everyone is convinced that you are rich and teaching here out of some exalted effort to uplift the poor miners."

"Nothing's farther from the truth," she replied, happy enough to have the matter out in the open. "My father was a hard rock miner in Colorado . . ."

". . . who owned half the mines on the Colorado Plateau. That's the rumor!"

"He never owned a mine in his life," Della said, dismayed that tales traveled at the speed of light in Carbon County.

They ate in silence for a few minutes, then the doctor put down his spoon. "I saw you in the Spanish Fork depot, talking to Jesse Knight. I *know* he owns half the mines in Utah."

"His wife and my Aunt Caroline Anders are distant cousins," she explained. "I was taking something to her from Aunt Caroline, and Uncle Jesse said he'd drop me off in Spanish Fork. That's all it was."

There was so much more she could have told him about

years of loneliness and humiliation, but she concentrated on her dinner instead. He seemed to sense her uneasiness and entertained her with stories of snakebites and lacerations from bar fights, which made her suspect he wasn't any better at small talk than she was. He stopped talking finally. "Are we the two worst people in the world when it comes to idle chatter?"

Della nodded. "It's a skill I never acquired."

"In that case, let me turn a corner in this conversation and tell you why, besides just wanting to get to know you, I asked you to dinner." He held up his hands in self-defense. "No need to be wary! It's this: I know you have a Finnish woman in your class."

"Yes. Mari Elvena Luoma," Della said, mystified. "She's newly arrived from Finland."

"Would you try to get to know her?"

"I'll be glad to." She peered at him. "Why her, in particular? I don't understand your interest."

Emil waited until the waiter removed their dishes. "It will come as no surprise to you that I'm the one who signs death certificates in Winter Quarters. I've noticed a preponderance of infant deaths in the Finnish community. I have my suspicions why."

"And they would be . . ."

"The families never call on me to assist in childbirth. Never. Granted, most women can do just fine without an attending physician, but not all. I've signed some death certificates I'd rather have avoided."

"They don't come to the hospital?"

"Few women do here, but I am generally in attendance in their homes. What the Finns do is give birth in one of their saunas and the women help each other." He interpreted her blank expression correctly. "It's a sort of bathing house, using heat to clean the body. Tough people, the Finns. The next step is to run outside and roll around in the snow."

"Uh, bare?"

"I suppose. I apologize, for this is a less-than-delicate subject. Apparently, the Finns use saunas for birthing rooms because they are clean places."

"If that's their choice, what can you do?" Della asked, curious more than embarrassed.

The look he gave her warmed her, because he must have realized her interest was genuine. "I've been here three, almost four years, Della. I'd give almost anything to convince those ladies to let me help in childbirth, but it won't come from me, I fear. Maybe you can gain their confidence."

"Does no one try?"

"No. Some of the people in the canyon don't even refer to them as white people, which seems odd," he told her. "I mean, with blond hair and blue eyes, they're whiter than every Welshman I see. But they're different, speak a well-nigh incomprehensible language, and keep to themselves."

"By choice?" she asked, remembering Aunt Caroline's first look at her, with her black hair, brown eyes, and decidedly un-Nordic nose.

"Hard to say," he countered.

"No, it's not," she replied. "Some people don't mind shunning those who are different."

Maybe she shouldn't have said that with such certainty, because the doctor gazed at her in a measuring way. "At least, that's what I suspect," she said, wincing at how lame she sounded.

"If you please, give it some thought," he said, then took the check from the waiter. "I care about everyone in the canyon. Each miner pays me fifty cents a month to provide health care. I'd like to earn my money with the Finns."

The sun was making its daily descent behind the mountains to the west that rimmed Pleasant Valley as they started toward the canyon. They walked through the little town, past the bank, the other restaurant, and two mercantile establishments. She saw two saloons down side streets and rows of neat little houses.

"You like it here, don't you?" she asked.

He nodded and tucked her arm closer to his side. "I suppose I'll move someday, because not many wives who had a choice would care for the winters here. For now, it suits me." His voice turned serious again, as it had in the restaurant. "Della, I'm not saying my glorified presence at a Finnish birth would make any difference, but I just want to have the opportunity to help if I'm needed."

"I'll do what I can," she said, touched by his concern.

He was kind enough to walk slowly, even though darkness came quickly after the sun went down. He also had no objection to stopping while she gathered her breath. "Promise me it gets easier," Della said, embarrassed at their snail's pace for her benefit.

"You'll be fine next week, and I'm in no rush tonight."

They entered the canyon mouth and passed Winter Quarters Saloon, which made the doctor shake his head. "You'd be surprised how much practice I've gotten here, suturing scalps split by liquor bottles."

"More than mine accidents?"

"Decidedly. These are safe mines, and Bishop Parmley runs them well. How safe were those mines on the Colorado Plateau?" he asked.

She knew he was just making conversation. What did he know about her father? "I suppose they were safe enough," she said, too shy to say more.

He walked her to Mabli Reese's door and shook his head when she invited him inside. Della held out her hand.

He took her hand in his. "Thanks for a pleasant evening, Della." He chuckled. "And thanks for not expecting silly small talk." He didn't release her hand. "If you ever feel like just talking, I always feel like listening. G'night."

Chapter 12

*D*ella thought about what Emil Isgreen said, long after she should have been asleep, wondering if he meant it. As a matter of course now, she traced "Olympia" with her finger in the dark, enjoying the feel of the wood. The room was warmer too. Owen Davis had come back and installed shutters on the inside of the windows, shutters with slats, so she could let in as much or little light as she wanted, and not worry about prying eyes. Della had opened one of the shutters to look at an inside slat. There it was, Angharad's red dragon.

In the morning, she hurried with Mabli through breakfast next door. There was even time for her to French braid her hair again and braid Mabli's hair too. The real fun was watching her landlady preen in front of her mirror, something she didn't think Mabli did too often. She also insisted that Della wear the brooch again on her green dress, which hadn't met with much argument. It did look nice on the polished cotton.

She was prepared for the opening hymn this time, listening with something close to bliss to the first verse of "Hark! The Children Sweetly Sing," and remembering to sing the chorus. She still couldn't help a look around. Obviously they must have thought every congregation in Utah sounded like theirs.

Rather than a duet during the sacrament, Richard Evans's exquisite tenor was joined by his wife's alto on "How Great the Wisdom and the Love," with a soprano and bass making up a quartet unmatched anywhere in the Church. Her pleasure at the beauty of their voices was equaled by her realization of just how much she had been looking forward to this all week.

Angharad and Owen Davis sat directly on front of her. He needed a haircut. She looked closer. Maybe he wore it long to cover a blue mark down the back of his neck, which went up his head well into his hair, as far as she could tell. Della leaned closer to Sister Parmley and whispered, "That's a strange birthmark."

"More like a slice of coal that nearly took his head off," Sister Parmley whispered back.

Shocked, Della stared at the blue line until little Florence had to nudge her with the sacrament bread again. She calmed herself by concentrating on the sacrament and then fell under the spell of the music, which this time was everyone humming "How Gentle God's Commands." The final hummed verse grew softer and softer until everyone dropped out, except a lone tenor. Bliss, then utter silence.

She went quietly to class as they all did, children filing out behind their teachers. She watched the children, knowing she would see some of them tomorrow in her classroom. She remembered a lesson on blessings that her favorite teacher had given in Young Ladies Mutual Improvement Association, which made her long to ask Uncle Karl for a blessing before each school year began. She never did.

Emil Isgreen sat next to her in theology class. It looked as though he had beat out Owen Davis to the vacant chair beside her in a dignified rush, well-mannered, but causing others to smile too and put their heads together, before the teacher asked for a volunteer to pray.

"Ooh, gossip, gossip, gossip," Emil said. "How are you this fair morning, Della dear?"

"Hush," Della dear said. "You're a distraction."

They were looking up the first scripture when a boy came into the classroom, glanced around, and handed a folded note to Dr. Isgreen. When the doctor opened it, all discussion stopped. One of the women in the room gasped, and Emil glanced at her, his eyes alert.

He stood up to leave the classroom. Della watched, curious, as other women looked at him, their eyes alert too. It was as though all the air had suddenly been whisked from the room. The men were watching him now, some even tensing to rise, Owen Davis among them.

"Steady, steady," he said gently. "Did you forget it's Sunday and the mine is closed? It's a broken arm in Finn Town. No worries." Everyone relaxed.

Before she had time to turn to the scripture, the door opened and another deacon came in. He looked at Della, nodded to her, and crooked his finger. "Bishop wants to see you," he said in the hallway.

Sister Parmley had whispered something earlier about the bishop issuing church callings during Sunday School. *I hope it's Young Ladies*, Della thought as she knocked on his door and smoothed down her dress.

Bishop Parmley opened the door and ushered her in to the tiny space. "Ready for school?" he asked, when she was seated.

"Willing and able," she said. "I've visited the homes, and my room is ready."

He leaned back in his swivel chair. "I tell Brother Bowman this, and I'll tell you too—if you find a student that can't afford a slate, let me know. I always have Clarence Nix order extras for the store." He smiled at her expression. "Sister Anders, sometimes there are definite advantages to being both bishop and mine superintendent. I like to know what my ward families need, and that goes for all the miners. Every child in this camp is my responsibility."

"I'll let you know," she told him.

He steepled his fingers and observed her for a moment, almost as if he was wondering what to say next. Della observed his expression, silently amused.

"I . . . I really like working in Young Ladies," she hinted, as the pause went on.

"That's not the call, Sister Anders," he said finally. "But I have to tell you, the more I think about the one I'm going to issue, the better I like it." He leaned forward then, looking into her eyes, completely serious. "I'm extending a church call for you to be secretary to the choir."

Della gasped and sat back. He couldn't be serious. Choirs didn't need secretaries. She drew her lips into a firm line as her amazement turned to irritation and then beyond irritation to something she hated to think was anger. This was a church call from her bishop, after all.

"That's the *only* way he thinks he can get me in the choir!" Della burst out, then put her hand to her mouth, ashamed of herself for speaking that way to her bishop. She felt tears start in her eyes. "I told him I wasn't going to join the choir and he's determined! Oh, Bishop, I'm sorry."

Quietly he handed her a handkerchief from a little stack beside his chair, but she could see her reaction was troubling him. She wanted to leap up and leave the room.

"Calm, calm! Sister Anders, I asked the heads of organizations about staffing needs, and several responded. Yes, it was Owen Davis who requested you and Richard Evans agreed. I prayed about all the requests and that's the one I couldn't get out of my . . ." He paused. "I was going to say 'my mind,' but I have to tell you, that's the one I couldn't get out of my heart." Another pause, then finally, "It appears you don't agree."

"I've never turned down a church calling, bishop, never," she said a long moment later, when she could talk. "Choirs don't need *secretaries*! Owen Davis is a dirty bird and a bully."

Bishop Parmley swiveled his chair toward the window and sat there for the longest time while she blew her nose again and looked in the other direction, embarrassed. It sounded like he was clearing his throat. *Oh, Heavenly Father, please don't let him be laughing!* she thought, in misery. *He'll think I am an idiot. No, he already knows I am an idiot.*

"You'll . . . uh . . . have to ask the dirty bird why he needs a secretary," he said finally.

"I wouldn't ask him for the time of day if he had the only watch in Winter Quarters," she snapped.

He turned around then, but not before she saw the ghost of smile. "Are you turning down this call? Think carefully, Sister Anders."

Della hesitated. "I don't know what I want to do," she said finally. "I really don't."

"There seems to be a little more here than I may have realized," he said, after another long pause.

"I'm sorry, Bishop," she whispered. "I was rude."

"Maybe not." He leaned toward her across his desk and took her hand. It was a warm grip and a rough one, reminding her where she was and what he did. "Think about it. You don't have to give me an aye or nay right now. Will you think about it?"

Della debated a long moment before she nodded.

"Give it a week. A fortnight, if you need more time."

His expression was kindly now, which made her throat constrict. She stood up. "I'll think." She gestured with the handkerchief. "I'll return this next week," she said and hurried out.

She didn't waste a moment leaving the meetinghouse. Thankfully there was a back door by the bishop's office, so she didn't have to face anyone in the corridor. She wiped her eyes, tying to stop her tears, but they fell anyway. Only the greatest force of will kept her from sobbing out loud. "You're a bully, Owen Davis, and I just can't face you," she muttered under her breath as she hurried to Mabli Reese's house, which she knew was thankfully empty right now.

Inside the house, she slammed the door to her room. It wasn't loud enough, so she opened it and slammed it again, then threw herself on the bed, the one the dirty bird had carved so beautifully. She couldn't think of a time when she had been this angry, or maybe a time when she had felt able to express such anger. She wasn't sure which, only that her mind was in a jumble. She closed her eyes in utter sadness and slept.

Della wasn't certain how long she slept. The room was light, so she didn't think it was much past noon. She opened her eyes, relieved that she had left the meetinghouse so no one had to see her behave like a baby. With any luck, no one would ever know what a fool she had made of herself in the bishop's office. She knew Bishop Parmley would never say anything about her childish behavior; he was a bishop, after all. *I could probably tell him anything*, she thought suddenly. *For that matter, I could probably have told my bishop in Salt Lake anything too. Was I more a fool then or now?*

It took more time, but she willed herself to calmness. Maybe by two o'clock she would have the courage to go to sacrament meeting. She didn't have to tell anyone why she had left Sunday School. It was between her and the bishop, and he had given her two weeks to think about the most stupid calling any bishop had ever issued.

She lay still, composing her mind, thinking of school to start tomorrow. Soon she would be busy with pupils and teaching, and there was the library three nights a week. She closed her eyes in agony. *Oh, please let Owen Davis not want to read the newspaper!* She knew she would have no trouble in school, separating Angharad from her father. That sweet child would never know how badly her teacher had been bullied; if Della had learned anything at university, it was to maintain a professional attitude. *I have to settle my mind and think through this calling*, she told herself. *It's going to take at least two weeks to work up the gall to turn down a calling from my new bishop.*

She heard Mabli's front door open; Sunday School must be out. She had promised Mabli she would help in the boardinghouse kitchen. But those weren't Mabli's light footsteps. Della felt her stomach tense. The footsteps paused outside her door.

"I'm so sorry. I don't know what happened, but forgive me."

Never, she thought. *Not ever.* Silence. He walked away ,and the front door closed quietly behind him.

It took every ounce of courage Della possessed to walk to sacrament meeting at two o'clock.

The choir was sitting on the stand for sacrament meeting. Della sat with Mabli on one side of her and Sister Parmley and her family on the other. *I can do this,* she thought. She closed her eyes during the sacrament prayer, concentrating and hoping the Lord wasn't too displeased with her. This time, a soprano sang, her voice so achingly lovely that Della sighed with the beauty of it. She thought about not taking the sacrament, but she knew with all her heart just how badly she needed it. Besides, she wasn't angry at Owen Davis any more, just sad and discouraged. She couldn't blame him for what he didn't know, but she also knew she had better not see him or think about him for a long while. If that unaccepted calling had to hang over her head like a wet sheet, so be it.

He made no move to talk to her after church, which relieved her further. Back from the morning's emergency, Emil Isgreen was kind enough to walk her home. As they strolled along, he told her about the little boy with the broken arm.

"They had taken him to the sauna," he told her. "I've never been in one before."

"Was it steamy?" she asked, curious.

"Oh, no. Just cool and so clean. It was an easy break. I could have fixed it anywhere, but they wanted the cleanest place, I guess." He nudged her shoulder. "He'll be one of your students, I think. He's seven."

"Yes, one of mine."

When they passed the school, she looked up at her classroom windows, with their construction-paper leaves. Soon there would be more. She felt her anticipation returning, until she saw Miss Clayson looking at her.

I could ignore her, Della thought. She waved instead. She couldn't be certain, but she thought the principal moved one hand just a bit. Ah, well. She had nine months to try to sweeten up a prickly woman. *And is that prickly woman her or me?* Della asked herself, not even sure where that thought came from.

"Have the first day jitters?" Emil asked, when she was silent.

"Not at all," she told him. "I'm ready."

They walked in companionable silence the rest of the way to Mabli's. He agreed to come in for chocolate cake, downing two pieces before she had finished even one. Mabli watched him eat, her eyes bright.

Mabli put another slice in a pasteboard box. "Take this with you. It's a long way to the canyon mouth!"

Della walked the doctor outside. He paused on the step and gave her that half-friend, half-physician look she was already familiar with. "I guess you didn't realize it, but you made it all the way from the meetinghouse to Mabli's without needing to stop and gasp your lungs out. I'm about to pronounce you cured of altitude-itis. You're an official Winter Quarters resident now."

Della curtsied playfully.

"We could celebrate with dinner next Saturday night," he said. "Interested?"

A second date. Time to nip this in the bud. She shook her head. "Not right now. Let me get a week or two of school behind me, and then I'll know if there is life after three o'clock every day."

Emil nodded. "I'm harmless."

"I know that," she said quietly. "I just need a little time."

When she returned to the house, Mabli was putting on her hat again. She picked up the rest of the cake. "Speak now or hold your peace," she said.

Della shook her head. "It was lovely, and my clothes still fit."

Mabli stopped at the front door. "I invited Owen and Angharad over to help us finish it, but he mumbled something about a sore throat. He doesn't lie any better than he cooks, but I said I'd take it to him. Want to come with me?"

It was Della's turn to mumble something, so Mabli shrugged and said good-bye.

Della stared at the closed door for a long time, a sinking feeling in her heart. "I'm making a mess of this. I never intended to," she said out loud, then went to her room and quietly closed the door on a Sunday she wanted to forget.

She sat on her bed, feeling that unwelcome numbness she remembered from earlier days in Salt Lake. Maybe she couldn't run away from it after all. Maybe she wasn't trying hard enough.

Someone knocked on the door, and she sighed, put upon. Mabli had gone to her brother-in-law's house, so it wasn't Owen. She went to the outside door and stood there, her hand on the knob but so unsure. "Yes?"

"Andrew Hood, your Sunday School superintendent. My son Milton wanted me to ask you something."

Della opened the door. "Come in, please. Do have a seat."

"No Mabli?"

"She took some cake to Owen and Angharad." Della sat down so he would sit down too. "Milton. Let's see, I believe he is six and this is his first year of school."

"Exactly so. That's probably why I'm here."

He didn't speak for a moment, and she began to wonder what errand a six-year-old could send his father on the day before school started.

She had to smile. "Please tell Milton that he might be

afraid, but I *still* expect to see him tomorrow! Please assure him that we will have fun. I believe in fun."

That was all it took to break the ice. Brother Hood laughed. "Here it is, miss," he began in his forthright way. "Every year I give my children a father's blessing before school starts."

"What a wonderful thing to do," Della murmured, thinking of the years when she could have used precisely such a priesthood gift.

"I imagine most of the fathers in this canyon do that. Well, my dear, I gave Milton his very first before-school blessing. When I barely had my hands off his wee head, 'Papa,' says he, 'I don't think Miss Anders has a papa here. Do you think she is nervous? Maybe she needs a blessing.'"

"What a kind child," Della said, touched.

"He is that. Takes after his mum," Brother Hood said. "He kept after me, and then so did Rupert—he's in your class too. I promised them I'd ask if you wanted a blessing before the start of school. Well?"

"My goodness," she said, her voice soft. *I could say no and continue to ruin what is already a dreadful day,* she told herself. *Or I can say yes and begin again.* "I would like that more than anything, Brother Hood," she told him.

"Well, then," he said. "Your full name, my dear?"

"Della Olympia Anders," she said, barely able to speak as the whole force of what he was about to do settled gently down on every pain she had felt all day, sweeping them away.

"A lovely name for a lovely lady."

She closed her eyes as he put his hands on her head and gave her the father's blessing she had craved for years with all her heart, without even knowing what it was she wanted until it was happening to her right there. She listened closely as he blessed her with good health all year and an understanding of her students, many of whom came from so many different places in the world. He prayed for the Lord to keep her and her loved ones safe that year.

I have no loved ones, she thought, but as he said it, she wondered if that was really true. Maybe she would find some this year. She could already count Mabli, if she wanted to, and Angharad. As he gave her a priesthood blessing, everything suddenly seemed possible.

He paused then, and she almost wished him to continue, even though he must be done. Or maybe he wasn't. His hands, already firm on her head, seemed to press with more strength.

"Bless this dear child of thine, Father. Let her be more brave than she has ever been, and more kind too."

He took his hands off her head. Della stood up and held out her hand, but it wasn't enough. He held open his arms, and she was in them in a moment, letting him hold her as he probably held his own children, this generous man.

"Brother Hood, I don't know what to say, except thank you from the bottom of my heart," she told him. "You can give Milton and Rupert a good report."

"Aye, lass, I will." He went to the door and let himself out as quietly as he had entered.

Chapter 13

On Monday morning, as Della stood at the window and watched the children, she wondered if she would ever anticipate the beginning of a new school year without enthusiasm. Maybe if she ever did, then that would be the time to find a new career.

She walked into the entrance hall as the children came up the stairs. Her satisfaction deepened as she saw Milton Hood, who had engineered her blessing last night, generously sharing his own father with her. She couldn't thank him today—separation of church and state, after all—but she knew where to find him on Sunday.

There wasn't any law against touching his shoulder as he came in the door, eyes wide, some fear in them. "Milton, you're a prince. Thanks for coming to my classroom today."

His smile brought one of her own and must have been contagious, because it spread to other youngsters his own age, students new to the business of learning.

Angharad Davis came with the Evans children, so Della knew Owen was in the mine. Della stayed in the hall, and her pupils naturally clustered around her. Before directing them downstairs for the opening assembly, she admired Angharad and Myfanwy's starched pinafores and Billy Evans's handsome cravat, probably a relic of his father's.

His arm in a sling, the next little boy through the door must have been the Finnish child whose arm Emil Isgreen had set yesterday during Sunday School. Della made a mental note to ask him if he needed a pillow to rest his arm on, in class. She accepted a flower cleverly folded from newspaper, then came to Mari Elvena Luoma, who lingered in the doorway.

"Good morning, Mrs. Luoma," Della said. She pointed to the basement stairs and held out her hand. "Come with me?"

Mari nodded. Holding hands, they waited together until the last child was in the building. Della felt the woman's hand tremble in hers, but Mari did not hesitate to go down the stairs.

The students had gathered in the gymnasium, seating themselves on the floor and looking at Miss Clayson, who stood before them, dressed always in black and tapping a ruler in her hand. Israel Bowman stood beside her, a big grin on his face.

Nothing seems to daunt him, Della thought with amusement. A weekend in Provo with his fiancée must have been a positive restorative. She reminded herself that she was brave too because she had been given a blessing.

With a little squeeze of reassurance, Della released Mari's hand and joined her fellow teachers in front of the students. While they waited in silence for a few tardy scholars, Della admired the Winter Quarters Elementary School students—clean faces, well-combed hair, and an air of expectancy. The Parmley children were dressed a little better than the others, but not by much. She suspected Sister Parmley was far too wise to flaunt her family's superior status.

With an ache in her heart, Della remembered her first day at Stake Academy in Salt Lake City, wearing the best she had, because Aunt Caroline had made no effort to buy her anything better to replace the clothes she had worn in her own mining camp classroom, where everyone was equally poor.

Della glanced down at her own tidy shirtwaist with its small green and white flowers, and gold watch pinned there, a far cry from Miss Clayson's funereal black. She smoothed her brown skirt. *Two inches from the ground and just brushing my shoe tops*, she thought, remember the Rules for Teachers. *I can't do anything about my wild hair, Miss Clayson, but I am a teacher.*

At eight thirty on the dot, Miss Clayson began what was probably her usual first-day lecture, full of admonition and warning, as she continued to tap that ruler. Breathing heavy and their cheeks flushed from running, two children came in after she had begun. Miss Clayson paused and gave them an icy stare that made Della's stomach start to ache, and *she* had arrived on time.

"Starting tomorrow, *that* will earn you an hour after school, writing 150 times on the blackboard, 'I will never be late again,'" the principal commented. She continued her speech, after another glare at the two offenders, paler now than snow.

When she finished speaking, the gym was absolutely silent. Della couldn't even hear anyone breathing and wondered for one irreverent moment if Miss Clayson had included not breathing in her lengthy list of things not to do in school.

She wasn't through. As Miss Clayson took a leisurely look around the silent gym, Della had to grudgingly admit that the principal knew how to command a crowd. Not a child moved.

Miss Clayson turned to her left and indicated Israel Bowman with a flick of the ruler that made him flinch involuntarily. "You older students remember Mr. Bowman. He is teaching the fourth through sixth grades."

Della couldn't help but notice a sudden relaxation among the students in that age group, and a few smiles.

"Mr. Bowman is from Provo," Miss Clayson explained, giving *Provo* the weight of a word not generally spoken of in polite society or groups younger than twelve.

Heavens, even towns don't measure up, Della thought.

"He is a graduate of the University of Utah and has been teaching here for three years."

She turned to her right, and Della felt her stomach tense. "Miss Anders will be teaching the first through third grades," Miss Clayson said. "She is from Salt Lake City and has a teaching certificate from the University of Utah." To Della's ears, the way she said teaching certificate made it sound like an object scraped from the bottom of a shoe.

"I have the seventh and eighth graders," Miss Clayson concluded.

Della had to bite the inside of her cheek to suppress the laughter that threatened. Everyone not in grades seven and eight had audibly sighed, even Mari Elvena Luoma, who didn't speak much English. Had he been in attendance, Della doubted that even Bishop Parmley could have resisted a sigh of relief.

Her amusement was followed by shame. Since she was standing so close to her, Della couldn't overlook Miss Clayson's own little sigh at the students' involuntary reaction. She thought of Andrew Hood's blessing, and his admonition to think of others kindly. *I can begin here,* Della thought. *I'm not certain how, but I must.*

Della jumped, along with everyone else, when Miss Clayson slapped her ruler in her hand. "Classes dismissed. Pupils, follow your instructors!"

Miss Clayson looked at her first, and Della nodded, struck again by the slightest wounded look in the principal's eyes. Della turned her attention to the littlest ones in the room. "Come, children," she said. "Let's go learn."

When the warning bell clanged at five minutes to three o'clock that afternoon, Della looked up in surprise from the table with all the construction paper leaves, wondering where the day had gone.

"We have run out of time," she said to her students, who clustered around the table, turning in the leaves with their names spelled on them. "Let's put these on our tree tomorrow morning, before we begin our arithmetic. Do you remember what I have asked you all to do tonight? Make sure you take some of my magic paper with you. Remember: draw me a picture of something you did this summer."

Each student selected a piece of shirt cardboard, the magic kind from the inside of men's ready-to-wear shirts. As she watched them, Della congratulated herself again for rescuing all the paper from her summer job in Auerbach's Menswear department. She had applied for the job on a whim, never thinking the menswear department would have her. Her employer assured her that ladies made the best salesmen. Once she survived her initial shyness, she had proved him right. One reward was all the stiffened shirt paper she wanted that would have been discarded.

Her first week's salary meant a mound of Franklin Rainbow Crayons from Auerbach's stationery department. Her triumphant return upstairs after lunch, with a stack of Rainbow Crayons, had made her boss laugh and tell Samuel Auerbach himself. That afternoon, the boss of all bosses had asked to meet the lady in Menswear who bought crayons with her first week's salary.

When Della calmed her nerves and told Mr. Auerbach she wanted them for the Westside School, which couldn't afford much, he had generously bought her even more crayons, presenting them with a flourish on her last day of summer work. She had left those crayons for Westside and still had enough for Winter Quarters too.

It was a pleasant memory. "You each have a box of crayons now. Take them home tonight but bring them back tomorrow, along with your picture. We will have Mr. Bowman's class select the best one of all, and I will send it to a kind man in Salt Lake City. Agreed?"

"Agreed," her students chorused back to her. They were learning already.

The bell clanged and class was over for the day. "Draw something lovely tonight," Della told them.

When the last student left her room, she sat down and leaned back in her chair, pleasantly tired.

Israel Bowman stuck his head inside her open door. "Survive it?"

"Yes, indeed," she told him. "We've learned our names and can spell them mostly." She clasped her hands on her desk. "Israel, I'm wondering just how much Miss Forsyth taught them last year."

He came closer and perched on her desk. "Between you and me and almost everyone in this canyon, Miss Forsyth didn't have much on her mind except the mining engineer."

Della rolled her eyes. "Checking my older students' reading comprehension today, I was afraid of that! I'm quite tempted to teach *all* my students this first quarter at a sec-ond-grade level. The third graders will get rudiments they lack, and my bright little first graders will probably shine at that grade."

"Why not? Do it." He looked around, then picked up a ruler from her desk and slapped it in his hand like Miss Clayson, then whisked it close to her nose. "And *don't* fall in love with anyone in Winter Quarters Canyon!"

She crossed her heart and pretended to spit in her hand. After Israel returned to his own classroom, Della straight-ened up her room and looked over the stack of slates on the table next to her desk, checking addition and subtraction on the older students' slates, and numbers from zero to nine on her little ones' slates. She had taken three slates from the closet to give to those without them and thanked Bishop Parmley in her heart for the extras.

She looked at the Regulator on the wall. If she hurried, she could thank him in person, if he happened to be in the Wasatch Store. Quickly, she swept out her classroom, took a good look at the broom, and carried it next door to Israel's classroom, where he was going over class work too.

"Going to find a new mode of travel in and out of the canyon?" he joked and ducked when she pretended to throw the broom at him.

"How does your fiancée tolerate you?" she teased in turn.

"She thinks I'm wonderful."

She held the broom up to her. "Remember what Miss Clayson told me about Billy Evans?"

"Ah, yes. He's the little fellow who just can't seem to read." He tugged his hair as though to pull it out by the roots. "Miss Forsyth used to tug at her hair whenever she talked about him. I swear she developed a bald spot."

"Don't joke. He needs to learn to read," Della retorted. "When I asked him today, he took this broom, held it like I'm holding it, and promised me he'd read when he was taller than the broom!"

"I give him credit for quick thinking," Israel said. "Trouble is, he doesn't seem to grow much."

She returned to her classroom, taking one more look around before she closed the door. Indecisive, she stood in the hall a moment, part of her wanting to stick her head in Miss Clayson's classroom as casually as she had dropped in on Israel, to ask how her day went. The discretionary part of her suggested she tiptoe from the building so Miss Clayson wouldn't hear her leave. She listened to the discretionary part.

She was in luck at the Wasatch Store. Bishop Parmley was just coming down the outside stairs as she started up. She stepped back and waited for him, still embarrassed about her reaction yesterday to his innocent church call.

"Bishop, I owe you an apology."

He waved her to silence, his expression good-natured. "My, dear, it's now a matter between you and the Lord. When you two decide, just let me know."

She continued home, happy to unhook her shoes and just wiggle her toes and flop on her wonderful bed. She closed her eyes and thought about her students and then about the builder of her bed and his quiet apology outside her door yesterday.

"I should apologize to him," she murmured to the ceiling. "Better than that, I should explain to him why I didn't like being bullied."

She thought about apologizing all during supper preparations next door, where, thankfully, Mabli was moving too fast to wonder why Della was so silent. After a close call with her fingers as she grated carrots, Della forced herself to pay attention to supper. While eating in the kitchen, she turned around in surprise to see the French miner and the German miner standing in the doorway.

"We're going to escort you to the library," the Frenchman said. Maybe it was the French way; there was nothing in the tone of his voice that indicated she might have a choice in the matter. In fact, the slightly militant look in his eyes told her what he thought about a Frenchman—even a coal miner—allowing a lady to walk *anywhere* unescorted after dark.

Della also remembered Brother Hood's blessing and decided to be kind, particularly since she probably didn't have a choice in the matter. "Your escort is appreciated," she told them, touched to her heart.

Theirs was a quiet walk to the Wasatch Store that evening. The Frenchman's initial burst of solicitude was followed by amazing shyness. His German friend was no more loose-tongued. Surprising even herself, Della kept up a mild chatter about her school day and about the little boy who wasn't planning to read out loud until he was taller than the broom. It was enough conversation to carry the three of them down the hill and into the library, where the two men went immediately to the newspaper table.

Della was not surprised that few children came to the library that night. She knew her class was drawing, and she suspected Israel and Miss Clayson had given their own assignments. She half hoped that Owen Davis would drop by to look at the newest Merthyr Tydfil paper. He didn't. Half of her was relieved and the other half worried that he might be embarrassed to see her. Neither half gave her much comfort.

As it was, she had ample time to draw her own picture for Samuel Auerbach, thinking she would send it along with the others that they chose. She was no artist, and heaven knows she was the smallest cog possible in the well-oiled machinery that was Auerbach's. Still, even a department store owner would recognize the lady in wildly curly hair who was ringing up a purchase for a gentleman in Menswear and stashing another sheet of "magic paper" behind the counter.

She looked up to see Levi Jones, book in hand, staring down at her drawing.

"I had a summer job working in the menswear department at Auerbach's Department Store in Salt Lake," she explained as she checked out his book. "That's where I got the paper your Myfanwy is probably drawing on right now. It's that sheet of stiff paper found inside ready-made shirts. I saved the thin cardboard and bought crayons with my first week's salary."

He gave her a puzzled look, and she understood two things with perfect clarity—Levi Jones had probably never worn a manufactured shirt in his life, and he must be wondering why someone named Anders needed a summer job.

"Brother Jones, I'm a poor member of the Anders clan," she said, suddenly ready to answer the question this polite man would never dream of asking. Maybe they all needed to know. "I'm part of the Anders family tree that has to work, same as you do."

He digested that but still shook his head. "Maybe they should have taken better care of you."

Maybe they should, she thought, struck by another fact: The Welsh with their welcoming ways would never have treated her like Aunt Caroline, not in a million years. It was going to be an evening of revelations—epiphanies, as her more worldly professors at university would have said. Through some unlooked-for miracle, she had fallen among good people.

"I'm no artist," she admitted, keeping her voice low, although she suspected every man was listening.

"Oh, I don't know." He pointed to her little figure with the curly black hair. "I would know that was you in a roomful of paintings. *You* really sold shirts?" he asked, as though he still couldn't quite believe it.

"And socks, suspenders, collars, and other things a lady never mentions," she whispered back.

He threw back his head to laugh, then remembered he was in a library and closed his mouth, his dark eyes merry. He gave her a courtly bow and left the library.

The clock was striking nine o'clock when Owen Davis came in. At first she wondered if he had waited for the last minute because he was afraid she would be angry with him. She decided to err on the side of charity; he had probably waited until Angharad was asleep, whatever his business.

He stood by the newspaper table until the other library patrons left, except for her self-proclaimed escorts. *I owe Brother Davis an apology*, Della thought.

The French boarder came closer. "Miss Anders, should we wait for you?"

"Yes, please do," Della said as she stood up. "I'll be down directly. You might . . . you might just wait belowstairs." *No need for everyone to hear me apologize*, she thought.

"We walk her home," the German explained to Owen, distinctly proprietary. "She shouldn't walk by herself here."

"I agree," Owen said. "Would you let me walk her home tonight?"

The Frenchman and German looked at each other, then at Della.

"He can walk me home, just this once," she told them.

They left, but not without a backward glance that

Owen seemed to have no trouble interpreting.

"If ever two men wished me to the underworld . . ." he remarked. "And I don't mean a mine! Sister An—"

"I'm so sorry I was rude," Della interrupted, talking fast in her embarrassment. "I didn't expect a calling to be a secretary in the ward choir." She took a deep breath. "Why? Choirs don't need secretaries."

If she thought that would bother him, she was wrong.

"Ours does. It's because of Eisteddfod." He straightened up the newspaper. "I'm interrupting you here. I can explain Eisteddfod to you on the walk home." He seemed to know what she was thinking. "Angharad is asleep. She specifically wanted me to talk to you about her drawing. I didn't come here to make you apologize."

She thought about that frank statement as she extinguished the lamps. He stood by her desk, looking at her drawing. "I saw Levi Jones as I was walking here. He told me about your summer job."

"In almost three months, I accumulated a respectable stash of thin cardboard and bought crayons," she told him as she closed the door, knowing Clarence Nix would lock it later.

There was enough light at the foot of the stairs to see the question on his expressive face, but Della didn't give him a chance to ask it. "Tell me what Eisteddfod is and why you think you need a secretary."

He winced. "I know skepticism when I hear it. Eisteddfod is a poetry and singing festival. It's probably been going on in Wales since my relatives worshipped trees. We started our American Eisteddfod three years ago. Last year the competition was in Huntington. The year before in Wales—not that Wales!—in Sanpete County. The first year we held it here, and next June, we'll hold it here again."

Owen seemed in no hurry, and she couldn't think of any reason to jar him into motion. The night was cool but calm and he said Angharad was asleep.

"Are they all Welsh choirs?" she asked as they strolled along.

"Less so here in America. We sing in English and Welsh." He stopped so she stopped. "We need a secretary to send out letters informing the choirs and handling any correspondence."

"There's not a soul in your choir already who couldn't do that," she pointed out, walking again.

"You're right," he admitted, surprising her. "I want you in the choir too, because you have a very nice voice. I enjoyed your voice last Sunday when Angharad and I sat in front of you. We sat there on purpose, to spy out your voice."

"You're honest."

"Of course. I'm not a bully, though. I'm sorry you felt I was."

She was silent, concentrating on her steps because the ground was uneven. "I'd rather not talk about it," she said finally.

"That's your privilege," he said. He stopped again. "I would never bully a woman. I just can't imagine anyone not wanting to sing with us. And now you're wondering how one man can be so arrogant."

She shook her head. "I don't know you well, Brother Davis, but I do know this: You're pretty much clear as water and far from arrogant. Now tell me, what was Angharad's concern about the drawing?" *I dare you to unchange that subject*, she thought.

"She had to use a lot of the red color because she wanted to draw the red dragon," he said. "She wanted me in the picture too, so I helped her. Was that allowed?"

"Of course. Oh, I see. Is she afraid she used too much red, because now the crayon is shorter?"

"Exactly. I told her you probably didn't mind, because that's what colors are for."

"You tell her I don't mind, and I'll tell her too."

"I'll wager more little boys used black for the mines."

"Surely not," she said. "They're too young, and I wanted *their* summer, not their father's."

"Don't be too surprised by what you get, then," he said mildly. "Mining is a family business."

They walked on in silence. The wagon road was empty now, and lamps went out in homes as they passed them. In another moment, Owen started to sing "Lead, Kindly Light." Della could have sighed with the pleasure of his voice.

"You sing too," he said after the first verse.

Della shook her head. He shrugged and sang the second verse. The third verse brought them to Mabli Reese's house. He opened the door for her, then glanced at the boardinghouse.

"Hark there. Your escorts don't trust me."

Della waved to the Frenchman and the German who stood on the porch. "Good night, sirs!" she called.

She stepped inside. "I believe everyone in this canyon is determined to watch out for me."

"I believe we are," Owen said, and it warmed her heart.

Owen seemed to understand her shyness. "It's time someone did look out for you. I hope you'll think about that calling."

"I told the bishop I would," she assured him. "I'm going to take a walk on Saturday. It's a good time to think."

"Don't get lost," he told her as he went to the door.

"I won't. I just want to take that upper wagon road. I'm no adventurer."

He stood in the doorway a moment longer. "You *are* an adventurer. You're in Winter Quarters, aren't you? Good night."

Della closed the door quietly, stood there until he had time to walk away, and then opened it again. Sure enough, he started over "Lead, Kindly Light." She hummed the alto line along with him until his voice faded in the distance, perfectly in tune with himself.

Chapter 14

*W*hen her students arrived the next morning, Della had propped her drawing against the chalk trough. Riku Kokkola, he of the broken arm, handed her another flower folded from newspaper and stared at her picture.

"You really did work in a big store?" he asked.

"I really did. I sold socks and shirts and cravats."

His astonishment was as obvious as Levi Jones's last night. "Do you mean men in Salt Lake City do not have wives who knit socks and make for them shirts? What a strange place is this Salt Lake."

Della laughed. "It's 'and make shirts for them.' Do you think people in Salt Lake are strange?"

"Maybe."

He took his seat, after handing her his drawing and the Rainbow Colors.

"This for you, Just Miss Anders," Mari told her.

"Oh, it's just . . ." Della laughed. "Call me Miss Anders, if you please, Mrs. Luoma."

"You call me Mari, if you please. I am a student here."

Della glanced down at her drawing and sucked in her breath. The whole panorama of what must be Finland spread before her on a modest sheet of thin cardboard—coastline, water impossibly blue, and birch trees lining the shore. In the foreground, Mari Elvena had drawn a ship's railing and a woman's hands on them.

Della looked up. "My goodness, Mari, you were leaving Finland. Was it hard to leave?"

Mari leaned toward Juko her interpreter, who whispered in her ear. She shook her head and whispered back. Della nodded to Juko, who cleared his throat.

"She said, 'Not so hard. Heikki was here.'"

Angharad handed in her drawing last, and there was no overlooking the worry in her eyes, even though Della was certain her father had told her not to be concerned about using a lot of red. "My goodness," she said again.

The red dragon of Wales glared back at her, but he rested on a table, where two people—one a young girl, and the other a man with a thin blue scar on his neck—were looking down at him, the girl holding a crayon.

"Da said you wouldn't mind if he helped me. He draws figures better than I do. And I'm still sorry about all that red," Angharad said.

"You drew the dragon, I am certain," Della told her. "Colors are to be used. No fears."

"Aye, miss. Da said you would tell me that, but it's still a prodigious amount of red."

Only the greatest force of will kept Della from laughing, wondering how often Angharad's father used that word. "Prodigious, yes, but I never argue with artists. Do be seated, my dear."

Della looked at her class, everyone seated now, most of them with their hands clasped on their desks, as she had requested at the beginning of each day. She saw no fear on anyone's face this morning, the second day of class.

Della stood by her desk, amused to see the little girls' eyes on her shirtwaist and skirt, reminding her of the way she had observed her own teachers in the mining camps, wondering how they could afford such lovely things. She had made the light-blue shirtwaist herself, and the skirt came from ZCMI's bargain aisle, a reject because there was a tear easily mended. *They're admiring me as I used to admire my teachers*, she thought and stood a little taller.

"I *was* going to start this morning by handing back

your arithmetic and reviewing it," she said, duly noting the disappointment. She held up her hand. "However, I believe we should turn our attention first to these marvelous works of art. Agreed?"

"Agreed!" everyone said.

On her direction, each student came to the front, took a drawing, and explained it, while Della stood in the back of the classroom to observe. The range of expertise varied from stick figures to an accomplished drawing of a girl kneading bread as her mother watched. Mary Parmley's drawing of a girl gathering wildflowers told her worlds about a Parmley summer. *When I was her age, I was washing dishes in a boardinghouse*, Della thought.

Bryn Lloyd stood with his picture, a boy standing by his father in the mine.

"Bryn, that's interesting, but you were supposed to draw me *your* summer, and not your brother's," she said.

The other children tried not to giggle. Della thought they were laughing at Bryn first, but realized they were trying not to be impolite and laugh at their teacher. She looked closer at the picture. The boy was Bryn. She could tell by the way his black hair curled around his ears, wearing a too-big miner's cap with a wick lamp. He was eight years old and he was in the mine with his father. He was also one of the students with a slate from Bishop Parmley.

"I was wrong, Bryn. That's you, isn't it?" she said. "What are you doing in this picture?"

"I'm a boney picker, miss," he said, and there was no disguising the pride in his voice. "I pleaded to help my family, and my da finally said aye."

Della, say the right thing, she told herself, swallowing. "You're a fine lad to help your family. What is a boney picker?"

The children looked at each other, as if amazed there was an adult in the world who didn't know something that simple. Della laughed at their expressions. "You have to help me! Remember, I sold shirts and socks to gentlemen last summer!"

She had given them permission to laugh at her ignorance, and they obliged her. Bryn stood by his desk and hushed the others with one hand. *I see a leader*, Della thought, waiting.

"I pick out the rock from the coal that Da mines," he explained.

"You do this in the . . . the pit? Isn't that what you call it?" she asked, interested.

"Pit. Colliery. 'Tis the same," he said in his musical Welsh way. "Any road, the checkers and weighers give Da more money when the rocks are gone."

Another hand shot up. She called on Roderick Farish, who stood beside his desk now, his eyes eager. "Next year, t'bishop says I can be a gate holder in the summer, and open and close the mine doors."

"My goodness. You'll be nine then, and in Mr. Bowman's class," Della said.

He nodded.

"Doors where?"

"On the Farish level," he said proudly, looking around. "My papa and his brothers mine that level, and so shall I someday."

"You have your own level?" Della looked around her classroom. There was no disguising the look of admiration on the students' faces.

"Aye, miss. We Farishes are that good!"

Heavenly Father, let me teach them all I can, but oh, let me learn about families from them, Della thought. She admired the line of cardboard shirt drawings telling the whole story of Winter Quarters canyon, then pointed to the horses.

"Whose is this?" she asked. "Horses in the mine?"

"I feed and curry them when they come out, miss," Juko Warela said. "There's a barn by the Number Four mine. Isä—Papa—mined in Rock Springs before we moved here.

I learned about cowboys and horses there." He glanced at Mrs. Luoma. "When I grow up, I am going to be a cowboy *and* a translator."

Della clapped her hands. "I think you should!"

She turned back to the drawings. To choose only one or two would be sheer silliness, she decided.

"I am going to send all of these drawings to Mr. Auerbach," she announced. "I'll hand them back now. Write your name on the back, and a short sentence about what you're doing in the picture. Tell Mr. Auerbach what your fathers do too." She noted their skeptical expressions. "I can promise you that he doesn't have the slightest idea what happens in a mine. It will be your job to educate him."

"Please, miss, so far, all I can write is my name," Angharad said.

"Six-year-olds, come to my desk, and I'll help you." She looked at the older students. "Turn your desks together and help each other. Sing out if you get stuck, and don't be too noisy."

The children did as she said, bending to their work, talking softly, laughing a little. When the Parmley girls and Myfanwy Evans finished, they went to her desk and offered to help the little ones. By the time the bell rang for recess, the drawings were done and lined up in the chalk trough again. After they left the room, Della looked at what they had written on the back of the cardboard. Margarad Llewellen had even written a recipe for oatcakes, promising Mr. "Owback" she would make him some, if she ever went to Salt Lake City. "They're best with butter, but butter is dear," she wrote. "Sometime Mama takes lard from Da's lamp and we use that."

Della blinked back tears at that one, nodding to herself. She would write a letter to Mr. Auerbach and attempt to explain these modest lives to a man who lived in a mansion. Clarence Nix probably had a small box in the Wasatch Store, one just big enough for the whole story of Winter Quarters.

She looked through the drawings again, fascinated and maybe even envious. Except for Mari Luoma's picture, every picture had more than one person in it. Victor Koski had crowded six blond children sitting close together onto his magic cardboard. They appeared to be sitting in clouds or steam. All she could see were faces with sweat pouring down in big drops, bare legs and feet.

Curious, she turned over the picture and laughed out loud. "Is sauna and we are getting clean," Victor had written. "Come to Finn Town. You get clean too."

"Mr. Auerbach will think I have lost my mind," Della murmured to herself as she wrote the day's arithmetic lesson on the chalkboard.

"I already think you have." She turned around to see Israel Bowman lounging against her open door.

"No, no, it takes more than two days of class for that," she joked back. "Look at the wonderful drawings."

"The ones my class is going to judge?" he asked.

"Changed my mind. I'm sending them all to Mr. Auerbach." Della dusted off her hands. "What do you think?"

"Magnificent," he told her.

"Do you ever find yourself learning more from your students than you teach them?" she asked.

"Every doo-dah day," he replied quietly. "Don't tell Miss Clayson. She'd call us derelict in our duties to these poor miners' children." He nudged her arm. "You're already under their spell? That's some sort of record. It took me a whole week."

"I had a head start," she told him and took a deep breath. "I'm a miner's daughter."

"I wondered," he said. "Something you said on the train made me think you were. You already know how hard it is. Why are you here? Come to think of it, you're the lady with more advantages than all of us put together, aren't you?"

"Think again," she said. She knew she had said too

much, and she prayed for the bell to ring to end recess. When it did, she couldn't help her sigh of relief. "And that's all I'm saying. Shoo! Back to your class."

When the warning bell rang hours later, Della looked up in surprise. *You'd think I was a first-year teacher and hadn't a clue about pacing myself through the day,* she scolded herself. "Where does the time go, William Perry?" she asked the little boy finishing his arithmetic on the board.

Puzzled, he looked at the clock. "It's right there, miss," he pointed out.

"Of course." She clapped her hands. "Tidy up your desks. We look like ragbags." It touched her to see they looked as interested at three o'clock as they had at eight thirty in the morning.

She cupped her hands around both ears. "What is it you're supposed to remember that we learned this afternoon?"

"Do not touch blasting caps!"

"Louder. I couldn't hear you."

"Do not touch blasting caps!" everyone shouted.

"Excellent. Scram now. It's a lovely day out there."

They left in a good-natured jumble, slowing down immediately when they saw Miss Clayson standing just outside her door.

Miss Clayson just stood there. *What have I done now?* Della asked herself.

"We were rather loud this afternoon," Della said tentatively.

Miss Clayson came into her classroom and marched to the closet, flinging it open to see Franklin Rainbow Colors neatly lined up, all of them with a child's name.

"What game are you playing, Miss Anders?"

Della opened her mouth, but she could tell from Miss Clayson's frigid expression that the principal didn't want her to talk.

"All the students could talk about was the pictures you had them draw on . . . on . . . magic paper!"

"Cardboard liners from men's shirts," Della said, stung by Miss Clayson's lack of imagination.

"And these crayons! Everyone was talking about those too. We use pencils and pens in this school, Miss Anders, and while I'm at it, don't let them call you just 'miss.' It's a British Isles affectation, and I'm trying to root it out. Here you are *Miss Anders*. If I heard them say 'aye, miss,' to you once, I heard it a hundred times! And why on earth would you tell them to 'scram'? Miss Anders, must you bring vulgarisms into my school?"

Della was silent.

"What do you have to say for yourself?"

Della looked at the floor, suddenly twelve again and under the thumb of someone else who didn't want her. She willed her mind to go blank, as it used to go blank, but something had happened. Maybe it was Brother Hood's kindly blessing Sunday night. Maybe it was the children's pictures of their brave little lives with parents who loved them, drawn on magic paper. Maybe it was Angharad's red dragon, fierce and bold, or the blue scar down her father's neck, or even the rough French and German boarders, determined to keep her safe on lonely walks. *If I cannot be as brave as my students and these miners, I don't deserve to be here*, she thought suddenly.

It took all her strength to look into Miss Clayson's angry face. This was usually where she mumbled and apologized to Aunt Caroline, but maybe there would always be Aunt Carolines.

"Well?"

"I'm not sure where to begin, with so many accusations," Della said. "I do know this: I have been assessing this year's second grade pupils, and Miss Forsyth did them a great disservice. So did whoever else tried to teach them last year. The third grade pupils have not progressed either."

Della paused and made a discovery: Bullies don't like to

be challenged. "Magic paper, crayons and 'aye, miss' aside, Miss Clayson, I intend to reintroduce the third graders to the essentials. I'll bring along the first graders, who seem quite bright to me. We'll have a meeting of the minds in the second grade level and see where that gets us by December."

"If you're still teaching here then," Miss Clayson snapped.

"I will be," Della replied. "I wouldn't dream of leaving Winter Quarters Canyon." She went to the closet and took out the broom, thinking of Billy Evans. "I will teach Billy Evans to read, and . . ."

The closet seemed to remind Miss Clayson. "Those crayons! We are not so frivolous here. These are poor children who need all the education they can get, to find their way out of the mines. Maybe you cannot assess such needs, considering your own background."

"It is precisely because of my background that I know their needs," Della fired back, wondering where her courage was coming from. "They don't know they're poor! Their parents love them and they do the best they can." *I wish I had been blessed with half their advantages*, she nearly said, but stopped herself in time.

Della began to sweep the floor as Miss Clayson seethed.

"I could dismiss you right now," she said.

"I doubt you could get another teacher here this year," Della said, her voice calm as she swept around her desk. "I have excellent references and have done nothing to warrant dismissal. Each student will be working at grade level by May, when school ends." She stopped sweeping and looked Miss Clayson in the eyes again. "We will have fun along the way, with magic paper and crayons. We might even sing and dance a little, if the mood is on us."

Silence hung in the classroom like a foul odor as Della kept sweeping. When she finished, she put the broom away and began to erase the board, pressing hard because her hands were beginning to shake.

She turned around and nearly gasped to see Miss Clayson coming closer, her eyes alive with anger now, as though she had been deliberately stoking some inner fire that Della could not understand. She pushed Della aside and picked up the drawings in question, flipping one after another faster and faster. She stopped on Bryn Lloyd's drawing of him and his father, standing close together in the mine.

"What is this?" Miss Clayson snapped.

"It's . . . it's Bryn and his da . . . his father. Bryn is a boney picker in the summer because it helps the fam—"

"This is the very thing I am determined to squelch!" Miss Clayson shouted. "You're encouraging them! You're glorifying life in the mines!"

"No, I—"

"I want them out of the mines!" Miss Clayson waved the picture, then clutched it in both hands, as if to tear it in half.

"Don't you dare!" Della said, trembling in her own anger. "I asked my children to draw me a picture of something *they* did during the summer. This is what Bryn Lloyd did. That is all. I am not glorifying *anything*, Miss Clayson. I merely want to know my children!"

"Your children! They are *pupils*. Students. We are to mold their lives!"

Della was pleading now. "Don't tear that picture. I couldn't bear it if Bryn ever found out what you think of him and his family. Don't. Just don't."

Della held out her hand, even though it trembled. "I will educate them to the best of my ability this year, but I refuse to even suggest that the work their fathers do is anything less than noble labor."

The room was silent, except for the ticking of the clock and Miss Clayson's labored breathing. Miss Clayson flung Bryn's picture at her and stalked from the room, slamming the door behind her until the windows rattled.

Della sagged against the desk, then sank to her knees to retrieve the picture, drawn so lovingly. She picked it up and set it carefully on her desk with the others. She heard a sound and looked up in fear, not certain she could withstand another visit from her principal.

Israel Bowman stood in the door now, his face white. Della just shook her head and got to her feet. She shouldered past him and hurried down the back steps. Hanging onto the swings, she threw up on the playground.

When she finally looked up, humiliated, Israel was sitting on the back steps, a glass of water in his hand. She sank down wearily beside him and accepted the glass, drinking it down.

"I heard everything," he said. "My word, I think Winter Quarters Canyon heard it all!"

"Oh, no," she whispered.

"No fears, Della," he said, getting up to pump her another class of water. "I'll wager you'll have a canyon full of champions, if word of this gets out. How dare she bully you like that."

She drank, then gave him a weak smile. "I hope to high heaven there weren't any students in the building."

"Not too many," he told her, attempting his cheerful self again, although she could tell he was still shaken. "Just a Parmley, a Pugh, an Jones, and a Llewellen in my room, their eyes like saucers! I told them to scurry out the back way. Pretty fleet children." He put his arm around her shoulder, gave her a squeeze, and let her go. "Della, you'll do. She didn't bawl me out quite that bad my first week here. Walk you home?"

She nodded, grateful for his solicitude. She looked at the mess she had made by the swing set and groaned.

"I'll sluice it away while you gather up your pictures. I certainly wouldn't leave them here. Della, those pictures are probably even more wonderful than you know. You're really going to send them to *the* Mr. Auerbach?"

He kept up a soothing conversation all the way to Mabli Reese's, after a quick stop at the Wasatch Store to rummage through a pile of boxes until she found the right one. Clarence Nix assured her he would get a package in the outgoing mail tomorrow morning, if she would bring it by on her way to school.

"You going to be all right?" Israel asked, as he walked her to her front door.

"I am, thanks to you," she said.

He held up his hands. "I can't take credit for the way you handled Miss Clayson. See you tomorrow, Della. I'll, uh, scram now."

Della went inside and closed the door, just leaning against it, relieved to be home, relieved to have half a canyon and a closed door or two between her and the wrath of Clayson. With a sigh that ended in a ragged sob, she unbuttoned her shirtwaist and had it off, trailing behind her, by the time she collapsed on her bed. After a few minutes, she sat up and looked at the two red dragons at the foot of her bed. She left her bed and picked up the small carved box on her bureau, turning it over to see Angharad's little signature dragon there. She went to the wooden shutter and found the dragon. Her heart seemed to lift as she suddenly realized she was surrounded by the protection of dragons.

She lay down again, exhausted, and thought of dragons and *bwca* and singing and brave men with coal scars who worked underground. "Owen, you're no bully at all," she murmured. "I'm going to be stubborn, though. If I went to choir practice tonight, I would just cry."

She slept for an hour, then woke up, put on her old dress and apron, and went next door to help Mabli get supper for the miners. By the time the girls had cleaned the kitchen and carried their portion of food home to their families, her heart was good again.

$\mathcal{C}$hapter 15

⌒⟨◈⟩⌒

$\mathcal{D}$ella stayed up too late, writing her letter to Samuel Auerbach, telling him of her students and their drawings on the cardboard from Menswear. Mabli came in when she finished setting tomorrow's bread at the boardinghouse. Indignation burned in the woman's eyes. "Little Doris Pugh told me."

Della put down her pen. "Miss Clayson's just a bitter woman, for some reason." She sat back, suddenly tired. "I choose not to become like her."

Mabli brewed them chamomile tea to serve with her shortbread biscuits. "I made extra for your class tomorrow," she said, then picked up her knitting.

"Mabli, are the dragons good or evil?"

"They are neither. They are *defiant*." She stood up then, kissed the top of Della's head. "Good night, my dear. God grant you a good sleep."

He will, Della thought. She finished the letter, read it again, and set it in the box with the heart and soul of her students, her amazing, unexpected reward after only two days of teaching in a mining camp. Maybe she would write to Uncle Jesse Knight tomorrow night in the library, when she wasn't so upset. She had promised the Knights a letter.

But it was late and Mabli had to get up early to fix breakfast. She might lie in bed all night and toss and turn, but she wouldn't disturb her landlady. She was unbuttoning her shirtwaist again and thinking about an apple in the kitchen—dinner had been gall and wormwood—when someone knocked softly on the door.

Her heart in her throat, she imagined Miss Clayson there with some giant powder to toss in the room and blow Mabli's tidy house to smithereens. *Della, you're an idiot*, she thought. She edged toward the door, unwilling to open it.

Another knock and then a woman's voice, with lilting accent, and not Miss Clayson's.

"Sister Anders, it's Annie Jones. Do let us in."

Della let out her breath and opened the door, stepping back in surprise to see Sister Jones followed by a dozen others. As she looked at them, she realized this was the Pleasant Valley Ward choir and wondered what Owen Davis was up to now.

Sister Jones seemed to have appointed herself spokesman. "Forgive us for the lateness of the hour, but we were talking about the drawings after choir practice and wanted to see all of them. We've only seen our own children's drawings."

They don't know about my confrontation, Della thought, relieved not to tell them. "Come in, all of you. I'll pass them around." She laughed. "I had them sign their names small at the bottom on the front. You know, as great masters like da Vinci and Raphael signed their work. On the back, I wrote a little about the picture too, and so did they."

She took the pictures from the carton, grateful she had not packaged it to mail yet and handed them from parent to parent. Della's heart felt at peace again to see Billy Evans's father nod his head to see his son fishing in Winter Quarters Creek. She had to dab at her eyes as she watched Sister Margarad Terfil run her fingers gently over the picture of her showing Maud how to knead bread. Rachel Hood laughed to see her daughter going underwater as her husband baptized her in the creek, dammed up for just that occasion, according to Alice's account.

"We wait until summer, when the creek water is warmer," Rachel confided.

"I was ten when I was baptized," Della told her. She realized with a start that she had never told anyone even that much about her own baptism, because Aunt Caroline had thought it shameful for her brother-in-law to wait so long.

She looked around, pleased at the sight of satisfaction written so large over something so small. There was Owen Davis, taking Thomas Farish's good-natured teasing because he didn't have a boney picker of his own, but just a daughter. The pictures drawn on magic paper with Rainbow Colors went around again, and then the parents filed out as silently as they had come in, except for Owen, who held up his hands in self defense.

"Not guilty! Sister Jones insisted we disband c-h-o-i-r early so we could see the masterpieces."

He had spelled out the word, which made her laugh. "You're i-n-n-o-c-e-n-t," she spelled back. "Probably as p-u-r-e as Ivory Soap too." She opened the door for him.

She thought the others had gone, but they were standing outside in a semicircle. When Owen joined the men's side, someone gave a note, and they began to sing to her in Welsh. Della leaned against the doorsill and listened, her heart full now where only an hour ago it had been empty. When they finished, they walked slowly away, Owen tagging behind again.

"What was that song?" she asked him.

"A welcome. "And now *nos da*, good night." He turned away to join the others.

"*Nos da*," she said softly into the night.

The next morning, Della opened the front door to see purple thistle, yellow flowers she couldn't identify, and white straw flowers tied together in a bundle with red yarn. It was wrapped in a Finnish newspaper, so she looked up the canyon toward Finn Town, a smile on her face. She hurried to put them in water, then grabbed up the package of pictures and hurried to the Wasatch Store.

Della gave the package to Clarence Nix to mail for her, and he whistled to see it addressed to Samuel Auerbach, care of Auerbach's Department Store.

"You certainly know all the right people," he said to her.

"Very few," she assured him.

"Oh, let's see," he said, counting on his fingers. "Karl Anders, Jesse Knight himself, and now *the* Mr. Auerbach?"

All Della could do was shake her head and hurry on, determined not to even approach being late, not with Miss Clayson probably still on the warpath. Let Clarence think what he wanted; everyone else already did.

Miss Clayson must have declared a weird sort of truce, Della decided by the end of the day. It was probably too much to think she regretted her outburst, but the principal was her usual surly self, without yesterday's added vitriol.

Still, there was something vaguely disturbing in the air, familiar to her because she had a sixth sense about trouble, ingrained in her from life with Aunt Caroline. Her students were not as exuberant as yesterday and there was no mistaking the way they seemed to make themselves small against the wall as Miss Clayson welcomed them into the school building.

Once they had negotiated the perils of the front hall, her students settled into their classroom with relief equal to her own, because she knew it was their refuge too. Every eye went to the bouquet of wildflowers she had brought along.

"A bird told me this was from one of our Finnish classmates," Della announced. "Tell me, Pekka Aho, how do I saw 'thank you' in your language?"

Pekka looked around. "It's not allowed."

"It is in my room," Della said, her voice firm.

"Kiitos," he replied, his voice equally firm.

"Kiitos," she repeated, then took a small yellow flower from the bouquet and angled it into her curly hair.

After school, Miss Clayson walked by her classroom several times but made no move to enter. Della corrected papers, one eye on the door, until she could have chewed nails with her disgust at herself for being so fearful. Wearily, she returned her attention to the work in front of her, dreading nine months of this.

"Ready to go?"

Della looked up a few minutes later to see Israel standing in her door. Bless his heart, he was going to escort her out of the building.

They walked down the front steps together, Israel with his coat slung over his shoulder. He looked around and breathed deeply.

"Ah! The fragrance of coal and sulfur," he said, which made her laugh softly. "Or maybe it's fire and brimstone coming from the belly of the school, where the imps of the underworld reside."

"That's coming a little strong," she scolded.

"I know. Did I tell you that my Blanche worked here two years ago? This is where we met."

"Then why . . ."

". . . isn't she still here? Miss Clayson just doesn't seem to want anyone to be happy. Sad, but there you are. It bothered me to watch her try to intimidate Blanche, as though daring her to teach these lovely children with her whole heart. Something burned that woman somewhere. Wish I knew what." He turned to face her. "Keep teaching with your whole heart. We owe it to them, and you owe it to yourself."

Della thought about his words that evening as she set out the latest newspapers in the library. She had brought her flowers to the library, unwilling to let them languish at school while they wilted. Better to get another few hours of use out of them. Using the window as a mirror, she put another yellow flower in her hair.

Dr. Isgreen commented on her flowers when he stopped in, still carrying his medical bag.

"Putting on airs, Miss Anders?" he teased.

"Of course! Two wildflowers that are nameless and homeless," she replied. "I am radical."

"What I would like you to be is my dinner guest this Saturday evening again. I mentioned it earlier. Any thoughts on the matter, or must I dine forgotten and alone?"

There it was again. "I can't this Saturday," Della said. "I am going on a long hike and will probably be sunburned and unfit for company when I return." *I'm not really putting you off*, she thought. *Just sparing you from bad news.*

The doctor took her refusal in stride. "I'll just to ask you again next Saturday." He tapped her desk. "You can congratulate Joe Padfield on Sunday. He's now the father of another son."

"I shall, Emil," she said gently.

"Was it something I said?" he asked, his voice equally gentle.

"It's hard to explain," she whispered.

"Find someone to explain it to," he said, and she heard nothing but infinite patience. "It could even be me. I'm known in some circles as a good listener. G'night, Della."

She knew it could have been worse. She sat at her desk, wondering where her usual patrons were. She went to the window, looked down, and felt her heart miss a beat. A group of men and some women had gathered below. Clarence Nix had joined them. He just shrugged and up they came, orderly and quiet, but with something more in their eyes.

The women looked at her. She tried to interpret their expression as she thought over her day and the awful day before. Surely they didn't think she was the author of that bit of nastiness, brought on by her principal.

"No, I . . ." she said, then stopped as they came closer. She backed up until she was pressed against her desk. Suddenly it was too much, and she put her hands up to protect herself. In another moment, she had covered her eyes, twelve again and afraid.

"Wait a moment. Stand back, please. You're frightening her, and you don't mean to."

Owen stood there, moving them back. Della opened her eyes, startled now to see concern on those faces that had looked . . . she wasn't sure how they had looked. Maybe it was her imagination; there were too many of them.

He said a few quiet words in Welsh, and the women took hold of their husbands and tugged them back. He turned around, and she flinched from habit.

"Calm now," he said, speaking as soft as Dr. Isgreen had spoken. "We're your friends here, and we've just heard something that made us fair angry at your principal. Please, Della, we're your friends."

With a sob, she went to the other side of her desk and sat down hard, then leaned her forehead on her hands. She heard a few more quiet words in Welsh, then English, and the room was silent. Annie Jones knelt beside her, her hand gentle on her back. She handed her a handkerchief, and Della took it with shaking hands.

"Bishop's here too," she whispered to Della. "Oh, my dear, what did you bear for us?"

Della pressed the handkerchief to her eyes and forced herself to breathe slower until her dizziness passed.

Anne began to caress her back. "My son was afraid to say anything, but he told my Levi tonight. What Gwilym heard from Mr. Bowman's room was too many unkind words directed at you. That's what we *don't* like, as God is our strength."

Della raised her head from the desk. Maybe if she looked only at Annie, the rest of them would disappear. But there was Owen, looking at her with so much concern. She turned all her attention to Annie Jones, who had given her bread.

"All I did was ask your little ones to draw me a picture of something they did this summer."

"I know," Annie said.

"She doesn't understand miners, does she?" Della asked. "And when your children say 'aye, miss' to me, she thinks it keeps them Welsh, or English. I think she means well, but she doesn't understand miners. I do, actually. My father was a miner. He died in a mine."

Della put her head down again. She didn't want an audience for such childish behavior, she who was supposed to be dignified and professional and their children's teacher. What must they be thinking?

She swallowed and set her lips in a tight line, demanding order from a heart that could barely beat. In another moment she was in control. It might last long enough for her to get back to Mabli's house and her little refuge with all the dragons. She glanced at the clock through blurred vision.

"I should have stayed in Salt Lake," she whispered to Annie, and maybe to Owen too, because she looked at him next.

"No, miss. We need you here, think on," he said with the ghost of a smile. He leaned closer, his words for her alone, and Annie backed away, understanding. "I know you better now. I could smite myself for bullying you."

His face was close enough to hers to sniff the odor of coal and sulfur, but she was getting used to that. "You didn't mean to," she whispered.

"I never will again, miss."

She smiled this time, not much of a smile. "Thank you. That's all I need to know."

He stood up, apparently satisfied. Annie touched her shoulder. "Do you want us to say anything to Miss Clayson? Strength in numbers."

Della shook her head. "It's my fight. She didn't say anything today, so she might be regretting what happened. I will teach the way I know best. If at any time *you* are not satisfied, tell me." She managed a shaky laugh. "Just one at a time, though."

That seemed to satisfy the parents. They looked at each

other. Some nodded good night to her and left the library. Others made themselves comfortable at the newspaper table. Annie plucked another yellow flower and tucked it in Della's hair. She whispered in Della's ear. "Myfanwy is desperate for curly black hair. I don't know what to do!" She kissed Della's cheek and left with Levi.

Soon it was just Bishop Parmley standing there with Owen. He came closer. "I'm quite willing to rescind that call, Sister Anders."

"No, sir. I promised I would think about it, and I will."

"I can also say something to Miss Clayson. She has to listen to me."

"It's my battle."

"No, actually, it's the battle of every immigrant. Just say the word." The bishop touched his finger to his forehead in salute and left.

"Going hiking on Saturday still?" Owen asked.

She nodded. "I don't need any company."

"You're so certain, miss?"

I'm not really, she thought. *What I am is confused, and I don't need an audience for that.*

"Aye, mister."

She wished his eyes weren't so kind, but they were, pools of brown with real depth.

"That's 'aye, dirty bird,'" he reminded her.

"Don't tempt me. *Nos da*, dirty bird."

Della watched him leave. "You're short for a dragon," she murmured too low for him to hear. She turned her attention to the sheet of paper in front of her, where she had written, *Dear Uncle Jesse and Aunt Amanda*. She picked up her fountain pen, pleased to see that she was not trembling now. *Let me tell you about my interesting students,* she wrote.

Chapter 16

*D*ella heard thunder Friday night after the Frenchman and the German walked her home, but the storm blew over. Saturday came cool and fair, perfect hiking weather. Breakfast was soon on the boardinghouse tables—platters of sausage smelling strongly of sage, hash made from yesterday's beef and potatoes, and canned peaches.

When the dishes were done, Della sliced some cheese and leftover hash to put between two slices of Annie Jones's oat bread that had mysteriously appeared during what was probably Levi's walk to the day shift. Mabli filled a pint jar with water, adding it to a cloth bag, with the admonition not to be late getting back, and to sing as she walked, in case there were bears about.

"You're *not* going to discourage me," Della scolded mildly.

"I would never! Stay on the road, though."

"I will. You're a dear to worry about me."

She put on an old skirt and shirtwaist and only one petticoat this time. She had an equally old sweater that she knew would end up knotted around her waist, but it would feel good right now. She subdued her curls with a bandanna that used to be her father's.

Outside the front door, Della smiled to see an elaborately carved walking stick, with a note skewered to the end. She detached the note. *This was my Da's. Use it to ward off bears and bullies. O*, she read.

The day shift was already in the mines, so she had the

road to herself as she swung along, getting used to the feel of the stick. She stopped once to look and found more than one dragon wound about the beautiful staff. Obviously, Owen's father had taught his son everything he knew. She thought about that and wondered what her father had passed down to her. She knew she looked nothing like Frederick Anders with his tall, blond good looks and eyes blue enough to challenge the skies, or grey when things weren't going well. As she remembered, they were mostly grey in his final few years.

She remembered how much he liked to read and had taught her when she was younger than most. One luxury she recalled was the Sears and Roebuck catalog. In good years, there were two, one for the back house and the other to read. After she was baptized, he had scrounged up a Bible from somewhere. She never had a Book of Mormon and took his word for it that there was such a thing and she should believe in it.

But the catalog was a constant. Once or twice, when the mine paid, Papa actually ordered a few things for her from the catalog. Most Christmases, she and Papa decided what they wanted from the catalog, cut out the pictures, wrapped them, and gave them to each other.

She started her climb up the switchback road behind the Parmleys' house and the other, nicer homes that belonged to the foremen and checker and weigher men. The road was steeper, and she used the walking stick, glad of it. She perched for a long while on a boulder that the sun was beginning to warm, hiking up her skirt because there was no one to see her. She gazed down on Winter Quarters Canyon, pleased with the view.

She was too far away now for the noise to reach her. There was no smell of coal or sulfur, just the clean odor of grass dried for months by the sun and still giving off the fragrance of August. She lay back on the rock and watched a hawk wheel high overhead, noodling along on air currents, probably looking for voles or field mice.

She slept then; the sun was just warm enough. Even the red dragons on the end of her bed hadn't been much protection against bad dreams of Miss Clayson chasing her and throwing Rainbow Colors at her, which exploded against the blackboard. When she opened her eyes again, a chipmunk observed her from a nearby boulder.

Refreshed, Della continued her climb, stopping to look back and get her breath. Soon the canyon below was out of view. She climbed for an hour, leaving the road to gather thistles and something resembling Queen Anne's lace. Yellow flowers like the ones in the bouquet Mari Elvena had given her seemed to grow out of the rock, a testament to grit and ingenuity. She stuffed the flowers here and there around the bandanna, reminding herself to take them out before she returned home.

Finally she reached the point where she could look down on hawks below her now in the canyon. She was on a ridge, following it south, keeping company with quaking aspen that she knew would turn yellow in a few weeks.

The road continued along the ridge, and she almost followed it, remembering those trails she and Papa had traveled, her trudging along behind on shorter baby legs.

She left the road and walked into a wide meadow there at the top of the world. She found another boulder and sat on it, removing her sweater, and then her shirtwaist, shy at first then confident. No one was nearby. She unbuttoned her camisole too and let the breeze play on her. This wasn't a corset kind of day. She sighed with pleasure and closed her eyes again.

All was silent except for an occasional birdcall. She thought through the humiliation of the week from Miss Clayson, then measured it against the concern of Israel Bowman, Dr. Isgreen's gentle insistence that she have supper with him again, Angharad's dragon on the magic paper, and Annie Jones's second loaf of oat bread.

Thinking of the oat bread made her hungry. Della sat

up and buttoned her camisole again. She ate the hash sandwich. She looked inside the satchel to see that Mabli must have added a fat dill pickle, confined in a twist of waxed paper. A bite of pickle and a bite of sandwich gave her a meadow banquet, swigged down with slightly milky water from a pint cream jar. After lunch, she felt disinclined to move. The sun had peaked overhead and was beginning its slow descent. Clouds billowed to the west, inviting more raptors to coast by on air currents, one audacious hawk even dropping down to eye her as potential carrion.

"What, pray tell, Della Olympia Anders, are you planning to do about your call as choir secretary?" she asked out loud.

She sighed. The bigger question was how could she remain in this close-knit, gossipy canyon and convince its inmates that she wasn't what they thought, without revealing what she was?

Della held up her hand and spread her fingers, looking through them to the sky. "It probably can't be done," she said.

She wondered again what maggot in her brain had compelled her to snatch that job opening off the board in the education department. She could have found an inexpensive flat in the west side near her school and moved from the Anderses' house on the avenues. The city was big and she was anonymous. Instead, she had come to a mining camp, trying to find what?

She looked around her, realizing why she had gone no farther. This meadow looked something like the meadow where she had spent most of her childhood. True, the mining camp of Hastings on the Colorado Plateau, home of the Molly Bee, was higher, unlike this meadow, which seemed to be part of a ridge. The flowers were the same; so was the fragrance of drying grass, and the breeze that she knew from experience would turn into a howling rage in winter.

Maybe some ill-natured imp had made her pluck that

job card off the bulletin board, tricking her into thinking she could go home again. The more mature part of her brain assured her that she could not. The other side, the one that had been so terrified only a few nights ago, was looking for something or someone, dead or gone or never there in the first place.

She knew that to accept the bishop's calling was to open herself up for the first time in years. One glance at her students' lovely pictures lined up on the chalk trough had cemented them firmly to her. She knew these children because they reminded her of herself. Maybe coming here was one way of going back to see a younger Della Anders, and maybe change the course of events for them, if not for her.

It was a jumble in her mind and she didn't understand it. Sitting there cross-legged in the high alpine meadow, maybe she hoped to glimpse that little girl again and tell her not to be so fearful. Even if she couldn't change her own childhood, maybe she could understand it.

As she sat so still, she heard water running, gurgling over rocks. She stood up and stretched, took care of personal business, then walked farther into the meadow, holding her hands out to touch the waist-high grass. She found the creek and filled her pint bottle for the return trip, flicking some of the icy water on her face, which felt tight from the sun. As she walked, she decided she liked the people a few thousand feet below her too well to tell them much about herself. Bishop Parmley had said he would rescind the call. She would request that on Sunday.

Funny, though—her decision, once made, left her more hollow than usual. She knew she should pray about it but discarded that thought almost immediately. It was just a silly calling, mattering little in the great scheme of things. The bishop could find her a spot in another organization. She closed her eyes as she walked, remembering how Bishop Parmley had told her he felt it was right in his heart.

Feeling awkward, even in the middle of nowhere, Della knelt and folded her arms. She had no idea what to ask for, except maybe one more chance to tell her father thank you for what he tried to teach her, even though Aunt Caroline had not a good word to say about him.

It was probably no prayer. All she said was "Oh, Father," not even sure which father she was addressing, maybe both. After a long, silent time on her knees, she said "Amen," rose, found the walking stick, and started back.

The road was right where she left it, and there was nothing faulty about her sense of direction. She was in no hurry, even though the sun seemed to speed its descent, once it had passed the arc of noon. The clouds boiling from the west rose higher, and she knew there would be rain tonight; this one wouldn't blow over. She liked the sound of rain on the roof and she figured Mabli's roof was watertight, considering that her brother-in-law seemed the sort of man to look after his relatives. She could read a book in bed and look at the red dragons between her feet on the footboard.

She realized she had walked much farther than she probably should have. Well, her time was her own and it was Saturday. No harm done. She started humming "Choose the right, when a choice is placed before you," because it had a quick, no-nonsense beat that would keep her moving. Her active conscience made her think of the words, and she wondered again about her decision to tell Bishop Parmley no. The succeeding verses did nothing to assuage her, so she switched to "Put your shoulder to the wheel," which speeded her walk but left her dissatisfied, too. "We all have work, let no one shirk," was not a chorus designed to comfort the unwilling.

"Della, *you* are the dirty bird," she said. Maybe "Columbia, the Gem of the Ocean," would get her down to Winter Quarters canyon without a guilty conscience.

She started to sing then stopped; someone else was singing. "Oh my," she murmured, as her face turned red. The owner of the walking stick must have wondered if she was planning to return it.

She stood still in the road, irritated with herself for spending so much time in the meadow that Owen Davis felt she needed to be rescued. Another thought filled her mind, giving her the clearest indication she could have wished for, that her awkward, two-word prayer was about to be answered. Out of habit, she rejected it immediately, then had the grace to reconsider.

Della listened. The tune was familiar, but the words were Welsh. She hummed along, then harmonized softly. She stood there, wracking her brain, until she remembered "Men of Harlech," which the glee club boys had sung one year. She continued down the slope.

The singing got louder, and then she turned a bend in the trail, and there Owen was, swinging along at a steady pace. He smiled to see her and elaborately wiped imaginary sweat off his forehead.

"There now! I thought I would have to walk to Sanpete County to find you."

"I wasn't running away."

"I should hope not. I stopped in at Mabli's after my shift. *She* was getting worried, which meant *I* had to do something about it. Such is the way of women."

"I'm sorry," she said, and meant it.

"No fears," he replied, turning around when she reached him and starting down slower now, to match her stride. "I wanted to talk to you anyway. Was this the worst week of your life?"

She could tell from his tone that he was trying to joke, but she couldn't help her reply. "Heavens no! I've had far worse weeks."

That couldn't have been the answer he wanted, because he puffed his cheeks and let out a whoosh of air. Still, he didn't seem to want to turn the idea loose. "Surely it's in the top shelf of bad weeks."

"No, not really," she said again, hoping she sounded matter-of-fact enough, because she didn't want his pity.

He seemed to think a change of subject was in order. "Did you walk as far as the alpine meadow?"

She nodded. "Lovely."

"Aye, miss!" he teased, then grew serious. "I went there after Gwyna died, when I had no earthly idea how I was going to survive her loss and raise an infant."

Della stopped walking, ashamed of her whining. "My worries are paltry by comparison."

He nudged her into motion again. "I doubt that. Did you arrive at any decisions? I know I didn't."

"I didn't either," she told him. "Guess it's not much of a meadow, eh?"

He laughed and said nothing more until another bend in the road. He stopped and faced her, hands on his hips. She had no choice but to stop too and turn his way, to be polite.

"Della, I'm no bully and a dirty bird only on occasion, but you have to tell me what's going on."

"No, I don't," she retorted but did not move. His eyes wouldn't let her.

"You do. You're carrying a burden I made worse, even though I don't know how, really. Could you share it?"

"Why would you want that?"

He shrugged. "I like you. You came to our canyon, and we take an interest in people here. It's the Welsh way."

"The nosy way?" she challenged.

She didn't get a rise out of him. He shrugged and started walking again.

"Wait. Wait. Don't leave me here alone." She winced, unwilling to sound so pathetic, but unable to take back words spoken.

He looked at her and nodded. "You afraid of heights?"

"I don't think so."

"Take my hand."

She let him lead her off the trail and up the slope to an outcropping of rock.

"I call it Arthur Pendragon's Seat. Angharad and I come here when we want to talk. Let me help you seat yourself. If it makes you nervous, we'll go back to the road."

She sat and dangled her legs over the rock. She said nothing, afraid to begin.

"Here's what I know about you," Owen said, just when the silence was starting to make her wary. "You're an Anders, so you come from a wealthy family in Salt Lake City, and you're working in a mining camp. But you tell me your father died in a mine. Everyone thinks he was a mine owner, but I have my doubts."

Della took a deep breath. It was now or never. She let her breath out slowly, prepared to say nothing, until Owen leaned closer, his shoulders touching hers.

"He died and left you at the mercy of your relatives, didn't he?"

She nodded. "There were times when I hated him for doing that," she began, her voice tentative. "That sounds wicked!"

"It's not. Have you ever heard of the Abercarn Horror?"

She shook her head.

"On September 11 in 1878, my da and two brothers went into the Cwmcarn pit at the Prince of Wales Colliery. They and 265 miners never came out. There was an explosion and a two-month fire that was put out with thirty-five million gallons of water. They were tombed in there, and they remain there still. My brother William was sixteen, and Alfred was eighteen. A year later when I was ten, I became a boney picker like little Bryn Lloyd in your class. When I was thirteen, I went into the pit."

"Why?" She couldn't help her anguish. The pressure of his hand increased.

"We had to eat, and the Davises know mines. But let me tell you, Della, there were times when I was underground that I hated my da too. It passed." He shook his head. "There were more times when I wonder if Da, Al, and Will had drowned or burned up in the explosion. Too many nightmares."

Della couldn't help the shudder that ran through her. "When my father died, I was alone because I had no mother. How could he *leave* me?"

"Not his choice," Owen replied frankly. "A silver mine?"

She nodded. "The Molly Bee, close to Hastings. We lived there off and on, for all of my life in Colorado."

"What happened?"

"A cave-in, Papa and two others. He's buried in Hastings, so I at least know where he is. I asked my aunt and uncle once if they would have his body moved to Salt Lake's city cemetery. Uncle Karl asked Aunt Caroline to look into it, so Papa remains in Hastings."

He nodded, silent for a long time. She waited; she knew Owen Davis was bright and would figure it out. He sat silent for a long while, as the sun slipped lower. He began tentatively.

"Your uncle is a busy man, eh?"

"Very. When I showed up on his doorstep with a tag around my neck reading *Karl Anders, Salt Lake City*, he turned me over to Aunt Caroline."

"What did she do for you?"

For the first time since she had sat down on the rock overlooking the road below, she turned to look at Owen. To her relief, there was nothing but concern in his eyes. "Absolutely nothing."

He moved restlessly, then spoke as if to himself. "A grieving girl . . . you were . . ."

". . . almost thirteen . . ."

". . . comes to her house and she does nothing."

Della nodded. "Uncle Karl sat me down and made me tell him what had happened to his brother. He said he would take care of me and said he would enroll me in Salt Lake

Stake Academy. He did. He told Aunt Caroline to get me some better clothing. She smiled and nodded—she could look so serene!—but did nothing. That was the pattern."

"He didn't notice?"

"I wondered about that at first, but Uncle Karl was seldom home, except for dinner." She shrugged. "Whenever anything came up concerning my care, he just looked at Aunt Caroline and told her to take care of it."

He absorbed that. "I gather times had been hard at the Molly Bee."

"The worst. I came to Salt Lake with one skirt—too short—a shirtwaist and a petticoat, and that's what I started school in."

The look in his eyes was starting to bother Della. "It could have been worse! I had a room of my own, and the food was better." She chuckled. "When Mabli told me one night that nearly everyone in the canyon was living on oatcakes, I was reminded of Lumpy Dick."

"Who?"

"More like what. You boil water, add flour, and stir until it thickens. If you have some raisins too, that's Lumpy Dick. I ate a lot of that in Hastings. We all did."

"I'll stick with oatcakes, think on." He sighed. "So there you were in a good school, dressed in mining camp clothing."

"I can't begin to describe the humiliation," she said. "I had two girl cousins a grade or two ahead of me. They told me in no uncertain terms that I was never to pal around with them at school. I started hiding out in the school library during lunch. The librarian was kind to me."

"Bless her heart."

"I was afraid of everyone and everything. Then the worst thing happened: I started to grow." Della stopped, feeling her face growing warm. "It's rather personal." She glanced at him, still seeing nothing but kindness. "If you'd rather I didn't say any more . . ."

"Speak on." It was his turn to look shy. "I'm already dreading what happens when Angharad starts to turn into a woman, and I'm the one required to provide the education! At least, if that's what you're driving at."

He didn't seem to mind, which set her at ease. "That was it. I grew taller until I couldn't let out the hem in my skirt any more. And . . . and there was nothing I could do about my shirtwaist. It just got tighter and tighter. And then oh dear."

She couldn't tell him about the awful day when she didn't know what was happening, except there was blood. Maybe he would understand. "I . . . I started crying in the library, because I thought maybe I was dying."

He understood. "No lady had taken you aside to explain?"

She shook her head. "The librarian put her arm around me, and I told her." Della couldn't help her smile. "She was so kind! She helped me and even gave me a book that she kept under the counter. What a relief to know I wasn't going to die!" She nudged his shoulder. "Courage, Owen! You have Mabli to help you, and Angharad is only six. Maybe you'll marry before the dread talk."

"Maybe I'll marry just so I don't *have* to give the dread talk!" he teased in turn, then turned serious again. "So there you are, turning into a woman."

"Every night I prayed that I wouldn't grow anymore, because I only had the one skirt. I prayed so hard, but I kept growing. Then I . . . I started hunching over, because that shirtwaist . . . Oh, gracious."

"Shame on your aunt," Owen said, his voice hard. He looked away. "Well, don't stop there. I'm really counting on that librarian like I have never counted on anyone before, Della."

It was hard to continue. She wasn't going to cry, but the memory of her rescue still had the capacity to reduce her to tears of gratitude for that tall, boney spinster who kept the books of stake academy in order and had enough heart to include a terrified girl in her stewardship.

Della fumbled in her satchel for the handkerchief. She pressed it to her eyes. "Miss Ordway marched me to the domestic science teacher. Between the two of them, I learned to sew. She bought me a long skirt—claimed it was an old one of hers—and I spent my lunch hours for the next month, cutting out and sewing two shirtwaists." She shook her head, back in that domestic science room again, thirteen and desperate. "They couldn't do anything about my shoes, but wouldn't you know, Miss Ordway found a pair of shoes in the back of her closet."

"She bought them for you."

"Of course she did. I believed her, though, because in spite of what Aunt Caroline told me every day, I couldn't bear to think I was a charity case. I learned to shelve books, and no one is better at alphabetizing. I had to think I was paying Miss Ordway back for her kindness."

"You were."

"I hope so." She blew her nose, which set two birds to flight.

"Were things better then?" he asked, his words tentative. It warmed her heart to hear the hope in his voice, and it surprised her too that anyone could become so invested in such a horrible story. *Maybe I could have shared this sooner*, she thought. *It's been a burden.*

She shook her head. "I had clothes now, but there wasn't anything Miss Ordway could do about the teasing."

Della could see he was puzzled. "If you have better clothes now, why the teasing?"

"You won't like this much. I know I don't."

She shivered. She untied her sweater from around her waist and put it on. "It's getting cold."

"No, it's not. Tell me, Della."

"My father was the family black sheep. He never went to church and left home for the silver mines as soon as he could. He lived rough, and along the way, met a Greek woman named Olympia. She had a baby and left him and the baby as soon as she was able."

"That would be you?"

"It would be." She took a deep, ragged breath and wasn't surprised when his arm went around her shoulders. He was kind that way; maybe she could actually tell him and get it over with, let him think what he will. She couldn't stop the sudden flow of words. "They never married. I'm illegitimate, and my cousins spread that story far and wide at school." She sobbed in good earnest now. "Every single day, someone would whisper to me, "Della, Della, who's your mother?'"

Chapter 17

❧

*B*ecause his arm was around her, she felt his flinch, heard his sharp intake of breath. *I should never have told him*, she thought in misery. *What must he think of me?*

"Hand me that," he ordered, holding out his free hand for her handkerchief.

She gave it to him. He found a dry corner and blew his nose. She winced at his fierce look, until it dawned on her that his anger wasn't directed at her, not at all. She let out her own breath in a sigh of relief.

"Della, I would never scare you! I'm . . . I'm just fair stunned that the people who should nourish you would be so cruel."

She shifted a little, and he released her, apologizing, but did not move away. He stared across the ridge as though trying to regain his composure.

"I can't tell you what a refuge Miss Ordway and the library were," she said, anxious for Owen to move on. His anger at her treatment startled her. "When Clarence Nix asked me if I would like to be the librarian three nights a week, I wanted to jump up and down. Until . . ." She stopped, angry at herself. It seemed that every avenue she traveled down was leading her back to her life with the Anderses. She had been foolish to think it would not follow her into Winter Quarters.

Owen looked at her again, not taking his eyes from hers. "That's really why I came here this afternoon. I don't give a fig what you decide about the calling. It's this: I don't think anyone else noticed your terror in the library the other night, but I did. All of us coming toward you, looking like the wrath of demons. I was watching your eyes, and I saw your fright. Forgive us for frightening you for even a moment. We didn't know you had been bullied by masters for years and years."

She nodded. "How could you know? I never said anything." She took her own turn, looking across the canyon. "You can see why I never wanted to say anything. The shame . . ."

He gave her a blank look then. "Who's shame?"

"Well, mine!"

His arm went around her again, more gentle this time. "Maybe I don't understand what you are telling me. Two people meet, mate, have a baby and it's the baby's fault? I can't buy that."

"You mean that, don't you?" Della asked when she thought she could speak without tears. It sounded so simple when he said it.

"With all my heart." He stood up and held out his hand. "We'd better start back. You keep talking, and that's an order. If I punch a tree, just remember, you're not the reason. I *really* don't like Aunt Caroline."

She smiled at that as she took his hand and let him haul her easily to her feet. "I'll tell the good stuff then."

"I need that right now. *Diolch*. That's thank you in Welsh."

"*Diolch. Diolch*. I'll try to remember that." They started walking slowly. "About a month after I had that skirt and nice shirtwaists, Miss Ordway told me about a little job in the branch library near our neighborhood. It was just a few hours after school each day, for fifty cents a week."

"Coal pays better, but not much," he commented, and she laughed, touched beyond measure by his attempt to cheer her.

"For the five years, I walked a mile to the public library

after school and shelved books. After another month, I was able to buy a pair of shoes and stockings. Call me proud, but I returned the shoes to her that she had given me, because I think I was desperate for dignity."

"You wanted to let her know you were self-sufficient at thirteen. You're a wonder."

"No, I'm not. *You* were in the pit at thirteen," she reminded him.

"Aye. Maybe I'm a wonder too."

They looked at each other in perfect charity. She continued. "Soon I could buy a new petticoat, and eventually . . . other lady things."

"Good!" He chuckled. "Gwyna gave me a look hot enough to coke coal once when I complained after she bought a wee bottle of rose water. It was a week before she let me off the sofa and back to bed."

Della plopped down on a rock by the road and laughed. It was a small boulder, but Owen sat beside her, laughing along. "It's a good memory now. Thanks for reminding me, Della. It's easy for a husband to be a fool. Ask any wife, think on."

"When school was out, the neighborhood library asked me to work six mornings a week," Della said when they started walking again. "By the time school started in the fall, I had several skirts and shirtwaists and a coat that was nearly new."

"The taunts?"

"They never went away, but I had Miss Ordway and the library," she said. "Isn't it amazing where books can take you?"

"Aye, miss."

She nudged him hard enough to make him lose his balance, then grabbed his arm before he fell down. He just laughed.

They walked in silence. Della watched dusk come.

"Was church any kind of a refuge?" Owen asked finally.

"Wait a minute. You said your father was the black sheep. Were you even a member?"

"Aye, mister," she teased back. She thought before she spoke. Maybe he wouldn't notice that she wasn't answering his question. "Funny thing about my father—he vaguely remembered that children were supposed to be baptized. He thought it was ten."

"Better late than never. Did you know anything about the church?"

"Not a thing. One morning, Papa told me we were taking the train to Pueblo. Said we'd walk around until we found a Mormon bishop."

"Did you?"

"Finally! It was late afternoon when Papa found him. It was hot and I was tired." Della chuckled at the memory. "He was an undertaker. When Papa told him what he wanted, the bishop sat me on a coffin in the display room and told me what baptism was. I didn't have a white dress, but he found one in the mortuary. Oh, don't shudder!"

"I'm not. I'm just trying not to bust wide open with the biggest laugh you'll probably ever hear, considering my enviable vocal range," Owen said with a perfectly straight face.

"We found a dammed up creek and he baptized me. It was either eat dinner or buy two train tickets home, so we ate dinner. Papa helped me onto a flatbed, jumped on afterward, and we rode home to Hastings." She made a face. "I seem to have a long history with flatbeds."

"That's not your average baptism, I hope you know," he said, much subdued now. "Had you even seen a Book of Mormon?"

Della shook her head. "The bishop told me it was true, and I trusted him until I had a chance to read it and find out for myself." She looked at him, remembering. "When I finally read the Book of Mormon, it kept me alive, especially that part in Mosiah where God hears the silent prayers of the people of Alma and makes their burdens light."

Owen didn't say anything. Della handed him the soggy handkerchief, and he took it without a word.

They walked steadily, off the ridge now. "There is one thing—give me your opinion, Owen."

"Aye."

She looked around—no trees to punch. "It's this: Aunt Caroline let everyone at church know about, well, what I told you."

He interrupted her there, holding up his hand. "I was wondering if you were going to answer my question about the church being a refuge."

"You should have been an attorney," Della said mildly. "She told me she did that because she didn't want someone to think I was something I was not."

He muttered something in Welsh; she knew better than to ask him to translate.

"When I was older, a young man I met at the library asked me out for ice cream. When he escorted me home, Aunt Caroline told me I was obligated to tell him everything if he did that again, so he wouldn't be fooled."

"What did you do?" His voice sounded tight, and Della was afraid to look at him.

"I fobbed him off and he quit asking. Mostly I just don't get involved with people." She ignored his silence and forged ahead. "It's this: Emil Isgreen asked me out to dinner last week and I enjoyed his company. He asked me again this week and I put him off." She stopped walking, turned around, and started up the slope again, agitated.

"Come back." He said it so soft.

She turned around, wanting the distance. "Aunt Caroline is nowhere near me now, but I still hear her voice reminding me I'm poor and illegitimate."

"It'll take time. We have lots of that here, especially in winter. As for Emil, tell him yes! It's no one's business." He held out his hand. "Come on. We have something to do, and we're almost at the spot."

Mystified, she joined him, not taking his hand but walking beside him. He pointed to another outcropping and walked up to it.

"Take my hand and come on up."

She did without question.

"I want to sing with you, and this is a nice, resonating spot. Believe me, I know them all."

"You're serious?"

"Never more so. Let's sing, um, let's sing . . . 'Did You Think To Pray.' Know all the verses?"

"I think so."

"I'll sing the melody in my range, and you sing your part."

"I'll need a note, since I'm just a poor Greek-Scandinavian girl," she said, happy to joke, if hesitant to sing with a master.

"Easy. I'll give you your actual note in your range. I'm amazing. Listen."

Della listened. He gave her four beats and they started to sing. It was the simplest of church songs; she could have sung it in her sleep. *I sound so good when I sing with this man*, she thought, then surrendered to the song, the words, and everything in her heart.

She faltered a little on the verse that began, "When your heart was filled with anger, did you think to pray?" but Owen took her hand and kept singing, until she was ready to match his voice, if that was even possible. Singing there with him, anything seemed possible.

It was her turn to squeeze his hand tighter on the next verse when he struggled over, "When sore trials came upon you," and "when your soul was full of sorrow." He had lost the love of his life when Gwyna died in childbirth. She used to think that her sorrows were the worst in the world. Maybe she was wiser now.

The chorus seemed to soar: "O how praying rests the weary! Prayer will change the night to day. So when life gets dark and dreary, don't forget to pray."

They were both silent a long time. "Why that one?" she asked finally.

He shrugged. "Della, you have a fine voice." It was getting almost too dark to see him, but his voice sounded full of humor again. "Be a good girl and tell this dirty bird thank you. No apologies, no, 'oh, but I'm not as good as you.' Just thank you."

"Diolch," she said, remembering, which made him take a deep breath of his own.

She released his hand and they continued down the slope, until she stopped. It was too dark to see, and she wasn't sure of her footing. He took her hand again, twining his fingers through hers this time.

"Well, miss, this calls for the coal miner's song: 'Lead kindly light, amid th'encircling gloom,'" he sang. "'Lead thou me on.'"

"'The night is dark and I am far from home,'" she chimed in, harmonizing.

"I know where I'm going," he assured her, "and I don't need a light." He walked her home, her hand in his, and his staff in the other.

"Where's Angharad?" she asked.

"Playing at the Evanses'. Tell me something: Do you write to Miss Ordway?"

"I wish I could. She died the summer I graduated from stake academy."

"A pity, that," he said. "I hope she knew you were headed for university and a teaching certificate."

"She did. In fact, oh, my." Della stopped. They were passing the bench at the lumber area where the two of them had sat only two weeks ago. She sat down. "Is there any hope for that napkin?"

"Beyond resuscitation," he replied. "I have a shirttail."

"And I have a petticoat. It's dark enough! I had a summer job, but all my contriving couldn't come up with

189

enough for tuition and books. It wasn't much, I suppose, but I didn't have it. I mean, fifty dollars or five dollars, if you don't have it, you don't have it."

"Aye to that, hence oatcakes in August. What did you do?"

"It's what Miss Ordway did. The librarian at the public library wrote me of her passing. I was a kitchen flunky for a crew stringing telephone wire so I missed her funeral, sad to say. Just as I was about to withdraw my university application, I received a check for thirty dollars from her estate. It was all I needed to make up what I lacked. Owen, she was still watching over me."

"You've been blessed, Della," Owen said simply.

"And there's this. You know that fifty cents a week that the public library paid me? There wasn't any job; she told them she would pay it, and *they* would give it to me."

She went for her petticoat while Owen tugged out his shirttail.

They continued their slow walk to Mabli's. She asked him in, but he shook his head. He looked at her, and she knew the signs now.

"What?"

"Let me tell your whole story to the bishop tonight. Ah, now, now. He'll find a way to inform others that you're an ordinary person like all of us, even if you *are* named Anders."

"I couldn't bear it if . . . well, you know . . . *that* detail."

"No fears. Tell Mabli what you've told me. She'll be judicious in what she passes on. I know it." He scratched his head. "We'll have to be quite circumspect around the Finns, or they might take the train to Salt Lake City and burn down your uncle's house."

She put out her hand. "All right. I trust you."

He shook her hand. "Don't give the choir a thought. See you in Sunday School."

Della began hesitantly that night, telling Mabli what had happened. Mabli's reaction put Della's mind at ease.

If anything, she was even more indignant about Aunt Caroline's treatment. Between the two of them, they cried and ate almost a whole batch of ginger snaps.

"I'll pass some of your story on to Annie Jones," Mabli promised. "We talk in this canyon. We also stick together." She sighed. "All those years and no one to talk to . . . It's over now."

"I hope so," Della said. "If you hear something long enough, you start to believe it."

"Then unbelieve it," Mabli declared, ever practical.

Della yawned. "There is one thing I believe: Owen was kind to find me. He said you were worried and sent him out to look."

"He doesn't lie any better than he cooks!" Mabli retorted. "*I* knew you'd be back. Who can get lost on a wagon road? He came off the day shift like he was shot from a cannon, cleaned up, and told me he was going after you. You have a champion."

"I need one," Della replied, choosing honesty over embarrassment. "Tell me, Mabli, how did he get that blue scar on the back of his head?"

Mabli poured them both some warm water from the cookstove's reservoir and they washed for bed. "My lovely Gwyna had been dead about a month, and Owen was trying to work and take care of an infant. He was getting so little sleep. I think he just got careless in the mine—so unlike him."

Della shivered. "I wonder why he didn't give up mining altogether after that."

"He thought about it." Mabli took the pins from her pompadour and brushed her hair. She put down her brush and her gaze turned inward. "My Dafydd called it the lure of the mine. They can't leave it behind, drat them."

"But if something happens to him . . ." Della thought of her father. "Angharad will have no one."

"Not true!" Mabli said stoutly, then repeated it softly.

"Not true, my dear. You would never have been treated so poorly if you had been in *our* canyon."

Mabli picked up her hairbrush. "And now you *are* in our canyon for better or worse, think on. So is Angharad." She had to smile at that. "Every nursing woman in Winter Quarters owns a part of Angharad. When I think of all the breasts that suckled her! I doubt my brother-in-law has a single blush left in him. He took his baby from breast to breast until she was weaned."

"He's a good father."

"The best. Now, go to bed!"

"Not yet," Della said, looking away, shy. "Mabli, could we say our evening prayers together? I've never done that and I would like to, if you don't mind."

"Mind? Never. Let's kneel by your bed."

They took turns. Mabli's prayer was longer because she had more people to pray for than Della's paltry contribution of students and Jesse and Amanda Knight. She finished her prayer in Welsh.

Della climbed in bed, punching her pillow until it was concave enough to handle the exuberance of her tangle of curls. To her surprise, Mabli tucked the blanket up higher on her shoulder and gave her a pat. No one had done that since her father was alive. After Mabli blew out the lamp and closed the door, Della added a postscript: *Father, keep us safe in this canyon, and bless my landlady.*

She lay in bed, a smile on her face as she listened to the wind suddenly pick up, and the low growl of thunder from the west. The clouds she had watched in the canyon had finally made their way to Winter Quarters.

She listened, alert now, for the next sound. It received a welcome in her own dusty heart. The rain came, washing the canyon clean and sluicing away the sorrow in her heart. She knew that Owen had dislodged it that late afternoon, forcing her, in a gentle way she didn't understand, to root out the festering sores in her life by telling them to another human being. Maybe the Welsh really did know something about the healing power of conversation. Whatever it was, she was grateful. She knew she owed him a debt she could never repay. She was trusting Owen with her dreads and secrets and had given him permission to tell another her story.

Chapter 18

❧

Sunday morning, Della took extra time for her hair, that cross of hers to bear that had formed a love-hate relationship with her from the time she was old enough to brush it. Soon she had her mass of curls corralled into as sedate a bun as she could manage.

Time was passing, but she looked at herself in the little mirror over her bureau, pleased with what she saw. In a moment of bravery, she turned slightly sideways to see her Greek nose in profile, happy with it for the first time.

In a rare burst of candor—for her, anyway—she had once confided to Miss Ordway in the library that no one else had a nose like hers. In answer, Miss Ordway had marched her to the stacks, to the section on Greece. She found a book then pointed in triumph at a statue with Della's precise profile, right down to the full lips so mysteriously smiling.

"She could be your ancestor," Miss Ordway had pointed out.

"I'm not a statue," Della had protested.

"Someday you will see yourself for what you are, Della, and when you do, I'll expect a thank you," Miss Ordway had told her.

Della looked at her face now, with its olive complexion, deeply porched eyes, full lips, and nose of character. "Thank you, Miss Ordway," she said to her reflection. "I wish I could tell you in person."

Walking quickly in the Sabbath stillness, Della couldn't

have said just when she decided she was beautiful, but it had happened, as Miss Ordway had somehow known it would. Between the meadow yesterday and her entrance into the Pleasant Valley Ward meetinghouse, Della just knew. Just knowing made her stand taller.

It was early. Della knew that priesthood meeting was probably concluding right now. She waited in the chapel, happy to sit there in the quiet for her turn.

The building emptied quickly as priesthood holders hurried home to escort their families to Sunday School. When all was quiet again, Della went to Bishop Parmley's office.

"Sister Anders, you look finer than five pence this morning," he said, standing up to shake her hand, then gesturing to a chair. "Any news for me? I'll take whatever you give me."

"Bishop, it's yes. I'll be secretary for a choir that doesn't need one."

Bishop Parmley nodded, obviously pleased. "I prayed you would accept the call. It's a calling you'll enjoy."

The old Della almost said, "I doubt it," except that the new Della who had looked out of the mirror at her that morning was in charge. "I know I will. Thank you."

Della sat close to Sister Parmley again that Sunday. Mabli sat next to her, with Angharad. Della looked for Owen, then noticed he was seated at the sacrament table this time, looking vaguely disgruntled. *Well, Brother Davis, it appears that someone didn't see a happy face in* his *mirror this morning*, Della thought with amusement. She whispered to Mabli, "Your brother-in-law looks discouraged."

"He was uncharacteristically dramatic this morning," Mabli whispered back. "Claimed he was doomed to disappointment. I haven't a clue what he means."

Della shook her head, striving for a sympathetic look. She would have to watch his face when the bishop made his announcement. She noticed Dr. Isgreen, seated beside

Brother Hood. She caught his eye and smiled, thinking that if the new Della still had the nerve today, she might ask him if the Saturday dinner appointment could be revived.

After Brother Hood's opening remarks, Richard Evans invited his talented congregation to sing the "Never Be Late" song, which still didn't perk up Owen Davis. Angharad didn't notice because Mabli and Della both sang directly to her, "Try to be there, always be there, promptly at ten in the morning."

Bishop Parmley rose to announce new callings, new teachers for the Primary Association and Relief Society. Then the bishop looked at Della.

"Will Sister Della Anders please stand?"

She did, her face rosy, seeing the sacrament table out of the corner of her eye and Owen's sudden interest.

"Sister Anders has accepted a call as choir secretary."

Owen's head went back in surprise.

"All in favor? Vote for yourself, my dear," Bishop Parmley said.

She did, making it unanimous. Apparently everyone in the Pleasant Valley Ward harbored the illusion that their choir needed a secretary. How wise of them.

This time the YL class sang "We Ever Pray for Thee," during the sacrament, and Della was ready for their lovely voices. Once she had taken the bread, she closed her eyes, letting what she was doing assume its rightful importance over the sound of voices, singing even softer as Owen raised his hands and blessed the water next.

She opened her eyes and watched the progress of the goblets as parents sipped, then helped their children. No one said anything, the quiet as eloquent as the music had been. Without a word, Brother Hood rose and gestured people toward the door and their classrooms.

Emil sat next to her in theology class. "Well done, Sister Anders," he told her. "You're just the person to whip that choir into shape."

Della laughed softly. "I am certain that's why I was called," she said, turning to Exodus as the teacher wrote verses on the blackboard. *Now or never, Della*, she told herself. "Emil, does your Saturday night invitation stand?"

"Pending any emergency, oh yes," he replied, ruffling through his scriptures.

When Sunday School let out, Della prepared for her usual mad dash up the canyon with Mabli to get dinner on the table for the boarders.

"Take your time," Mabli told Della. "I can get this dinner myself." She touched Della's arm. "Better yet, I'll get Angharad to help me. See if you can coax Owen up the hill with you. What we're eating has to be better than oatcakes."

Emil strolled with her out of the meetinghouse, where Owen stood with the Evans family. Owen glanced at her and Emil once, and he seemed shy for some reason that eluded her, especially since he knew her now better than anyone in the canyon. For one terrible moment, she feared he knew too much. But that was the old Della, talking in one ear.

She said good-bye to Emil and joined the Evans family. "Brother Evans, I am now your secretary," she said, standing by Owen. "I trust you and your assistant here to invent any number of ways to keep me attending every choir rehearsal. Probably singing too."

Sister Evans turned away to laugh, and Richard Evans reeled back theatrically, as if she had dealt a body blow. "Owen, you never warned me about her skeptical and sharp tongue," the choirmaster exclaimed.

"She's shrewd, is Sister Anders," Owen said.

"She's also hungry, and the assistant choirmaster has been appointed to escort her to the boardinghouse, since his sister-in-law has invited him to dinner," Della told the Evanses.

"Now then, you had me going," Owen said as they walked up the slope.

"I'm not in the habit of turning down callings, even manufactured ones," she said.

Apparently Owen decided not to let that embarrass him. "I'll have a letter about Eisteddfod scratched out by Tuesday and a list of addresses for you to send it to. You can make any corrections you choose."

She nodded, almost too shy to say what she wanted. "Did you . . . did you talk to the bishop about, well, you know?"

"Aye, miss. He's a discreet man, so the right word will get around. And Mabli?"

"She knows now."

"How do you feel about this?"

Della thought about his question, and her conversation with the new Della in the mirror that morning. "Like a boulder is off my shoulders," she said finally

"It needed to be done."

They walked in silence for a few minutes, and then she spoke. "You were wrong about that meadow, though. It was a very good place to reflect."

"I'm glad someone found it useful."

She glanced at his profile and saw the small muscle working in his cheek. Yesterday's Della would have remained silent. Today's Della nearly did. "You have your own boulder."

He nodded, silent.

"I can listen too," she offered and said no more.

When they passed the school, Della looked to see Miss Clayson standing in the window, dressed in black as usual. She could not help her sigh.

"You have your work cut out there," he commented.

"I'm already thinking of what I will probably do this week to incur the wrath."

"As a parent, let me say that I am delighted with Angharad's progress," he told her.

"Tell me something. Last week, Miss Clayson's tirade

included scolding me for . . . for glamorizing the mine. She doesn't want a single boy to go into the pit. They should all be doctors and lawyers."

"Those doctors and lawyers will get a little chilly, when winter comes and there's no coal," he said with a laugh.

"What about you? Do you want Angharad to marry a miner?" Della asked.

He considered her question. "What I want—perhaps what any miner in this canyon wants—is for children to have a choice. Some of us never did."

Della thought about Owen's words that afternoon as the four of them walked back for sacrament meeting. It was still on her mind in the morning as she hesitated and then joined Miss Clayson inside the front entrance of the school, ready to welcome her pupils too. Before anyone came inside and even though her stomach was churning, she stood beside the principal.

"Miss Clayson, I angered you last week," she said. "Here is what I do at every school where I teach: I pledge myself to educating each child in my charge, boys and girls equally, so they will have a choice someday. Mining is as noble a profession as any."

Miss Clayson did not raise her voice. "Mines kill," she said, with such infinite sadness that Della looked away.

"I know," she said softly, "but these children love their fathers." *And I loved mine*, she thought. "They are also proud of them. I will not confuse these children and divide their loyalties. It isn't in me."

The children were coming inside now, the boys flushed from running, and the girls more sedate, some walking arm in arm with their sisters or friends. Della's heart warmed to see the greeting in their eyes when they saw her. She ushered them toward their classroom and waited another moment as Mari Luoma came up the steps.

"Good morning, Mari," Della said.

Mari blushed and looked toward the outside door. Della saw Heikki beaming at his young wife, nodding his head in encouragement.

"Good morning, dear teacher. I am so pleased to see you," Mari said in careful English, almost as though she didn't want to wear it out.

"Excellent! I am pleased to see you too."

Mari giggled, both hands over her mouth. All during recitation and arithmetic board work, Della tried unsuccessfully to erase Miss Clayson from her mind. During lunchtime, she tried to talk to Miss Clayson. She reached the stairs leading to the basement just as she heard the woman's door close.

Della walked back into her classroom, supremely dissatisfied with herself, until another thought surfaced. She stood still, suddenly aware that perhaps others' lives could be as distressing as hers had been. *But isn't now*, she thought with amazement. *I have been blessed.*

By the time her students trooped back in, ready for the treat she had promised, she was ready. She held up the book, one of several that Clarence Nix had ordered on her request.

"Here are the rules," she told her students. "You have to get comfortable and not worry about recitations or whether three plus three equals seven . . ."

"Miss Anders!" Eddie Williams said promptly. "It's six."

She smiled at the bright faces looking back at her, eyes merry, then slapped her forehead. "You're right! But we're not supposed to worry about that during story time. We are going to read *Black Beauty*." She opened the book. "'Chapter One. The first place that I can remember was a large pleasant meadow with a pond of clear water in it . . .'"

She walked home after school in perfect charity with herself, accompanied by Mari Luoma and her other Finnish students. Other students had trailed along too, dropping off with a wave to her when they reached their own homes.

When Della stopped at Mabli's house, Mari put her hand on her arm. "You come with me?" she asked, pointing farther up the slope. "Finn Town?"

"I will come with you to Finn Town, but not today," she said and looked at Pekka Aho to translate. "Please tell her I have to help Mabli Reese in the boardinghouse kitchen and then go to the library tonight. Maybe another day?"

"You are a busy teacher," Pekka said, then translated. Mari continued up the slope with the other students, her long, blonde hair in one braid down her back. Della watched them until they were out of sight beyond the bend, because she thought little Tilda Koski might look back and wave. She did, to Della's delight.

The library was pleasantly full that evening. It was becoming such a social place that Della had put up a sign last Friday: "Please keep conversations to a dull roar, unless the building is burning, in which case you may shout *Fire!* in the language of your choice." Everyone coming in laughed, but the resulting volume probably would have suited even Miss Clayson.

Owen came in just before closing again and put *The Jungle Book* on her table. "We loved it," he whispered. "I was only frightened one night."

Della laughed out loud. When Owen put his finger to his lips and shook his head, she mouthed, "Dirty bird."

"Care to recommend another, oh Greek oracle?" he asked.

Della crooked her finger and he followed her. "The Little Prudy books. There's not a girl alive who doesn't like them. There are six, so you can get started."

He took the book from her and turned the pages. "Anything for an older reader who will be thirty-one in January?"

He followed her to the D's, and she handed him *A Tale*

of Two Cities. "Ever read it?" she whispered. "I cried until my nose ran."

Owen leaned his forehead against the bookcase and put *Little Prudy* to his face to stifle his laughter. "I'll take it," he whispered back. "Since I'm here, may I ask to escort you to choir practice tomorrow night?"

"Afraid I won't show up?" she teased.

"No! I like your company."

Chapter 19

Choir practice began promptly at seven o'clock Tuesday evening in the chapel, with the men gathering in one corner to sing "Men of Harlech" as a warm-up. Owen helped Della off with her coat and joined the tenors and basses.

"They like to show off when someone new arrives," Martha Evans whispered to Della. "We humor them."

The ladies giggled. Della was impressed with "Men of Harlech," but she had to smile. "Tell me this: Does the Pleasant Valley Ward choir *really* need a secretary?"

The ladies looked at each other, hands to mouths, which told Della everything she needed to know. "Are all the men in this choir as unprincipled as Owen Davis?"

"Aye," Martha said promptly. "It's a sad fact and true about men. Better you learn now than later. They do anything to get what they want." She put her hand on Della's arm and leaned close. "But here is the truth—we prefer this unprincipled Owen to the one that never smiled."

"And I want to sing," she said simply.

When the men finished showing off, Richard Evans beckoned Della forward. "At long last, we have a secretary," he said, which made everyone laugh, including Della, after she glared at Owen. "I know there will be some correspondence in the early spring as we get ready for Eisteddfod in June."

"Owen—Brother Davis—promised me there would be letters to send right now," Della said. "Told me Sunday he was composing a letter."

"He lied," James Gatherum, a Scot, told her with a perfectly straight face. "'Ave ye no' heard of 'welshing,' Sister Anders? There's a rrreason."

"Lads, lads, kindly don't malign me," Owen said in good-humored protest at their laughter. "I walked her here and I'd like to walk her home, if she is still speaking to me after you *bwca* finish."

"I suggest we pray, if anyone can do it with a straight face," Richard Evans said. "Martha?"

"Only because you're my husband," she said.

After an opening prayer, Richard Evans had his choir take their positions behind the pulpit. He directed Della to stand between Tamris Powell and Claudie Jones. He sang a note and they began running up and down scales in chromatic intervals. When they finished, he handed out well-thumbed Deseret Sunday School songbooks.

"We usually just call for suggestions," Brother Evans explained to Della as he handed her a book. "We sing a special number twice a month in sacrament meeting." He turned to Della. "Since you're our newest member, you choose a hymn, my dear."

"That's easy," the new Della said promptly, getting into the spirit of the rehearsal. "Since you are picking on Brother Davis, how about 'Let Us Oft Speak Kind Words'?"

"Excellent choice," Brother Evans said, as the basses and tenors hooted. He looked around. "Silence, ye fiends! Do you miscreants want a note or not?"

And so it went all evening, to Della's amazement and delight, as the choir sang and teased and argued about what to sing on Sunday. She had never heard anything like it, and she was sorry when it ended.

Or almost ended. After a glance at her, Owen raised his hand. "One more, Richard," he said. "Just Sister Anders and me, if she will."

"Oh, but . . ."

"'Did You Think to Pray?' We sounded nice the other

night. Here's your note and the beats." His hand was already moving, not giving her a chance to protest further.

I'm being railroaded by a master. Thank goodness he's not a bully, Della thought, as she sang with him, timidly at first, but strong by the chorus, because he was easy to sing with. When he gestured, she left her place between Tamris and Claudie and stood beside him. When they finished, everyone applauded, which made her blush.

"Perfect," Brother Evans said. "You two can sing in Sunday School during the sacrament. Any other business?"

Della held up her hand.

"We won't take no for an answer," the choirmaster told her.

"I wouldn't dare object," she said tartly. "I just want to know why no one uses the piano. Don't tell me it's because no one needs it." She looked around at the friendly faces. "I'm the secretary, and maybe I should ask those things, since *no one else* has anything for me to do."

"It's badly out of tune and we can't afford to hire the piano tuner from Provo," Tamris said. "I wish we had a piano too."

"Maybe we need a fund-raiser. You know, a little here, a little there. It will add up to a piano tuner eventually."

"What do you have in mind?" Brother Evans asked. "We're challenged in the wallet."

"A pie auction. Every household makes a pie or a cake and we auction them, either by the pie or the slice." Della looked at the ladies. "We did this in Colorado, where my father mined. We were challenged in the wallet too, but we pooled our resources."

This was the test. Della glanced at the choir as they considered her idea. From their expressions, no one seemed to be wondering why someone named Anders would hint at her own poverty. Owen had spoken correctly; a few words in the right place had changed her life in the canyon.

"I think it's a good idea," Tamris said. "Della, would you like me to help you organize such an event?"

"Certainly. We'll invite everyone in the canyon."

Brother Evans looked around. "Any objections?"

Owen raised his hand. "You say, each household? I'm no cook."

"I guess you'll have to do your best, Brother Davis," Della said.

"Only if you promise to bid on it," he countered.

"Never."

The tenors and basses hooted again, and Brother Evans gave up. He shrugged his shoulders and looked at Della. "You can probably still get out of this calling."

"And miss all this fun? I wouldn't dream of it."

"Still talking to me?" Owen asked as the others peeled off and they continued toward the Edwards boardinghouse.

"Of course I am. I don't know when I've enjoyed an evening more. I'm going to be scared to death up to and including Sunday morning, when we sing, though."

"No need. Everyone listening is a friend." He laughed softly. "I might lie about a secretary, but I'll never give you a wrong note! Pie auction?"

"That's how the miners in the Molly Bee raised enough money to bury my father and put me on the train to Salt Lake City."

He didn't say anything, but he clasped his arm around her shoulder as they walked slowly along. In another minute he was humming "Lead, Kindly Light." She joined him on the second verse and was still humming it after he had said good night.

Almost without knowing it, Della settled into the rhythm of Winter Quarters Canyon, ruled by trains twice a day, the growl of the tipple, the occasional distant rumble that meant blasting in the mines. In her own world, there was the smell of chalk dust and library paste, and as autumn deepened, the odor of children dressed in woolen stockings and coats. Miss Clayson was as prickly as ever, but Mari Luoma was learning English, and there was always Saturday night in Scofield with Emil Isgreen. That became her time to hash over the week, and maybe even solve the problems of the world, if dessert was slow to get to the table. The doctor listened, offered advice, and kissed her on the cheek after each walk home.

Equally fun to Della was the letter she received from Amanda Knight in answer to her first letter. To her delight, even Uncle Jesse had found the time to include a note. His totally unrepentant apology when she took him to task about his Pleasant Valley Ward choir comments was so funny she read it aloud to the choir.

"He had me thinking I was on my way to help out a fatally flawed choir," she told them when the laughter stopped.

Her reply to the letter was easy to write. There was always something to tell the Knights about her children, the choir, and life in a mining camp that churned out more than half of Utah's annual coal output, according to Uncle Jesse, who never joked about profit.

The return letter a week later included an invitation to Provo for Thanksgiving, which made Della sit in silence for a long moment. When some of her old fears surfaced, she showed the letter to Owen Davis, her eyes anxious. "Should I say yes?" she asked him the night Mabli invited him and her niece to the boardinghouse kitchen to learn about pie dough.

"If you don't, I'll write it for you," he told her, as he tried to roll a circle. "Sometimes you're a butterbean."

"At least I can make a circle," she answered, taking the rolling pin from him and deftly creating a bottom crust. Her acceptance letter was on its way two days later.

With permission from Mr. Edwards, she invited her

students to the boardinghouse dining room the first Saturday to make posters for the Pleasant Valley Ward pie auction. To her delight, Mari Luoma brought along Pekka Aho's mother, who carefully copied the words for the announcement onto the large sheets of paper Della had wheedled out of Clarence Nix. She added stunning backgrounds of canyons and trees, turning modest posters into masterpieces. By unanimous consent, Mrs. Aho's posters went to the Odd Fellows Hall in Scofield and Scofield's bank.

Well-fortified with Mabli's cookies and snacking on dried apples, the children finished their posters, and Della arranged them around the dining room to dry. Billy Evans finished his last, after most of the children had left. Della stood in the doorway between the kitchen and dining room, watching him survey his little effort with all the panache of a Renaissance artist.

"He learns at his own pace," she whispered to Owen, who had arrived in all his day shift finery to retrieve Angharad.

He stood next to her but not close, still dark with coal around his eyes and caked into the sharp lines beside his nose.

"Billy Evans is the little one who said he would read when he was taller than your broom?" Owen whispered. "Any luck with that?"

Della shook her head. "He's not growing and he's not reading. From the little he tells me, I think Miss Forsyth ridiculed him."

"But you don't."

"Never! I sit next to him in our reading circle, hug him close when he lets me, and put my finger under each word as the others read aloud."

"I have an idea," he whispered.

"I'll take any suggestions. I know he's tracking the words with his eyes. He's just not brave. Believe me, I can understand that."

"When you think he's brave enough, just tell me."

"What will you do?"

"My secret," he said. He went into the dining room to stand by Billy and his poster, admiring it too until Angharad joined him and the three of them left together.

Well, Mr. Enigmatic, I'll try anything, she thought.

He looked back at her from the doorway, a child on each side of him, Angharad lugging his empty lunch pail. "It's going to snow tonight," he told her. "Time to change your autumn leaves for snowflakes."

Owen was right. There was just enough snow in the canyon next morning to coat the ugly machinery. It was gone by noon, except in those places were the sun's rays couldn't penetrate. He was also right about the bulletin board, which had given Miss Clayson something to complain about through September and into October.

The leaves had been green when school started, and the children wrote their names on them. By two weeks into school, the cardboard tree had fully leafed out, now including spelling words from that second grade level that Della chose for all three of her classes. They had added yellow leaves next, fortified with more spelling words, which drifted down to the bottom of the board like the quaking aspen in the canyon.

Della would have removed the leaves and put up another display, but Mari Luoma had drawn more leaves from orange construction paper and used a dab of glue to adhere them to the wall underneath the bulletin board, as though they truly fell from the tree. The children were agile enough to appreciate writing their spelling words on the wall's leaves and soon, the floor. By the second week in October, the leaves were glued to the floor and headed toward the windows, which made Miss Clayson sigh and purse her lips every time she passed the classroom door.

She had complained once about the clutter, until Della showed her the spelling test results. "Even my first graders have learned the second level words," she pointed out. "I've started challenging the third graders with words from their own level now, and they're doing well. They're catching up."

With Owen's coaxing, Israel Bowman's support, and Emil Isgreen's encouragement, Della had stood up for herself, respectful but persistent. The terror of the first time made her lose her breakfast on the way to school, darting around one of the machinery buildings to vomit. With her stomach empty, toes practically digging into the floor through her shoes, Della had presented her results, which left Miss Clayson with nothing to do but nod and agree.

The principal had even smiled when she walked by the door one afternoon to see brown and gold leaves high on the walls in circles. "Now I suppose you will tell me that a big gust of wind blew them there!"

Della had nodded and laughed out loud. Miss Clayson couldn't bring herself to go that far in public, but Della could have sworn she saw the woman's shoulders shaking when she walked away.

Della usually sat with her class for lunch, fixing herself a sandwich from the table in the Edwards boardinghouse where the miners selected their lunch. She nearly cried the morning all the miners presented her with her own miner's lunch bucket, a two-tiered, round container with the bottom level reserved for water. Someone had painted a garland of roses around the bucket.

"Della, that's a treasure," Mabli told her. "Since you don't need that larger compartment for water, let's fill it with cookies."

"Mr. Edwards won't mind?"

"Hardly! His boardinghouse is full for the first time in ages. Men have been transferring from the other houses."

"I can't take credit for that!" Della protested.

"*I* would, if I were you," Mabli replied with a laugh.

Knowing Mabli, she probably would have credited the

steady increase in library traffic to her "interesting beauty," as Dr. Isgreen put it one Saturday night, perhaps when he felt more bold than usual. Della knew better. Every week, Clarence Nix put a new book and one or two magazines on her desk. Soon the wives were coming by twos and threes to sit together and read *McCall's* and *Harper's Bazaar*.

Owen and Angharad dropped by regularly. He returned *A Tales of Two Cities* and assured her that he only sniffled a little when Sydney Carton declared, "'It is a far, far better thing I do than I have ever done.'"

"You have absolutely no romance in your soul," Della whispered, and he just grinned in that maddening way. She held out another book. "Here! Read some Stephen Crane!"

Maybe it was the order she craved. Her classroom was lively every day, and Della found something soothing in the calm of the library, with only low murmurs and page turning. She settled in comfortably that night, eager to browse the latest *Saturday Evening Post*.

Della looked up when the door opened, surprised to see Bishop Parmley wearing miner's clothes, his tin pot lamp fixed to his cloth hat. She knew he wasn't usually in the mine. Something must have happened. Everyone else had the same thought, apparently, if the sudden tension in the air was any gauge.

The bishop nodded his apology to her, then looked around the room. Dr. Isgreen was already on his feet, pulling on his coat. Owen and Levi Jones stood up, and the bishop gestured them closer. Every eye was on him, the women alert and intense.

"There's been a cave-in in Number One," he said, his eyes softening when two of the women groaned. "Doctor, come right now. Owen, I need you for timber work."

"Aye," Owen said. He looked at Angharad, then at Della.

"She can stay here with me," Della said, crossing the room quickly to sit beside the little girl, who looked bewildered as the library began to clear rapidly of miners and wives. "Angharad, you'll help me shelve some books?"

The child nodded, then looked at Owen. "Da . . ."

Owen kissed her forehead and headed for the door, stopping to look over his shoulder at Della. "If I'm not back by nine . . ."

"She'll come home with me," Della finished. "Nothing simpler."

"Just until I get back." He smiled his thanks and left right behind Emil Isgreen.

Angharad edged closer to Della. "I don't like it when he leaves so fast," she whispered.

"I wouldn't either," Della told her, pulling her close. "Oh, look! Everyone left in such a hurry. We have magazines and newspapers to straighten out. Do you want to straighten the magazines?"

"Aye, miss," Angharad replied and started to gather magazines. Soon she was humming to herself, which told Della worlds about how the Davises coped.

When they finished, Della went to the shelves and found *Captain Horace*, the third Little Prudy book. "I think we should read while we wait for your father." She sat down and held out her arms. With a sigh, Angharad climbed onto her lap.

Della was still reading at nine o'clock, even though Angharad had felt heavier and heavier for the last fifteen minutes, as though she slept. Della closed the book and remained where she was, comfortable and warm.

At nine fifteen, Clarence Nix came upstairs to see why the lights were still on. When he saw Angharad asleep, he tiptoed closer, kneeling down by the chair.

"They're still in the mine. Mr. Parmley's put Owen to work shoring up the timbers. They're taking out the bodies now," he whispered. "One Finn and a miner from one of the boardinghouses."

"Oh, no. Do you know who the Finn is?"

"Matti Aho."

Della bowed her head over the sleeping child in her lap. Matti Aho was Pekka's father. *I know how Pekka feels*, she thought, anguished for her student.

She waited until Clarence left to wake up Angharad, who yawned and then remembered where she was. "Da?"

"He's shoring timbers. You'll come home with me. Aunt Mabli is probably setting bread dough."

They walked up the wagon road. Angharad's hand tightened in hers as they passed the Number One portal, lit now with lights rigged by the mechanics. She turned her face into Della's skirt as one of the women standing there started to wail.

Her heart in her throat, Della picked up the child, tucking her face tight against her chest to blot out the frightening sight of a bloody sheet on a stretcher. As she walked fast, the cars from Number One continued to dump coal in the tipple. The rumble drowned out the shrieks.

Can't it stop for death? Della thought, aghast. *Is coal that important?*

Mabli was looking out the kitchen window toward the Number One portal when Della entered, carrying Angharad. She took the child from her and held her close while Della removed her jacket. "Do you have room for her in your bed?"

Della nodded. "She's small. Owen said to leave your front door unlocked. Will he come and get her?"

"He'll try. I trust you to tell him to let her sleep so he can sleep. He's on day shift, you know."

"No rest for him?"

Mabli shook her head. "They don't mine coal, they don't get paid. I'll be next door."

It was a simple matter to help Angharad prepare for bed. "Let's do what your da does every night," Della suggested.

Angharad nodded and knelt beside the bed, reaching for Della's hand. She twined her fingers through Della's, then picked up Della's other hand and placed it over her free hand, binding them together.

"That's what Da does. You go first, miss," Angharad whispered. "Then it's my turn."

Della bowed her head and prayed for her students, for the men in the mine, and for the dead miners and their families. She said amen and kissed Angharad's head. "Your turn."

The child prayed in Welsh, the lilt soothing to Della's heart, even though none of the words were familiar. She recognized *Amen*, added her own, and then helped the child into bed.

"I like your dragons," Angharad said, her eyes on the footboard. "I asked Da why he put them on the inside of the footboard. He told me they were your protectors." She yawned. "Now you sing 'Ar Hyd y Nos,' like Da."

"I don't know it," Della said, chagrined to see disappointment in the little girl's eyes.

"You have to sing it or I'll never get to sleep," she said firmly. "Everyone knows it." She patted the space beside her. "You have to lie down too."

"I can do that," Della said, taking off her shoes. "Maybe you could sing to me this time."

"It's not done that way," Angharad insisted, then sighed. "Ah, well. I'll sing."

Her voice was sweet and sleepy. After only a few bars, Della stopped her, relieved. "I *do* know that song, my dear. Would you mind if I sing it in English?"

"I thought you would know it," Angharad said. "Teachers know everything."

I know so little, Della thought, touched. "Give me a note, like your father does."

Angharad did. Della sang: "'Sleep my child and peace attend thee, all through the night. Guardian angels God will send thee, all through the night. Soft the drowsy hours are sleeping, hill and vale in slumber sleeping, I my loving vigil keeping, all through the night.'"

She sang it again as Angharad joined her in Welsh. "Da will teach you," she said when they finished. "Just ask."

"Now what do I do?" Della asked.

Angharad pointed to her forehead and then each cheek. "You kiss me for the Father, the Son, and the Holy Ghost, and then once on the lips like Da, and another for my mother."

Della did as she was asked, tears in her eyes. "Do you want me to stay here until you sleep? What does your father do?"

"Da generally tells me to behave and then goes in the kitchen and starts carving." She laughed, a low, sleepy sound. "Sometimes I peek around the corner and watch him. Sometimes he chases me back to bed, and sometimes he lets me sit on his lap." And then she closed her eyes.

Della stood a long time in the doorway, keeping her vigil.

Chapter 20

*D*ella sat in the front room after Angharad slept, chilled to the bone to hear the shrieks of the women coming closer. She peeked out the window as a procession wound its way toward Finn Town, the dead man on a stretcher and women and miners behind. The unearthly keening sent goose bumps marching down her spine in ranks.

She put her hands over her ears, then went into her bedroom to watch Angharad, praying she was deep in sleep. The child slumbered, unaware.

Mabli let herself in quietly a little later, then sat with Della a few minutes. "Dafydd died in a cave-in," she said and went into her own room.

Della sat up another hour. When the clock chimed twelve times, she gave up and joined Angharad in bed. She quickly grew accustomed to the child's even breathing and appreciated her warmth.

She woke hours later, not certain why, until she realized Owen was kneeling by the bed, saying her name softly. The room was completely dark. As she came awake, she wondered at first how he could see so well in the dark, then reminded herself he was a miner.

"I'm awake," she whispered.

He went into the front room. She put on her robe and followed him.

"What time . . . ?" She peered toward the clock.

"After three," he whispered.

"Have a seat," she said, still groggy and wondering how to treat a guest at three in the morning.

"I'm too dirty."

"Yes." As her eyes became accustomed, she still had trouble seeing him, because he was black from cap to boots. "Just let her stay here tonight."

"I was going to ask that," he told her. "I'm going to wrap myself into a blanket I keep just for times like this, and sleep on the floor in my house. No point in washing and changing, because I'm on the day shift."

"Won't Bishop Parmley let you stay home today, since you've worked half the night?"

"I don't mine, I don't get paid. I did the timber shoring on my own time."

"Did you have a choice?"

"I could have refused, but more men might die. I'm the best timberman at Winter Quarters," he told her.

"It's not fair!" she said, wide awake now. She saw him then because he smiled, and his teeth were so white.

"You sound like Angharad. Nothing's fair, Della."

"You just spent six dangerous hours in a mine where men died." She turned away. "Don't worry about Angharad. I'll get her to school just fine . . ."

"You're thinking of your father."

She turned back, surprised. "No, I wasn't. I was thinking of you." She rubbed her arms, suddenly cold. "Poor Matti Aho. His wife and Pekka were wailing and his brother Victor. I don't like this."

"No one does, I assure you."

He opened the door and just stood there. There was enough light for her to see sudden indecision on his face, and she went toward him to reassure him.

"I'll tell Angharad when she wakes up that you are fine."

"That's not it. I hate to tell you this. The other miner who died was your Frenchman."

Della gasped. Owen guided her to a chair. The room continued to spin, so he pushed her head down gently, using only two fingers on the back of her neck.

"I'm coal black," he apologized. "It'll never show in your hair. I'm sorry, Della. I didn't want to tell you." The pressure of his fingers increased when she tried to move. "Just stay that way a moment more. Sit up slowly now."

She did as he said, taking easy breaths until the room held still. She thought of the courtly way her Frenchman from the boardinghouse and his German friend had of waiting for her each night she was in the library, adamant that she not walk home alone.

"He didn't speak much English," she said finally. "His name was Remy Ducotel and he was from Alsace, where the coal mines are." She looked at him, puzzled. "Why do miners do it?" She hadn't meant to ask that. "Those men are dead, and the women and children were wailing!"

"What else can we do?"

She knew it was not a question she could answer, but she tried. "Anything but mining. Those shrieks, those wails!"

"Men wail too, when their wives die," he said, the words wrung out of him. "Death is not exclusive to a mine."

The old Della would have stopped, but the new one couldn't, especially as Della remembered the look in Angharad's eyes when Bishop Parmley came to get her father in the library. "You're the only parent Angharad has."

"And this is news to me?"

She stood up suddenly and staggered, but steadied herself. She clapped her hand hard against his shoulder, not caring about the coal dust, wanting to jerk him around and shake him, in her anxiety. "Now I *am* thinking about my father. Good night, Owen."

He left without saying another word.

"Shame on me," she said out loud. "Shame on me to remind him."

Angharad came awake easily in the morning, when Della sat on the bed and touched her shoulder.

"Your father is fine," she said first.

There it came, Angharad's little sigh of relief. Della's hand went automatically to the child's head. "He stopped by early this morning and didn't want to disturb you." She leaned closer. "If you can hurry, I will have time to make you a French braid."

Angharad dressed in record time and was soon sitting sideways on a chair in the kitchen. Della brushed the hair almost as dark as her own, trying to hear only the companionable chatter of the little girl and not think about the Frenchman and Pekka Aho's father, dead today, where yesterday it had only been another afternoon shift in the Number One mine. With a clarity that startled her, she relived the last morning of her father's life. He had kissed her as usual, reminded her to be a good girl in school, and promised they would have a picnic in the canyon on Sunday, since the leaves had turned and fallen, and there were few good days left before winter.

She braided Angharad's hair, expertly twining the strands of hair from one hand to the other, finding peace in the simple task. When she finished, she steered Angharad in front of her mirror.

Like every lady, young or old, since someone discovered mirrors, Angharad turned her head this way and that, pleased. She hugged Della around the waist and declared solemnly, "I am truly beautiful."

"I agree! Should I do that to my hair too?"

"Aye, miss." Angharad frowned. "Do you have time? Doesn't Mabli need you?"

"She does, but you could do my early-morning job and help Mabli. Then I'll have time."

Angharad dashed out the back door. Della dressed quickly and took her turn before the mirror, wishing her hair was not so curly but straight like Angharad's. Since she already knew wishing never changed anything, Della soon had her hair subdued enough to twine it back and forth too and anchor it.

When she was hooking the elastic around her shoe, she heard the front door open.

"Angharad?" Owen stood in the doorway, his face and hands clean, still dressed in yesterday's clothes.

"She's next door helping Mabli," Della said, holding a shoe. "Look, Owen, I . . ."

He held up his hand to stop her. "You were right last night, but things aren't likely to change. Can you accept that?" He sighed. "You have to accept that in a mining camp."

"I don't have to accept anything, Owen Davis," she told him, not mincing her words, even though she hated to see the cloudy look that came into his expressive eyes. "Maybe I'm no better than Miss Clayson."

"Maybe we'll just have to not discuss this subject." He chuckled, with no mirth in the sound. "It can probably join a number of subjects not to be discussed in this canyon, because it's bad luck. Next door?"

"Aye," she told him, which made his smile genuine.

She put on her other shoe and followed him to the dining room, where Angharad dished out scrambled eggs to the boarders. Della couldn't help but notice how quiet the dining room was this morning.

Mabli carried in a platter of sausage. "Eat with us, Owen?"

"I already ate," he said, but Della watched his eyes linger on the sausage.

Della knotted three links of sausage into waxed paper and handed it to him. "Man does not live by oatcakes alone," she declared.

"This man does, but he also knows better than to argue with determined women," Owen told her. "I learned that early, because I was a diligent husband. *Diolch yn fawr iawn.*"

"I know *diolch*," Della said, "but . . ."

"Thank you *very much.*"

He put the sausage in his lunch bucket, where she

doubted there was anything more than everlasting oatcakes. He knelt by Angharad for a moment, speaking to her but not getting too close. When he finished, he held out his index finger and she did the same, touching one to the other. A word or two in Welsh and he was gone.

When she finished and took the bowl back to the kitchen, she whispered to Della, "They told me I was the best ever at serving eggs." Her face fell. "I wish I had saved some for me."

"We did." Della held out a plate with eggs and sausage that Mabli had put in the warming oven.

Della sat with her, eating a boiled egg. Angharad ate in silence, savoring the eggs, probably a rare treat, and the sausage, even more rare. Her satisfied sigh when she finished went to Della's heart.

"Miss, the men in there said it was Pekka's da who died."

Della nodded. "We'll have to think of something nice to do for Mrs. Aho. Remember the pretty posters she made for us?"

"He won't be in school today, will he?"

"Probably not."

"We should visit."

"I agree."

They walked to school in relative silence, Angharad's face pensive. She slowed as they passed the Number One portal. She shook herself visibly, as if trying to dispel an unwanted sight.

"What did you tell your students at your Westside School?" she asked, turning her face resolutely away from the Number One.

Della gave her a puzzled look.

"I mean, when the miners died?'

Della knelt in the wagon road and put her hands on Angharad's shoulders. "There weren't any miners' children in my Westside School, my dear. Nobody's father died in the two years I taught there."

The disbelief in Angharad's eyes felt like a spike through Della's heart. She gently pulled Angharad closer. "Not everyone is a miner, my dear. Some fathers are constables or farmers or lawyers or teachers or greengrocers."

"And they don't die?"

Della gathered her close. "Everyone dies eventually, my dear, but don't worry. Not everyone has dragons." It sounded stupid when she said it, but nothing else came to mind.

Angharad clung to her, wordless. In another moment, she released her grip on Della and stood back, smoothing her pinafore, womanlike, even though she was only six years old. "Aye, we do have dragons." She took Della by the hand again and led this time.

Her students already knew. All Della could do that morning was stand before them and say simply, "Pekka has lost his father. What can we do to help him?"

Everyone was silent for a long moment. From Mari Luoma, tears in her eyes, to the youngest-six-year old, they looked at her with the patient gaze of people who expected her to do more than she knew what to do. She was their teacher, and they expected her to know. She glanced at her arithmetic book lying open to today's lesson and closed it.

"I have an idea. Should we make cards for Pekka and Mrs. Aho? We can tell them how sorry we are and we can take them to their home this afternoon."

"May we use the magic paper?" Mary Parmley asked.

"Most certainly. If we fold it in half or lengthwise, that would make a good card." Della went to the closet and took out the thin cardboard. She folded one piece in half, and her students smiled their approval. "Well then. Let us get our Rainbow Colors too."

She took their suggestions and wrote them on the board, crafting a sentiment both simple and profound in that way of children. "Dear Pekka and Mrs. Aho, we know you are sad, and we are sad with you," was the result. Della could see no way to improve on their heartfelt message, but she added, "You may also write what else you wish."

As she looked around her classroom, she understood with painful clarity the weight each of them carried when their fathers went into the mines. She made her own card, then drew a picture for Mr. Auerbach of her children working to make sympathy cards for one of their own. She decided to write him a letter that night and tell him what had happened in their canyon.

When everyone was finished, she collected their cards, admiring them. Tommy Pugh's card made her blink back tears. He had drawn Pekka, complete to his blond hair and blue eyes, and the knit cap he had started to wear. Pekka's eyes were red with weeping and tears fell down his crayon cheeks. She motioned Tommy to her desk.

"You did a fine job drawing Pekka," she said. "He's so sad. How did you know to make his eyes so red?"

"When my uncle died last year in Number Four, my eyes were red and they hurt," he whispered back. "Mama gave me a wet rag for them."

"My eyes were red and hurt after my father died in a mine," she told him.

They looked at each other with perfect understanding. She spent the rest of the morning reading *Black Beauty*. At first she wondered at her wisdom in reading, because they had reached that part of the story where Beauty is driven by Reuben, who is drunk and ignores the nail in Beauty's foot, as she limps in the rain.

She looked up when the children started to sniff and wipe their eyes. "Should I stop?" she asked, anxious.

"No, miss!" came the chorus. She kept reading, after sending around the bottom of her lunch bucket filled with cookies from Mabli.

"Will your mothers and fathers mind that I am giving you cookies before lunch?" she asked, not so anxious now.

"No, miss!" they said again, and some of them giggled, the crisis over.

The afternoon passed quietly, the children content to return to their studies, helping each other as she had taught them. When the closing bell rang, Della gathered up the cards. "I'll take these to Pekka," she told them as they pulled on their coats. "You may come if you like. I'll walk slowly."

She walked with Mari Luoma, as she had chosen to do, more and more. Juko Warela walked beside them. He had turned into the best kind of interpreter, quiet, speaking low and translating promptly.

"Juko, ask Mari if Mrs. Aho has a place to go," Della asked.

He didn't need to translate the slow shake of Mari's head. "Maybe she will take in boarders now," he said on his own. "Or laundry." He shrugged. "If not, she will have to leave, because the company owns her house."

Della nodded, her eyes on the little shack by the Finn Hall, the one with the coffin in the front yard. The coffin was empty and there was no lid that she could see. "Where is . . . where is Pekka's father?" she asked Juko.

"In sauna," he told her. "It's a clean place, and the men have washed and dressed him." He pointed to a small building behind the Finn Hall, where the men stood outside, hands in pockets, heads close together, talking and smoking.

Mrs. Koski, Tilda's mother, came out of the house with the coffin in front and walked to Della, holding out her hands in welcome.

"We're so sorry," Della said, her voice low. "Pekka's friends wanted to make cards." She held them out to Mrs. Koski.

The woman put her hand on Della's waist and led her inside the Aho house, which was crowded with women. Another woman directed her toward Mrs. Aho, who sat so still, a man's handkerchief in her grip. Pekka sat beside her, dressed in what must have been his native garb from Finland, a red and white striped vest and wool knee pants with bright red stockings. Della put her arm around his shoulders. She kissed the top of his head and put the cards in his lap.

"We want you to know we are thinking of you, my dear," she whispered. "Everyone made you a card. Me too."

He nodded and looked at Tilda Koski. "Tilda says you read *Black Beauty* today too."

"We did." Della hugged him. "When you feel like it, I will come to your house, or you can come to mine, and I will read you those parts you missed. Will that do?"

He nodded. Della looked over his head to his mother. "Mrs. Aho, we feel so sad for you." She had a fleeting memory of a funeral in her Salt Lake ward, where Aunt Caroline brought food the cook had made and sniffed into a lace handkerchief. Before she left, she told the new widow to only ask if she needed something, all in a matter of two minutes. "Is there something I can do for you right now?"

Mrs. Aho shook her head, but Della looked beyond her to the kitchen, where cups and plates were mounded high. "I see something I can do. Tilda will help me."

More people were coming to pay their respects, so Della went into the kitchen and rolled up her sleeves. She filled the sink with hot water from the stove, swishing around the iron soap saver until she had a few bubbles. By then, Tilda Koski and two other classmates had joined her, everyone with a dishtowel.

Della started washing dishes, chatting with her students, reducing the mound to order. By the time she finished, the Parmley girls were there to dry the dishes. Myfanwy Jones brought a loaf of bread from her mother. Through the window over the sink Della saw Angharad standing by her father, her hand on his shoulder. Della watched as he carved on the coffin lid.

"He's carving Mr. Aho's name," Tilda told her.

"No one will see his beautiful work in the ground."

"God will."

Drying her hands, she walked outside. By now, the

coffin was outside the door to the sauna. She turned away, unwilling to watch what she knew was coming. She looked at the Davises instead. Owen watched the sauna, as Angharad drew a freehand dragon, a small one, below the elaborately carved name.

Owen wiped the wood chips from his arms. "I asked Victor Aho what his name meant. He said 'aho' was a glade, or an opening in the forest." He pointed with his carving tool. "I hope I caught the essence."

"You did," she told him, tracing the outline of trees and the open space.

"Can't get too fancy with pine," he said, with all the apology of an artist. "I'd have preferred oak." He chuckled at that. "Artists. Slap me silly if you think I need it."

"No! Now who's the butterbean?"

He turned his attention to Angharad, who had opened a small pot of red paint. Her eyes fierce with concentration, she took a delicate brush and traced the dragon, then filled it in. She stepped back to observe the effect.

Della turned around to see the Finns carrying the shrouded corpse of Matti Aho to the coffin. Owen glanced too, then tightened his arms around his daughter. He kept her facing the coffin lid until the body was safely stowed in the cloth-lined box.

"Walk her around to the front and keep going," he said to Della as he picked up the lid. "Nice work, my beloved," he told his daughter. "Go with Miss Anders."

Della did as he ordered, going against the stream of women who came out of the house, their tired faces etched with grief. She kept walking away from Finn Town, as the wails and shrieks began again. Soon she was carrying Angharad, whose face was turned into her neck. "You did a beautiful thing for Pekka's da," she whispered.

Angharad helped her and Mabli in the boardinghouse kitchen, her face solemn. She arranged the rolls neatly on the serving table, striving for symmetry and order in an unhappy, disordered day, or so Della thought as she watched.

She was standing there, her mind on Finn Town, when her German came into the dining room. Della felt tears in her eyes, remembering the Frenchman. Mabli had said his coffin was in the front room that Mr. Edwards used as an office.

"Fraulein," the German said, holding out a small box.

She took it from him, a question in her eyes.

"Open it."

She did and sucked in her breath. A gold sheaf of wheat no larger than her thumb lay nestled on a piece of cotton. She picked it up. It was a brooch with a simple clasp. "Mr. Muller, it is lovely, but I . . ."

"Remy would have wanted you to have it. He never talked much about his wife—she died in Alsace—but she was his treasure. I put her wedding ring on his little finger."

"I'll wear it and think of him," Della said simply. "Mr. Muller, isn't it strange where in the world people end up? He's so far from Alsace."

After Owen came to get Angharad, she put the wheat sheaf pin in her carved box. She stared at it a long time before she closed the lid, missing her Frenchman, so far from home but so kind to escort her each night from the library. Before she prepared for bed, she stood outside as dusk turned to dark, looking toward Finn Town, her mind and heart on fatherless Pekka Aho, her student.

"We are all far from home, dear Father," she whispered, her heart full of Matti Aho and a wooded Finnish glade carved in pine, with his own Welsh dragon.

Chapter 21

*D*ella wrote a long letter to Mr. Auerbach that night, telling him about the cave-in and Pekka and *Black Beauty* and magic cards. Wishing she had some skill, she sketched a poor drawing of Matti Aho's name on the coffin lid and a tiny red dragon. *I've learned that babies are born in saunas,* she wrote in conclusion, *and people are laid out for burial in saunas too. Beginnings and endings, Mr. Auerbach. I am learning so much in this canyon. Yours sincerely, Della Anders.*

The little house seemed so quiet when she finished the letter. She got up, restless, ready to go next door and help Mabli with the everlasting bread dough, when Owen knocked. She knew it was him: two knocks, a pause, and then a third one.

"Come in."

He stood a long moment in the doorway, and he looked so tired. He shook his head. "It's just this: the ward choir is going to sing at the funerals tomorrow morning. You too of course."

She knew better than to argue. "What are we singing?"

"That's the right question," he said with a faint smile. "'Lead, Kindly Light,' the miner's song. Richard wants to sing 'Nearer, My God, to Thee,' as well. He's in the pit tomorrow morning, so I'm conducting."

"A practice?"

"No time. I'll practice with you right now."

They sang "Lead Kindly Light," together, then he

handed her the hymnbook for "Nearer, My God, to Thee." When they finished, he nodded to her and said, "It's a good voice you have, miss."

"What's wrong, Owen?" she asked quietly, but she thought she knew. "It's Angharad, isn't it?"

He nodded and went to the door again. "Things like this happen, and she clings." His hand was on the door-knob. He faced the door as if he could see through it. "She knows too much about death."

He left, closing the door quietly behind him. She stood there and listened, but he did not sing as he walked away, which meant her letter to Mr. Auerbach had a lengthy postscript.

Della was prepared for the walk to Scofield's cemetery, but the next morning as she joined others of the Winter Quarters community heading to the canyon mouth, she saw wagons there, two with coffins, and others for the mourners. She walked past the wagon where Pekka sat, so close to his father's coffin. She held out her hand and Pekka grasped it for a moment, his face stern, almost. As she glanced around, she saw that same look on other children, as though they controlled emotions they already knew too well.

"Pekka, you come back to your class when you feel like it," she said gently. "And it had better be soon!"

He grinned; to her relief, she saw the little boy still there. He gave her hand an answering squeeze.

She sat in the wagon with the choir, pleased to see the Welsh women wearing their distinctive red skirts, aprons, shawls, and curious stovepipe hats. She sat next to Tamris Powell, who had bundled her infant in her voluminous shawl. Maryone's alert face peered out through the fringe.

"That's clever," Della said. "You have her bound in there really tight."

Tamris leaned toward her, her eyes lively. "Practical, more like. I can nurse her and no one's the wiser. You marry a Welshman, I guarantee someone will give you a shawl too, as a bride present."

"Not a chance, Tamris. After this school year, I've decided to find a teaching job in Arizona, because I think we're going to have a cold winter here."

"Oh, you think that?"

"What?" Della countered, amused. "The cold winter, Arizona, or the need for a shawl?"

Tamris just shrugged and moved closer to her to accommodate Annie Jones and Martha Evans. Owen helped Angharad into the wagon and took a hand up from one of the basses.

A wind-scoured place of rocks and weeds, the cemetery dominated a small ridge north and east of Scofield. Della stared at it and turned to Tamris, not sure how to phrase her question.

Tamris knew. "If the miner is from the United States, his body is shipped home by the company. If from Wales, he stays here. Or Finland, or France. This is the last stop before the resurrection, courtesy of the Pleasant Valley Coal Company, unless that miner has relatives on the other side of the mountains."

"My father is buried in Colorado."

"Then you know," Tamris said, her voice soft.

Remy Ducotel's burial came first. He had no mourners beyond the cluster of miners from Mr. Edwards's boarding-house, chief among them the German, who stood with head bowed by the grave. Bishop Parmley read from the book of John, reminding everyone of many mansions in a place far away from the shacks of Winter Quarters, a place where winds blew warm and miners didn't die in cave-ins.

Taking a deep breath, Della walked to the grave and stood beside Mr. Muller. She fingered Remy's little wheat sheaf pin as the men took turns shoveling dirt on the coffin. She looked down, touched to see *Ducotel* carved beautifully on the lid, with French fleur-de-lis surrounding it. She glanced back at Owen Davis, who was looking at her, and put her hand to her heart. No wonder he looked so tired. He must have carved late into the night after his shift.

After the German shoveled some dirt, he handed the shovel to Della, a question in his eyes. She took the shovel. "He was my faithful escort," she whispered and added her portion to the growing mound on the coffin. When she finished, she rejoined the choir, as they sang "Lead, Kindly Light."

It was Matti Aho's turn next. This time Bishop Parmley read from the book of Job of man born to trouble, as the sparks fly upward, with the comforting promise of seeing God someday. He stood at the head of the grave, a short man surrounded by the much-taller Finns. There was a sudden flurry of motion as Mrs. Aho fainted, but the other women supported her.

Della stood next to Owen, shoulder to shoulder as the choir crowded together to make room for all the Finns. In a moment, she felt his hand reach for hers, then twine his fingers through hers. She leaned toward him. "There are too many of these, aren't there?"

"One is too many."

"Thank you for carving Remy's name on his coffin."

"He was your escort."

Matti's brother, Victor, read from his Finnish Bible next, when Bishop Parmley finished. His words were lost because the wind had picked up, driving in from the northwest. Her heart heavy, Della looked down on Scofield and across the broad meadow, buttoned up for winter. The railroad's steel ribbon of track stretched straight across the valley. She watched as a train came out of Winter Quarters canyon to the south, laden with coal for Salt Lake City's homes and smelters, mined at great cost this week. *And no one knows except us*, she thought. *Would it make a difference if anyone knew?*

CARLA KELLY

Della wore the wheat sheaf brooch on Monday. The wind that had blown without reprieve since Saturday's funeral relented, although the air was chill. The sunshine cheered her. It was the kind of morning where children would leave their homes bundled up and forget their jackets by afternoon's closing school bell. She would have to remind them not to leave their coats behind.

To her delight, Pekka Aho was sitting in his usual place in her classroom. Della knelt by his desk. "We missed you."

"Mama said I could stay home longer, but I told her that you needed your paper monitor."

"I do," Della replied, understanding as never before the resiliency of children. "Would you please hand back the papers on my desk?"

He nodded, ready for his assignment. *All anyone wants is something to do*, she thought.

At midmorning, while her older students took turns reading softly to each other on one side of the room and she sat with the six-year-olds, sounding out simple words, Miss Clayson came to her door and gestured. Della told her charges to copy the words and went into the hall, feeling that familiar lump in her stomach.

"Yes, ma'am?"

Miss Clayson looked at her for a long moment with an expression Della couldn't interpret. It seemed to contain equal parts of exasperation and bewilderment, with a dash of surprise in the background.

"I want you in my classroom as soon as school is out and the building is empty," she said, turning on her heel as soon as the words were out of her mouth.

Della stood there, suddenly limp, wondering if the principal had found a replacement for her early grades teacher. "Arizona, here I come," she muttered under her breath as she went back into her classroom.

The day dragged, as though capricious time had decided to toy with her and draw out all the dread in the universe. When the building was empty after three o'clock, Della wiped off the blackboard and returned Owen's wonderful wooden letters to their compartments. She touched the letters and wondered if this was her last official duty as the early grades teacher. She straightened her skirt, tucked some stray curls into place, and squared her shoulders for the tumbrel ride to the guillotine.

"Come in," Miss Clayson said, her voice perfectly neutral.

Della did, her eyes going immediately to the thick white envelope in Miss Clayson's hands. Her eyesight was good enough to see the stamp of the school district in the upper left corner. *I had so much to teach here,* she thought, saddened and trying not to show it. *And who will run the library?*

Miss Clayson held out the envelope. "Read it."

Della willed her hand not to shake as she took the envelope. With a deep breath, she lifted the flap on the envelope and pulled out the folded sheet of paper.

Sure enough, it was from the superintendent of schools. Della stared at the words, thinking of Billy Evans's difficulty in making sense of letters. Now she would never have the chance to see if she had taught him anything.

The letter was written to the attention of Miss Clayson. Della looked up, puzzled.

"Read it."

She did, dread in every bone of her body. Her eyes opened wide as she scanned the typewritten page. She sucked in her breath and sat down in the first student desk. "My word," she said finally, without looking up. Following the instructions on the superintendent's letter, she turned next to an envelope still inside the larger envelope and took it out, barely able to contain her excitement as she recognized the distinctive Auerbach's Department Store logo.

"Read it out loud, Miss Anders."

Della opened the letter addressed to the superintendent

from Samuel Auerbach himself, telling of his delight in receiving pictures from Miss Della Anders's early grades class at Winter Quarters School. "'We were all amused last summer when Miss Anders carefully saved the extra pieces of cardboard from our shirts,'" she read. "'Imagine my surprise to see them returned to us, with wonderful drawings of life in the canyon. Miss Anders also made us laugh last summer when she spent her entire first week's paycheck on crayons from our stationery department.'"

"Your entire paycheck?" Miss Clayson asked.

Della nodded. "I still thought I would be teaching at the Westside School again, and I *knew* those little ones had never seen crayons before. I wanted them to have *too* many, because they never had too much of anything."

"Some people might consider you improvident," Miss Clayson said, but there wasn't any sting to her words.

"I suppose I am," Della agreed happily. "I just loved those little children. Oh, I *know* I am improvident! After I took the job here, I spent my last week's paycheck to buy more crayons. I left the first crayons at Westside School and bought more for my students here." She laughed and dared a gentle joke. "I'm not so improvident, Miss Clayson. Auerbach's gives a five-percent employee discount on anything we buy in the store."

She thought Miss Clayson may have chuckled, but that seemed impossible, so she returned her attention to the letter before her. "'I like to collect good art, and I always pay for it,'" she read. "'I've had these pictures framed and they are now on display outside my office, with the children's comments printed underneath. Is five dollars enough?'" Della sucked in her breath. "Miss Clayson! Five dollars for the drawings!"

Miss Clayson came around the desk and picked up the envelope. "I don't think you perfectly understand. Open this." She held out a fat brown envelope.

Della gasped as she stared at twenty-five five-dollar bills, as crisp as if someone from Housewares had ironed them. Knowing the meticulous Samuel Auerbach, that was probably what had happened. "Five dollars *each*? Miss Clayson, these children have never seen five dollars in their life!"

"I know. I was as stunned as you, Miss Anders." She sat down in a desk opposite Della and reached into the envelope again. "You're not done yet. Look at this."

Della looked at the smaller envelope. She read the writing on the outside, still in Mr. Auerbach's familiar handwriting, the one that circulated on memos in the store. "'Miss Anders, use this for whatever you need, and let me know how I can help. Samuel Auerbach.'" Della ran her finger over his signature, almost afraid to look inside the envelope. When she did, she felt tears start in her eyes. She pulled out three ten-dollar bills. "Miss Clayson," was all she could say, as she reached for the handkerchief in her pocket.

She blew her nose and sat back, stunned. "I . . . I just wanted to show him how I was using that shirt cardboard, since he teased me about it before I left. That was all." She looked away as she dabbed at her eyes. "Maybe I wanted him to know how wonderful our children are."

"You have succeeded." There was no mistaking Miss Clayson's pride. The principal folded her hands on the desktop. "How would you like to use that thirty dollars?"

"You decide. I'm in shock!"

"I think you know what to do with it. I may wonder at your methods, but your instincts are sound." She folded her arms and looked out the window to the children's playground.

Della closed her eyes, seeing Pekka Aho behind them, and his serious face as he rode to the cemetery on his last journey with his father. She opened her eyes. "Let's give it to Pekka's mother. Heaven only knows what is going to happen to her when she has to leave company housing."

"I like that." Miss Clayson leaned toward her across the desk. "Would you do this too? When you write your thank-you letter to Mr. Auerbach, tell him about Mrs. Aho. I've seen the posters she drew for your pie auction. Maybe he needs someone like Mrs. Aho in his department store."

"What a wonderful idea!" Della exclaimed. "I'll just mention her talent, because there is not an Aho alive who would want me to beg."

"No, there isn't," Miss Clayson agreed. "Just plant a seed, Miss Anders, something I think you are good at."

A compliment from Miss Clayson; Della couldn't have heard right. At the principal's insistence, she took the money to her room, where she tucked it in her lunch bucket and fairly floated up the hill toward the Wasatch Store, where she bought small envelopes. That night in the library, she wrote notes to each of her students, telling them where their five dollars had come from.

Della stayed up late at the kitchen table, writing a letter to Mr. Auerbach but not sealing it. Tomorrow, she would have all three grades write individual thank-you notes for their composition class. She wrote where the thirty dollars was going, telling her summertime employer about Mrs. Aho and her lovely posters advertising a pie auction to raise money to have a piano tuned. She wrote about the widow's uncertain future and her brave children.

When she finished, she read through her lengthy letter and realized that Winter Quarters was no longer just about a school. Maybe it never had been about a school. She realized that for the first time since she left Colorado, with a name tag around her neck, that Winter Quarters was more than teaching school or even mining. Winter Quarters was her home, for good or ill.

A week later, before the pie auction, she sent a similar letter to Jesse and Amanda Knight, telling of the funerals, describing what Samuel Auerbach had done, and the aston-ishment on the faces of her students when she handed each of them an envelope with five dollars in it. She wrote of the bewilderment on the faces of her younger children, most of whom had never seen actual money in their short lives since their fathers were paid in scrip, good only at the company store. She wrote of the dozen beautifully embroidered dish towels left outside her door with a note from Mrs. Aho. She had sent the note and half of the towels to Mr. Auerbach, as Mrs. Aho had requested.

She had an appreciative audience in Owen Davis, as he sat at the kitchen table a few nights later and she showed him how to French braid Angharad's hair.

"Have you thought of copying each letter you send to the Knights and to Mr. Auerbach and keeping it?" Owen asked, putting his hands around hers as she wove the braids. "I'm not going to be good at this."

"Oh, ye of little faith!" Della chided. She felt the pleasant sensation of his breath on her neck as he stood so close, holding his daughter's hair. She had decided that the faint odor of sulfur and coal was not unpleasant, mingled with Pears Soap and a freshly laundered shirt. "Now hold these strands in this hand—that's it—and weave these strands through."

"Da, you're tugging my hair," Angharad said, the soul of patience.

"Never," he joked. "That's Della." He narrowed his eyes in concentration.

"No, it isn't," Angharad contradicted. "She *knows* what she is doing."

A true artist, no matter what the medium, Owen was not satisfied with his effort. He wanted to start over, but Angharad vetoed his wish, reminding him that Mabli needed them next door to practice pie dough. "Another thing I am not good at," he grumbled as he let his daughter tug him to his feet. He gave her a kiss and sent her ahead.

"Seriously, copy your letters. Someday you can look back on this school year and remember us." He handed back her hairbrush. "Tamris Powell said you're going to apply to teach in Arizona next year. You'll never find a choir there like ours."

"No, I won't," she agreed. "Probably never find such humble second tenors either. What am I thinking?"

"I don't know," he said, serious now. "Don't be in a hurry to leave us."

He was certainly standing too close. She knew she should move back, but there she stood, hairbrush in hand, admiring a man's brown eyes and wondering if coal was permanently etched in the lines around his mouth. She suddenly wanted him to kiss her, but she stepped back instead, gathering up her hairpins on the table, feeling her face growing hotter by the minute. *Conversation, Della*, she told herself, startled at the direction of her thoughts. *Something trivial.* "What kind of pie are you going to make for the auction?" she asked, wishing she did not sound breathless.

"I think humble pie," he said with a smile. "And if I can't find a can of that in the Wasatch Store, I might try . . . oh, I don't know. What should I do?"

Kiss me, she thought. "How about a vinegar pie?"

"You're serious?"

Way too serious, she thought, dismayed at the unruliness of her thoughts, and suddenly thankful she had a harmless topic. "I learned to make it in Hastings, when we didn't have anything else in the house. Yes, a vinegar pie. And don't look so skeptical!" *Better yet, don't look at me at all, unless you're on the other side of the room.* "It's inexpensive, tasty, and better than oatcakes."

He gave her a small salute and went next door for his piecrust lesson. Della stared after him, wondering at herself and hoping Owen Davis wouldn't need any more French braiding lessons.

*C*hapter 22

*A*fter a week's discussion with herself, Della decided there was nothing as good for her wandering thoughts as a vinegar pie, tasty and tart in turn. She had wanted to say something to Dr. Isgreen during their dinner in Scofield, but she knew better. One didn't talk about a man to another man, especially one content to kiss her cheek after each walk up the canyon.

There wasn't a single woman in Winter Quarters Canyon she could talk to, either, about feelings she had never experienced before. Aunt Caroline had drummed in her head the improbability of any man ever wanting her, once he knew of her less-than-stellar origins. The old Della had taken Aunt Caroline's harsh lesson to heart; the new Della wasn't so sure. It was perfectly obvious to her that Owen and Angharad Davis were favorites in the canyon, especially since all of the nursing mothers six years ago had given their milk to Owen's infant daughter and probably felt they had a share in the little Davis family. She chose not to say anything, which made the old Della nod and the new Della fret.

On the Saturday before the auction, she made a vinegar pie, pleased with its unexpected sweetness. Papa had requested it for his birthday every year, which was a good thing, since they seldom had the money for an actual cake with flour, sugar, and icing. She could have left it alone, but there was a dab of heavy cream in the icebox left over from one of Mabli's more grandiose desserts. She whipped it into stiff peaks, then cut herself a sliver of pie. She took the first bite plain, as she remembered from life by the Molly Bee. A dollop of whipped cream turned the second bite into a little bit of heaven. Funny how vinegar pie could be such a surprise to the taste buds.

Owen stopped by with Angharad before he left for the afternoon shift. He had taken to leaving Angharad with her and Mabli—"Giving Martha Evans a break" was how he put it. She sat him down for pie and whipped cream. He ate the dessert quickly, then held his plate out for more, which told her something about the state of the lunch bucket at his feet. She sent him into Mabli's house on a fictitious errand and quickly added another sandwich to the bucket, while Angharad watched, sworn to secrecy.

"That's vinegar pie," she told him when he returned. "You probably have every ingredient in your own kitchen right now, except maybe the egg and allspice."

"You're putting a lot of misplaced faith in my kitchen," he told her. He gave Della a look, which she could only label sly. "If you two make that pie for next Saturday night, I'll carve you a box to give to the Knights for a Thanksgiving gift when you go there."

"What do you think, my dear?" Della asked his daughter. "Should we do his dirty work?"

"We'd better," she replied. "If someone bought the Davis pie at the auction and died, we would be in trouble, wouldn't we?"

"*He* would be. Not you," Della pointed out. "Aye, we'll make your pie." She tried to end her sentence on that Welsh up-lilt, which only made him shake his head and call her a butterbean on his way out the door.

"A butterbean, am I?" Della asked, pleased.

"He calls me that and then he tells me he loves me," Angharad said, which gave Della food for thought that tasted better than vinegar pie.

Della mailed her thank-you letter and all the letters from her students. With some reservations as she left the Wasatch Store, she wondered if she was relying too heavily on Mr. Auerbach to pick up on her unspoken wish to do more for Mrs. Aho. *These dear people have become my concern*, she thought more than once during the week. Pekka Aho had already told her that he and his mother and his sister had moved into his Uncle Victor's house, since they were no longer eligible for company housing. Since Victor was a bachelor, he had only two small rooms.

She still had to nearly flog herself to volunteer information to Miss Clayson, but the letter forwarded from the district superintendent seemed to have turned some sort of page in the principal's own book of life. Taking Owen's advice, Della had copied the letter she wrote to Mr. Auerbach and showed that to her principal.

"I . . . I wanted to achieve a balance in my comments about Mrs. Aho," she told her principal. "If he picked up on it, he might be inclined to help her. If I say too much, he might think I am encroaching. What do you think?"

It was the right question, Della realized later, noting how Miss Clayson's eyes had lit up when Della asked her opinion. She told Dr. Isgreen about their conversation that Saturday night.

"If you include her like that, she might start to see you as an ally, and not a . . . a . . ."

"Butterbean?" Della asked, which made him choke on his pie. "That's what Owen Davis calls me."

"That's it!" He sobered immediately. "Let's hope Mr. Auerbach finds you just interesting enough to want to continue his help." He gave her hand a brief squeeze. "I find you interesting."

They walked back to Winter Quarters that night through a light snowfall. He took her hand to steady her when the road seemed slippery and kept her hand even where it didn't.

At Mabli's door, he kissed her cheek as usual. "What pie should I bid on, if I want to share it with you?"

"Pumpkin," she said and kissed his cheek for the first time.

"Butterbean, indeed," he said as disappeared in the swirling snow. "I'd never call you that."

But I like it, she thought as she closed the door.

It snowed all night, making church the next day a challenge. She and Mabli struggled through the growing drifts, Mabli wishing out loud, not for the first time, that she cooked for a boardinghouse closer to the chapel. By the time sacrament meeting was over that afternoon, a dismaying amount of snow had filled in whatever path they had cut that morning.

"What do we do now?" she asked Richard Evans.

"I put my littlest daughter on my shoulders and break a trail for Martha and assorted offspring," he joked. "Let Owen give you a hand down to the railroad tracks. The company keeps those clear."

"The railroad tracks?"

"Aye, miss. Coal has to go through. You'll be using the tracks this winter to get to school. You shouldn't have any trouble finding a willing man to help you up the embankment, when you get where you're going." Richard smiled at her, his eyes kind. "Just so you know, my dear, you're a source of comment in the Number Four mine. Three-quarters the single men there want to ask you out, but lack courage."

"I never knew," she said, her face rosy.

"'Tis true." He nudged her shoulder. "I suspect they're mainly afraid that Miss Clayson will murder them if they do. We hear she went into quite a rage when that mining engineer ran off with Miss Forsyth."

She could enter into the spirit of the thing. "You have my permission to let drop a little rumor that Miss Anders has no intention of running off with *anyone* in Winter

Quarters Canyon. That is, unless they're willing to follow her to a teaching job in Arizona, where it's warm."

"Actually, some of the men are quite nice. And here is Owen. He'll give you a hand down to the tracks."

"Aye. Hang onto your hat, Della."

Without even straining, Owen picked her up and carried her down the snowy slope to the tracks. "You really should put me down," she protested as he carried her.

"When I get to the tracks, I will," he assured her. "Della, I load two tons of coal a day with a shovel. You think I can't carry someone—let me judge—who weighs a mere one hundred and twenty pounds?"

"One seventeen," she said, trying not to laugh.

"I added two pounds for the hat and overcoat," he said, as he set her down. "And one pound for shoes." He climbed the slope to retrieve Angharad. With Angharad on his shoulders, they walked along the tracks, Della minding her steps. When they passed the Wasatch Store, Clarence Nix came out waving a telegram.

"Miss Anders, this is for you," he said, coming gingerly down the snow-covered steps to the rail line.

She wracked her brain for bad news and couldn't think of any. "How bad can it be?" she murmured. She opened the telegram, gasped, and handed it to Owen. As he read it, his expression mirrored hers. "You need to take this to Mrs. Aho! Angharad and I will go with you."

She took back the telegram from him, thanking Mr. Auerbach in her heart and mind. She read the simple message again: *Does Mrs. Aho speak English? Can you send me one of those posters immediately? I have a plan. Your favorite art dealer, Sam A.*

"I don't understand about Auerbach's," Owen said as they continued. "It's a department store?"

"ZCMI's competition. Auerbach's has the most wonderful window displays—pilgrims and turkeys at Thanksgiving; Santa and elves at Christmas and a train going around and around a tree; cupids in February; leprechauns in March," she said. "And you should see the Fourth of July display. Mr. Auerbach has a terrific window dresser."

"And maybe he wants Mrs. Aho?"

"I have no idea, but I'm hopeful." She took his arm. "Owen, this is an opportunity."

He nodded, pleased, if the look on his face was any indication. He stopped and she stopped, since her arm was looped through his now, better for stability, she assured herself. "You're going to make Winter Quarters the best place you can, aren't you?"

"I hadn't planned to, but why not?" she replied.

He helped her up the slope in Finn Town until one of the Finnish miners noticed them down below and reached his hand to her, towing her up as easily as Owen had carried her down.

Victor Aho's house was crammed with his brother's family now, plus a dog. Angharad went right to Pekka, and Della sat next to Kristina Aho. The widow read the telegram and looked at Della with a question in her eyes.

"Why does he want to see me?"

Della explained about her thank-you letter. "I didn't tell him you were looking for employment, because I didn't want him to think we were demanding anything. We have our pride here."

"You too?"

"Yes, indeed," Della replied. "I'm a miner's daughter, remember? There are a lot of things you could do in a department store, Mrs. Aho. With your permission, I'll mail him that poster in the Scofield Bank and—"

Kristina put her hand on Della's arm. "I have a better idea."

She went to a chest by the window and pulled out two framed pictures, one of bluer-than-blue water flowing in front of a log cabin, and the other of a village square. "There is no place to hang them here. I painted these in Finland, so

I would never forget my home. If he can return them . . ."

"I will make certain he does," Della said. "This could be our lucky day."

"I could use a lucky day," Mrs. Aho said simply.

Della mailed them on her way to school, wishing there was some way to speed them down the snowy canyon on sled runners and onto Samuel Auerbach's desk. "Just put it out of your mind now," she murmured as she hurried the rest of the way to school, arriving with enough time to tell Miss Clayson what was going on. Propped against his classroom door, Israel Bowman listened, nodding his approval.

"I hope you're not setting her up for a disappointment," Miss Clayson said.

"If I don't try, nothing will happen," Della told her emphatically, quite willing to overlook Miss Clayson's familiar frown she knew so well by now. This time, she didn't even have to reach down deep to gather up the courage to speak. "The Ahos need our help."

There was no mistaking the cloud that came over Miss Clayson's face at those words. "Then try, Miss Anders," she said. "Do more than I ever did!" She turned on her heel and went into her classroom.

Dismayed, Della looked at Israel, who shrugged. "I've been here three years, and I don't begin to understand Miss Clayson," he said. He shook his head. "You know something? I don't even know her first name."

"We should remedy that."

"You're braver than I am."

The first order of business on Saturday was to make a pumpkin pie. Since Owen was sleeping off the effects of last night's late shift, Mabli bundled up Angharad and took her niece to the boardinghouse kitchen. Della made two pumpkin pies, letting Angharad decide which looked better. The other one joined the ranks of pies cooling for the noontime dessert.

Under Della's supervision, Angharad rolled out the crust for the vinegar pie. The leftover piecrust became cinnamon and sugar piecrust cookies. Della tied a dishtowel around Angharad's neck as she ate those little bits of pastry heaven no child in the world could resist.

Angharad made the vinegar pie, ready for praise when she cracked the egg without getting shell in the bowl. The pie went in the oven with two apple pies, one of which Mabli was taking to the auction.

"I'll tell you a secret," Angharad said, when Della took her next door for a wash in the tin tub.

"I like secrets," Della said, pulling the child's smock dress over her head and testing the water. "In you go. Don't splash, because it's my turn when you're done and I need more water than you do. What's your secret?"

"Da told me that William Goode in Number Four likes Aunt Mabli."

"Maybe he'll buy her pie and they can eat it together."

"I don't know," Angharad said doubtfully. "He's English."

Della splashed water on Angharad. "You're a snob! Hold still and I'll wash your hair."

When Angharad was done, dried, dressed, and settled in Della's bed for a nap—the auction would keep her up later than usual, and Owen had insisted—Della closed the kitchen door and took her turn in the tub. She washed her hair, hoping there was enough time for the curly mass to dry before the auction.

She was stepping out when she heard the familiar two knocks, pause, and one knock on the outside door. It opened, and she heard Owen calling for his daughter.

"She's sleeping in my bed," Della said through the door. She dressed quickly and wrapped a towel around her hair. She decided Owen wouldn't be too shocked to see her. After all, he had been a husband once.

"How do you even manage to get all that hair under a towel?" he asked when she opened the kitchen door. "And how on earth do you comb it?"

"I told you my secret: olive oil." She saw the carved box in his hand. "That's my payment for the pie?"

"Aye, miss. Is there a pie somewhere?"

"Next door. Angharad made it all. I just supervised. Your honor as a family is entirely safe and you may keep the box."

"Oh, no. Take it to the Knights at Thanksgiving."

Owen sat down as she unwrapped the towel around her hair, then dabbed a little olive oil on a wide-toothed comb. He watched with interest as she combed her hair, wincing along with her when she winced at the tangles.

"Drat," she muttered, as the comb got stuck in her curls.

"Let me try," he said, standing up and taking the comb from her.

He hummed softly as he pulled the comb through her curls. He did it with more force than she was accustomed to, a man's hands, but he didn't tug on tangles. "This is a challenge," was all he said.

When he finished, he handed back the comb. "Fun," he said and went to the door of her room to wake up his daughter. Della sat half asleep, almost lulled into slumber by the feel of strong hands in her hair, yet at the same time, supremely aware of his presence.

Angharad came out of Della's bedroom, rubbing her eyes. "My pie?" she asked when she saw Della.

"Next door. You're a true pastry chef now, Angharad."

The chef smiled at Della's compliment. "We didn't need you, Da," she told her father. "I'm sorry, but it's true."

"I'll bear up under the strain. Let's get your pie and go home." He nodded to Della. "*Diolch yn fawr.*"

"*Â chroeso,*" Della said promptly. "Mabli taught me 'you're welcome.'"

He looked at her a long moment, just long enough to make her feel shy. "You continue to surprise me, miss."

"Don't know why," she told the closed door after he left. "*You* can't help being charming, and *I'm* a butterbean."

Della took a last look in the mirror and picked up her pumpkin pie. She walked carefully on the wagon road, which had been cleared off and on when the snow had let up during the week. In the church basement, she and her little committee hung the construction paper chains that the Primary children had made that week, during what would have been lesson time. Butcher paper from the slaughterhouse above Finn Town covered the tables, which were already filling up with pies and the occasional cake.

The old Della made her panic for a moment. Suppose no one showed up? The whole thing was her idea, and it could be a perfect failure. She looked at Tamris Powell, who had taken a moment to nurse Maryone under her all-encompassing shawl. "Will people come?"

Tamris just rolled her eyes. "You're about to discover how much everyone in this canyon likes a party! Did Brother Richard tell you there will be dancing too?"

"My goodness, no. But the whole purpose of this is to tune the piano, so how . . ."

"Violins, a guitar, drums, more violins, and even a bagpipe, unless someone hides it from Brother Hood! You worry too much, Della."

"I suppose I do," Della said. She pushed the old Della into an empty closet in her mind and locked the door.

She wondered why she had ever worried. The low-ceilinged hall underneath the chapel was full of canyon-dwellers and families from Scofield, ready to auction pies.

Bishop Parmley's biggest contribution of the evening was Andrew Jackson Franklin, from Number Four, via North Carolina, who proved to be an actual auctioneer. "I heard him muttering to himself in the pit one day, when the Welshmen were singing," Bishop Parmley said. "Andy, you have the floor."

The miners looked at each other when the auctioneer held up a cherry pie and started his bid-calling patter. Their fervent applause at his double-tongue ability made him stop and bow before continuing. The cherry pie sold for fifty cents, which astonished everyone.

"It's just cherries, not solid gold," the cherry pie maker said, dazed. "I give the credit to Andy. He can auction *anything*."

When Andy held up the vinegar pie, looking humble as all vinegar pies look, and announced its ingredients, Della raised her hand. "I love vinegar pie," she announced. "Fifty cents."

Andy grinned and pointed his gavel—someone had borrowed the gavel from the Odd Fellows Hall. "Trust the little lady down front with the curly hair! Fifty now fifty now fifty, what am I what am I bid what am I bid bid bid?"

He got the pie up to two dollars and declared Della the winner. She held up her hand. "Not so fast! Angharad made this, *not* Owen! It's edible."

Owen clutched his chest to Angharad's delight. She propped him up. "Really, Da."

With a grin, Andy pointed his gavel at Della. "But you're the one paying. It's a bargain now."

"*I* want a piano tuned, and I know Angharad is a pastry chef," Della said. "We didn't even let Owen *touch* it."

Andy kept going as his audience laughed, then nickled and dimed the price up another dollar, still declaring her the winner. Della elaborately counted out three dollars and handed it to Brother Evans with a flourish. She curtsied when Angharad handed her the pie, with a flourish of her own.

"I'm having fun," Angharad whispered. "So's Da, and that makes me happy."

Della looked around the room. People were eating pie and some were dancing. She glanced at Owen and Emil Isgreen, standing together and laughing. She made another discovery—just a modest one: She was happy too.

Chapter 23

wenty, twenty-five, thirty." Tamris Powell looked around at the choir. "Thirty dollars for one piano tuner."

"We are rich," Angharad said solemnly, sitting on her father's lap, her eyes half-closed.

Owen put his arms around his daughter. "It was positively cutthroat." He looked over Angharad's head to Della. "And when those men in your boardinghouse ganged up on Dr. Isgreen over your pumpkin pie . . ." He shook his head. "I anticipated bloodshed."

"Tell me, Della, is this one of those skills you brought from Salt Lake City?" Richard Evans asked as he took the money from Tamris, stared at it a moment, and handed it to Bishop Parmley.

"Brother Evans, I have never organized anything in my life! Choir secretary may be the best thing that ever happened to me," Della said as amazed as any of them.

"Then you'd better set your goals a little higher," Tamris teased. "Five dollars for a pumpkin pie?" She laughed. "And pumpkin pie only has a bottom crust. My dear, you are the belle of Winter Quarters Canyon!"

"Oh, that was just a boardinghouse of miners pitching in two bits each," Della said, embarrassed. "They probably just don't want me to spit in their scrambled eggs come Sunday morning." She blushed and glanced at the bishop. "Oops. 'Scuze me."

"Then explain why they all insisted on dancing with

you?" Tamris asked, when the laughter died.

"Whatever it was, we can get the piano tuned now," Richard said. "Della, could you write your Provo relatives and see if they know of a piano tuner willing to risk life and limb to come here in winter?"

"I'll do it tomorrow," she said, happy to change the subject. Her feet ached from all that dancing, and she wanted to hurry home and soak them in hot water before bed. "How about this? In her last letter, my Aunt Amanda told me I could invite someone to come along for Thanksgiving. That's as good a time as any to make arrangements for a piano tuner, and at no cost to anyone except train fare."

"I believe you're right," Richard said. He looked at his wife. "I'd send Martha, but who would cook the Evanses' turkey?" He looked at Owen next. "I believe we should send the worst cook with you, Della. No one wants him here at Thanksgiving."

"I second that," Tamris said.

Owen looked down at Angharad, asleep now. "She goes where I go. Is there room?"

"There is if she doesn't mind sharing a bed with me," Della said. "I'll write the Knights tomorrow." She looked around at the choir. "I never thought to ask: Does anyone here actually *play* a piano?"

Half the hands in the choir shot up. "I might have known," she murmured.

"And that's not even counting the congregation," Bishop Parmley said. He stood up. "Scatter away now, all of you! Priesthood meeting is still at eight in the morning."

Tired down to her toenails, Della pulled on her coat and looked out the door. Snow was falling again, but lightly this time, almost like a benediction to the success of the evening. Satisfied, she watched the choir members and their families walk away together, laughing and talking, bumping into each other the way people do who know each other well. As she started up the slope alone, she missed Emil

Isgreen. He had been called away to a delivery, which meant she lost her escort.

She saw Mabli walking ahead of her, but William Goode walked beside her. Angharad had been right—the shy Englishman had bought Mabli's apple pie for an impressive dollar and a quarter.

"Slow down there, miss. Where's the fire?"

Pleased, she turned around. Owen had roused Angharad enough to put her on his shoulders, but her head drooped over his. "I'm not gentlemanly enough to walk you all the way to the boardinghouse, but only because Angharad is sleepy."

She waited for him. "I never expected it."

"Maybe you need bigger expectations, Butterbean."

"Would I know what to do with them?" She fell silent then as they passed the school. Della looked back and saw a light burning on the lower level, where Miss Clayson lived. "Do you know, I didn't even invite her," she said. "I should have." She shook her head. "Life is full of a lot of 'should haves,' isn't it?"

"Too many by half," he agreed. "How is Billy Evans doing now?"

She knew a change of subject when she heard one. "I know he knows how to read, because his eyes follow the words when I point them out, and he can answer most questions about the book. He's just not brave."

"Do this for me: Monday afternoon, measure Billy, then leave that broom outside your class. I'll get it on the way up from the pit. It'll be long after school is out and he has gone home, because I'm staying late to shore some timber. I'll have the broom by your classroom door on Tuesday morning. Have Billy measure himself against it."

"I'll do it. Have you decided what reward you want if—"

"When."

"—when Billy finally reads?"

"Still thinking. Remember, Monday afternoon."

She did as Owen asked and leaned the broom against the wall outside her classroom on Monday morning. As she started for home, Della looked back at the Wasatch Store and nearly succumbed, before reminding herself that it was too soon for Mr. Auerbach to respond to her latest letter about Kristina Aho. She also resisted the urge to write to Mr. Auerbach, telling him about the pie auction. *He'll think I am a pest for writing so often, and I do want that summer job again*, she told herself.

She had thought there would be plenty of time to read a magazine while she sat in the library, but she was wrong. Between recommending books, checking out others, and chatting with the patrons, the Regulator chimed nine before she knew it. She started arranging the newspapers and was soon joined by her German and a swarthy man from Italy who bowed like a count and informed her that he had come to take the place of Remy Ducotel. "I am Nicola Anselmo, strong man," he said in careful but fervent English as he pounded his chest.

She hid her smile and nodded graciously in turn, already knowing how futile it was to argue with men possessing limited English but boundless chivalry.

When she got home, she went to the boardinghouse kitchen, where Mabli was still cleaning up. "You seem to have lost your cadre of helpers," Della said, tying on an apron.

"I don't mind," Mabli said as she swept the floor. "What that tells me is that their fathers and brothers have plenty of work in the mines now and don't need a handout, no matter how we try to disguise it." She leaned on her broom. "How many hungry days did you have at the Molly Bee?"

"Probably as many as . . . as my friends have here," Della said, "only I didn't have a kindly Welsh lady who ran a kitchen."

Mabli winked back tears. "I wish there had been someone to help you."

"You can't help everyone in the world," Della told her, touched. "My Aunt Caroline assured me my growth was stunted because my father was a miserable provider."

"Shame on her!"

"I don't fault her now," Della said, surprised at herself for coming to the defense of such a woman. "She just wanted me to be tall, blond, and blue-eyed, like all the Anderses. I used to wish for that too."

"But not now?"

"No. I like what I see in the mirror." She giggled and pounded her chest. "I am Della Anders, strong woman!" she declared, which meant she had to tell Mabli about Nicola Anselmo, her new escort.

The broom was waiting outside her classroom door the next morning. She thought Owen might have left a note, but there was none, which disappointed her. When the children hurried outside for their midmorning recess, she kept Billy Evans back a moment and asked him to line up beside the broom.

"But I did that yesterday, miss," he reminded her in his polite Welsh way.

"I know, but let's see if you grew overnight," she told him. "You won't miss more than one minute of recess, I promise."

He lined up obediently next to the broom, and his eyes grew wide. "Miss! I did grow!"

"It appears that you have," Della agreed, quite aware now what Owen had done. "Ah well, you're still not tall enough to read though, are you?"

"No, miss."

"I wouldn't rush it."

There was no mistaking the relief in Billy's eyes. *Owen, I* will *know when he's ready*, she thought, suddenly understanding this little fellow. *I'll see it in his eyes.*

When Billy ran outside to join the others, Della took a good look at the broom, amused to see that Owen had carefully trimmed the head. No one would notice; there was still plenty of straw for sweeping. "I never would have thought of that," she murmured.

All week Della focused on school (Miss Clayson grumbled about children tracking in mud and snow); choir (the entire choir was happy to wish Owen and Angharad away for Thanksgiving to find a piano tuner); and the library, where Clarence Nix presented copies of Sherlock Holmes's short stories, and a copy of *Tess of the d'Urbervilles*. "It's racy," Clarence had warned her. "Keep it in your desk, and no one under twenty-one gets it."

"I'll keep it next to *Barry Lyndon*,'" she assured him, and then she couldn't resist. "They probably won't mate," she teased, which made Clarence blush as red as his bow tie.

All the focus in the world couldn't disguise her longing to check for mail, every hour on the hour, at the store, wondering when Mr. Auerbach would respond. "I won't, I won't, I won't," she muttered each day, determined to wait until Friday.

Thursday afternoon, she swept out her classroom and put on her hat, testing her resolve to avoid the store, when someone knocked on the doorframe. She turned around to see the bishop dangling a letter in his hand.

"For you, Sister Anders. I think you've been waiting for this," he said, as she hurried toward him.

It was a thick letter, with the Auerbach Department Store logo. She took a deep breath. "Pray, Bishop," she murmured.

"All the time," he assured her and handed her his penknife to slit the envelope. "I'm just nosy enough to want to know what it says."

She gestured him inside her classroom and he squeezed himself into a desk. She sat across from him, took another deep breath, and pulled out a letter and train tickets. She couldn't help herself. Tears came to her eyes before she even opened the letter.

Nonplussed—hadn't he been bishop for years?—Bishop Parmley handed her his handkerchief and she blew her nose.

"You read it," she said, her face still deep in the handkerchief.

"'My very dear Miss Anders, I need Mrs. Aho at the earliest possible convenience,'" he read, and his voice wasn't so steady. He read ahead and chuckled. "'My traitorous window dresser's assistant has abandoned me for my rival, ZCMI, so we are glum, what with the holidays approaching.'" Bishop Parmley took his own deep breath. "'Will you please ask Mrs. Aho if she and her two children will visit me as soon as possible? Send me a telegram and I will have someone meet them at the depot. Monday would be good, but Tuesday will do. If she's agreeable, I'll make arrangements for housing and school. I'll pay all her expenses for this visit. Be persuasive, my dear Della! Your friend, Sam.'"

The bishop looked at her, tears in his eyes too. Wordless, Della handed back his handkerchief. He blew his nose vigorously. "Well, well. You organize a pie auction and find employment for a widow. Della, are you a genie let out of a bottle?"

"I never was before I came to Winter Quarters," she assured him. "Bishop, this means the world to them."

"I know," he said, equally serious. "I sometimes hate that I have to run a business here and evict good people who have nowhere to go. It pains me." He gave her a long look. "Sister Anders, the Lord is well-acquainted with you." He couldn't say any more. He pressed his hand to the bridge of his nose and left the room quietly.

She sat there until the shadows started to shift across the canyon. When the Regulator whirred and prepared to chime four times, she leaped up and pulled on her coat, grabbing the letter and its contents and started running up the road toward Finn Town.

She stopped twice to gasp and wheeze, bent over and wishing she hadn't laced her corset so tight that morning. "Vanity, vanity," she mumbled, as she tried to draw a big enough breath to get her up the road, which suddenly felt as steep as a coal chute.

When she stopped in front of David Wilson's home, Emil Isgreen opened the front door, looking at her with some concern. He came down the steps toward her, doctor's bag in hand.

"Is there something I can do?"

She shook her head. "Corset," was all that came out.

"I can remedy that right here," he said with a wink. "Trouble is, I'll lose my job and so will you."

She waved her hand weakly and tried not to laugh, mainly because she couldn't. Wordless still, she held out the letter from Mr. Auerbach. He read it and had the same reaction Bishop Parmley did—a sudden urge to look away and fumble for a handkerchief.

"All I run into are crybabies," she said.

"We won't get fired for this," he said softly as he kissed her cheek. "Get moving, Della. You're the bearer of glad tidings."

She waved at him and continued at a more sedate pace past the tipple and into Finn Town. Pekka was sorting through a pile of rocks and lumps of coal by his uncle's shack. He brightened to see her.

"Miss! Stop and visit," he said, as hospitable as his mother, who was standing at the door now, her hands on her cheeks, her eyes on the letter in Della's hand, her expression close to hopeful. Della held out the letter.

"Mrs. Aho, I think you're going to celebrate Christmas early this year."

Her hand to her throat, Kristina Aho read the letter once, then read it again. She took out the train voucher and stared at in disbelief. She just stood there looking at Della, her eyes full of wonder and hope.

"What does the assistant window dresser do?" the widow asked, clutching Della's hand to her breast now.

"She paints the backgrounds on all the window displays in Auerbach's Department Store," Della said. "There are many windows and many holidays and seasons. Oh, and there are displays in women's lingerie and Housewares."

Suddenly Kristina's legs couldn't hold her. She sat down on the front steps, unmindful of the cold, and stared at the letter again. She turned to Della, her expression intense now. "Could I live on what Mr. Auerbach would pay?"

Della nodded, confident she knew Mr. Auerbach's heart. "He would never offer you a job if you could not support your family with what he will pay you."

Mrs. Aho pulled Pekka close to her and whispered to him in Finnish. He nodded, serious, seven years old and the man of the family. "Miss, could you send this nice man a telegram, telling him to meet the Monday evening train in Salt Lake City?"

"I'll do it right now."

Della stood up. She turned to start down the slope, when Mrs. Aho grabbed her hand and kissed it. Della gathered the woman close. "I'll miss Pekka," she whispered, "but this will be so good for you!"

Della joined the group of friends and relatives Monday morning early, as they waved good-bye to Kristina, Pekka, and little Reet from the depot in Scofield. She was there on Friday afternoon, standing in the snow with the others as the train brought them back, triumphant and employed.

Exhausted but happy, Kristina told Della about the house on the west side that Mr. Auerbach had arranged for them. "He said the rent would be small, so I could get on my feet again." She giggled and rested her blonde head on Della's shoulder. "I didn't know what he meant by getting on my feet because I was standing right next to him, but I think it is good!"

"It *is* good," Della assured her. "It means he'll be watching out for you."

"As you have done here," Kristina said simply. "Pekka is already enrolled in your old Westside School." Pekka whispered to her in Finnish. "Ah, yes. Your principal Mr. Oldroyd said to send him more good students anytime."

In his role as mine superintendent, Thomas Parmley arranged for the train that carried the Scofield miners to Winter Quarters Canyon to take the Aho family and their few possessions to the depot on Monday morning early. Miss Clayson surprised Della by giving her permission for the lower grades class to go along and wave good-bye, as the Scofield spur to Colton took the Aho family to Salt Lake City and a future.

When they returned to their classroom, cheeks ruddy from the cold and excited about their impromptu train ride to Scofield, Della unrolled a narrow strip of butcher paper for her students to draw a picture of themselves waving good-bye to Pekka.

"Draw yourself, and then put your name underneath your picture," she said. She pushed back the desks so they could stretch out the strip of paper on the floor. "John Farish, you draw the engine. Janey Wilson, you draw the passenger car. We'll send this to Mr. Auerbach."

Angharad tugged at her sleeve. "Miss, may I draw you when I finish my own drawing?" she asked.

"I'd appreciate that. I need to write these arithmetic problems on the blackboard."

They worked quietly and soon the train was drawn, the tracks lined with students waving goodbye. Some of the figures cried, some laughed. There in front, waving a red handkerchief, was a medium-sized woman with a mound of curly black hair. She had a prominent nose, the Greek kind, and eyes as dark as her hair. Della looked closer and swallowed back her tears—so unprofessional in a classroom. Angharad had drawn a small red dragon beside her, waving to another small dragon on the roof of the passenger car carrying the Ahos.

"They might need a dragon," Angharad said.

"They will," Della whispered back. "So do I."

$\mathcal{C}$hapter 24

❦

$\mathcal{T}$rust Uncle Jesse. In the Knights' return letter, welcoming her and the Davises for Thanksgiving, he had included travel vouchers on the Denver and Rio Grande Western Railway, good for a year. "'My dear niece (or whatever you want to dub our relationship), one of the perks of being a substantial stockholder in the Tintic Mining District Railway is a certain caché with the Powers That Be in Denver. Consider this an early Christmas present.'"

Wonderful. This trip won't cost Owen or the choir anything, she thought jubilantly as she opened Aunt Amanda's letter. The first paragraph made her frown. "'Since our Anders cousins aren't expected back from Europe before December, I have invited your Uncle Karl to Provo for Thanksgiving. I knew you'd be pleased,'" Della read and felt anything but pleased. She kept reading. "'I'm looking forward to meeting the Davises. You mention them in nearly every letter.'"

She sat down on her bed, supremely dissatisfied with herself. Surely she hadn't mentioned Owen and Angharad *that* often. She picked up the letter again. "'We have found a piano tuner. He's a timid soul, so Jesse may have to include another year's pass on the D&RGW to get him to Winter Quarters Canyon. I assured him it is a small price to pay for harmony—forgive my punning, dear—in the Pleasant Valley Ward Choir. See you soon!'"

Della thought it prudent to leave the letter home when Owen escorted her to choir practice, but she brought along the railroad vouchers.

"What a kind man is your uncle," Owen said, looking them over. "If you don't think I'm being forward, I'd like to write him a thank-you note."

"Three Ninety East Center Street, Provo," she said. "He'll be pleased to hear from you."

"I've carved a little box for him."

"You'll be the best guest he ever had," Della said. She frowned.

"What's the matter, Butterbean?" he said gently. "I know that expression from the upper wagon road. Hoped I wouldn't see it again."

"Aunt Amanda invited my Uncle Karl for Thanksgiving too, and I'm . . . not quite ready to see him."

"You won't be alone, Della," he told her. "Come along now, or we'll be late. You have to call the roll, remember?"

"And that is as big a lie as I hope you ever tell me!" she said, happy to be diverted. "The choir does not need a secretary."

Owen tucked her arm through his to get her in motion. "*I* need a secretary. And you *won't* be alone." He chuckled. "Angharad is so excited. This will be her first trip outside of Pleasant Valley. Think of that."

She did, in the week that followed before the holiday, touched at the way the women of the canyon, Angharad's many mothers, saw that Owen's daughter had a new dress for Provo; a real hat and not a knit cap; and a pair of new black shoes that Annie Jones insisted Myfanwy had only worn once before they were too small.

Even the Finnish women transferred a portion of their affection from Della to Angharad. One afternoon after the day shift, Heikki helped Mari Elvena carry her large leather suitcase to Della.

"I want you and Angharad to lend this for to pack both your cloe and her cloe," Mari said, with great concentration, followed by a wry expression. "I do not think that is quite right."

"Very close," Della said. "Angharad and I can *borrow* this. And I think you mean *clothes*. There is no singular to clothes, although I do believe cloe is more logical."

"English is not logical," Mari said with a sigh. She brightened and took hold of Della's arm. "When you return, you are invited to sauna with us."

"Sauna? Oh, my."

Mari nodded, then took Heikki's hand. "We only invite our friends. What you did for Kristina Aho . . ." She stopped and stood a little taller. "Friends do not forget friends. Not ever."

Angharad could barely contain her excitement as she brought her clothes to Mabli's to pack after school let out early on Wednesday. "Will I like Provo?" she asked, handing her much-worn flannel nightgown to Della, who folded it tighter and made a note to herself to sew Angharad a warmer one for Christmas.

"You will love Provo," she assured the child. "I am going to take you to the Palace Drug Store for a cherry phosphate."

"Will I like that?"

"Are you human?"

They laughed together. Della wrapped Myfanwy's shoes in a dish towel and put them in the suitcase, along with her rose talc, after Angharad had a good whiff and declared it heavenly.

"I'm taking along my five dollars," Angharad confided. "I want to buy my da a new cravat for Christmas and maybe milk chocolate, if I have enough. He loves chocolate."

"When he's talking to the piano tuner, you and I will shop," Della assured her. "You will have enough."

They were packed and ready to leave, Angharad impatient in Mabli's front room, and Della watching out the window for Owen. She knew he had worked six days straight through, except Sunday, to make up for the lost days coming up in Provo. Still, she wasn't prepared for the look of exhaustion on his face as he approached Mabli's house. He couldn't see her as she stood back from the lace curtain. With a pang, Della watched him square his shoulders, obviously determined not to show his exhaustion to his daughter.

"Why do you have to mine coal?" she murmured.

Della assured Owen she could carry Mari Elvena's suitcase as far as the tipple, to ride the coach reserved for Scofield miners heading off shift. He wouldn't hear of it and carried it over her protests.

"Back off, ye black-faced boyos," the engineer growled, as he spread out a blanket on a bench for them. "Ladies, have a seat, if you please. Owen, you're clean. Sit here too, but mind your manners."

She hadn't thought he would ever blush, but Owen did, which made his friends laugh. He said something that must have been pithy in Welsh, because the laughter stopped, even if the grins didn't.

"Tight fit, this," he murmured, taking Angharad on his lap. "Warm too."

"Owen, it's snowing and ten degrees," she pointed out, then was kind enough to look out the sooty window and try not to laugh.

Uncle Jesse's vouchers impressed the stationmaster at the depot in Scofield. Others headed elsewhere for Thanksgiving filled up the single railcar as the coal cars were coupled on behind, with a bump, a nudge, and a creak of wheels for each car.

Owen glanced behind him and kissed the top of his daughter's head. "One of those cars has coal your da mined today," he said, and there was no mistaking the pride in his voice.

He must have seen something in Della's expression. "How did your da feel about silver?" he asked.

"The same," she told him simply.

The train had its head of steam when Israel Bowman

jumped on. "We can leave now," he said, and everyone laughed.

Owen set his daughter by the window, and she stared out as the train started. "I am satisfied," she announced. She caught her father's grin and gave him a look of some dignity. "That is a spelling word for the third grade."

"Can you spell it?" he asked.

"S-A-T-I-S-F-I-E-D."

"You're right," Della said. "Angharad, Myfanwy Jones, and John Farish take the third grade spelling test every week, as well as their own. That makes me as proud as coal makes you proud."

"Makes me more proud than coal, I vow," he told her.

He looked out the window. "I haven't left this valley in seven years, and Israel Bowman goes to Provo every week to see his sweetheart. Is my world too small, Della?"

She thought about it. "I don't know. You're the one to decide that."

He returned his gaze to the landscape. Della watched dusk come quickly, steeling herself against fear as the train, pushed by tons and tons of coal in the railcars, picked up speed and started down the mountain. She couldn't help sucking in her breath every time the engine braked, and every time the tracks curved to follow the contour of the mountains. She closed her eyes, afraid, as she remembered the ascent in late August and how much it had terrified her then. The descent was more frightening.

"Come here, Della," Owen said, startling her. "Sit next to me. You're afraid."

She did as he said without a word. "Aren't you afraid?" she asked, wanting to lean against him.

"I mine coal," he said. "Why would I fear this? Don't think me more forward than the average man, but could you use a cuddle like Angharad?"

She nodded, afraid that if she spoke, her voice would betray her. He put his arm around her and pulled her close to him. He was kind enough not to comment on her tremor, every time the engine braked and the cars swayed from side to side. She glanced at Angharad, who was tucked closed to his other side, her eyes big with fright too.

"Good thing you have two sides," Della murmured.

"Just as nature planned, Butterbeans," he told them both. He leaned toward Della. "I was in a cave-in in Number Four a few years ago. We secured ourselves behind a brattice—it's a canvas curtain to channel air. Two tenors and three basses. We sang until they dug us out. Want to sing, you two?"

Della nodded.

"Any favorites, Angharad? Della?"

"'A Happy Band of Children,'" Angharad said promptly, her eyes still worried.

"You give the note. It's a G," he told her. "Just close your eyes and think it through, and let's see how close you get."

Della watched as Angharad did as her father said, then sang a note as pure as any note he ever sang. She held her breath, hoping the child was right, and smiled when Owen nodded, obviously impressed.

"Right on, sweetheart. I couldn't have done it better." He kissed Angharad's cheek. "I suppose you can stay in the family now."

"Oh, Da," Angharad murmured.

"Give me the note again, and we'll start. Oh, yes." He pulled a copy of Deseret Songs from his overcoat pocket and handed it to Della. "For the less gifted."

Della cracked him on the head with it.

"Need another note, Butterbean?" Owen asked Della. "Sing loud now," he said and began. "'A happy band of children, all joyous, blithe and free . . .'"

As they sang the first verse, soprano, alto, and tenor, the passengers stopped talking. By the second verse, others joined in. After the last line—"And bless Thy church and kingdom, Thy little servants pray"—the non-singers applauded.

Della felt the fear leave, thinking of the line before—"O Lord, do Thou watch o'er us, And keep us day by day"—as the branch train loaded with coal and little servants raced, jerked, and braked its way down the steep incline toward Colton and the main line. She probably could have told Owen she wasn't so afraid now, but his arm around her was comforting.

Other hymns followed until they reached Colton, but Della remembered what Bishop Parmley had told her. *The Lord is mindful of me*, she thought.

Della knew Jesse Knight would have a carriage waiting for them at the depot when the train pulled into Provo after midnight, but she hadn't expected him to be there with Aunt Amanda too, her arms out to welcome them. Her generous embrace soon included a sleepy Angharad, held in Della's arms as Jesse Knight shook hands with Owen.

When they reached the house, Aunt Amanda took her and Angharad upstairs to her turret sewing room, where the couch Della had slept on last fall had been replaced by a bed. "You and Angharad can sleep here. Every little princess needs to wake up in her own turret. I'll leave you to help her."

"Better ask Owen up too. He and Angharad always have a prayer," Della said, as she helped the child from her clothes and into the lovely flannel nightgown that Aunt Amanda had left on the bed.

"Da?" Angharad asked.

"Right here," Owen said from the doorway, hesitant to enter.

"Come on in," Della said. "It's a tight squeeze. Aunt Amanda let me sleep here last fall, just because I wanted to. I'll leave you two to have prayer."

Owen came into the room, skirting past her, and took her hand when she started to leave. "Pray with us."

She knelt beside the bed with Owen and Angharad,

watching how they twined their arms. When Owen held out his arm, she hesitated, then twined her arm through his, bowing her head as Angharad prayed in Welsh and then her father.

"Your turn," he whispered.

She prayed for her students and the Knights, the prophet and everyone in Winter Quarters Canyon, then said amen. Owen kissed his daughter and tucked her in bed. He sat beside her and sang "All Through the Night" in Welsh and then looked at her.

"Your turn," he said again.

She sang the first verse in English, and Owen harmonized in Welsh. By the time they finished, Angharad was breathing evenly, her face relaxed. Owen watched her a moment.

"Does she look like her mother?" Della asked.

"Very like," he said. "Gwyna was a beautiful woman, and so her daughter will be."

"What does her name mean?"

"Beloved. Gwyna named her before she died." He closed his eyes. "I'm tired."

"Don't know why," she said, as she followed him down the winding stairs from the turret. "You've only been working six days straight, mining a couple tons of coal."

"I would like to sleep late, maybe to seven o'clock," he told her as they entered the main hall, where Amanda waited.

"All tucked in, Mr. Davis?"

"Aye. Angharad is of a more practical turn of mind than her da. I believe she would give up the bedtime rituals, but I am not ready yet." He yawned. "Do forgive that."

His hostess laughed softly. "Jesse already bailed out. Della, I put Brother Davis in the room with the blue wallpaper. Show him down there, then come to the kitchen for a moment, if you please."

Della nodded and led the way down the main hall to

one of the guest rooms. "Here you are. You'll find everything about where you would in your own place, except there is an indoor lavatory at the end of the hall."

He took that in, his own eyes drooping. "And how do I . . . uh . . ."

Della smiled, unembarrassed. "Just pull the chain. Good night."

Amanda was sitting at the kitchen table, looking at the carved box Owen must have given her when she was getting Angharad ready for bed. "This is exquisite," she said. "Would it be rude of me to ask him to carve me two of these before Christmas so I could give them as gifts? I would certainly pay, and pay well."

"I'll ask him. If he has time, he'll oblige you." She rubbed her eyes and leaned her head on Amanda's shoulder, gratified as her aunt's arm went around her waist. "Oh, Aunt, all he wants to do tomorrow morning is sleep until seven! He worked six straight days so he could not lose any hours in the mine."

"How do they do it, my dear?" Amanda asked. She ran her hand over the box. "Tell you what: *Nobody* will wake him up. Maybe he'll sleep until the dissipated hour of nine."

They laughed together, then Amanda kissed her forehead. "Go to bed! Cook and I will have the turkey in the oven. The pies are done, and all you have to do is look pretty tomorrow." She made her own assessment. "I'm not sure what it is, Della, but you have a certain something about you I never noticed before."

Della smiled and went upstairs. She was out of her clothes in a minute and in bed beside Angharad, who burrowed close to her. *It's confidence, Aunt Amanda*, she thought before she slept.

She woke at nine to snow falling outside and breathed the fragrance of cooking turkey, which drifted up through the vent. The house was quiet, so she hoped Owen still slept.

She closed her eyes, revisiting the pleasure of his arm around her on the train. She thought of his question. *No, your world isn't too small, as long as it includes me*, she told herself, then turned her face into the pillow, shy to even think something like that, no matter how farfetched she knew it was. Owen Davis knew more about her than anyone in the canyon, but he didn't seem to mind being her friend. She hoped it would be enough. The old Della would have said it was, but the new Della wasn't so sure.

Angharad came awake slowly and peacefully, something she probably always had done, even as a baby, even during days that must have been desperately sad for her father. Some children were blessed with a calm disposition; she must have been a comfort. Della tried to imagine such hardship, trying to work and tend to a helpless infant. Her own father had done that too, but it wasn't a time Della remembered; she was too young. By the time she was aware she had no mother, it hadn't mattered, because she never had a mother.

She looked at the child beside her, a beloved daughter who had many mothers in Winter Quarters. *I suppose I am one more*, she told herself as Angharad opened her eyes.

"Is Da still asleep?" she asked.

"I hope so."

Angharad sat up and looked around, delighted at the little room. "Am I in a castle?" she asked as she got out of bed.

"Very like. Aunt Amanda lets me sleep here when I visit, and she thought you would like it too. I suppose this means we are both princesses."

"*You* are. I would be satisfied, s-a-t-i-s-f-i-e-d, with black curly hair," she said and bounded back into bed for another cuddle.

"That's what makes a princess?" Della asked.

"I think it must be," Angharad replied, serious. "Da says you look like a princess."

"No. He calls me a butterbean," Della told her, even as she blushed at the secondhand compliment, handed out in that artless way of children.

"No. No. He says you are beautiful," Angharad insisted. "I was not supposed to tell anyone, but he probably meant anyone but you, since you're beautiful and probably already know it." She yawned and returned to sleep.

Della dressed quietly and went downstairs on tiptoe. The main hall was still dark, which pleased her. She wondered if Owen had ever slept past seven in his life, even when he was on the late shift, because he had to take care of Angharad.

She went into the kitchen, and there sat her Uncle Karl Anders. She stopped in the doorway, her heart pounding, then remembered that Aunt Caroline was still in Europe.

"Happy Thanksgiving, Uncle Karl," she said when he looked her way.

Her uncle stood up and held out his hand to her. She crossed the room and took it, releasing it just as fast. He sat down and looked at the pile of letters in front of him.

"Amanda let me read the letters you've been sending her," he said, picking up another one. "You're having a good time in a pretty hardscrabble place."

"Hardscrabble?" she asked, puzzled. "It's a mining camp, and I know those well. Uncle, the people are so kind."

He nodded, indicating her aunt. "Amanda tells me you brought two of them with you, intent upon finding a piano tuner."

Maybe it was the way he said "them," as though miners were a species apart. "They're kind," she said again, but it sounded feeble to her own ears. She felt herself drifting back into the desperately sad, lonely child who had come to this man's door with his name and address around her neck on a placard. "We had a pie auction to raise money for a piano tuner," she said, forcing herself to speak to her uncle. Maybe she could change the subject. "What . . . what do you hear from Aunt Caroline and my cousins? Are they still in Europe?"

"No. They're in New York City, spending my money," he said with a rueful shake of his head. "You should have gone along, Della. You are generally the voice of reason." He laughed too heartily. "You could have stopped them and saved the family fortune!"

"They didn't invite me," she reminded him.

He gave her a look of genuine surprise. "I told Caroline to invite you."

"It must have slipped her mind," she said, wondering if any subject was safe. "I could never have accepted anyway, since I had to teach school. They'll be home soon?"

"Next week." Uncle Karl frowned. "She didn't invite you?"

"No, but I assure you I couldn't have gone." *This has to stop*, she thought. *Someone help me.*

Someone did. Even from the kitchen, she heard Owen Davis singing. Uncle Karl was listening too. "Amanda, your guest likes to sing in the shower."

"And he's marvelous," Amanda said. "Jesse thinks he sounds that good in the shower, but he doesn't."

They laughed, and soon Karl and his wife's cousin were talking of family matters. Della quietly left the kitchen and sat on the stairs, closing her eyes in gratitude. When Owen finished with "Our Mountain Home So Dear," sung with even more gusto than the song required, he segued into "Men of Harlech" and then the sound of running water stopped.

"Did Da break it?"

Della turned around to pull Angharad onto her lap. She had dressed herself, but she handed her hairbrush to Della.

"No, he just turned off the water," Della said, brushing the child's hair. "I'll show you how to take a bath in there tonight, with lots of running water. Want a French braid?"

By the time Owen came out of the bathing room

wearing dark trousers and a turtleneck sweater, Angharad's hair was braided. He joined them on the stairs.

"I could like indoor plumbing," he told them.

"You're supposed to," Della teased.

"I only wanted to sleep until seven," he said, sounding apologetic. "It's nearly ten."

"Excellent! There is nothing here for you to manage, and I still do a better French braid," she told him. She handed the brush back to Angharad, who took it upstairs. "All you have to do today is eat and be thankful." Feeling bold, she nudged his shoulder. "That's what President McKinley said in his proclamation last month."

He shook his head in disbelief. "And here I am sitting on the stairs in *the* Jesse Knight's house." It was his turn to nudge and tease. "Do you *know* who he is?"

"What my father used to call a shirttail relative, the nicest rich man I know." She stood up. "Now it's time to gird your loins and meet my bona fide uncle."

The two men shook hands in the kitchen. She felt her face grow warm when Uncle Karl looked down at his hand when they finished, maybe thinking it would be black. *The coal washes off in the shower*, she thought, embarrassed, hoping Owen didn't notice her uncle's involuntary glance. No such luck. Owen was quite aware; she saw it in his eyes.

Chapter 25

Owen insisted on a long walk after Thanksgiving dinner that afternoon. The snow had let up, and the scrape of snow shovel on sidewalk was heard up and down Center Street. After dinner, Owen had asked Amanda if he could shovel in front of the Knights' home, but the Knights' handyman beat him to it.

"You'll just have to be a guest," Amanda told him, her eyes merry. "You too, Della. Put down that dishtowel and step away from the sink!"

"Is she always so kind?" he asked, when they strolled down Center Street with Angharad skipping ahead.

"Funny, I never really knew her before I went to her house in August," Della said. "When I went there with my Aunt Caroline, I was in the kitchen, doing the dishes." She stopped walking. "I'm sorry my Uncle Karl is so condescending to you."

Owen just shook his head. "Never apologize for your relatives."

"Easy for you to say!" she retorted, amused. "Mabli is a delight."

"You never met my relatives in Wales! Aye, it is easy for me to say." He took her arm. "March now. If I don't work off that dinner, I'll never be able to squeeze under a ledge of coal and set a charge!"

They walked north, past Brigham Young Academy. "Uncle Jesse says the academy will keep growing," she told him. "You can send Angharad." Her arm was pressed to his side, and she felt his silent laughter. "I'm serious!"

"I know you are. I just can't help thinking how those relatives of mine would be astounded at a Davis in a college. It would never happen in Wales. It can happen here in America."

"It *will* happen here, and for Angharad. I may not agree with Miss Clayson . . ."

"You seldom do, if memory serves me."

"I do appreciate her passion to see our students in places just like this." She stopped and faced him. "Here's the difference: she doesn't seem to understand that probably all of you in the canyon have exactly that same passion, and that is why you work so hard."

"You've found us out," he said simply.

She looked at the broad stairs up to the entrance, room for all. "We have to work and wait, to see how many canyon children end up here."

"Your life's work?" he asked, as they ambled toward Center Street again. "A noble one, but suppose you decide to marry? Schoolteachers aren't allowed."

"No, they're not, but I don't see a mound of marriage offers coming my way."

They walked in silence for some distance before he spoke, and she could hear the hesitancy in his voice. "Della, you have only one fault that I can see."

She laughed out loud, which made Angharad smile too, even though her father's voice was low and not intended for her ears. "I am managing, cranky, and dictatorial! Just ask Angharad."

"She's not, Da," Angharad contradicted.

"I didn't think so. Run on ahead and lend a hand to that old lady shaking out her tablecloth." He watched her go. "It's this—you still don't think large enough yet."

He must have decided the conversation was getting too serious. "Besides, Dr. Isgreen seems happy to buy your dinner every Saturday. *He's* not interested?"

No, I'm *not,* she thought suddenly. *Emil is charming and he kisses my cheek once a week, but . . . but what?* "I think he's mostly interested in my connection to the Finnish women." She felt her cheeks grow warm, despite the cold air. "He really wants me to find ways to get them to call on him when they . . . when they think they're . . ."

"With child?" Owen concluded. "They do keep to themselves, and the women are shy about that. All women are, if my own wife was any indication."

She nodded, shy herself.

"You did a wonderful thing for the Ahos," he reminded her. "You'll find a way to gain more of their confidence."

"I think I have," she told him. She lowered her voice, even though the nearest listening object was a cat licking its paw on a back porch. "Mari Luoma wants me to sauna with them after we return."

Owen gave her a sidelong look so arch that she laughed. "I'm not quite sure what that means, except Emil did mention something about rolling in the snow." She stood on tiptoe, so no one else could hear her. "Um, in broad daylight?"

"Not likely! Do it, Della. I've heard rumors, and you can tell me all about it."

"I wouldn't breathe a word, you dirty bird," she said.

"You haven't called me that in a while."

"You haven't deserved it," she said, watching Angharad shake out the tablecloth, then skip toward them. "Maybe you don't think large enough, yourself."

"You'd be surprised," was all he said, taking her arm again.

Uncle Karl left that evening for Salt Lake City, but not before insisting that she spend Christmas with them. "Your cousins will have stories of Europe, and you'll spare me their chatter," he said, as she helped him into his overcoat.

"I think you'll enjoy knowing how they spent your

money," she teased, wrapping his muffler tighter. They stood just outside the front door now.

"I have some satisfaction in knowing how *you* spent my money, Della," he told her. "I do wish you had stayed at the university for a four-year degree, instead of just a one-year teaching certificate."

"It was all I could afford," she said, before she thought. Her stomach dropped to her shoes as she watched his expression. "I mean . . ."

"I told your Aunt Caroline to make all the arrangements," he said, wary now. "Didn't she?"

"Maybe it skipped her mind," Della said, her old fears returning. "I could only manage one year there because all I had was my library job."

He sucked in his breath. "But you volunteered at the library, didn't you? That's what Caroline assured me."

She shook her head, wanting to end this conversation, because his expression was set now, his eyes troubled. "It doesn't matter, Uncle Karl," she said hastily. "I'm doing well."

"In spite of us?" he asked, thoughtful. He put on his hat and walked slowly to Uncle Jesse's waiting carriage, appearing to Della like a man who had aged suddenly. He looked back at her once.

Della went inside and leaned against the closed door. "Please forget you invited me for Christmas, as you have forgotten everything else you should have done," she said into the wood grain.

"You're talking to yourself."

Surprised, Della looked closer in the dimly lit hallway to see Owen standing there, hands in pockets. With his dark hair and dark clothing, she hadn't noticed him. She sat by him in one of Aunt Amanda's uncomfortable hall chairs.

"Owen, Uncle Karl had no idea that my aunt never paid my tuition at the university and never invited me to Europe."

"Do you think he will say something to her about it?" Owen asked.

She shook her head. "I'm beginning to suspect that Uncle Karl is afraid of her too."

"'Tis a sad state of affairs for a marriage," he told her. "Are you feeling a little sorry for him?"

"I'm not sure what I'm feeling," she said frankly. "It's nice to know I managed that year at university by myself. As for Europe . . ." She laughed softly. "What a nightmare that would have been!" She turned to look at him in the low light. "Owen, have you ever felt like you avoided certain disaster, even if you didn't know it at the time?"

He nodded. "Aye, miss! Two years ago, the entire Relief Society Presidency of the Pleasant Valley Ward was certain they had found me the perfect wife. She was English and visiting the Parmleys—lovely to look at, liked my daughter, found miners interesting, and even had a little private income."

"Sounds good to me," Della said. "What happened?"

"I didn't love her," he replied simply. He made a great show of trembling. "The entire Relief Society Presidency told me what they thought. Oh, Butterbean, Welsh can be a nasty language when women are fierce!" He shrugged. "I was right. She married a mine foreman at Castle Gate, and from what I hear, she has been plaguing his life evermore. I got off easy with just a few well-chosen and pithy Welsh curses."

"The Relief Society would never!" Della declared.

"You're such a wee babe," he told her. "Let's get Angharad to bed."

After their prayer, they both sat on Angharad's bed, Owen's hand on his daughter's head like a benediction. "Was it a good day?" he asked her.

Angharad nodded, her eyes sleepy. "I ate turkey and dressing and was satisfied with pumpkin pie." She reached up and put her hand over her father's. "And you slept late."

279

"That's us. What about Miss Anders here? Did she have a good day, do you think?" he teased.

Angharad composed herself for sleep. "Aye, Da. She made you laugh."

Owen kissed his daughter, murmuring to her in Welsh. "Don't look for logic in the six-year-old mind," he told Della as they left the room.

"I never do. I teach them, remember?" she pointed out.

Aunt Amanda had Friday planned out like a general on campaign, and she went into action as soon as her husband and Owen left the house. She watched them on the sidewalk, moving slowly, heads together as they talked.

"I so appreciate that nice man distracting him from business today," she told Della, who joined her at the window. "After they do a deal with the piano tuner, Jesse wants to take him to visit the Bullocks, who are building a new house and need some advice on woodwork." She clapped her hands together. "And we have some serious shopping."

"After a stop at the Palace Drug Store," Della said. "I promised Angharad a cherry phosphate."

"Only if we can sit at the counter," Aunt Amanda said.

"Of course! You're aware that most of Provo will think you have taken leave of your senses," Della joked.

"I might even slurp my straw," the woman said. "Put on your hat, Della. Duty calls."

The cherry phosphate, which made Angharad wrinkle her nose at the fizz, was followed by a serious discussion at the counter. Angharad held out her four dollars and fifty cents—fifty cents had already gone to Bishop Parmley as tithing—and her carefully written list, which included a silk cravat for Da, milk chocolate candy for the same, and new shoes for Myfanwy.

"Sister Jones said Myfanwy has outgrown these shoes I'm wearing . . ."

"And they're lovely," Aunt Amanda said.

"I think she just said that so I would have new shoes for this trip," Angharad told her. "Can we find a nice pair for my friend, after I have bought Da's Christmas presents?"

"I am certain of it," Amanda said with no hesitation.

"I'd also like something for my Aunt Mabli, if there is enough. She likes lemon drops."

Della pointed Angharad down the street to Taylor Brother's Emporium. "You'll find everything there, and you can hold the door for that nice lady. Go now." She took her aunt's arm. "They have no idea that they are poor," she whispered. "I never really knew *I* was poor, until I went to Salt Lake and found out."

"I feared that, Della, but it was never my place to say anything. Or maybe it was, and I ignored it." She leaned toward Della. "You've turned out so well, in spite of a great deal, I suspect. And Angharad? She's rich in love." She took a deep breath and collected herself. "I'll have a word with Brother Taylor. Steer Angharad to the cravats and find a good one."

Della reached in her purse, but Aunt Amanda put her hand over hers. "No. This is my Christmas present. I won't get a better one, even if Jesse does buy me that gazebo for the backyard I've been hinting about."

Della found Angharad looking at the cravats, her face serious. "I like them all," she whispered to Della. "What on earth am I to do?"

"Do what all women do in such a dilemma: we buy the man in our life *two* cravats. I believe there is a sale on. It happens after Thanksgiving," Della whispered as she peered into the glass case. "Pick your two favorites."

"Do you have a man in your life, Miss Anders?" Angharad asked.

"No. I'm just telling you what I would do."

"Da thinks it's Dr. Isgreen," the child said, persistent. "We could buy him a cravat too."

Della felt her face grow warm. "He's my friend, but he's

not the man in my life. No cravat for Dr. Isgreen."

Angharad frowned. "I don't understand how a lady knows if she has a man in her life or not. I like Johnny Farish, but he pulls my hair."

"I don't know either," Della replied with a laugh. She turned Angharad around to face the glass case again. "Two cravats for the man in your life who will still be there when Johnny cries off!"

When Brother Taylor himself came over to help, he nodded his approval where Angharad pointed and took out the two cravats. He looked over his spectacles at the little girl in front of him, her expression earnest, her hand on her purse.

"My dear, you are in luck. Those very cravats are on sale today and tomorrow." He leaned closer. "I can let them go for seventy-five cents."

"My stars," Angharad said, her eyes wide. "This is my lucky day."

Della glanced at Aunt Amanda, who was struggling to keep a straight face and failing so monumentally that she had to turn away and stare at a mannequin.

To the amazement of his clerk, Brother Taylor insisted on wrapping the cravats himself as Angharad watched. When he asked for her finger to hold the ribbon so he could tie a knot, she was ready. He handed the package to her with a flourish. Angharad counted out seventy-five cents, her expression intent.

"She looks that way in my classroom over math assignments," Della whispered.

Della watched as the little girl stood on tiptoe and beckoned the dignified man to bend down. When he did, she kissed his cheek. Amanda looked away again, her struggle different this time. She grasped Della's hand. "How did you get so lucky to teach what I suspect is a whole canyon full of dear children?"

"Some of them are ragamuffins and rascals," Della

whispered back. "I love them all." She leaned against Amanda for a moment. "Wouldn't you think I was due good luck?"

"Overdue." She hesitated, opened her mouth to speak, closed it, and opened it again. "While you're at it, take a good look at her father, Della."

"Maybe I should," Della murmured.

They found the right shoes next at the Provo Co-operative Mercantile Institution, after Amanda Knight's quick word with Brother Esplin. There were lemon drops too, and then a whispered conference between Amanda and Angharad, which resulted in Della being led away by her aunt to stare at woolen underwear.

"I'm supposed to distract you so she can buy something for you," Amanda said. "Let us examine the merits of woolen underwear versus jersey."

"Woolen," Della said decisively. "You'd be amazed how wind can whistle up your . . ." She laughed. "It's a cold canyon."

Shopping done, Amanda sent their purchases home with a delivery boy. By common, unspoken consent, they returned to the drugstore for the dissipation of hot fudge sundaes, even though it was snowing outside.

They walked home in the snow, Angharad skipping ahead, then breaking into a run, hands held out, when she saw Owen and Jesse on the porch, still talking, heads together. Owen picked her up and gave her a whacking kiss that made Della laugh.

"Are they ever apart much?" Amanda asked.

"When he's in the mine, of course," Della said, her eyes on the Davises. "The Evans family watches her when he's on late shift, but lately, she's been staying with me and Mabli, her aunt."

Standing there in the lightly falling snow, she told Amanda what Owen had told her about those desperate days after his wife died, how he carried his infant at all hours from breast to breast in the canyon, as other nursing mothers kept his little morsel alive. She told Amanda how Owen had come by that blue scar on his neck and how the others tended him and his child.

In the telling of it, she felt her heart give up more of its callus at the hands of her relatives. As onerous as her life after her father's death, it couldn't possibly come close to the pain Owen must have felt, struggling with death and keeping his child alive in a place so difficult. "I can't imagine how hard that was, Aunt Amanda, and I can imagine a lot," she said quietly.

Amanda looked at her with the same seriousness. "Until I die, I am going to regret that I did not step in when I thought life was overwhelming you."

"No need," Della said. "I think it made me strong. It might even have made me good." She took a deep breath. "Aunt Amanda, I'm in love, aren't I?"

"I know you are," her aunt said without batting an eye. "Have you any idea how your eyes follow him? Or how you perk up when he comes into a room? Jesse and I sat up in bed late last night, wondering if you had any idea."

They stopped walking. Amanda took her arm. "I couldn't be more pleased, but Della, a miner."

"That's hardly an obstacle, because there is a bigger one—he's still in love with his late wife. You should see his face when he talks about her."

"You have lots of time, dear!" Amanda said, patting her face. "This is our little secret and I won't say a word."

"He tells me I don't think big enough," Della said, her arm through her aunt's as they walked slowly toward the house. "Life isn't really made up of big things, is it?"

"Not the things that matter. He'll figure it out, but time is on your side."

No one really wanted to leave the next morning. Still in her nightgown, the one Aunt Amanda said she could take with her, Angharad walked around the turret room as if memorizing it. She asked for a piece of paper and quickly drew a dragon to leave on the bed.

"Sister Knight might need a dragon, even if she does have a lovely house and all the hot fudge sundaes she wants."

"You and hot fudge sundaes!" Della chided gently, folding their clothes and Christmas gifts into Mari Luoma's big suitcase. "I can't believe you dragged your father to the drug store after dinner last night for another one!"

"He loved it," Angharad said complacently. "I still have a quarter left."

"Thank goodness! No one should go home entirely broke." She grabbed Angharad and sat down with her on the bed, holding her close. "My father taught me that years ago."

"What happened to your da?" Angharad asked suddenly.

I can't tell you, Della thought in panic. "He died." *Dear Father in Heaven, don't let her ask me how.*

"How?"

They were both holding each other now, almost as if Angharad knew. "In a mine," Della said, her voice muffled in Angharad's hair.

Angharad said nothing, but Della felt her enormous sigh, more than she heard it. After a moment of silence, Angharad pulled herself away from Della to look at her. It was a woman to woman look, startling in a child so young. Through a blur of unshed tears, Della gazed at the face of dignity.

"I pray every day for every man in Winter Quarters," she whispered. "Do you, my dear?"

Angharad nodded. "We all do," she said, her voice turned into Della's breast. "We pray that at Brother Evans's house when I stay there, and every morning before Da leaves for Number Four. He and I touch fingers and he says, 'Leave it in God's hands.'" She leaned against Della, a child again. "Could we do that now, *os gwelwch yn dda*? Please, I mean."

Wordless, Della put out her finger and touched Angharad's. "Leave it in God's hands," she murmured. *Leave it all in God's hands*, she told herself as she held the child close. *This is my secret. Pray I will not be impatient, because Aunt Amanda is right: I have time.*

Chapter 26

❧⟨◦⟩❧

$\mathcal{I}$t was easy to say, leave it in God's hands, but harder to do, as Della discovered the next day as they took the Denver and Rio Grande Western back to Winter Quarters in a snowstorm. Trust Owen to know how frightened they were, Della told herself, even though neither she nor Angharad said a thing. She wanted to close her eyes and scrunch into a little ball, but there was Angharad, expecting her teacher to act like an adult.

His arms around both of them again, he told them about the piano tuner, coming next week. When that brought no response, he tightened his grip on both of them. She closed her eyes when the train abruptly pulled to a siding as a coal train from Winter Quarters clacked past, the vibrations adding to her terror.

In a better setting, Della knew she could have better appreciated his one-sided conversation about his visit with Jesse to David Bullock, and their tour of the Bullocks' new home. "Imagine, he wanted my opinion on the wainscoting in his dining room. I made a few suggestions." He laughed softly and nudged Della. "Butterbean, this is where you are supposed to say, 'Oh, really?' or maybe, 'Just think.'"

"I'm scared to death," she murmured into his vest.

"I know, I know," he crooned. "Don't leave our canyon again, eh?"

"Not until I am old and toothless with failing eyesight," she joked, discovering it was easier to joke when she kept her

287

eyes closed. "Or maybe until I go to Salt Lake for Christmas. Horrors! I'm going to rethink that."

"No, no. You should visit your relatives. Pay attention now to what Brother Bullock said."

She nodded.

"I told him that coal gets slow, along about July and August. He asked me to come to Provo for that time and install the wainscoting myself, and build his closets. What do you think?" He gave her a gentle shake. "This is where you nod your head, Butterbean."

She nodded again, then finally heard what he was saying "Really? Owen, that's wonderful. You could have another career."

"I'm a miner," he reminded her, "but that would ease the summer gap. Believe *this*, if you can. I barely do. Your aunt contracted with me for three carved boxes."

"She said she might," Della said. Owen had kindly pulled his overcoat over both her and Angharad and she couldn't see the snow any more.

"She is paying me twenty dollars a box—sixty dollars! I make that in two months in the mine. It's too much."

"Owen, you're the butterbean. Your boxes are *that* beautiful."

He shook his head. "I'll believe you, even though thousands wouldn't."

He hummed to them as the train racketed along, and she slept, worn out with worry. When she woke, the train was silent. They had stopped. She sat up, alarmed.

"Now, now," he soothed. "Snow's blocking the tracks, and they've called for all able-bodied men to shovel. I am good at that. Keep my darling warm, will you?"

She did as he said, holding Angharad close, as the child slumbered on. He and the other men climbed back on an hour later. The train built up steam and they started again, slower this time, because they had lost momentum.

"We could have used another helper engine at Thistle," he said, wrapping his overcoat around them again, even though it was cold and snow-covered.

"Da, your nose is red," Angharad said.

"Thank goodness it's not long and Greek like Miss Anders's nose, or it probably would have grown icicles," he teased.

Della laughed and Angharad giggled, after she took a good look at Della's nose. "Da, Miss Anders is beautiful. You said—"

"I said we'll be home in an hour," he interrupted hastily, which made Della smile into his overcoat, more flattered now than fearful.

Two hours later, the train struggled even slower in the dark. Della heard Owen's stomach rumbling, so she took out the turkey sandwiches Aunt Amanda had provided and the vanilla cake with chocolate icing that Angharad pronounced almost as good as hot fudge sundaes.

"Your daughter has become quite a woman of the world," Della told Owen later as Angharad slept, her head on his lap. "Cherry phosphates and hot fudge sundaes."

"She had a good time. So did I."

He yawned. "If you won't be afraid, I'm ready for a nap. Wake me up if you're frightened." He closed his eyes, his hand curved protectively over his daughter.

Della watched them both, drowsy herself but determined to stay awake, because she was certain it was her force of mind keeping the train on the tracks. She closed her eyes too. When she woke later, his other hand was curved around her.

"Almost home," he whispered.

"What a relief. I have a job here, and the ward choir needs a secretary in just about the worst way," she said promptly, which made him laugh.

He was silent as they crossed the broad meadow. The snow had stopped and the moon was full and high. Della looked out the window, knowing it would be a cold walk to Winter Quarters, unless someone happened to be heading that way with a wagon. It was too late for the branch line. Good thing all she owned were sturdy shoes, the kind teachers wore.

Owen cleared his throat, and she looked at him, noting some uncertainty in his expression. "Della, I've decided on my reward when Billy Evans reads for you."

"And that would be . . ."

"I get to kiss you."

You could kiss me now, she thought, calm with the idea and welcoming it. She saw his hesitancy, clearly understanding what he was asking, what it meant to a man who had loved his wife, dead six years.

"You know, it might be a while until . . . until Billy is ready to read," she said, hoping she was right. "I hope you're not in a big hurry."

"No, miss. I mean . . . Billy needs to think about this and take his time. I'll just take a little off the broom head, here and there, until he thinks he's ready. You'll know."

It's not Billy, is it? she asked herself. *It's you. And it's no peck on the cheek, either.* "I agree completely. Billy will know."

He smiled and looked out the window then, his relief almost palpable.

Monday morning meant spending more time than usual, talking about Thanksgiving and turkey with her students. Della asked them to decide whether they wanted construction paper snowmen or icicles for the bulletin board. The result was a tie, so there would be both.

During lunch, Mari Elvena showed her how to fold the paper a new way to make a series of snowflakes. After reading, recitation, and arithmetic, Mari showed the whole class how to make an indoor paper snowstorm. By the time the bell rang, snowflakes were everywhere, looped from window to window, each with a spelling word or a math problem.

Mari lingered after class. "Miss Anders, I have for you . . ." She held out a folded piece of paper. Curious, Della opened it and read the note from Mrs. Koski. Here it was, the invitation to a sauna she had been dreading.

"Mari, I don't know . . ." She hesitated, her face red.

Mari held out her hand. "Come to see Mrs. Koski with me after school."

Mrs. Koski held out both hands and drew Della into her home in Finn Town.

"Mrs. Koski, I've never . . ."

"This is how we ladies want to say thank you." She gave Della shrewd look. "You would not want to make us unhappy."

"No, never," Della agreed. "Very well." She looked around; no men in sight. Kari and his brothers must be on the afternoon shift. "Please tell me that the men . . ."

"Just ladies for you this time!" Mrs. Koski assured her.

"What do you mean, '*this* time'?" Della squeaked.

Mari and Mrs. Koski laughed. "We are joking you," the older woman said. "Families sauna together."

She said something to Mari, who nodded solemnly. "We will assure you that if *any* man in Finn Town thinks he will spy, *all* men will be sleeping alone in their front rooms until the winter thaw! Thursday night? You do not have the library that night."

Della gulped. "Do I bring a towel?"

"Yes. Don't look so worried! We all look alike, Miss Anders. Even schoolteachers!"

Mabli's mouth dropped open when she told her what was going to happen Thursday night, but she was more philosophical, to Della's surprise.

"Owen tells me that the Finnish men are the cleanest men in Winter Quarters," she said. "He wonders how they do it. Maybe you'll find out."

"Mabli, I came here to teach!"

"Didn't you plan on learning anything new along the way?"

To her chagrin, the next three days shot by. On Thursday, Della waited until the canyon was completely dark. Owen stopped by to wish her well, which made her frown at Mabli.

"You weren't supposed to say anything!"

"I couldn't resist," Mabli said. "This is too good not to share."

"Care for an escort to Finn Town?"

"Not. On. Your. Life," she said, biting off each word, which made him turn away, his shoulders shaking. Angharad looked from one to the other, mystified.

"She's going to take a bath in Finn Town," Mabli explained to her niece. "You can help me roll silverware into napkins next door, and we'll expect your father to behave himself."

"He always does," Angharad said.

"I am escorting you to Finn Town," he declared firmly.

"Very well," she said grudgingly, picking up her towel.

"You're a good sport," Owen said as they walked the short distance to Finn Town.

"I like these women, and I promised Dr. Isgreen I'd do what I could," she told him. "There really isn't any point in being embarrassed around you, is there?"

"None at all. What you did for the Ahos was life changing, and every Finn knows it. We don't understand them too well, and I'll confess that some of us don't treat them as well as we should. It's more than a bath tonight, Della, a lot more." He tipped his cap to her. "Good night, Butterbean. Enjoy yourself."

"Is he your man?" Mrs. Koski asked as she came closer to the ladies by the Finn Hall.

"I doubt it," Della replied, hoping Owen was far

enough away not to hear either of them. "He *is* nice."

"That's a start. The sauna is back here," she said. "Some families have their own, but this is the largest one."

When in Rome, Della reminded herself, as they went into a side door in a small frame building. She stood in the doorway, noticing that someone had built a snow bank about six feet tall around the little structure.

"My Kari thought that would be the kind thing, since you have shy ways," Mrs. Koski said.

Della nodded, relieved. She looked around. They were standing with ten other women in a chamber with benches and hooks. Some of the women were already undressing. *Oh, dear*, she thought. *I'm not so sure about this.*

Uncertain, she stood next to Mari, who was taking off her petticoat.

"Take a deep breath, and take off your clothes. Not cloe," Mari teased, making fun of herself. "All of them. Clothes."

Della did as she said, staring straight ahead at the hooks on the walls that were rapidly filling with dresses, petticoats, and drawers. Her shoes and stockings went first, and her skirt and shirtwaist were easy enough to shed. The petticoat came off slower. She had not bothered with a corset, but she unbuttoned her camisole and just stood there. She glanced around. Few of the women were as well-endowed as she was. "Heaven sakes, Della," she muttered under her breath, and took off her camisole. "Everyone here has two."

Her drawers took a little longer, until Mari whispered, "You won't surprise us."

Della laughed and pulled off her drawers, her face on fire. She hung them up with her other clothes.

"Leave your towel too," Mrs. Koski said.

My stars, what am I in for? she thought. Eyes down, Della followed Mrs. Koski into the next room.

She took another deep breath and regretted it, because the heat seemed to vibrate from the very walls. She looked at the iron stove in the middle of the windowless room, with rocks placed on it. A bench held branches tied in bundles with dried leaves on them. There was a barrel of water, a dipper, and white enameled dishpans. Against two walls, benches on two ledges faced each other, the stove in between.

She admired the women's easy grace and lack of embarrassment around each other. "I think I am the only one who is shy, Mrs. Koski."

"Call me Eeva," the woman said promptly. "It's hard to be formal standing in the nude."

Della laughed and the others joined in, as if given permission to tease her a little. "Miss Anders, if you make a naughty wish about a man in sauna, it comes true," someone joked. "Sauna once a week will keep your rump as smooth as baby's bottom," someone else said. "Men like that," said another.

Della took her hands away from her breasts and nether parts and put her hands to her flaming face. "Do they really?" she teased back, which earned her a dipper of cool water on her backside from Eeva.

"You're frisky already," Eeva remarked. "Are you so sure your man doesn't know he's your man?"

"Positive," Della said, then, "Maybe," which earned another laugh.

"Here's what you do now," Eeva said. "Hold still." She poured a dishpan of water over Della, then handed her a tied bundle. "Take this *vasta*, and dip it in the water. Lay it across the stones. Watch Mari."

She followed Mari's lead, watching as her vasta's leaves seemed to reconstitute themselves and give off the pleasant odor of birch.

"We will sit here," Mari told her, as she picked up her vasta. She pointed to the lowest level.

"Why not up there?" Della asked, as the other women sat on the upper ledge.

"More heat there. It would . . . might be hard for you," she explained. "As for me . . . I am with child, so I sit lower. Same reason." She turned her fine eyes to a woman, much farther along, who sat opposite them. "When her time comes, she will have her baby here, in sauna. Very clean."

Della nodded, remembering what Emil Isgreen had told her. She sat down beside Mari. "I'm happy for you," she said. "You will still come to my class?"

"If I can," she said. "I do not think Miss Clayson will care for big belly."

"Probably not," Della said. "Mari, my eyeballs are cooking!"

The other ladies laughed. Before she climbed to the upper level, Eeva took another dipper of water and splashed it on the hot stones, making them pop and hiss. The rocks were so hot that the steam vaporized.

"Now we sit and enjoy," Mari sat, closing her eyes. "Someone will toss more water on the stones later, or not."

"It's not steamy," Della said, surprised.

"Just hot. Lie down if you want to, but sit up slowly or you might faint," Eeva said from her higher ledge. "If you have questions, ask."

Della nodded, watching her skin turn red and then begin to sweat. She did as Eeva suggested and lay down on the bench, not shy anymore. Sweat rolled off her body and dripped from her curly hair. Some women sat and some lay on the ledges, their expressions remote, probably much like her own. She felt herself relax as she sweated.

She heard a faint swishing sound and looked around to see some of the women gently slapping themselves with their birch bundles. Della did that too, enjoying the stimulation to her skin. Then it seemed like too much effort, so she stopped.

Mari touched her shoulder a few minutes later. "Let me pull you slowly upright," she whispered.

Della held out her hand and let Mari help her. "Slowly

now. If you feel faint, tell me," Mari said. "Dear teacher, we go outside and lie down in the snow." Mari spoke to the more pregnant woman in Finnish, who was already on her feet. Della steadied her and the woman smiled a drowsy thanks.

The three of them walked into the next room and left by the door that opened onto the snow-fenced field behind the sauna. Della looked up at the stars, so clear in the night sky, big enough to touch almost. *I am hallucinating*, she thought but felt surprisingly unconcerned. She reached up to touch them, then laughed at herself.

"Roll now," Mari said, after helping the more pregnant woman down.

Della sank down, not cold at all, but relieved as the snow contacted her sweating body. With a sigh, she lay full length and rolled in the snow, content to lie there, stare at the stars, and pull snow over her like a blanket. *Everything washes away*, she thought. *Maybe fear and anger.*

She turned her head when the door opened and other women came out. Eeva sank down beside her. "What do you think?"

"Bliss," Della said. "May I go back in?"

The ladies around her laughed. "Still no men in there," someone called. "What a pity."

"No matter," Della teased in turn. "I wouldn't know what to do with one, anyway."

"You'll figure it out," another lady said.

Mari stood up. Della could see now that she had lost her waist and was gently round. *Maybe someday for me*, she thought. Anything seemed possible, after sauna.

Mari held out her hand. "I will not go in again. Come with me. We will sit in outer room and dry us."

"Ourselves," Della corrected.

She followed Mari back into the first room, drying herself, then sat on the bench, content.

"I'll see you tomorrow, dear teacher," Mari said and left.

The room was full of women now. Della followed them back into the sauna, pouring water over herself this time and lazily slapping her bare body with the vasta. When she felt drained of all the sweat in the universe, she looked at Eeva. "Tell me. Can I soap myself and wash off in here?"

"Yes. In fact, some of us are done. We will do that too, then go in the snow again. These other ladies are tough." Eeva smiled at their mild catcalls. "I will finish when you do."

Every inhibition was just a distant memory now, as Della soaped her body, unselfconscious, relaxed. She breathed deep, her eyes closed. Eeva poured cool water over her and washed away the soap.

After a last roll in the snow, Della sat for a long while in the outer room, wrapped in her towel, clean as never before. "It's more than just a bath, isn't it?" she asked Eeva.

"It is sauna. I cannot explain it more. You understand now."

Dry, dressed, and comfortable, Della let herself out of the sauna and walked around the Finn House. A door opened in the house across the road, and Owen came out. She looked at him, surprised.

He turned and waved to the miner in the doorway, then took her arm. "Victor Aho thought you should not walk home alone after sauna, so I waited. He said some people get dizzy. Well?"

"The Finns must be the cleanest men in the mines. My goodness, Owen, that was wonderful. Every single pore in my skin worked overtime."

He smiled at that. "You didn't feel, well . . ."

"Shy? At first. It didn't last too long. Don't let me embarrass you, but Mari reminded me that we all look alike. You should try that. Know any Finns?"

Owen threw back his head and laughed. "One or two! And I have my own invitation tomorrow night. Should I?"

"You won't regret it. Aren't you always telling me to

broaden my horizons? Take your own medicine, Owen Davis. Finnish men probably look like Welsh men. I know that much, even if I teach the lower primary grades."

"You're saucy tonight."

"Blame it on sauna."

Chapter 27

*S*auna became part of Della's rapidly filling week. It took her three Thursdays to work up the nerve to do what Dr. Isgreen wanted.

"Mari, do you know Dr. Isgreen?" she asked one Thursday, addressing her friend, but speaking loud enough for all to hear. "He takes me to dinner every Saturday night."

"Oh, ho, we know what that means," Eeva said. "Soon you'll be knitting booties and cooking for *him*." She shook her birch bundle at Della. "Is he tall and handsome?"

"Tall, anyway," Della said. "He kisses my cheek every Saturday."

One of the women hooted. "*How* long have you been eating dinner with the doctor?"

"Since September."

"So slow! Find a Finn," she told her. She looked closer. "You're not smiling."

"I have something serious to say to you, my friends," Della said. "Dr. Isgreen wishes you would let him help you when you know you are with child."

The sauna was silent. "Are you shy about a man who is not your husband, seeing you in those private places?" Della asked simply. "I would be too, but I would go anyway. If I loved my husband, I would want to do everything I could to have a healthy son or daughter."

"I'm too embarrassed," a woman said. The others nodded.

"Oh, now," Della chided gently. "I had to get brave to

take off my clothes, and here I am every week."

More silence, but it was a thoughtful silence. "Think about it. That's all I could ever ask." She looked at Eeva, who seemed to be the group's natural leader. "I'm not saying birth would always go well if Dr. Isgreen attended you, but who knows?"

"It is still in the Lord's hands," Eeva said.

"It is, but the Lord expects us to help ourselves, doesn't He?"

"That's where I left it," she told Emil that Saturday.

"I can't ask any more." He gave her that frank, admiring look she had come to expect. "Della, you're amazing, do you know that? Few ladies would bare all for medicine."

"I bared all out of curiosity," she assured him. "*Your* interest was a by-product. I go there once a week because I get so clean and I am welcome. Still, I hope some good comes of it."

"It has," he told her. "Ordinarily, I never talk about my patients, but Mari and Heikki Luoma asked me to come to their house yesterday. They were scared silly and shy, but I do pride myself on my bedside manner."

"Emil, I'm so pleased."

"So am I. She's doing fine and I will check her every month. I've promised to deliver their baby in June in the sauna. Others will hopefully follow." He took her hand. "Della, what new worlds will you conquer now?"

"I'm trying to work up my nerve to invite Miss Clayson to come to Salt Lake City with me for Christmas," she said and made a face. "My uncle invited me and a friend, and Owen thinks I should go."

"Can't be any scarier than stripping off in a sauna for the first time," Emil said cheerfully.

Yes, it is, Della thought, after Emil walked her home and kissed her cheek. She had showed the letter to Owen after Sunday School, when he and Angharad walked her back to Mabli's. "It's the first letter Uncle Karl has ever written me, but I'd rather stay here."

"Let them see you as the confident lady you are," he told her.

"Have I really changed?" she asked, wanting to know what he thought.

"You're a long way from the frightened girl in the high meadow."

She thought about that as they walked home from church. *He thinks I'm confident*, she told herself. *Let's see.* "Owen, please cut off some more of that broom head. Billy Evans is getting closer."

"You think so?" There was something shy and hopeful in his voice that touched her heart.

"I think so. I'm watching him pretty closely these days."

"I trust you to know," he said simply. "I mean . . . you're his teacher."

"I would not for the world hurt Billy."

"He knows that." He hesitated and she waited, hoping no one would stop to talk with them and silence this man so ready to speak. She could have cried when he broke his own spell. "Maybe it's still too hard for him."

Della gathered her courage and tried again. "Something holds him back," she said, her voice soft. "I wish I knew what was troubling Billy."

"He'll tell you sometime."

School kept her too busy to worry about Owen, but not too busy to worry about Christmas with the Anderses. She wrote a letter to Uncle Karl, telling him she would arrive a few days before Christmas. In the Wasatch Store, she held the letter so long before giving it to Clarence Nix that he cleared his throat several times.

"Miss Anders? I, uh, need to put a stamp on that," he said.

Embarrassed, she handed the letter to him and two

cents for postage. "Are you going home for Christmas?" she asked.

"Too far to Texas," he said, shaking his head.

She took her courage in hand the next morning before school and stopped in Miss Clayson's classroom. *I've helped some Finns and I've tried to help Owen*, she told herself. *It's your turn, Miss Clayson, whether you want help or not.*

The principal looked up, annoyed, when Della knocked on her open door. "Well?"

"Will you come with me to Salt Lake City for Christmas?" Della asked. The invitation sounded as forlorn to her as the last cricket still chirping and hiding somewhere in her classroom. "My uncle asked me to invite someone, and I want to invite you."

All she can do is say no, Della told herself. *No is just no. You've heard worse from Aunt Caroline.*

Miss Clayson folded her hands together on her tidy desk, oceans more organized than Della's desk. Della knew her principal was not a woman to betray any emotion in her eyes, but she saw something. Maybe it was a trick of the light. Maybe Della was dreaming. *Please, Father*, she prayed. *I can be her friend too.*

There was a look of triumph on Miss Clayson's face. "So. You've conquered the Finns, and I am your next target."

Della's courage, last seen running for cover, stopped running and turned around, irritated. "You could say that, except something bothers me," Della said. "I've been here since August, and I don't even know your first name. Shame on me."

"Lavinia. Lavinia Augusta. My relatives weren't quite as ridiculous as your Olympia, but they came close. What can you do with Lavinia Augusta?"

"Vinnie? Gussie?" Della asked, amused now. "Sounds better than Oly. Lavinia, will you come to Salt Lake with me?"

Miss Clayson started to shake her head, then stopped.

"I am planning to go to Boise and spend Christmas with my sister. I . . . I could spend a few days in Salt Lake. Why not?"

Della clapped her hands. Miss Clayson sighed. "Don't be so childish. Miss Anders, you're a professional!"

"A happy one now." *Resist that*, Della thought. "I'll take you to Auerbach's to meet Salt Lake's most discriminating art collector. Maybe you'd like to visit Mrs. Aho and Pekka."

"Maybe I would. I owe Mr. Auerbach a personal thank-you." Miss Clayson looked at her clock. "Unless your noisy pupils have suddenly turned into angels, you might want to, uh, mosey to class." She looked down at the papers on her desk.

"Well, well, Miss Clayson," Della murmured as she hurried toward the front of the building. She even blew Israel a kiss, which made him stagger back in shock as she passed his door.

She stood in her own doorway for a satisfied moment. They were by no means angels, but she loved them. She walked down the center aisle, enjoying their resounding, "Good morning, Miss Anders!"

She turned around. "Good morning to you. This is it: If you score well enough on today's tests, we will spend the remainder of this week preparing for our Christmas party. Pencils? Paper?" She turned to the blackboard and raised the maps covering each grade's arithmetic test. "Remember our rule: Third graders do third grade work, and the rest of you can do your grade and all the rest. Ready? Go!"

Sitting at her desk that afternoon, grading a day's worth of tests, Della sat back in complete satisfaction. Everyone was working at or exceeding grade level now. Some of the first graders—Myfanwy and Angharad for certain—should probably be moved into third grade next fall. She would discuss the matter with their parents in May before school adjourned for the summer.

Funny thing about life: She had taken the one-year teaching certification course because she could afford nothing else. Her goal had always been to be a librarian, like the kind woman who nurtured her and healed her broken heart at Salt Lake Stake Academy. On a whim, she had come to a mining camp, where she found eager students, a library, a choir in need of a secretary, a sauna, and friends. She went to the window and looked toward the canyon mouth. And dinner with a doctor every Saturday night. She leaned her head against the widow frame, her breath blotting the view. And a kind man wanting to move on in his life but afraid to take the next step. Aunt Amanda was right: time was her ally.

The Christmas party was a roaring success, even if the snow falling all day had put the matter in some jeopardy. In his role as mine superintendent, Bishop Parmley had authorized the coal train and its one passenger car to make several trips back and forth to Scofield, giving everyone the opportunity to crowd into the Scofield school's larger gymnasium for a combined party.

His eyes full of terror at his huge audience, but grimly determined, Danny Padfield recited, "A Visit from Saint Nicholas." When he finished, the roaring acclaim made him rush from the makeshift stage and bury his face in his mother's lap. Angharad, Myfanwy Jones, Bella Williams, and Nancy Fergusson followed—equally terrified, equally determined—with their rendition of "I Heard the Bells on Christmas Day," sung in two part harmony. This time there were sniffles in the audience.

"Softies," Della heard Lavinia Clayson mutter under her breath, from their vantage point at the edge of the stage, herding performers on and off.

"Don't you ever cry at sentiment?" Della whispered.

Miss Clayson actually smiled. "Miss Smarty, I'll have you know that when I was your age, I wept bitter tears when the Little Match Girl was found frozen on Christmas morning!"

After the last, "We wish you a Merry Christmas and a Happy New Year," from the combined schools, the boardinghouse cooks outdid themselves with iced Christmas cookies. Mrs. Schmidt, a miner's widow who ran the company's newest boardinghouse, contributed two *stollen* from her native land. Mrs. Petrakis had created the Cypriot version of Greece's *baklava*, which meant everyone was sticky from all that honey. Two of the French miners from Mr. Edwards's boardinghouse had talked their way into Mabli's kitchen to produce *éclairs*.

"There is no more cosmopolitan dining in Utah than found here in Pleasant Valley," Emil Isgreen declared. He leaned closer. "I'm only grateful no one could find a sheep's stomach, so we were spared Brother Hood's haggis!"

"Are you going home for Christmas?" she asked him.

"After Christmas. I convinced Miss Harroun, my Salt Lake nurse, to relieve me then. Uh-oh, trouble," he said, eyeing a little boy coming toward him with a note. He read it, then kissed her cheek. "Babies never wait. Merry Christmas, Della. See you in 1900."

She couldn't leave until the following Monday, since the choir was singing "Silent Night," in sacrament meeting. Richard Evans followed with "O Holy Night," so lovely that her heart nearly stopped beating. Since she sang lower alto, Richard had placed her next to the second tenors. "My goodness," she whispered to Owen when the last note faded in the packed chapel. Richard bowed and returned to his place as choirmaster.

Owen just nodded and reached for her hand, holding it by his side where none of the other tenors and altos could see. She twined her fingers through his, which produced no noticeable effect beyond a slight color to his cheek. *Bill Evans, hurry up and decide to read*, she thought, then concentrated on the closing hymn, since Brother Evans was giving her the fish eye now.

That evening, Owen and Angharad brought by the

three carved boxes for Amanda Knight. Mari had loaned her larger traveling case again, so there was room.

"Here. Give this to your uncle from us. Will it fit?" he said, handing her a carving of the name Anders, outlined with thistles like the ones she remembered from the high meadow.

"I'll make it fit," she told him. "It's beautiful."

He nudged his daughter forward. "Angharad made this for you. I only helped a little."

Della knelt beside her student and took the package from the child. "May I open it now?"

Angharad nodded, too shy to speak.

It was an oblong carved box, smaller and just right for letters. "It's lovely," Della said. "But what . . ." Her fingers traced a mountain and what looked like waves lapping on a shore made of oak.

Angharad looked at her father for encouragement. "Da thought you might like the Aegean Sea. That is Mount Olympus."

She kissed Angharad. "Your da was right."

"He usually is, miss. Happy Christmas. *Nadolig Hapus.*"

Della handed Angharad a package, the rose talc she had bought in Provo on their shopping day, and another gift to Owen, a copy of John Taylor's *Mediation and Atonement.* It had seemed like a dry tome to give to a man so important to her, so she had crocheted a little bookmark with his name on it. "You have to wait for Christmas, you two."

Owen produced an envelope with her name on it. "It's not much. Stick this in Angharad's box and take it with you." He pointed to what he had written on the envelope below her name: *Open early if you think you need it.*

"What on earth does that mean?"

"If you need it, you'll know."

"Now you're going to help me in the kitchen, Angharad," Mabli said, taking her niece by the shoulder, leaving them alone in the front room.

"Thank you for Mount Olympus," she told him.

"It's our version, so it looks a bit like that mountain you can see from the high meadow." He took a deep breath. "Do you think Billy Evans is getting close to reading?"

She nodded, nearly overwhelmed. "Any time now. After that last bit of straw you sliced off, I don't think you can remove much more and not make him suspicious." She laughed softly. "Or leave me much to sweep with!"

"I'm not entirely out of ideas about that broom, and I have faith in Billy."

She looked at him, loving the honesty in his eyes. "I'm afraid to go to the Anderses and still scared of the canyons. Since you won't be along to cover my head with your over-coat"—he chuckled at that—"would you give me a blessing? It's my right to ask."

He nodded and pointed to the floor. She knelt and he put his hands on her head, blessing her with courage and fortitude. He finished in Welsh, then said amen and kissed the top of her head. He left without a word. She stayed on her knees, praying for Billy Evans to grow over the Christmas break.

Chapter 28

⚬⚬⚬⚬⚬

*T*he canyon was as frightening as ever. Della took so many deep breaths that she felt light-headed by the time they reached Colton. Miss Clayson had buried her nose in a copy of *Daniel Deronda*. When her terror lessened, Della observed with unholy glee that her principal hadn't turned a single page since they left Pleasant Valley.

"One more canyon," Della said. She pulled out the latest copy of *McCall's*, purloined from the library, and turned to the short story.

"Miss Anders, you really should read more elevated material," her principal scolded.

"At least I turn the pages," Della teased and turned a page.

Miss Clayson had the good grace to laugh. "What's the story about?"

"A secretary in a stenographic pool in New York City who falls in love with her boss."

"Preposterous!"

"I know," Della said, unruffled. She rummaged in Mari's suitcase and pulled out a month-old copy of *Saturday Evening Post*. "There's a great story in here about a young lady who goes to cook for a rancher in Wyoming. I guarantee you won't even think about snow towering over the train. Live a little, and laugh some more. My father used to say that."

Miss Clayson decisively snapped *Daniel Deronda* shut and took the magazine. In a few minutes, she was engrossed and turning pages, to Della's delight.

During the Provo stop, Della hurried from the train with Owen's three boxes and handed them to Amanda Knight, who waited at the depot.

"Since it's Christmas, I added another ten dollars," Amanda said, handing over seventy dollars in an envelope.

"All that will make him do is deduct ten dollars from the next box he makes for you," Della told her. "I'll spend it for him and buy him new shirts from Mr. Auerbach. He'll be the envy of Number Four mine."

"Do that." Amanda touched her forehead to Della's. "I'll be thinking of you in Salt Lake. If it gets too awful, you know where we live."

The train began to fill up, stopping at little towns all along the way to Salt Lake. After Miss Clayson put down the *Saturday Evening Post*, Della told her about her life in a mining camp on the Colorado Plateau, her father's death, and the pain of growing up in a household where she wasn't wanted. She spoke of the stigma of her own birth. Miss Clayson just nodded, her expression thoughtful.

"My father was a railroader," she said, when Della finished. "We had to glean coal from the tracks to heat our house in winter. I got pretty good at fighting for a lump of coal." Miss Clayson hesitated. "It may have made me less . . . less kind than I should have been." She picked up the magazine again, then put it down. "Thank you for telling me. I had heard some rumors, but nothing more."

"I should have said something sooner. I hope the Anderses will be on their best behavior, since I have brought along a guest."

"How will they treat you once I leave for Boise?" Miss Clayson asked quietly.

"I have no idea," Della replied, her voice just as soft.

She had some idea when they arrived at the depot in Salt Lake City and found no one waiting for them. "Well, that's embarrassing," Della said. "I was hoping Uncle Karl might send his coachman."

Miss Clayson just shrugged and picked up her bag. "I see a trolley platform over there. Will it get us anywhere near your uncle's house?"

"Pretty close, and I do like to ride the trolley."

Della couldn't help herself; the closer they came to the Anderses' house, the more quiet she became. When they came to their stop, she got off and just stood there.

"I trust you remember where you live," Miss Clayson said, her voice surprisingly gentle.

Della pointed. "Two blocks that way. I took this trolley a million times to my library job after school."

She couldn't help her relief to see few lights on in the house. Even if no one was home, the housekeeper would let them in. "This is it."

"My stars. It's a mansion," Miss Clayson said, properly awed.

It was never a home, Della thought, wishing herself back in Mabli Reese's tiny front room. If Miss Clayson hadn't been there, she would have turned around.

She rang the doorbell. After a long wait, a maid she didn't recognize opened the door. "The Anderses are out," she said.

"I'm Della Anders, and I was invited to spend Christmas here with my aunt and uncle," she said. "Uncle Karl is expecting us."

The maid nodded and opened the door. Della unbuttoned her overcoat and handed it to the maid. Miss Clayson did the same. "Is Mrs. Mabry downstairs?"

The maid smiled at that, maybe relieved that she wasn't going to be responsible for letting in strangers. "She is. You can go downstairs."

"I know the way. Would you ask Mr. Mabry to put our luggage in whatever room Aunt Caroline said?"

"She didn't say anything, miss," the maid said. "Are you certain she was expecting you?"

Ashamed, Della glanced at Miss Clayson, who was

regarding the maid with a frown. She took Uncle Karl's letter out of her handbag and handed it to the maid, who glanced at it.

"He probably didn't mention it to Mrs. Anders."

I was afraid of that, Della thought. "Miss Clayson? Let's go downstairs." Her face burned with humiliation as they started down the hall.

Miss Clayson touched her arm, stopping her. "You are welcome to come with me to Boise. Oh, Della."

"We'll be all right. Mrs. Mabry is my friend."

To Della's relief, but not her surprise, Mrs. Mabry held out her arms and gathered Della close. "My little pet," she crooned. "Mr. Anders said you were coming!"

I'm too old to cry about this, Della told herself and kept her face turned into the housekeeper's generous bosom until she felt in control again. "Mrs. Mabry, this is Miss Clayson, my principal from Winter Quarters School. The maid had no idea where to put us . . ."

"Pleased to meet you, Miss Clayson. You'll be in your old room and Miss Clayson will be next door. Ned will see to your luggage, and I will find a little something for you to eat. Everyone else is out."

Mrs. Mabry's "little something" turned into roast beef sandwiches, leftover potato salad, and cake with chocolate icing. "That's especially for you, dearie," Mrs. Mabry said as she sliced off a tile-sized slab of cake. "It's her favorite, Miss Clayson. Eat it all. You're looking a little puny."

Miss Clayson didn't try to hide her smile as Della tucked into the cake first.

"Shame on me," Della said, feeling not even slightly repentant. "I've walked that vertical canyon so long that I can easily work off a cake or two before New Year's!" She put down her fork with a sigh when she finished and turned her attention to the roast beef sandwich.

Mrs. Mabry sat down. "We worry about you in that canyon, Ned and I."

"No worries," Della assured her. "The mines are good, my students are willing, and I'm secretary of the choir." She held out her glass for more milk. "Did my cousins buy out Europe?"

"Very like. Cressy fancies herself only a little bit lower than the angels, and Ellen is too good for the University of Utah. She's after your uncle to send her to Vassar, wherever that is."

The front doorbell rang. Mrs. Mabry stood up. "I expect they're home. Go on up, dearie. Face the music."

The old Della took over for a moment. Della felt her heart begin to race, and the color leave her face. As her panic rose, she reminded herself that Uncle Karl had invited her to his house for Christmas. "I am twenty-four and an adult," she murmured, her lips barely moving, as she walked upstairs with Miss Clayson.

The Anderses had removed their wraps and were settling into the parlor when Della came in. Uncle Karl stood up and held out his arms awkwardly. "Della, you're a welcome sight," he said in the vicinity of her ear. "Caroline, think how much you and the girls have to tell her about Europe!"

The briefest glance assured Della that none of the Anders women had any desire to even mention the continent across the Atlantic and certainly not its various parts.

"What a treat," Della murmured and introduced Miss Clayson, who said all that was proper.

"How long will the two of you be staying?" Aunt Caroline asked, not suggesting that either of them sit down.

With a frown, Uncle Karl ushered them to a settee. "I invited Della for the holidays, and I believe Miss Clayson is on her way to Boise in a few days."

"The holidays?" Aunt Caroline asked, as though her hearing was faulty. "The holidays?"

Della tightened her grip on the settee, ashamed that Miss Clayson should hear such rudeness. She thought of

Annie Jones's lovely offering of oat bread and Eeva Koski's generous invitation to sauna, and felt her blood run in chunks. "I will leave shortly after Christmas," Della said.

"I am leaving the day after tomorrow. Early," Miss Clayson said, her voice smooth and dangerous to anyone who knew her, which, luckily, Aunt Caroline did not. Della felt her heart begin to beat again because she suddenly realized she had an ally.

The silence seemed louder than the roar of the tipple. Uncle Karl clapped his hands together, which made Aunt Caroline jump. "Excellent! We're having a dinner here tomorrow night. Just a few businessmen. I think they will be diverted to hear what life is actually like in a coal camp."

"Diverted," Aunt Caroline said. "Will we have room at table for two more people?"

"It'll be the driest dinner in the history of this house," Cousin Cressy said. "Mama, I'll happily relinquish my place."

"Me too," Cousin Ellen chimed in, then spoke in that wheedling voice Della remembered so well. It had gotten Ellen blended perfumes and kid gloves and was probably going to get her Vassar now. "Besides, Mama, *our* friends are going caroling to the less fortunate that night." An Aunt Caroline in training, Ellen smiled at Della. "You know, cousin, those people you used to teach on the west side."

"Yes, I know. My lovely, kind students," the new Della replied, which startled Ellen, who hadn't expected a comment at all. "I plan to visit a few of them tomorrow. I'll let them know about the treat that's in store."

Ellen frowned. Cressy took the lead, mumbling something about a headache, and Ellen was happy to follow her out the door.

"You can certainly entertain our guests tomorrow night with stories about the coal miners," Aunt Caroline said, staring after her daughters as if she wished to follow them.

"I really don't think we can *entertain* anyone with

something as ordinary as mining," Della said. "I'm certain Miss Clayson and I will be happy to talk about our students. Thank you for the invitation." Della glanced at her principal and saw all the danger in her bland expression. "As for me, and perhaps Miss Clayson, I'm tired after traveling. Would you mind if we, uh . . ."

"Not at all," Aunt Caroline said in her best company voice. "We breakfast at nine during the holidays, but you'll probably want to be on your little errands much sooner. Good night."

"Calm, calm, Miss Clayson," Della murmured as they left the parlor and went toward the backstairs. "I honestly thought she would be more polite, since you are a visitor."

She glanced at Miss Clayson. The principal's lips were drawn into a line tighter than the time last fall when Georgie Pugh brought a raw skunk skin for the seventh grade's Display and Discuss.

At the turn of the first flight, Miss Clayson must have felt she was out of earshot. She stood still. "Della, you may call me Lavinia anywhere now except during school hours. How on earth did you ever survive this house?"

"I kept out of sight and raised myself. And there was Mrs. Mabry," she replied simply. "When I get home, I might thrash Owen Davis for encouraging me to do this." She looked up the stairs. "One more flight. We're not quite under the eaves, but the beds are soft. Cool off, Lavinia. This is your room."

Della switched on the electric light in her old room. With a sigh, she heaved the suitcase onto her bed and unpacked. Tucked among her extra petticoat and drawers was the carved *Anders*, surrounded by thistles and leeks. It almost seemed a shame to waste it on the Anders mansion. No telling where Aunt Caroline would put the lovely carving.

She held the sign and traced it with her finger, feeling suddenly alone and among strangers. She had felt this way when she came to the house twelve years ago, and she felt that way now.

She found Angharad's carved box. She pulled off the top, remembering where she had put Owen's envelope. Starved and lonely, she looked at the words, *Open if you think you need it*, and opened it.

With a sigh of relief, she shook out a silk kerchief with a red dragon. The square was white on top, bright green below, and the dragon with upraised claw roared in the middle. At the bottom was the word *Cymru*. "Wales," she said. "Thank you."

Mrs. Mabry was happy to serve French toast at seven in the morning and offer advice. "Wear your best dresses tonight at the dinner, dearies."

"Who on earth is coming?" Della asked, holding out her plate for more French toast.

"You are a bottomless pit," Mrs. Mabry scolded, but loaded on another thick slice. "My goodness, who *isn't* coming? Some of your uncle's lawyer cronies, probably a typhoon or two . . ."

"Tycoon," Lavinia Clayson murmured, ever the teacher.

"Everyone kisses everyone else and says stuff they don't mean," Mr. Mabry said. "It happens every year."

They arrived at Auerbach's Department store at eight thirty. "Lavinia, look at that," Della said, her eyes on the largest display window. Although no observer of Christmas, Mr. Auerbach never spared any pains in creating the best nativity scene in the city, and the 1899 rendition was no exception.

Her mouth open like a child, Della admired the background scene, a star shimmering directly overhead. The rays cast a warm glow on date palms and sheep grazing on a hillside, with silhouetted shepherds leaning on their crooks, alert. In the distance, three camels and their riders approached.

Silent, they went to the next window and the next, charmed with elves in a Christmas workshop in one window, and desperate to own the lovely dresses set against a red velvet background in another window.

They went inside, and Della took the elevator to the third floor. She started down the familiar hall and stopped, her hand to her mouth. "He really framed them," she whispered to Lavinia. Silent, she walked past Bryn Lloyd standing beside his father in Number Four; Max Muhlstein drawing water from Winter Quarters Creek; Gladys Hood and her mother scrubbing the bare back of Brother Andrew Hood, crammed into a tin tub and turning from black to white; Angharad and Owen Davis, carving boxes; and little Mary Parmley helping Sister Parmley make raspberry jam.

She kept walking. "Oh my." Mr. Auerbach had even framed the long sheet of butcher paper the class had sent when they went to the depot to wave good-bye to Mrs. Aho, Pekka, and Reet. And there she was, curls practically bouncing in the wind, waving good-bye too.

"Lavinia, we have the best job in the world," she whispered. There was no reply; Miss Clayson was having her own struggle.

Mr. Auerbach's secretary motioned them to chairs, then went into the office behind her. In a moment she came out followed by Samuel Auerbach.

"Ladies, ladies!" he boomed. "You like my art gallery, do you? It's the best in town. ZCMI doesn't even come close."

"Mr. Auerbach, you're a prince," Della told him, which made him chuckle. "This is my principal, Miss Clayson."

He gave a courtly, Old World bow, which made Miss Clayson blush, then ushered them into his office. "Sit, sit. Tell me about your canyon," he said in his rapid-fire way, which meant conversation and laughter until Mr. Auerbach's secretary cleared her throat in the doorway and reminded him of his nine thirty appointment.

"Duty calls," he told them. With a flourish, he handed

each of them a voucher, good for a total of fifty dollars in his store. "Something nice for my children," he said. "Happy holidays!"

Outside his office, Della and Miss Clayson stared at each other and their vouchers. Before they could say anything, Mr. Auerbach opened his door.

"Della dear, there is more magic paper for you in Menswear—and a job this summer, no?—and all the crayons you need in Stationery. Miss Clayson, you're a lucky woman to employ her in your school." He thought a moment. "I'll be at your Uncle Karl's house tonight. Save me a seat."

"What should we get for the school?" Della asked, when they reached the main floor.

"You heard him: Something nice for his children," Lavinia said with no hesitation.

They spent the next hour buying books, journals, indoor play equipment for winter, and one new table for each classroom. The clerk in Shipping assured Della he could get it all to Scofield shortly after Christmas, and Mr. Auerbach had said the shipping was free. The remaining two dollars bought enough chalk for two years. They gathered up the promised Rainbow Colors and practically staggered under cardboard from Menswear. This meant another trip to Shipping and then a collapse in the ladies room.

"My feet hurt," Lavinia said.

"Too bad. The shipping clerk told me where to find Mrs. Aho."

"I'm not budging for ten minutes."

It was Miss Clayson's principal voice, so Della didn't argue. "That's fine. I have to pay another visit to Menswear. I'll be back here in fifteen minutes."

The fifteen minutes turned into twenty minutes, because selecting four shirts for Owen with a Christmas crowd meant standing in line, wondering at the wisdom of her purchases. She knew she had the right size, since she had sold these very shirts last summer and was a good judge of shirts. Three shirts were white, of course, but she couldn't resist a blue and white pinstripe that Della knew would please Angharad.

When she finally reached the register, Mr. Whaley presided, looking more frazzled than a mother with triplets.

"I could use you back here," he declared.

"Merry Christmas, Mr. Whaley."

"Buying shirts for a gentleman? Miss Anders, my congratulations."

He rang up her purchases while she tried to think of ways to explain four men's shirts. There wasn't time to explain that Owen Davis was overpaid for carving boxes and he needed a good shirt or two for next summer's Eisteddfod, but would probably never buy them on his own, because fathers were like that.

"It's a long and complicated story. I'm doing this for a friend."

Mr. Whaley wasn't about to let her off so easily. "'Long and complicated'? If I had time, I would tease you!" He handed her the shirts and wished her Merry Christmas.

Miss Clayson was ready when she came back. They went downstairs to other offices and found Kristina Aho, blonde hair in a tidy pompadour and trim in a dark skirt and blue shirtwaist, standing at a drafting table. She ran toward them, her arms open wide.

"I miss you all, but I have a good job," Kristina said, dabbing at her eyes. "Pekka comes by after school to sweep out Mr. Auerbach's office and empty the trash cans on the third floor. Reet stays with my landlady and her children during the day, and there is a Lutheran Church down the street." She took their hands in hers. "Come by on Christmas. Pekka will want to say hello." Her eyes grew wistful. "When he gets homesick for his friends and his teacher, he goes to the third floor and looks at your pictures on magic paper. What can I say? I owe you a debt I can never repay, Miss Anders."

"It's paid in full, if you are happy."

She hugged Della. "*Hyvää joulua*. It's a happier Christmas than we would have thought. I hope you have a wonderful 1900."

$\mathscr{C}$hapter 29

꩜

$\mathscr{C}$ousin Cressy proved to be monumentally wrong about the dinner that night. It may have begun as the driest dinner in the history of the Anderses' house, but it ended as the one no one ever forgot.

"Should I do this?" Della asked herself several times as she dressed in the dark green wool whose finest previous occasion was sacrament meeting in the Pleasant Valley Ward. As usual, there was nothing she could do about her hair. For courage, she pinned Remy Ducotel's wheat sheaf brooch to her lace collar and touched Owen's dragon kerchief for good luck before she knocked on Lavinia Clayson's door.

She wore her usual black dress, but Della admired the way her principal seemed to *will* herself taller. "We'll pull through this, but I wish you would come to Boise."

"I don't anticipate trouble from Uncle Karl's guests," Della told her as they went downstairs. "I've never been to one of his holiday dinners, so this should be instructive at the very least." *And maybe I'm a raving, hopeless optimist,* she thought, wondering again why she had accepted Uncle Karl's invitation. Maybe that corner of her heart or mind where twelve-year-old Della still lived, craved acceptance from hearts not inclined to give it.

They walked into the empty dining room, searching for their place names and found them next to Mr. Edwin Garland, another railroad lawyer, who was hard of hearing. Seated between her and Miss Clayson was an equally geriatric distant cousin of some sort who was only included in family occasions because Aunt Caroline held out the hope that he might keel over dead some day and leave some money to her daughters.

They went into the foyer to wait. When the dinner gong sounded—Miss Clayson jumped—the guests filed from the parlor on their way to the dining room. Della marched behind with her principal.

Perfect. The railroad lawyer was happy to ignore them, and the distant cousin focused his attention on Mrs. Mabry's renowned consommé, accompanied by olives, celery, and salted pecans. Interested, Della looked at the guests, pleased to see Samuel and Eveline Auerbach near the head of the table, engaged in animated conversation with her uncle.

Miss Clayson relaxed, to Della's relief. The roast goose that followed the soup practically crackled in its skin, and no one made better potato stuffing than Mrs. Mabry. Chicken croquettes with green peas came next. Maybe the guests were already full; maybe they were bored with holiday meals that left them stunned and groaning. Whatever it was, the conversation that had begun at one end of the table suddenly came their way, right when Della had a forkful of peas headed to her mouth.

"Della, my dear, Mr. Auerbach has been telling us about your students and their pictures of Winter Quarters," Uncle Karl said, raising his voice to be heard above the clatter of silverware. "He said you used shirt cardboard."

"I did. It's marvelous," she said, putting down her fork. "It makes the best paper for art work." She blushed when everyone laughed. "Well, it does."

"Della is determined to stamp out ignorance in coal camps," Aunt Caroline said. "We think it quite noble of her."

"There's no ignorance in the canyon to stamp out," she said, happy to discuss her friends. "I also help in the

Wasatch Store library three nights a week. The most popular book right now is anything by Dickens. *A Tale of Two Cities* is especially pop—"

Aunt Caroline laughed, sending warning prickles down Della's back. "What, do you *read* to the miners too? Really, Della, amuse us some more."

"They're quite literate," she replied, the prickles in her back marching in rows now. She tried to laugh, but it stuck in her throat. "I mean, how many of you can read another language? You should see the variety of newspapers we subscribe to." She felt the familiar dread again, when she had thought it was gone, banished forever by the new Della. "The ladies especially enjoy magazines like *McCall's*, and the men devour books like *Wealth Against Commonwealth*. They're very interested in corporate abuse . . . of power." Her voice trailed away as she looked around at her well-fed, powerful audience.

Shut up and eat, she told herself. She looked down at the peas on her plate, determined not to say anything else.

She wouldn't have, but Uncle Karl's law partner started to laugh. Some of the others joined in. Della kept her eyes on her plate.

"I wouldn't worry about the miners, unless little Miss Anders here is a fomenter of revolution, Salt Lake's own Mother Jones," the lawyer said. "She'll have to prod them. Men with any brains or ambition would never toil in a mine for more than five minutes."

Everyone laughed but the new Della just didn't see the joke. "They work in the mines because they are well-trained miners," she said, maybe speaking louder than she should have, because Aunt Caroline sent a glance full of daggers her way. "They work harder than anyone at this table, and they keep you warm all winter. They work so hard because they love their children."

Trust a lawyer to not let a good argument die. Uncle Karl's partner leaned toward the center of the table to see her better. "Why do you even bother to educate their children? They'll just go in the mines."

"Some will, naturally, but we teach them so they will have a choice."

Della looked up in surprise to see Miss Clayson on her feet, her eyes intense.

"Yes! If they choose to mine, they at least have a choice," Della said, slowly rising to stand beside her principal. "That's what we are providing—a choice. I have learned a lot."

"How to get coal stains off library books?" Aunt Caroline mocked.

"No, I . . ." She touched Remy Ducotel's brooch and looked around the table. "How many of you here take a bath every day? How many of you work *really* hard?"

"Della!" Aunt Caroline exclaimed. "Leave this table!"

"I will, Aunt Caroline," she replied, utterly calm now. She thought of her lovely Finns and the ward choir. She looked from merchant to lawyer to doctor, probably all of them stockholders in Utah's mines, who never knew—or cared—that their quarterly dividends came at a high cost in lives. "Seriously, though. Miners bathe every day. They scrub off the coal dust that you take for granted, and they are the cleanest people I know. They read to their children, and they sing while waiting out a mine collapse, and bury their dead and hope for a better future. As a teacher, I couldn't be in a better place." She took a deep breath. "You don't know what you're talking about."

Aunt Caroline was on her feet now, even though Uncle Karl tried to pull her down. She shook off his hand. "This is what happens when you . . . you give someone with no gratitude a university education!"

"You never paid a dime of my university tuition," Della said. "I came to you poor and sad, and I stayed that way." She looked at her uncle, into his stricken, weak eyes and realized with full clarity that *her* father had been the strong one. "I'm leaving."

She held her head up and looked around the table. "To spare her the bother, I'll finish what my aunt will probably say once I leave. My father was the family black sheep and he died in a mine. My mother and father were never married and she deserted him when I was a baby."

"They already know all that," her aunt said, triumphant.

"I thought as much. I'm sorry, Miss Clayson, that you had to hear this. I think I'll go home."

She willed her rubbery legs to support her from the dining room. She made it into the hall, then sank to her knees.

Miss Clayson helped her up and held her until she was steady. "My offer still stands, Della. Come to Boise."

"You must be ashamed of me," Della whispered.

"On the contrary. I've never been so proud of a teacher as I am of you! Let's pack and get out of here before fifteen minutes pass."

Miss Clayson helped her upstairs. Della heard doors opening and closing on the first floor, and she closed her eyes in shame. "What was I thinking?" she asked.

"Maybe that you have had a surfeit of wooden charity and misery," Miss Clayson told her, calm now. "I was going to say 'a bellyful,' but I still have my standards, Miss Anders!"

Della smiled. "Thank you, Lavinia. Fifteen minutes."

She packed as fast as she could, begging Heavenly Father to keep Aunt Caroline and Uncle Karl downstairs, because she had had enough barbs stuck in her raw flesh from her aunt and felt only disgust for her weakling of an uncle. "I'm going to thump you, Owen," she said, then took it all back when she looked at the dragon spread out by the foot of her bed. The woodcarving of the Anders name went back in her suitcase. Next summer she would take it back to Colorado and leave it on her father's grave.

They left the house by a side door, and Della felt her

spirits begin to rise. "I never have to go back, do I?" she said to Miss Clayson, who marched along grimly, the picture of indignation.

"Most certainly not! We shouldn't have a bit of trouble finding a downtown hotel. It's not that late and . . ."

She stopped speaking as a carriage came alongside, then she did something that endeared her forever to Della. Miss Clayson deliberately stepped in front of her, shielding her from whoever was driving by so slowly, ready to swing her suitcase if the door so much as opened a crack.

"Wait a minute, Miss Clayson!" came a familiar voice from inside the brougham. "Can Eveline and I interest you two in a place to stay the night?"

Della gasped out loud and put a restraining hand on her principal. "Mr. Auerbach! You're supposed to be eating dinner at my uncle's house!" She chuckled. "I ate the humble pie, but Mrs. Mabry makes wonderful cake."

As they stood there by the curb, the coachman leaped down and took their luggage, stowing it in the boot of the carriage. He held the door open with a real flourish and helped them inside. Della sat across from Mr. Auerbach, looking from him to his wife. "I'm totally a pariah," she said, doubtful. "Are you . . . are you sure you want to do this?"

"We've never been more positive," Eveline Auerbach said. "I had no trouble pleading a headache." She touched Della's hand. "Our leaving early will give them the chance to backstab the Jews too, so their evening won't be entirely wasted."

Miss Clayson put her arm around Della when she burst into tears, and Mrs. Auerbach handed her a lace handkerchief. Soon everyone was sniffling, except Samuel Auerbach, who was made of sterner stuff, obviously.

"Goodness, ladies! Della, I have a proposition from Menswear. Mr. Whaley came to me in utter despair at closing time and begged for more help to get him through to

Christmas. Will you help him? You'll be our guest and earn some money too." He laughed. "An Auerbach couldn't make you a better offer, and on Christmas too."

Della blew her nose and managed a watery chuckle. She nodded.

Mr. Auerbach took his wife's hand and kissed it. "I came here from Germany, my dears. Eveline was born in a gold mining camp in California. We understand immigrants and you are both precisely right. It *is* all about the children. Heaven bless you for understanding that."

Della saw Miss Clayson off at the depot early the next morning, then took a streetcar to Auerbach's. Mr. Whaley nearly fell down at her feet when she put on her nametag and stepped behind the counter. She protested when Mr. Auerbach insisted she attend the annual employees' holiday party later that week. She tried to remind him that she wasn't a full-time employee, but he wasn't buying it.

She sat next to Pekka Aho at the party, listening with huge delight and a little homesickness as he told her about his teacher at Westside School. "He does what you do, Miss Anders. We get a chapter a day after lunch, and two if we're really good."

The few evenings left before Christmas Della spent in the Auerbachs' parlor, listening to stories about Mr. Auerbach's early days in California mining camps, marriage to Eveline, and settlement in the City of the Great Salt Lake, opening an emporium with his brothers and having battles of wit—winning some, losing some—with Brigham Young.

At Mr. Auerbach's urging, she wrote a letter to the Knights, briefly describing what had happened. Amanda responded promptly and invited her to spend Christmas Day with them.

"Are you going?" Mr. Auerbach asked her over boiled eggs and toast on Christmas Eve. "We spend a quiet day

here on Christmas, but I assure you that Mr. Whaley would
be overjoyed to see you on December 26, for the dread
inventory."

"I'll stay here for that, if it's agreeable," she said, shy.
"You've been so kind."

"And you've been so helpful! Very well, then—write to
the Knights and tell them you'll see them December 27."

Della debated long and hard and sent a telegram to
Bishop Parmley, care of the Pleasant Valley Coal Company,
asking if someone could help her with her luggage to Winter
Quarters on December 27. She wanted to send that telegram
to Owen, but even Aunt Caroline had raised her better than
that.

She had the money to buy something nice for the
Auerbachs' for Christmas, but Della found a better way to
express her gratitude. She stayed up late on Christmas Eve,
drawing two pictures on shirt cardboard, one of Owen carving *Aho* on a coffin lid, as the men stood by the sauna with
Matti's coffin. She drew the Christmas party, with her girls
singing "I Heard the Bells on Christmas Day." She wrote
a brief description on the back of each picture and carried
them down to breakfast on Christmas Day.

"Happy holidays. More masterpieces for your art gallery. Mrs. Aho told me how she treasures knowing that
Matti has a beautiful coffin lid, even if no one sees it except
the eye of God."

"Pekka won't mind seeing this picture in my art gallery?" Mr. Auerbach asked.

"No. He told me he wanted us remember his father.
This is who we are," she said simply.

The Auerbach's present to Della were gifts for the
library, a copy of Jacob Riis's *How the Other Half Lives* and
a little replica of the Statue of Liberty. Della winked back
tears at their inscription in the book: *Dear Miners: We have
been where you are now. Courage and carry on. Samuel and
Eveline Auerbach.*

She had no plans to stop at the Knights on her return to the canyon on December 27. It was easy enough to side-step the matter in her letter and assure them that she would visit in the spring. She hadn't counted on Mr. Auerbach's telegram to Jesse Knight, which meant the Knights met her at the depot and climbed on board for brief hugs and kisses. The conductor on the Denver and Rio Grande Western Railway knew better than to argue with a major stockholder.

Concentrate on your magazine, she told herself after the train stopped in Thistle to take on two helper engines for the steep climb. Even a *McCall's* short story about a nurse who found her long lost lover on a battlefield in Cuba couldn't blot out the sight of snow towering on either side of the tracks. After nerve-wracking stops and starts, the train finally pulled into Colton, where the spur to Scofield was waiting. Knowing an equally frightening part of the climb lay ahead, Della asked herself again why she had turned down Mr. Whaley's perfectly good offer of full-time employment in Menswear, which paid more than teaching. It also guaranteed nothing more frighten-ing in transportation than a streetcar platform outside the store.

"Oh, well," she grumbled, gathering her handbag and wondering where the conductor had put her suitcase.

"'Tis here in my hand, Butterbean."

Startled, Della turned around and could not help her sigh. "Owen. What are . . . ?"

There he stood in the door of the railroad car with Mari Luoma's suitcase.

"Were you worried I would change my mind at Colton?"

"Nay, lass. You're solid and brave. I just didn't want you leaving deep grooves in the armrest because the canyon scares you." He came closer. "And you're welcome to slap me silly. I've seldom given anyone worse advice."

"Count your blessings you haven't relatives like mine!" she said, the sting suddenly gone.

"Not only did the bishop send me specifically to retrieve you, but also a large box of supplies for the school from Samuel Auerbach."

"On this train? We have a benefactor." She followed him from the train. "Mr. Auerbach even offered me a full-time job in Menswear so I wouldn't have to get on this train. Oh, and I bought you four shirts with the extra money Sister Knight gave me for your carved boxes and which I knew you wouldn't have accepted, because you'd see it as charity, and she sees it as Christmas generosity."

He turned around and stared at her, then shook his head as though to clear it. "To think I missed your scattershot conversation. Start over when we get on the branch line."

She did but not until his arm was around her, his overcoat ready in case the sight of more towering snow unnerved her. "I haven't decided if I'm more afraid when I can see the snow, or when I can't see it and imagine it taller."

"It's tall."

She scrunched down involuntarily, and his arm tightened around her. As he gripped her close, the train started with a lurch. She turned her face into his overcoat, and he started to hum a slow, drowsy version of "Take Courage, Saints, and Faint Not By the Way," which made her burrow in closer and shut her eyes.

The train started with fits and starts, and moved slowly. "How bad was it?" he asked after a few miles. "Might as well tell me what happened."

"Some of it was good," she said, reluctant to admit how awful her relatives were. "Miss Clayson and I visited with Kristina Aho and Pekka. They're doing ever so well. Miss Clayson is my champion."

"I didn't expect that," he told her, genuinely surprised.

"Here goes. It won't make you happy."

She told him about the dinner party and the guests' rude comments about miners.

"And you defended us," he said.

"We both defended you. Aunt Caroline was at her rudest, and Miss Clayson stood up for me. There we were, trudging to a streetcar platform, thrown out of the house, and Mr. Auerbach and his wife took us home. Miss Clayson went on to Boise, and I stayed with the Auerbachs and worked in Menswear during the Christmas rush."

"Della, you do manage to land on your feet, no matter what happens. I'm impressed."

Funny she hadn't seen it that way. She relaxed. "I have no plans to ever return to the Anderses' house."

"Wise."

"The Knights said I am always welcome in Provo. I'll leave it at that for now."

"Then I'd say you weathered a bad time with true grace, and a certain entrepreneurial spirit. You made yourself indispensable in Menswear."

"I suppose I did. Made some money too."

He laughed softly. "You're a Welshman's dream."

She couldn't have heard him right. She swallowed and her ears popped. It was the altitude, she decided. "I brought back your Anders carving. Wasn't about to cast pearls before those swine. Could you nail it over my bedroom door?"

"A bit grandiose, but why not? I'll do it tomorrow." He made himself more comfortable. "Now tell me about the shirts. Sister Knight did what?"

Della sat up and rummaged in her handbag, pulling out the envelope. "Here you are. Sixty dollars. Aunt Amanda wanted to give you an extra ten dollars, because it's Christmas. I told her I would buy shirts instead, since I know Menswear." He was warm and her eyes started to close again. "I bought you three white shirts, and a blue and white pinstripe because I liked it and thought Angharad would too."

"Three white shirts? Why on earth?"

She listened for some condescension or irritation but all she heard was genuine curiosity. "I thought it would be good for next June's Eisteddfod. Choir secretaries are supposed to think like that."

"I suppose they are, Butterbean. But three?"

She sat up to look at him. The light was going fast in the winter's darkness and the lamps weren't lit yet. "Owen, don't let me embarrass you, but I've noticed that you tend to sweat when you sing. Not always, but when you sing with Richard Evans, you sweat. Not when you sing with me, though, or Tamris or Martha, so I'm not certain what that tells me."

"It tells me that you're observant, and that I always feel a little inadequate when I sing with Richard. Such a voice he has. Three shirts was probably a good idea. Collars too?"

"Certainly. I told you I know Menswear."

"Aye, you did," he said, his voice gentle.

He hesitated then. She tensed, sleep forgotten, knowing too well that expression. "What happened?"

"It was a bounce in Number Four."

"A bounce?"

"That's what they call it here when the mountain settles. We put little wedges at the top of the timbers. Even before a bounce, the mine can settle and pop out the wedge. It's an early warning to run."

Della felt the familiar prickles down her back. "Who was it this time?"

"I hate to tell you . . . our best bass, George Grover."

"Oh, no," she murmured. "Bessie and Will are in my second and third grades. Is he . . . ?"

"Aye. The wedge popped out and hit him, a freak accident." He shifted restlessly.

"What of Sister Grover? My students?"

"She took George to Springville for burial and moved yesterday. Her family's there. Bishop has a key to the school, so he got their pens and slates from your classroom. I'm sorry, Della."

They were both silent then, the silence almost as painful as the sterile atmosphere in the Anders house. *What is happening?* she asked herself. *The mine is taking my students too.*

Chapter 30

There was so much she wanted to ask, but the train came to a sudden stop, which made her gasp and clutch Owen's coat.

"Steady now," he soothed. "I'll see what's wrong."

He went into the next car while she looked out the window, shuddering to see the mounds of snow crowding so close to the tracks. *Solid I may be after holiday eating*, she thought, *but brave I am not, Owen Davis*. She longed for him to return, even though he was just in the next car.

He came back and looked for his gloves on the seat. "There's snow all over the tracks. Make yourself comfortable. We're going to be here for a while."

The crew and few passengers were two hours shoveling snow off the track, as the cars grew colder and colder. Della shivered and shook. She dug in her suitcase and took out another pair of wool stockings, pulling them on because no one was in the car. She added a second petticoat and tried to draw herself into a little ball. When that failed, she started walking up and down the aisle, desperate to keep warm.

"I think we're going to be here tonight," Owen said when he came back in. He sat next to her, took off his gloves, and put his bare hands inside his jacket under his armpits. "I'd never be a railroad man!"

A few minutes later, one of the railroad crew came through the nearly vacant car, handing out blankets. "Stay close to each other," he warned.

Della took the three blankets he handed them and spread them around Owen, tucking the side closest to the window under his hips while he shivered. She pulled back the blankets and sat close to him.

"You know, you didn't have to come to Colton," she chided.

"No. I could have left you to freeze to death alone in this car."

"No one's going to freeze to death," she said in her best teacher's voice. "Are all Welshmen so dramatic?"

"I fear so."

Gradually, they warmed each other. Owen yawned and closed his eyes. "I'm no gentleman. I'm tired. Good night."

Her comment, "No gentleman? You shine better than most of the men at Uncle Karl's dinner," met with a mumble, more silence, then even breathing. She settled herself into sleep, doing her best to overlook the creaks and groans from the cars, the occasional hiss of the engine, and the fright that the entire canyon was going to send an avalanche of snow their way that would bury the train until a long over-due thaw in 1950.

A loud groan made her gasp, and she was convinced that the train was about to be buried under an avalanche. She shook Owen awake. "Don't you dare sleep when I am certain we are dying!" she implored.

He stared at her in utter disbelief, then laughed. She slapped the side of his head. "I mean it!"

"Remind me not to get on your bad side," he said, and grabbed her hands.

"You're on my bad side right now," she raged and then burst into tears, thoroughly embarrassed at waking up a defenseless man just because she was frightened.

He spoke to her in Welsh then, pulling her close, his lips on her hair, as she sobbed, crying every tear she hadn't shed in Salt Lake City because she didn't want her princi-pal to know how unprofessional she was, plus all the tears unshed during her visit with the Auerbachs, when she was determined to keep up his opinion of her.

"Just cry," he whispered. "Cry it all. You have stupid relatives who should be put in a vault and tossed in the ocean."

She took him at his word, sobbing into his handkerchief and then another one he pulled out when the first one was soaked. When he took out a third one, she stopped and dried her eyes, curious now.

"Why on earth do you have three handkerchiefs?" she asked, humiliated when she started to hiccup.

"I have four, actually," he told her, as calmly as if this happened to him every day. "Your Mr. Auerbach sent *me* a telegram addressed to Owen the Welsh woodcarver, Winter Quarters, Utah. All it said was, *Della's coming December 27. Rough time. Wolves for relatives*. That's why I'm really here."

"I think I love Mr. Auerbach," she said, blowing her nose on handkerchief number three. "So you came here to collect me and let me cry? Why are you so intelligent?"

He smiled at that. "Simple, Butterbean: I know women. I was married to one, and I am raising another. God bless the ladies, but you are a species apart."

She gave a little shriek when the train began to hiss and vibrate, then move in reverse. "What's happening?" she asked, not even trying to hide the quaver in her voice.

"I have my suspicions; you won't like this. Probably the coal train is coming down from Scofield, and coal waits for no man. That crew must have shoveled through to us. The train ahead will probably back us down to a siding, shunt us off and keep going."

Della moaned. "How far?"

"Not more than a half mile since our last siding. Buck up, Della. Things could be worse. You could be stuck in Salt Lake City with your relatives."

She gave him a fishy look, then started to smile. "I could

be. Instead, I'm having an adventure in the company of a man who understands the ladies. If I get really frightened and throw up, just overlook that."

"I didn't bring a bucket, so you're not allowed! That was the one thing Angharad did occasionally that made me go green."

"If you were a primary grades teacher, you would grow used to such emergencies." *That's it, Della, keep your conversation going*, she thought.

When the train reversed faster, she closed her eyes. "Sing to me," she whispered. "I'm afraid."

He started to sing "Sweet Is the Work," but got no farther than ". . . to show thy love by morning light," and stopped. She opened her eyes to see his eyes closed and a frown on his face. She thought to tease him—wasn't he supposed to keep *her* from terror?—but there was something sad in his expression that prevented her. She started to hum then, humming through all the verses as he remained silent. In her own concern for him, she forgot about her fear as their train backed down the mountain, pushed by coal that would not stop for anything or anyone.

Just as Owen had predicted, the train shunted onto the siding and the coal roared past, shaking the cars. Della breathed slowly in and out, calming herself and praying for the silent man seated beside her. Something had happened, and she didn't know what it was.

With a lurch and a hiss, the train started back onto the main track. Della hadn't realized she was breathing too fast until Owen put his hand over hers. She looked up, hoping his expression was more benign, but the sorrow lingered. Looking at his face, she thought of the high meadow, when she had bared her whole soul to someone she barely knew at the time, because her pain was so great. It was Owen's turn; Della knew.

"That fourth handkerchief," was all she said.

He took it out and tried to hand it to her, but she pushed

it gently back into his hand. "In the high meadow, you told me you had your own boulder."

"Aye, miss."

"Maybe you should tell me why 'Sweet Is the Work' made you so sad."

He was a long time silent. "It wasn't the song—it was what you said. Remember?"

She shook her head unsure. "I was afraid."

"You said, 'Sing to me. I'm afraid,'" he reminded her. He took a ragged breath. "That was what Gwyna said to me before she died. I had almost forgotten. I suppose I was feeling sad because I had almost forgotten."

"Maybe you're supposed to forget," she said, her words tentative. "Or at least not remember so . . . so relentlessly."

He gave her a measuring look, as though he wanted to argue, then his expression changed and became thoughtful again.

"Tell me about her. It's my turn to listen." It was also her turn to gather him close, as he had gathered her close on the trip up the mountain. "I owe it to you several times over. Tell me about Gwyna."

His expression grew wistful then. He waited a long time to speak, but she was patient.

"Gwyna was the wife of my heart. Her da was a miner too, and we were both in the Merthyr Tydfil Mission District. I don't even remember proposing to her because we were always of one mind."

He was silent, but Della wanted to know. "What did she look like? Beyond the dark hair and eyes, Angharad doesn't resemble you a great deal."

"Angharad is her mother's daughter. Gwyna was small, and she had a heart shape to her face, like our daughter. Little hands, little feet, and so graceful. She loved to dance, so we did a lot of that back home." He leaned back, his eyes closed. "Angharad doesn't understand why I don't like to dance. It's no fun now."

He looked out the window. "Seven, eight years ago, times were getting harder in the collieries of Glamorgan. We decided to come to Zion. Gwyna had a small legacy, and we used that to travel steerage in the vilest tub afloat. My goodness, I think I threw up everything except the soles of my feet during that crossing!"

There was just enough light from the lamp in the car to see his expression, not sad, as she dreaded, but simply the look of a man remembering. "We arrived in Salt Lake City on a Wednesday and were sealed in the Salt Lake Temple on Friday. By Monday I was shooting coal off the solid in Winter Quarters Canyon."

"Was Gwyna . . . was she . . . ?"

"Expecting Angharad by then? Aye, just barely." He settled back. "We hadn't known it until we got here at eight thousand feet that Gwyna had a bad heart. She couldn't walk from our home to the meetinghouse without stopping three or four times. All I know is mining and her sister Mabli was here. Could we leave? No. Should we have left? Aye, a thousand times."

You can do other things, Della wanted to say, but she had the wisdom not to.

"The doctor—Emil wasn't here then—wanted her to at least go to Provo during the last of her pregnancy. She was two days from going to stay with friends in Springville when she went into early labor." He spoke in a flat voice, almost like an automaton. "She didn't have a chance."

He put the fourth handkerchief to his eyes. A railroad crew member passing through the car stopped in surprise, but she shook her head at him. He continued on, looking back once.

"Gwyna hadn't the strength to deliver a baby. What still kills me—she knew it. She had been staring at death for nine months and she knew it." He leaned his forehead against his hand. "Gwyna said, 'Sing to me. I am afraid,' as you just did. I started to sing, 'The Lord is my Shepherd.'

She stopped me and said, 'If a girl, name her Angharad.' She cried out, 'Do your best,' and she died." A shudder went through him that Della felt in her own body. "The doctor pushed me out of the room, and he went to work immediately. I was on my knees outside our bedroom door when I heard Angharad's first cry."

He turned toward the window and cried. Della leaned her head against his back. "You haven't told this to anyone, have you?" she said.

"Not even Mabli," he said, when he could talk. He turned around to look at her, his face so ravaged she wanted to turn away, herself. "Especially not Mabli. I'm *doing* my best. Will I always feel so hollow?"

They sat close together in silence for the rest of the trip to Scofield. Every now and then, Owen shuddered, but he did not cry again. She thought he slept a little, but she was wide awake, deeply aware of him and filled with an enormous desire to protect him from his own sorrow. She had no idea how to do that, beyond listening, singing in the choir, and being his friend. Gwyna was still the sole possessor of his heart.

She knew that Arizona next year wouldn't be far enough. She decided it probably wouldn't matter where she went. She would always know that somewhere in the world was a man she loved, who was still in love with his deceased wife. It wasn't the news she wanted to lug into a new year and a new century, but there it was.

"Safe at last," he said when they pulled into Scofield three hours late. "Wouldn't you know it—there's Richard with a wagon for the treasure you and the redoubtable Miss Clayson bought for the school."

He was taking a light tone now, so Della followed his lead. "I was rather hoping he's still here because he wants his valuable secretary and his more valuable tenor."

"Aye to that."

He stood up. "Thank you for listening."

"Same to you."

He stepped back so she could stand in the aisle too. The door was open now, but she stood there, not on sure ground, because she didn't know if what was in her heart was true. *Hardly matters, Della*, she told herself. *He's tied to Gwyna still, even though I doubt that would please her, if she knew.*

"I'm completely out of order to say this, Owen, and it's taking all my courage." She looked for some sign on his expressive face that she should not say it, but she saw nothing. "I've never had a man or a baby, but I know children and love them. Gwyna knew what she was doing. She loved you so much and she wanted to give you the best gift she could. She did. Any woman would, who loved you. Good night now. Thank you again."

She hurried from the railcar, hoping he wouldn't follow, hoping he would.

"Della, wait a moment."

She turned around. She knew there wasn't a mean bone in his body. Whatever he had to say, she could bear it. He surprised her.

"Keep watching Billy Evans, will you? Just possibly he'll be ready sooner than he thinks." One deep breath followed another. "After all, he's almost eight and should be reading by now, shouldn't he?"

"I'll watch him closely."

Chapter 31

❦

$\mathcal{D}$ella decided there was nothing like the resumption of routine to soothe her heart. Even before the year turned and school resumed, she was back at her nights in the library and enjoying her Thursday sauna. When Miss Clayson returned from Boise, she spent a welcome afternoon with her principal, arranging and distributing Mr. Auerbach's largess in their school.

"I hated leaving you at the depot in such a state of mind," Lavinia told her.

"No worries. I was in good hands. Made some money too," Della replied. They looked at each other with perfect understanding.

No worries, really, except the anguish of sitting in the little desk occupied before the holiday break by Will Grover, whose father had died in a bounce.

"Pekka Aho. Will Grover. Bessie Grover," she said out loud. "Two men die and I lose three students. Four, if we add David Grover in Israel's class. This arithmetic does not add up."

She looked at the blackboard, comforted again by the words on the pegboard, which could only have been put there by Owen when he and Richard took the box of supplies to school. *Happy New Year, Butterbean. Keep your eye on Billy.*

Emil Isgreen was not back from Tooele yet, so there was no Saturday night dinner. Della wanted to talk with Mabli—for reassurance? for confidence?—but William

George was sitting in the parlor, so there was no opportunity. To give Mabli some privacy, Della walked to the Wasatch Store and took the key from the ever-obliging Clarence Nix. She let herself into the library, content to shelve books, straighten newspapers, and try to organize a disordered mind. *I'm wasting my time* warred with *He's worth the trouble*, until she wanted to take the next train out of Scofield. That always ended the struggle in her mind, because she was much too frightened of the trip to Colton, at least until spring.

"Penny for your thoughts, lass."

She looked up, surprised to see Richard and Martha Evans standing in the doorway.

"Do come in," Della said. "If I'm here, the library is open. Martha, we have a stack of new magazines. Richard, did you miss your choir secretary these past two weeks?"

"Aye, miss," Richard said. "'Twasn't much of a Christmas without your sharp tongue goading us on during practice!"

"I try to magnify every church calling I have!" Della teased.

They pulled up two chairs to her desk, settling in, their dark eyes kind.

"I'm making a muddle of things," Della said, knowing better than to stand on ceremony with them. She hesitated, and Martha put her hand out to touch hers, giving her heart. "It seems I want what I cannot have." Tears came to her eyes and she brushed them angrily aside. "I've cried enough for two women. I'm tired of tears."

Richard and Martha looked at each other. In her starved heart, Della wished there would ever be a moment when a glance like that would pass between her and Owen.

"You or me, *m cara*?" Richard asked his wife.

"Me," Martha said. "If it's any consolation, Owen doesn't know what to do either." She smiled at Richard. "No, he does, but it's a hard step for a loyal man to take."

"I never knew Gwyna, but she must have been someone special."

"Aye, miss," Richard said. "Do you know, not until you came to Pleasant Valley had anyone seen Owen laugh in years. And tease, and be so determined to have you in the choir that he would invent an unnecessary calling. He's fair amazing us, even though he is not moving fast enough for you, I fear."

Della nodded. "I think you are preaching patience, Brother Evans."

"I am."

They seemed in no hurry to leave, patient with her too. Della told them about Billy Evans and the broom, and what Owen wanted for a reward, should Billy read. Martha laughed softly. "That is so much what Owen would do! He's a sly one, Della. I should warn you about Welshmen."

"Too late," she said, looking away again until she had some control. "Suggestions?"

"Patience and time," Martha said. "Don't be in a pelter to leave us come summer."

"I have a job waiting for me in Salt Lake."

Martha shrugged. "Let it wait."

"I'm thinking about teaching in Arizona Territory next year."

"Arizona Territory will probably still be there in two years, things being what they are in the United States," Richard told her.

"You're wearing me down," Della said, with a smile.

"Good! That's why we stopped by, when we saw the light on," Richard replied, then stood up. "Come, *m cara*. Let's go home."

"What does *m cara* mean? Owen said it about Gwyna."

"'My love,'" Martha said. "If I know him, and I do, he's already thinking that about you." She leaned across the desk and kissed Della on the forehead. "Ye can't rush a heart that's mending."

"May I coax that heart a little?"

Richard held the outside door open for his wife. "Aye! And we'll pray that my scamp of a nephew Billy Evans decides to read before he is an old man. G'night now."

Della was in her classroom on Monday afternoon of New Year's Day, preparing new 1900 bulletin boards and laughing at Israel Bowman, who loped in looking disconsolate and missing his fiancée. Trust Israel to roll in just the day before the start of school on Tuesday.

"Shall I ask my class to make you a paper chain, 150 links long?" Della teased. "That way, you can take off a link for every day between now and June."

He at least had the good grace to laugh and waggle his finger at her. "Just wait until you fall in love and have three or four canyons between you and your fiancée!"

It'll take more than canyons, she thought, after Israel returned to his classroom, looking remarkably put upon. She got out Owen's chest of wooden letters and hung "Happy New Year in this new century!" on the pegboard. She prepared to rearrange the desks to accommodate the smaller size of her class, now that Bessie and Will were living in Springville. Israel said he would take the desks downstairs to storage, along with David Grover's desk from his classroom.

Before she moved a desk, Della took out a piece of shirt cardboard and drew the two desks, empty in a row with students sitting in the other desks. She wrote on the picture: "Empty desks because a miner died and his children are no longer here in Winter Quarters School." There was time to mail it to Auerbach's Department Store before school tomorrow.

When the desks were gone, Della looked at the rows, wondering who would be next. She sat at her desk, making lesson plans and idling away the afternoon, waiting for genius to strike. When it did, she thought she'd better give the credit to the Lord, since no one else probably knew what to do. She needed to enlist Lavinia Clayson's help, so she went to her classroom and rapped on the door.

No answer. She waited a while at the top of the stairs to the basement, still not sure of her reception in Miss Clayson's own quarters. Even though they were on far better terms, Miss Clayson had not invited her to her apartment in the basement. Timidly, she knocked on the door.

Lavinia opened it and stepped into the gymnasium, closing the door behind her. "What can I help you with, Della?" she asked, which Della considered a good start.

"I've been thinking about the challenge of exercise for the children, now that the playground is waist deep in snow. I'd like to teach my class the Virginia Reel. We could dance here in the gymnasium, and maybe your class and Israel's would want to join us."

She knew well that six weeks ago, Miss Clayson would have vetoed her request immediately, on general principles. She gave Della a thoughtful look, neither yes nor no.

"We haven't a piano, and there's no caller."

"I can ask the Evans brothers tomorrow night at choir practice."

"They're the brothers that have a little orchestra?" Miss Clayson asked, more interested.

"Yes, two violins, a guitar, and Richard Evans can sing anything. So can Angharad Davis's father, and others," Della explained. "As for a caller, Owen ... Mr. Davis ... tells me there is a miner in Number Four from Tennessee who calls. What do you think, Lavinia?"

Miss Clayson didn't rush her answer, but Della didn't expect her to. *Brother Evans tells me to learn patience*, she thought. Besides, at twenty-four, she was too old to hop from one foot to the other and pluck at Miss Clayson's sleeve.

"They're all in Number Four?"

Della nodded, hopeful. "They're on the afternoon shift this week."

"If they could come after lunch, that would give them

time to sleep in the morning, and make that shift. Let's do it. You'll make the arrangements?"

"Consider it done. There's something else."

Miss Clayson gave her a measuring look, but there was no malice in it. "Miss Anders, I have noted with you that there is always 'something else.'"

"I suppose there is," Della said, cheerful. "Mari Luoma—you remember, the lady in my classroom—well, she is expecting."

"I'm not surprised," the principal said, sounding as amused as she ever sounded. "I know what you are going to ask, and the answer is no."

"All I want is her to be allowed to stay in my class until she begins to show," Della said.

Miss Clayson thought a moment. "Why not? It's 1900 and we have entered the modern age."

Della walked home that afternoon happier than she had felt all week, accompanied by Mari Luoma, who was coming up from the Wasatch Store. Della took Mari's arm and told her that Miss Clayson said she could stay in the classroom until she started to show.

"I will have a . . . a plethora of English by then," Mari said.

Della clapped her hands. "My goodness! What a wonderful word, Mari!"

Mari blushed. "Heikki gave me dictionary for Christmas."

For choir practice Tuesday night, Della took her courage in hand and handed out an agenda with one item on it: teaching the Virginia Reel to the Winter Quarters School. "I need some musicians and maybe singers. One of you told me about a miner in Number Four who calls. I need him too. What about it?"

Tamris Powell and Martha Evans volunteered immediately.

"Richard, you and Owen can come too, since everyone's

on the same shift. Dance with your daughters," Martha said. "Your brothers can play their violins."

"I *could* use more fathers, since I have more girls than boys in my class," Della said. "What a good idea, Martha."

"I don't know . . ." Owen said with a frown.

"Brother Davis, *who* railroaded me into the choir?" Della asked in her sweetest voice, which made Martha and the other ladies smile.

"I did, but . . ."

"I knew you would want to do this for Angharad," Della told him, pushing back like the coal train in the canyon. "Richard, can you enlist your brothers for our music?"

"Aye, miss, with pleasure," he told her with an amused glance at his wife. "I'm certain Martha can fill me in."

"Possibly," his wife said with a straight face.

Owen didn't walk home with Della that night after choir practice but went his own way, head down. Della watched him and spent a long time on her knees that night beside her bed, giving the Lord all the good reasons she could think of why this was a good idea. Her reward was a peaceful night's sleep, even if she doubted that Owen slept well.

Since he was on the afternoon shift, Della wasn't surprised that Owen didn't stop by the library on Wednesday night. Angharad came in with Myfanwy Jones and her parents and went straight to Maria Nesbitt's *Darling Daughters* collection, Angharad's newest obsession.

She brought two of the *Darling Daughters* books to Della to check out, which meant Della let her stamp the book herself. Angharad leaned close, and Della got a whiff of the rose talcum she had given Owen's own darling daughter for Christmas. "Miss Anders, my father told me about the Virginia Reel this Friday," she whispered. "He's going to do it!"

It's just a gentle coaxing, Owen, she told herself as she smiled at Angharad. "You'll have fun."

She spent longer in sauna on Thursday night,

unconcerned now about sitting bare in a room with bare ladies. To her delight, the subject was the Virginia Reel. "We like to dance too," Eeva Koski said, tapping one bare foot. "May we all come?"

"Please do," Della told her and sat up. "Oh my, it's time for me to roll in the snow. Will I *ever* graduate to the upper bench?"

"Not unless you marry a Finn and you want to sit by him in sauna, just the two of you!" Mari teased gently.

"Mari, Heikki sits by you, way down there now! He must be in love," Eeva joked in turn. She leaned forward and playfully switched her vasta on Della's shoulders. "I think Della has someone else in mind besides a Finn. She'd rather sing than sit bare in a sauna."

Della dressed with special care Friday morning, confining her uncooperative hair into a single braid down her back. She knew anything that required more hairpins would never survive a reel. She tied the end with a red bow, took it out, and then put it back in.

The morning dragged, everyone anticipating the afternoon. When her students kept staring at the clock, Della gave up, took it down, and presented a lesson on telling time. During lunch, she sat with her students that brought their lunches and watched the others come back with fathers and mothers.

To her delight, she noticed that the Welsh and Scottish wore their native dress. The Finns were equally splendid, which made Miss Clayson smile and nod to Della.

While the violins, guitar, and banjo tuned up with each other and worked through one reel, Della enlisted Israel Bowman to help her teach the simple steps. Eyes bright, Angharad stood with her father, holding his hand. Della wasn't brave enough to look at his face. *If he never speaks to me again, I won't be any worse off that I am right now*, she reasoned, as Israel swung her around, a grin on his face.

"One line of four couples, facing each other," Della said, when David Evans gave her the high sign that the impromptu orchestra was ready. "Let's start small, while the rest of you watch. Mr. Bowman and I are here at the head. Just listen to Mr. Brock and do what he says. Let's start with Richard and Martha, Tilda Koski and her father, and Will Pugh and his mother." She nodded to the miner from Tennessee, then gave Israel her best curtsy to begin the reel.

Ten minutes later, Mr. Brock gave one last call and a final flourish. Out of breath, everyone stopped and clapped. Mr. Brock gave a rebel yell, which made Miss Clayson jump and glare at him.

"Well?" Della asked, when she caught her breath. "How about four lines of eight each now?"

Out of the corner of her eye, she watched Angharad lead her father onto the gymnasium floor. *Please, please, Lord, make this right*, she prayed. She noticed that the Evanses had joined him.

"Ready?" the caller yelled.

"As we'll ever be!" Levi Jones shouted back.

Della stared. Somehow, that brave man had coaxed Miss Clayson into a line. "The earth's axis just shifted," she whispered to Israel Bowman.

With more people, the next reel was longer. Happy, Della looked around to see everyone dancing. She got a glimpse of Owen in the other line and wanted to go to her knees in gratitude. He was whirling Angharad with all the delight of a man who looked like he didn't want to be anywhere else. "What's the matter, Della?" Israel asked, out of breath.

"Nothing. Just happy."

When they finished, some of the parents staggered to chairs and flopped down, laughing. Clutching his side, Richard nodded to Mr. Brock. "Let's give the man a rest from all that calling," he said, recovering quickly. "Dafydd, how about a polka? Everyone knows a polka."

Everyone did, from the nods all around. Some of the partners who had collapsed were getting to their feet again. Della laughed as Israel went to Miss Clayson, bowed, and took her hand. Pentti Hamalainen, a fourth grader, was bowing before Angharad.

"May I have this dance, Butterbean?"

Della turned around in surprise. "I'd be delighted."

She was no stranger to the polka. The summer she had spent in the canyon with the telephone line crew had seen a few spur-of-the-moment dances with nothing more glamorous than a band of one harmonica. Most of her partners had been much taller than she was. How nice to dance with a man and almost look him in the eyes. She looked and liked what she saw.

"Are we still friends?" she asked, as Dafydd nodded his head for the downbeat.

"We always were," Owen told her as they began to dip and glide. "Gwyna told me to do my best. I may have been interpreting that too narrowly."

It was a fast polka, but she was with a good dancer and it was a big gymnasium.

"You American girls are as light on your feet as Welsh women," he commented, expertly steering her away from a collision with two of her first graders.

"High time you learned that, Owen Davis," she replied, admiring his brass buttons because she was suddenly too shy to look at him.

"I was at Dafydd Evans's home yesterday," he said, leaning closer to speak in her ear. "Looks to me like Billy was saying his words to himself while his mam read to him. Any day now, Della."

Chapter 32

*D*ella watched Billy Evans all week, sitting close to him as always, reading and listening for his voice. "You're getting close, Billy," she whispered to him. "Do you want to measure yourself against the broom?"

He thought a moment, leaning against her, then shook his head.

"It's kind of hard, isn't it, to try new ventures?" she asked, thinking of Owen.

He nodded, and she turned her attention back to the students who were finishing their New Year's resolutions for the bulletin board, written on paper stars. She had them read their resolutions out loud. "I resolve to _____" had been the assignment. Answers ranged from "help Mam more," to "sweep better under little Gwyllum's high chair," to "think great thoughts," and "read *Oliver Twist*," from a precocious third grader.

"What about you, miss?" Maggie Forsyth asked.

Della thought a moment, then wrote her own resolution. "I resolve to . . ."

". . . read more than one chapter after lunch?" Timmy Pugh asked, impudent as always.

"No, you scamp! You already get away with that now!" she declared, which made them all laugh. "I resolve to be brave."

She could tell from their wry expressions that her students weren't impressed. "What, isn't that good enough for you perfectionists?" she asked them.

Hands shot up. She pointed to Sarah Powell, Tamris's middle daughter. "Miss, we think adults are just supposed to be brave."

Not this one, Della thought. She held up her hand, reached for another paper star, and wrote, "'I resolve to be as brave as coal miners.' Will that suit you?"

She could tell that it didn't, not in a canyon where children took their fathers' occupation for granted. "That's my resolution," she insisted and fixed it to the board with paste. "Remember, I'm from Salt Lake City where fathers work in offices and mercantiles. Oh, you are difficult to please today! Let's read a chapter."

After class, she sat with her elbows on her desk and her chin in her hands, thinking about Billy, Owen, and her own new ventures. Her mind turned to the theology class last Sunday, where the children of Israel, after forty years, were finally ready for their own new venture into the promised land. She looked in her desk drawer for the Bible and turned to Joshua, reading that part again where the priests carrying the ark of the covenant had to actually step into the fast-flowing Jordan before the river would stop flowing.

Maybe Billy and Owen weren't the only people who hesitated, she decided, as she read the end of the book of Joshua again. Maybe she wasn't quite ready either for that bold step. As Martha Evans said, she had time. No, it was Owen. He had loved, lost, and loved Gwyna still.

Speaking of bold steps—Della groaned as she stood on the school steps. She should have left with the children. The snow that had been falling all day was swirling in the wind now. She hesitated, then took her own medicine and plunged into the snow at the bottom of the steps. It was nearly thigh deep, and she floundered, telling herself not to panic. She knew where the wagon road was, and she could still see the tipple in the distance. She glanced away then looked again. No, it was gone now.

She struggled to the wagon road, wishing someone

would come along to at least break a trail in front of her. No such luck. She plunged through the snow, her teeth starting to chatter. She stopped and looked around. She should have passed the mechanical shed with its concrete bays, but she could not see it. She took a deep breath, forcing herself to be calm. She doubted anyone got lost in Winter Quarters Canyon, and she didn't intend to be the first.

But where was she? She looked back, thinking she could retrace her steps and just stay in the school; surely Miss Clayson wouldn't mind. The snow had already covered her trail. "Just go ahead," she murmured. "Not like you have a choice." She kept walking, turning her face to avoid the snow in her eyes and mouth, and realized she was traveling in an arc rather than a straight line.

"Can anybody hear me?" she called. No answer. The smart people in Winter Quarters Canyon were already in their homes, apparently. She faced into the storm this time, but she knew she was lost and getting cold. She looked up. The sun, never a long visitor in such a deep canyon, was nowhere to be seen. Soon it would be night and here she was.

Her only consolation was the knowledge that Mabli would miss her, since she usually helped with dinner in the boardinghouse kitchen. Still, she couldn't stand where she was and survive that long, not with the temperature dropping right along with the sun. She folded her arms, bowed her head, and prayed for someone to find her.

Keep walking, she told herself. She took four hesitant steps and bumped into a wooden building. She could have cried with relief. It was the lumber shed where she had sat with Owen Davis, trying to breathe, in her early days in the canyon. She felt for the open side and walked in, barking her shins on the piled wood. At least she was out of the snow.

Della worked her way to the back of the shed, crouching down by the end of the stacked wood, where the snow had not penetrated. Straw was piled in the corner, and burlap bags. She hunkered down and pulled the bags over her as she started to shake, more from fear than cold. She could have cried with the knowledge that all around her there were homes, even though she doubted her ability to find them; nothing was in a straight line in that narrow canyon. Each house by now was an island in a sea of snow.

She burrowed deeper in the rank straw, wishing for more burlap. When her mind settled, she remembered what Owen had told her about the Number Four cave-in when he and the other miners started singing. "'Lead, kindly light, amid th'encircling gloom, lead thou me on,'" she sang, then went through every song she could think of. She decided that alto parts were boring without soprano, tenor, and bass to buttress them. That would make a good topic for a Sunday talk: we all need each other. She sang the alto lines again, louder.

The cold was starting to drill a hole through the center of her forehead when she heard men's voices. She listened, groggy now, then closed her eyes in relief. They were calling her name. She sat up and tried to stand. She stomped her feet until they started to hurt, then felt along the boards to the front of the woodshed, where the snow was nearly chest high now.

"Della! Della! Della!" They said her name over and over. She couldn't think of a thing to do except scream and keep screaming until they found her. Trouble was, she couldn't stop screaming then, until someone grabbed her and pulled her close. It was Emil Isgreen, surrounded by snow-covered men.

"Della, can you walk?" the doctor asked.

"Barely."

"I'm getting personal now." He felt under her frozen dress and ran his hands down her legs. He pinched her ankle. "Can you feel that?"

"Yes! Stop it."

"Good."

All the men had crowded around the front of the shed now. She looked at their dear faces, seeing Finns and ward members and the men from her boardinghouse. God bless Mabli Reese, who had probably alerted everyone.

Someone picked her up. She looked close, then turned her face into his chest. It was Nicola Anselmo, her library bodyguard. "Thank you," she whispered. "I was afraid no one would find me."

"Remember, *signorina*, we are strong men."

Held in Nicola's arms, the men all linked arms again around her and started together up the canyon. All the men stopped as each man dropped off at his own home, where pinpoints of light gleamed in the darkness now. Everyone waited, silent, until an answering shout told them that the man of the house was home and safe.

When Nicola tired, he transferred her to Owen. "You scared me, Butterbean," he whispered in her ear.

"I didn't know where I was, and the snow was so deep," she whispered back. "I'm so sorry to endanger everyone. I should have just stayed at school."

"It won't happen again. When I think . . ." He stopped, unable to continue, and carried her in silence the rest of the way to Mabli's door.

Mabli tried to gather her close as Owen set Della on her feet. She hung on to his shoulder, wincing in pain. In a moment, her coat and muffler were off and Dr. Isgreen was leading her to the kitchen. Mabli yanked the tin tub off the wall and started pouring in hot water from the stove's reservoir, mixing it with cool water. Emil sat her down and pulled off her shoes and stockings.

Emil sat back, relief on his face. He felt her calf. "Wiggle your toes."

Sucking in her breath, she did as he said, then looked down, relieved to see normal white legs. "Pour in a little more hot water," Emil said to Mabli, after he tested it. Mabli did as he said, and he tested the water again. "A little more. That's good. Owen, help me pull the tub closer."

The men set her legs down gently in the warm water. Della flinched, then sighed with relief.

"Mabli, you keep adding warmer water as it cools down. Owen, you and Richard go next door to the boardinghouse and find some hot water bottles. We'll have Mabli get her into a nightgown and more woolen socks and we'll pack the bottles around her in bed. Della, you're sleeping with Mabli tonight. You need a warm body."

Della nodded. "I'm so sorry," she said again. "I had no idea the snow was so deep."

"That's the canyon for you," Emil said. "Perk up. No harm, no foul. I'd hate to have lost my dinner buddy, though."

Emil took her temperature after the men went next door. He nodded, satisfied with the reading. "Mabli, can you find her nightgown? I'll leave this to you two, unless you need some help."

"I can manage." Mabli left the room and came back with Della's nightgown. Emil left the room, while Della dried off her legs and pulled on a dry pair of woolen hose. Mabli helped her get her into her flannel nightgown.

"My bed's wider than yours. I'll take Dafydd's spot by the wall." Mabli took her hand and led her into her bedroom. With a sigh, Della lay down and let Mabli cover her.

Owen and Richard returned, and she heard them talking in the kitchen with Emil as they filled hot water bottles. She yawned, sleepy now. She opened her eyes when they brought in the hot water bottles, pulled back her nest of covers, and packed them around her.

"I'm staying here tonight," Emil told them. "It's too far back to the hospital. Richard and Owen are going as far as Richard's because Angharad is there. Warmth in numbers, eh?"

He went in the other room with Richard, but Owen

sat down on the bed, looking at her. "Words fail me, Butterbean," he said finally.

"That's rare for you. Do you know, I remembered what you told me about the cave in and I started singing. I sang 'Lead, Kindly Light,' first." She closed her eyes as the warmth of the water bottles penetrated her cold body. "The alto line is a bit dull by itself. I needed a tenor. A soprano would have been nice too. Bass was optional." She yawned. "Don't tell Brother Pugh I said that."

"I'm glad you can joke." Owen ran his hand down her shoulder. "How about a song now? A lullaby. You know the one."

He sang "All Through the Night" to her in Welsh, and she harmonized in English, secure, safe now, and drowsy. She wasn't totally sure, but it felt like someone fingered her curls when he finished.

Emil stayed the night, true to his word, checking on her every hour, warming the hot water bottles, and sitting beside Mabli's bed.

"It was a terrible scare," he whispered to her. "Once you were lost, you did all the right things."

"I didn't feel brave."

"You were, though." He chuckled softly. "If I could sing as well as Owen, I'd sing you back to sleep. I can hold your hand."

He did. She tucked it under her cheek, at peace.

It snowed for three days, which meant church and school were cancelled. Della heard the tipple, so she knew the men had gone into the mines. Nothing stopped the coal, but she already knew that. Mabli and the hot water bottles kept her warm that first night. By Sunday afternoon, the snow had stopped. The next sound was shovels everywhere as Winter Quarters residents dug out of their own snow caves. By Tuesday, there were paths everywhere and towering mounds of snow. On Wednesday, school resumed and life went on as usual.

Della's escort that night to and from the library was much more numerous, to her embarrassment. The latest train had brought a mound of newspapers, so she kept her newly appointed escorts busy sorting and organizing them. The talk around the table circled around a small article in the *Salt Lake Tribune*, announcing Pleasant Valley Coal Company's talks with the secretary of the US Navy. The men passed it around, discussing the news with each other in various languages.

"I thought it was just a rumor," Emil said, when he stopped in to see how she did and saw the article. "That would mean steady work here, even in the summer." He looked at her. "Why isn't that making you happy? Believe me, the miners will be thrilled."

"There's a man in Provo who wants Owen to put up the wainscoting in his dining room this summer and line his closets with cedar."

"Della, he's a coal miner, not a carpenter," he reminded her.

I know, she thought, irritated with herself. *Maybe I'm turning into Miss Clayson, wanting no one here to go in another mine.* "There are safer jobs," she said, but it sounded so puny.

He leaned closer, for her ears only. "Even school teaching has its perils, I will remind you. You came pretty close— too close—to peril."

"You know what I mean," she said, grouchy now.

"I do. All we do here in this canyon, or in Salt Lake, or probably even Timbuktu, is live our lives as best we know how. If danger comes, it comes. We do our best."

He was right; she knew it.

January faded into February, distinguished by even more snow and cold and school closings that just made her restless as she stalked about Mabli's small house. There was too much snow for sauna, sometimes too much snow even for church and the library, and definitely too much snow for Saturday nights in Scofield with Emil. Mostly there was too much snow for Angharad and Owen to visit. She also chafed, knowing she had no time to spend with Billy Evans and look for even the smallest signs that he was ready to read. There was never too much snow for coal, even though the miners had to trudge down the railroad tracks to get to the mines, and even walk up the long incline to Number Four, too slick and snowy for horses to haul the mantrip.

She reluctantly had to tell Mari Luoma good-bye. Her pregnancy was showing now, which probably bothered no one except Miss Clayson and the district school officials, if they had any inkling in the first place that the Finnish bride had been attending the lower elementary grade class. "I'll come see you before I go back to Salt Lake, and we'll figure out how to keep learning," she told her friend.

Della did go back a few days later when the Luoma sons brought their parents to Winter Quarters. The sons had pooled their resources and arranged for ship's passage from Finland for Aapi and Kaisa Luoma, since most of their sons and grandchildren now lived and prospered in Utah. "They are so pleased to be here in this good land," Mari told Della in her careful English. She patted her growing belly. "I will have an American citizen in June."

The first week in March marked the first week of no snow, and then another, which made Della smile. She stepped out of Mabli's house one Monday morning in mid-March to see the sky again, that intense blue found in high altitudes, and the sun so bright on the snow that it hurt her eyes. Sure enough, there was her escort, consisting of children now, older boys who had been told by their parents to make sure their teacher got to and from school. They helped her down to the railroad tracks and she floundered along with them, arriving tired at school, but at least arriving. They sang on the way, of course. "Daisy Bell" became a particular favorite once she explained what a bicycle built for two looked like.

She had thought that sunny day to stay after school and correct some papers, but her youthful escorts had other ideas. "Fifteen minutes," she begged. "You can walk ahead and look back and I promise . . ."

"No, miss," one of Miss Clayson's seventh graders told her firmly, already a leader. "My da hasn't spanked me in years, and I intend to keep it that way."

"I have a better idea." She took a quarter from her purse. "This is called a bribe. You five take it to the Wasatch Store and buy yourselves five cents each of penny candy. Eat it slowly. By the time you finish, I'll be ready."

The seventh grader laughed and caught the coin in midair that she tossed to him. Smiling to herself, Della finished grading papers in her empty classroom. They returned in half an hour, her chief escort waving two letters at her.

"Mail for you, miss."

She took the letters, one from Mr. Auerbach, always welcome, and the other from Uncle Karl, not so welcome. She felt the thick envelope, feeling another letter inside. Silent now, serious, Della walked with the boys up the canyon. She forced herself to laugh at their jokes as she asked herself why Uncle Karl had written. She hadn't thought she would ever hear from him again, not after that dinner party.

Another bribe to her escorts always involved cookies from Mabli, so she said thank you, shooed them next door, and opened Mr. Auerbach's letter first. It was nothing more than news from the store and the reminder that she was due to start work for him on June 1. She read it through twice anyway because she didn't want to open Uncle Karl's letter.

His letter was just a note on office memo paper, but it had her on her feet, reaching for her coat, unable to open the other letter. *I'm not that brave*, she thought as she left a note for Mabli so she wouldn't worry. She needed a brave man.

She hesitated to knock on Owen's door, but he opened it anyway. "I saw you coming up the walk. Why didn't you knock? Is Billy finally ready?"

She smelled food cooking. "I shouldn't . . ."

"Believe me, it's no loss to bother *my* cooking. Angharad's playing at the Parmleys'." He peered at her more closely. "It's not Billy, is it?"

Wordless, she held out the opened letter to him. He pulled out Uncle Karl's note. "'Dear Della, Caroline and Ellen are visiting Vassar right now, since Ellen is determined to go there this fall,'" Owen read out loud. "'I was going through old correspondence and came across this letter. It was never opened by me. Caroline read it, but I doubt she shared it with you. She should have. Your Uncle Karl.'" Owen looked up, a question in his eyes.

"The return address is from my father. The postmark is 1876," Della said. Her lips trembled. "I'm just not brave enough to read it. I need *you*."

He smiled at that, leaning against the doorframe. "I can't invite you in, Della. It wouldn't be proper." He thought a moment, just watching her. "I'll take the pan off the hob. I was going to the Parmleys' anyway to fetch Angharad."

He took her hand as they hurried along, slowing down when she struggled to keep up with him. Sister Parmley opened the door, a question in her eyes, when they stood there.

"The girls and I were going to walk Angharad home," she said, then looked from one to the other. "This is something else."

Della nodded. In the parlor, she stood by the window, wishing her hands were warmer, while Owen talked to Sister Parmley in a low voice and showed her Uncle Karl's letter. When he touched Della's elbow, she jumped.

"Sister Parmley says for us to use the bishop's study."

Della followed Owen into the study, where he shut the door. Afraid to look at him, she paced back and forth in front of the window as Owen sat in the easy chair and opened the letter from her father. She darted glances in his direction as he read but kept walking, as though trying to put miles between her and whatever bad news the letter contained.

She stood still when he finished the letter, searching for some clue on his face. When he started to smile, she sank into the chair next to him, her eyes still on his.

He held out the letter. "Don't be afraid. Take it."

When her hand closed around the letter, Owen sat back, his eyes intent on her face. She started to read the anguish of one brother to the other in Salt Lake City, as Frederick told Karl about her birth, and how her mother, Olympia Stavrakis, was pulled away from them both by her father, a miner from Cyprus, who swore never to give his daughter permission to marry an American, no matter how she pleaded. She looked up at Owen, tears in her eyes.

"Butterbean, she wanted you."

Gently, he took back the letter. "'He snatched her while I was in the mine, to where I have no idea,'" Owen read out loud. "'My neighbor said she was screaming and crying and clutching at Della, but he forced her to leave our baby.' Della, she wanted you very much." He swallowed. "Come here."

He held out his arms and she sat on his lap, her face turned into his chest, beyond tears now. She heard the door open, felt Owen shake his head, and heard the door close quietly. She listened as heavier footsteps went away—the bishop's. Wordless, she sat on Owen Davis's lap.

"How could her own father be so cruel?" she said finally.

"It happens. It's hard for some immigrants to leave the old country behind. He could just as easily have been Italian or Slovakian or . . . or Russian or German. Maybe even Welsh, though I doubt it. We are such kind, humble people."

Della chuckled at that, which she knew he intended. "She wanted me."

"Very much, think on. As much as Gwyna and I wanted Angharad." He held her off from him then, his hand under his chin to raise her view to his. "Della, can you live with this?"

She looked at his dear face and nodded. "I had a mother who wanted me."

"I would wager she still does."

Chapter 33

~⚬~

*T*he next morning, right after arithmetic on the board and a short review of the natural habitats of bears, Della sat next to Billy Evans while her students read aloud. She watched his face, noted his intensity, and decided he had been ready to read for a long time. *She* was the one who hadn't been ready, maybe even more unready than Owen.

Yesterday's letter had changed everything. As she lay in bed the night before, peaceful as never before, she thought that someday she might ask Martha or Richard if they had been giving both of them advice on patience. She decided she needn't bother; she knew what their answer would be.

"Angharad, I have a message for you to give your father," she said as she buttoned her student's coat at the end of the day. "Will you do that?"

Angharad nodded.

"Here's the message: 'Get the broom.'"

"'Get the broom'?" Angharad repeated, obviously mystified.

"That's the message."

His face expressionless, except for a lurking gleam in his eyes that seemed to be part of the Welsh national character, Owen picked up the broom the next day after he came out of the mine and cleaned up. "Time for the drastic step?" he asked. "You're certain?"

"Positive."

"Give me two days."

She nodded. "As long as you need," she teased back.

"For the broom, the broom," he retorted. "You've turned into a smart aleck overnight." He perched on the edge of her desk. "You obviously don't appreciate the planning, the cunning, the . . ."

". . . Welsh balderdash," she filled in, which made him laugh.

"Seriously, miss, I have been planning. I've asked his mam to put a slight hem in little Billy's trousers."

"Ah."

"What I want you to do in a few days is to remark that he seems to be growing. In another day, I'll ask Margarad to hem up another inch. You'll notice it, and then tell him a few days later it's time to measure against the broom. Make sense?"

"Completely. You are a shrewd man, Owen Davis."

"*Someone* has to be to kiss Della Anders," he said. "I'm leaving nothing to chance." He tipped his hat to her and left her classroom. She fanned herself with the day's theme on "The Coming of Spring and Why We Like It."

Two days later, she remarked to Billy in an offhand way that he seemed to be growing. "Your legs look a little longer," she told him.

He grinned at her, pleased. "That's what my mam said too."

After the weekend, Della found the broom waiting inside the door of her classroom when she arrived early. Owen had obviously left it before the early shift, because there was a note for her made with his wooden letters: "Della, oh Della, curly haired Della." She blushed and tried to take off the letters before anyone could see them, except that Israel Bowman stood in her doorway, laughing.

"Go away!" she exclaimed, removing the letters as fast as she could, before the children arrived.

"Della, oh Della, curly haired Della," she heard him sing as he walked toward his classroom.

She took a good look at the broom handle, impressed.

CARLA KELLY

Owen had cut off more than three inches, but only some-one who knew that could detect it, she decided. He had sanded the cut edges until they looked smooth from years of use. A little stain matched the rest of the broom. Smiling to herself, she put the broom in the closet. *I wonder what kind of a kisser he is*, she thought, and her cheeks flamed predictably.

When Billy arrived for school with his brothers and sisters, she welcomed him into her classroom. "Billy, have you grown again?" she asked, her eyes wide.

He nodded, pride showing on his face. "My mam thinks I'm fair astounding."

"So do I."

He looked at her expectantly, and she knew he wanted her to get out the broom. Owen was right; better to let him wait a few more days and think about it. Let him remind her.

"He's primed and ready," Della whispered to Owen before choir practice that night.

"Spring it on him tomorrow then." He hesitated. "You're sure he's ready?"

She looked him in the eye until it was his turn to blush. "I *know* he is."

"Ahem," Richard Evans said, tapping on his music stand. "Will the second tenor and lower alto pay attention?"

"June's coming. It's Eisteddfod business," Owen said promptly.

"Liar, liar pants on fire," Della said under her breath, which sent the alto next to her into a coughing fit that sounded suspiciously like laughter.

Della walked home after practice with Magarad and Dafydd Evans. "I'm going to measure your Billy next to the broom tomorrow," she told them. "I know he's finally ready to read."

"Owen's been a real help to you there now," Magarad

said. "He's good to do this. Why, do you think?"

"I suppose he's just interested in helping the school," Della told her.

"That's not the rumor I've heard," Dafydd said. "'Course, my rumor comes from the mines, and what do we know?"

She left it at that, changing the subject to the growing rumor about a US Navy contract, which interested Dafydd. It only earned her a measuring look from Magarad, one of the women who had nursed Angharad almost seven years ago, and who knew Owen Davis pretty well. Magarad squeezed her arm and mouthed "Good luck," as they said good-bye on Mabli's doorstep.

Della spent extra time that morning fussing over her hair, ready to be pleased instead of dissatisfied. The face that gazed back at her from the mirror was calm and had full lips, that handsome nose no one else had in Winter Quarters Canyon, and glorious hair. "This is my mother's face," she said to her image. "She was lovely and she loved me. Possibly, someone else loves me too."

She wore her favorite dark blue skirt and the shirtwaist with blue and white flowers on it. Remy's wheat sheaf pin went on next. She wore her red-and-white striped stockings. No one would ever see them, but they had been her favorite purchase at Auerbach's during the holiday break.

The wagon road was dry enough to walk on, finally. As she went down the hill toward school, she gathered children as she walked. Some were Finnish, others were the children of the Scots, the Cornish, the Welsh, the German, but they all knew "Daisy Bell," and knew it at the top of the lungs. Della waved to mothers standing in their doorways, watching her traveling circus.

Della, the Pied Piper of Winter Quarters, led her singing class past homes and mechanical buildings and the fire station and another boardinghouse to the school, where Miss Clayson stood on the front step, almost smiling. When they finished singing, they all dashed behind the school to the playground.

"You'll have to have them sing for our district leaders," Miss Clayson said. "They'll be here sometime in May." The familiar frown came back. "Perhaps there will be time for them to learn something slightly more elevated than 'Daisy Bell.'"

"Perhaps," Della agreed. She brightened. "We already know 'The Daring Young Man on the Flying Trapeze.'"

Miss Clayson flinched and looked over her spectacles at Della. "My dear, there are times when you are regrettably lowbrow."

"I know," Della said, happy to agree. "How about 'America Forever'? I'm teaching them that for our Dewey Day celebration on May 1."

"What a relief! I'm in favor."

When she released her students for midmorning recess, Della planned to ask Billy Evans to hang back for a few minutes. As it turned out, she didn't need to. As the others trooped out, he came to her desk.

"Miss? I think I'm ready."

"I believe you are too, Billy. Let's take a look at the broom anyway, just to make sure."

He nodded and went to the closet. She watched as he held it next to him. "Miss! Miss!" Billy's eyes were wide as he measured himself. "I am so much taller now!"

"I believe you are, Billy," Della said. She took the broom from him. "Let's make certain."

She measured the broom against the back of Billy's head and put her hand at the top, which was level with the little boy's ears now. "Billy, you are taller than my broom. Go pick out the book you want to read to me."

He put the broom back and went to the bookshelf. Decisive, he pulled out *David Copperfield*, which she had spent all winter reading to the class. She sat with him in the small circle of chairs she used for each class's reading recitation. He opened to chapter one, cleared his throat in an obvious but probably unconscious imitation of her, and began.

"'Chapter One, I Am Born. Whether I shall turn out to be the hero of my own life, or whether that station will be held by anybody else, these pages must show.'"

He read carefully, but he did not hesitate. When he finished the first paragraph, he looked at her for approval. "Aw, miss, don't cry," he told her. "I'm tall and I can read."

Della hugged him.

"Aw, miss!"

"Well done, Billy. Will you take your turn reading out of McGuffey after recess?"

He nodded. "As long as I can sit next to you, miss."

"As long as you need to, Billy. Better hurry outside now. I'd hate for you to miss recess."

With a blinding smile that Della knew she would store in her heart forever, Billy darted out the classroom door. Della closed her eyes and folded her arms. So much for the separation of church and state; so much for the Rules for Teachers—she thanked the Lord for Billy Evans and his amazing growth spurt that turned him into a reader.

Since the weather was so mild for March, Della easily convinced her youthful escorts to let her walk home alone. Billy lingered long enough to check out *Ragged Dick* from her classroom library, then ran after the others.

She was entering arithmetic grades into her gradebook when she heard someone humming, "Daisy, Daisy, Give Me Your Answer True," in a remarkably fine tenor voice.

"Come in if you're not too dusty," she said without looking up.

"I went home and took a bath. Well, do you have a new reader in your class?"

She stood up and met him halfway up the aisle, delighted. "Owen! He's marvelous! He read the first few paragraphs of *David Copperfield* to me and checked out one of Horatio Alger's little potboilers after school."

Owen grinned at her, his enthusiasm easily matching hers. "Did he even need the broom?"

"I'm not sure. It was all his idea, as you thought it might be. I think what impressed him most was the way he grew out of his trousers."

They looked at each other. "Well?" Della asked finally, when he seemed unable to move.

"I'm glad."

"Glad? You have a reward coming, I believe." Her face felt uncomfortably hot for an early spring day, but there he stood, taking not one step closer.

"Owen, what am I going to do with you?" she said finally. She took those three steps closer, put her hands on both sides of his face, and kissed him.

His arms went around her then; he pulled her closer until Aunt Caroline, Miss Clayson, and probably even the long-absent and frisky Miss Forsyth would never have approved. Never mind—none of them were there in her classroom, only Owen Davis.

She had probably had more recent experience kissing than Owen. After all, she had spent that summer before university in a canyon with telephone linemen, some of whom were her approximate age. What he lacked for in recent experience, he more than made up with technique. She hadn't noticed any women in the canyon with full lips like hers, but he made the most of her abundance, even catching her lower lip in his teeth in a provocative way that made her breathe a little faster. Whatever the length of his dry spell, Owen Davis hadn't forgotten a thing.

He broke away first, holding her off at arm's length and looking at her. "My word."

"Beginner's luck," she said, breathless. "Sort of."

He laughed out loud, which she stopped with another

kiss. Same result, except this time she was the one hauling him close. He offered not a single objection, other than a guttural sound in his throat that didn't sound like a complaint.

It was her turn to pull back. "I'm really glad Billy Evans was ready to read."

He smiled as though he had a private joke on her and sat down in one of the children's desks, keeping some wise distance between them. "Will you thrash me into next week if I tell you that Billy Evans has been reading at home for the past two weeks?"

Della gasped and threw an eraser at him. She put her hands on her stomach and started to laugh. She laughed so hard that she was desperate to loosen her corset strings, the very last thing she would do with Owen sitting right there.

"You're serious," she asked finally.

"Never more so. I went to the Evanses' house last week to suggest the trouser hemming, and Magarad confessed." He looked at her, as though measuring her capacity for amusement and his own culpability. "I, uh, had mentioned the wager to his brother Richard one slow morning in the mine, and one thing led to another. Evidently, brothers don't keep secrets."

It was Della's turn to look away. "I . . . I may have mentioned it to Richard and Martha once in the library." She laughed again. "But Magarad told you last week?"

"Cross my heart. I hadn't a clue before then." He sighed as though boulders had fallen off him. "She said everyone in the canyon wanted the best for us and knew it when they saw it, even if we didn't know it."

He walked her home, idling along, turning his face up to the welcome sun. "I hate being in a mine when the weather's like this."

"You don't have to be, you know," she said, tentative.

"And that's something else to discuss. For all that you probably have the most magnificent lips in the intermountain region, I'm not one to rush."

"I understand," she said, pausing at Mabli's door. She nudged his shoulder. "At least you have your reward."

He gave her a look of surprise, wide-eyed, amazed, and completely duplicitous; she knew him. "No, I haven't, Della. You'll recall that *you're* the one who kissed me in your classroom. *I* didn't start it. You still owe me. See you tomorrow."

She shook her head and watched him go down the hill, face up to the sun again. He turned around once to wave at her, and her heart was full.

There was a different feeling in the canyon Thursday afternoon, and it was nothing she could put her finger on. The first coal train had moved noisily past the school at the usual morning hour, but the late afternoon train still waited on the tracks, loaded with coal but not moving.

"That's a little strange," Israel said, standing beside her on the outside steps. "What's it waiting for?" He shrugged and ambled back to his classroom.

Della had removed the last of the construction paper snowflakes and clouds made of cotton wadding from one bulletin board. She was cutting out her stenciled "Think Spring!" sign to replace them when she noticed Owen, Nicola Anselmo, Victor Aho, Richard Evans, and Thomas Farish walking past the school, their children trailing after them. She looked closer. The children were carrying satchels. Curious now, she watched them go to the Wasatch Store. After a few minutes, Owen came back by himself. She waved to him from her window, and he took the steps two at a time, his face serious.

"What's going on?" she asked. "Something's wrong."

"Aye, miss. There was an explosion last night after the afternoon shift in the Castle Gate Mine."

"No, no," she murmured, putting down her scissors and coming to him as he stood by the door. "Please tell me no one died this time."

"No one died. Remember what I told you about

Castle Gate? It's a gassy mine and prone to methane. Because of that, the boyos don't shoot down the coal when they're in the mine. They set the charges at the end of their shift, which are detonated by an electric switch when everyone's out."

"I wish you did that here," she said. "It scares me."

"No worries, Butterbean. We're not a gassy mine."

"How can I not worry? What happened?"

"A sizeable portion of the mine exploded. Frank Cameron—he's the supe at Castle Gate—telegraphed Bishop Parmley and asked for a shoring crew. Bishop put me in charge and told me to get four of the best men. We're going to Castle Gate now to help their crew."

She reached for him, clutching his sleeve. He tried to back away, but she could tell it was a halfhearted effort.

"Nay, lass, I'm wearing my work clothes!"

"I don't care. What will you do there?"

"I won't lie. We'll be crawling over and under fallen timbers and trying to see how to shore it all up, so the men can go back to work." He looked toward the store. "I picked the best men I know. Richard's little and limber like me, and the others are taller and stronger. They can do the heavy lifting." He smiled. "And Tommy Farish is just the best miner I know." He touched the frown line between her eyes. "Hey, *m cara*, don't worry! We'll be fine."

"But . . . you told me you don't get paid if you don't mine."

"You may look Greek, but that's said like a Welshwoman! Bishop made an exception for us. We're actually going to be paid for something besides mining coal. Makes sense. If you can't get into a mine, you can't make money."

He came closer and put his hand on her waist. It was a tentative gesture and struck her as a little quaint, considering their fervent kiss yesterday. "I asked Angharad where she wanted to go. She wants to stay home, and she wants you to stay with her. I asked Bishop what he thought, and he assured me there's no impropriety. Will you? She'd rather be home."

"Of course I'll stay with her," Della said quietly. "Miss Clayson will understand. How long will you be gone?"

"Two weeks at the very least. Will Pugh will arrange the singing for Sunday and lead the rehearsals." He gave her a long look, as if he wanted to stay where he was. "And that's it."

"Are they holding the train for you and your crew?"

"Aye, miss. I have to go." He pursed his lips and regarded her long enough to make the heat rise from her chest to her neck. "You know, I still need to collect my reward, since you jumped the gun yesterday. Now?"

She nodded, and let him pull her close this time and kiss her with that same careful, methodical discovery of her lips. She already knew he wasn't a man to rush things, except this time there was a timber crew, a train with four engines on front, and many tons of coal waiting. His hands strayed a little from her waist, which wasn't part of the original agreement, but Della didn't care. She kissed him back, stroking his face, then running her fingers in his dark hair.

The whistle blew on the first engine and she jumped, which made Owen laugh. "I think they want me to hurry up," he told her, his lips still brushing against hers as he spoke. "We need to have some serious conversation when I return, think on."

She nodded. He left the school, running now. He looked back once. Della watched until she saw the train leave the canyon. "You called me *m cara*," she murmured. She looked at her shirtwaist, gray with coal in spots. She returned her attention to the canyon mouth, wishing he had not left.

Chapter 34

❧

*T*he shoring crew was gone three weeks. In that time, Billy Evans read five Horatio Alger books, and Della learned the first verse of "All Through the Night" in Welsh. She settled into Owen's little house, rearranged his spartan kitchen, and started cooking things on his stove that made Angharad assure her that nothing had ever tasted so good from that kitchen.

"Da told me once that the problem was his kitchen range," Angharad said one night as she spooned down a stew that Mabli had taught Della. "I sort of believed him."

"Now you know he was pulling your leg," Della said, and they laughed together about Da.

She relished the quiet moments with Angharad. When school was over for the day, sometimes Angharad would sit at her desk and draw. She had a flair for bulletin boards, which meant several little girls stayed after class and created a wonderful bulletin board to honor Admiral Dewey. The crowning glory was Dewey's battleship, its guns blazing, steaming into a Winter Quarters idea of Manila Bay. Myfanwy Jones had the good idea to make the ship gray using coal dust on the white construction paper.

"Papa told me there is going to be a dance in the new Odd Fellows Hall on Dewey Day," Mary Parmley told the other little girls. "He said everyone's invited, but we have to leave room on the dance floor for our parents."

Angharad went with her to the library three nights a week, which enlarged Della's escort supply. It touched her

CARLA KELLY

heart to see how much the older boardinghouse miners enjoyed being around children. Nicola had told her shyly one night that he was saving money to bring his childhood sweetheart from their Italian village to his Utah canyon. He had rolled his eyes. "And then, Signorina Anders, *bambinos* of our own!"

Angharad had asked her what Nicola meant, and Della explained as best she could that when two people marry, they liked to have children. It was enough of an answer to satisfy the child, but Della knew Owen was going to have to start supplying his own answers to such questions.

It could become my responsibility, Della thought that night after tucking Angharad in bed. She stood in the doorway of her little room, created out of Owen's only slightly larger bedroom. "Bambinos of my own," she whispered.

She carried that thought with her on Thursday night to sauna. Mabli had agreed that Angharad was too young for that experience, so she put her niece to work helping in the boardinghouse kitchen while Della joined her Finnish friends. The snow fence was gone from behind the sauna, so the women rinsed off with cold water from the creek, brought into the sauna in a big barrel.

Mari only stayed for ten minutes in sauna now. Della sat beside her, making her speak in English, because she suspected it was Mari's only chance right now to hear the language. One night, Mari put Della's hand on her belly to feel the baby kicking.

"It is Heikki's heartbeat in my body," she said in her quiet way.

Angharad's greatest pleasure came when Emil Isgreen bowed to the little girl in the library and invited her to dinner with him and Della. Angharad had insisted on her Sunday dress and French-braided hair for the occasion. Della loaned her the precious wheat sheaf pin, which Angharad touched all the way to Scofield, making certain she did not lose it.

She had spent a long time studying the half-page menu,

which made Emil smile at Della. He had laughed out loud when she solemnly declared, "This is a rare and memorable treat."

"Oh, you Welsh," he had said as the patient waiter, smiling, took away the menu. "You have a way with words."

He laughed when she declared in all dignity, "It is one of our many special gifts."

"I believe you, Miss Davis. Who wouldn't?"

She touched his sleeve, and probably his heart, when she asked, "Do you think that waiter would let me keep the menu as a souvenir?"

"Why don't you ask him?" Emil replied. When she left her chair to follow the waiter, he looked at Della. "I admire my canyon children. They have so little, but it never bothers them, because they have so much."

"'Your children'? You too?" Della asked softly, watching Angharad, who was returning to the table in triumph with the menu. "Amazing isn't it, how they wrap themselves around your heart."

"Speaking of hearts," he said after dinner, when Angharad skipped ahead on the road back to Winter Quarters, waving her menu. "Della, I've enjoyed our Saturday night dinners, but your heart is already taken, isn't it?"

She nodded, too shy to look at him. "It's probably not the wisest thing I ever did."

"Time will tell. I still intend to take you out to dinner every Saturday, unless a certain miner tells me to back off. And if he does, what will *you* say? It's a chancy life. You've seen what can happen."

"I honestly do not know what I will say."

She didn't. Maybe it was a blessing that Owen was gone for a few weeks. She had decided the first week that she would have some small idea how a life without him felt, even though the most intimate thing they had done was kiss. After all, she was nearly twenty-five, used to earning her own living, and confident that she could earn it any-where. She had written numerous letters to a school board in Phoenix that Miss Clayson had mentioned and torn up each letter.

By the end of the first week, she was nearly starved to hear Owen call her butterbean. Singing in church next to an equally fine second tenor who wasn't Owen Davis had felt like a desert. She realized just how often Owen had touched her fingers under the cover of the sopranos and first tenors in the first row.

She had broached her greatest fear to Annie Jones on the Saturday Angharad's friends had gathered by special invita-tion to a dollhouse day. Della had pulled the dollhouse into the front room so all the girls could fit around it and play. She and Annie made bread and butter sandwiches. Amazing how cutting the crust off Annie's oat bread, buttering it, and slicing it on the diagonal was enough to make the girls clap their hands in delight. Mabli's contribution of little cream puffs and actual lemonade had nearly been too much for the simplicity everyone was used to.

Della had sat with Annie and Martha Evans on the little front porch. She worked up her courage to ask them, "How do you keep from worrying every time a shift starts?" She put her hand to her warm face. "Maybe I should never mention it . . ."

Annie glanced at her friend Martha. "We were wonder-ing when you would ask us."

"Really. What do you *do*? I'm not sure I'm that brave, even though my father was a miner too."

"Has Owen declared himself yet?" Martha asked.

Della shook her head. "He's getting pretty close."

"I supposed as much, considering how you two hold hands in choir when you think no one knows," Annie teased.

Della laughed out loud. "And he thinks he's so discreet!"

"Men," was all Martha said, and it covered the subject.

"Seriously," she said. "I have to know."

The friends exchanged glances again. Martha took Della's hand in hers. "We just love them and hope for the best. When you have children of your own, they'll occupy your days and your thoughts. That helps."

"Even when you know something has happened?"

"Then you fall to your knees and pray," Annie said simply. "And when your man comes out of the mine with that dirty face and teeth looking so white when he smiles, you're not sure whether to smack him or kiss him. I can't answer your question." She looked at Martha again. "I think we all find our own level of coping."

"Annie, would you . . . would you marry Levi all over again, knowing what you know?"

"We married in Salt Lake Temple when we came here, same as Owen and Gwyna did. Levi is mine forever."

"But the now! I just don't know," Della exclaimed. She had spoken too loud, so she listened for the girls in the front room. She relaxed as their chatter continued. She looked across the wagon road toward the tipple. "Can I be that brave?"

"You already are," Martha said. "You just don't know it yet."

Owen wrote to them both, two letters in one envelope, the letters with coal dust fingerprints. Angharad had stared in awe at the unopened envelope, addressed to her. "I've never had a letter in my life," she told Della as they sat outside the Wasatch Store. Clarence Nix had presented the letter to Angharad, along with a stick of penny candy. "I always do that for a first letter," he assured the child.

Angharad slit the envelope with a hairpin and handed the letter to Della. "There are two letters. You take yours."

Eyes wide, Angharad unfolded the letter slowly, savoring the event. Della glanced at it. He had printed his letter to his daughter, so she would have no trouble reading it. Della opened her own letter. *Dear Butterbean, we're having a time of it here*, she read to herself. *There's no end of work, shoring up a blast sight. I don't envy the men in Castle Gate Mine.*

He had included little drawings of them sizing and sawing, then propping the timbers and nailing them in place. She held the letter closer. *I miss you. I know Angharad is in the best hands. I want her to always be in your care, no matter what.*

She looked away then, her eyes filling with tears. *Don't talk like that, it's bad luck*, she thought, thinking of the patient women on his porch, sharing their fears with her. She turned back to her letter. *Give me some time when I return, Della. Just a little time to think. Love, Owen.*

"He drew a picture for me too," Angharad said. She held out her letter, which had a little picture across the bottom of her father eating his sandwich and sitting next to Nicola Anselmo, strong man. She looked at Della's pictures and her face clouded over. "I like my picture better than yours."

Della put her arm around the child's shoulders. "I like your picture better too."

Her eyes worried, Angharad burrowed closer. "He asked me what I wanted for Christmas last year. I told him I wanted him out of the mine."

Della hugged her, her lips against Angharad's hair. "Tell him that for your birthday and for next Christmas too. And the one after that until he listens."

After an excruciating evening watching Mari's joy at her growing belly, Della finally took her fears to Mabli Reese. When Mabli went to Della's room to wake up Angharad for the walk to her own home, Della stopped her. "Let's talk first."

Silent, Mabli led her into the kitchen and closed the door. She poured them both some peppermint tea and brought a plate of oatmeal cookies to the table. Della shook her head.

"You've never turned down a cookie in your life, I'll wager," Mabli said. "Out with it. I think this conversation is overdue. You've been in love with my brother-in-law a long time, think on."

"Since at least Christmas." Della looked away. "Oh, who knows? Maybe since I saw his box of wooden letters in my classroom! Mabli, my heart's breaking. He told me about Gwyna's bad heart, but I think there is more."

"There is," her landlady said promptly. She pushed away the cookies, too. "Of course Gwyna knew about her bad heart! She knew before she was ten years old, and Owen was twelve and headed to the mines. The doctor sat us all down and told us, but she wasn't listening. She loved Owen when she first saw him too, I think. He has that way about him. Could a woman ever tell the man she loves about such a heart?"

Della shook her head and wiped at her eyes. Mabli handed her a napkin without a word, and kept the other for herself.

"When she was fourteen, Owen figured out that he loved her. He was a full-fledged miner by then. When he wasn't on the afternoon shift, he sat in our parlor and held her hand for four years! My stars, the man was persistent. He proposed when she was eighteen and she said aye without even a blink."

"Did anyone . . . ?"

"Try to reason with her? We all did. No one had the courage to say anything to Owen. Mam even sat her down and held her tight by the shoulders and reminded her that with her heart, to marry and then try to bear a child would be her death." Mabli looked away and put the napkin to her eyes.

Della grasped her hand. "I love that man too, and I know exactly what Gwyna told your mother." She waited until she could speak. "She probably said she would rather have a few months with that beautiful man, if that was all she was allowed, than spend a long life starving without him."

Mabli nodded, her eyes bleak. "Who can reason with that?"

"No one. I understand Gwyna completely." She squeezed Mabli's hand. "You should tell him what you've told me."

"Maybe someday."

She thought about Mabli's confession as she helped a sleepy-eyed Angharad through her nighttime rituals and tucked her in bed in her own bedroom. Since she was so tired, Angharad made no objection to Della singing "All Through the Night" in English this time.

"We should learn the other two verses," Della said. No answer. She smiled at the sleeping child and took the songbook into the front room. She read the second verse, nodding, but stopped on the third verse and closed the book. She set it on the floor. Once glance and the words had burned themselves into her brain: "Love, to thee my thoughts are turning all through the night; All for thee my heart is yearning, all through the night. Though sad fate our lives may sever, parting will not last forever . . . "

There was more; she couldn't read it.

Owen and his crew returned a week later, thinner, but with news that passed quickly from house to house, almost as soon as the crew got off the train. By early afternoon, the news traveled from classroom to classroom by that peculiar kind of osmosis common to public schools. The Pleasant Valley Coal Company had indeed signed a contract with the US Navy to provide two thousand tons of coal a day, starting May 1.

"That's good news," Israel Bowman had commented to Della after school. "Maybe I should throw over teaching and go into the mines." He laughed. "Heaven knows teaching doesn't pay!"

Owen had telegraphed ahead, so Della had already removed her clothing and personal items from his house before the crew arrived, or thought she had. He and Angharad came over that night, Angharad carrying Della's toothbrush.

"You'd have missed it before bedtime," Owen said. "Thank you for watching my daughter."

"Nothing simpler." She looked at him. "Didn't anyone feed you in Castle Gate?"

"We could have eaten more," he agreed.

She felt shy around him, considering their last kiss. Here he was, looking so calm, when all she wanted to do was kiss him again.

He seemed no more able to carry on casual conversation than she was, until she prodded him about the contract. "Is it a rumor or true?" she asked.

"True indeed. No oatcakes this summer," he said cheerfully. "And here's more good news: Bishop Parmley is toying with the idea of transferring his brother William to Castle Gate and moving me up to foreman of Number Four. I'd be salaried and working for the company instead of contracting coal. He hasn't decided, mind you, but he's considering it." He looked at her. "You're not exactly in transports of delight."

She tried to choose her words carefully, distressed that she sounded so wooden to her own ears. "You were going to do some carpentry work this summer in Provo."

"I'm a miner. That comes first," he reminded her, his eyes taking on a wary expression. "I didn't sign any contract with anyone in Provo."

She couldn't think of anything to say and hadn't the heart to remind him what Angharad had asked for last Christmas. From the look on his face, he wouldn't have heard a word. She went to the window, not willing to look at the man she loved, because she wanted to smack him into next week.

"Even your shoulder blades look upset," he told her, coming up behind her to rest his hands on those shoulder blades. "I'm a miner," he repeated. "My friends are all miners."

"You can make new friends in Provo," she said, her voice small, because she knew she had lost. "You can find plenty of work there."

"Gwyna is buried here." He removed his hands. "Well, she is," he said, defensive, as if arguing with himself.

"I know that, Owen." He wasn't going to change. She saw that clearly. She knew it was time to write a letter to the Phoenix School District and not tear it up. The mine had won.

Chapter 35

*D*ella was so frosty at church that *she* didn't even like herself when sacrament meeting ended. Worry in his eyes, Richard Evans asked her to stay behind for a chat. She mumbled something about spending the evening in her classroom, getting ready for Monday, and hurried up the canyon. Even the men in the boardinghouse steered clear of her as she slammed pie and cake on the dessert table and dared them to reach for it.

After a hearty bout of useless tears while Mabli was hiding from her in the boardinghouse kitchen, Della let herself into the school and unlocked the door to her room. She lit a kerosene lamp and put it on her desk so she could pretend she had something to do.

Drat that man, she thought, indignant. *Any woman who loves a miner should have her brain removed and washed.*

Out of sorts with everyone, she rested her head on her desk and closed her eyes. "I'm sorry, Heavenly Father," she murmured. "Forgive me."

When she felt better and sat up, she saw Owen Davis standing in her open door. Her eyes filled with tears. He didn't say anything. He went to the closet and took out his box of wooden letters. She heard him putting them back, then heard chalk on blackboard instead. She looked away resolutely.

When he finished, he nodded to her and left the classroom. She sat a long moment without turning around, then she sighed. *Time to take my medicine*, she thought. *How bad can it be?*

She turned around and read the board, both hands to her mouth. "'I'm not one to court. I only know how to be a husband,'" she read, shocked. "'Marry me? Or at least come to the dance with me?'"

"You are hopeless," she said out loud and erased the blackboard. Dusting off her hands, she went into the hall. No one there. She opened the outside door, and there he sat on the steps.

She sat down beside him, not quite close enough to touch him. Neither of them said a word. Gradually, she felt herself leaning slightly in his direction. Gradually his arm went around her waist, which meant that to be comfortable she had to rest her head on his shoulder.

"I'm being childish, and I can't stand myself," she said finally.

"I'm stubborn and mired in the past," he said. "Can we bend a little?"

Silence.

"I don't want you in the mine."

More silence.

"It's what I do best."

She looked at him then, and he turned to look at her. He was an honorable man, a good father, a churchgoer, a wonderful singer, an excellent woodcarver, and a skilled miner. To take one characteristic meant to take all. He wasn't an apple bin, to pick and choose from; he was the man she loved.

"Can I bend? I honestly don't know," she told him finally. "Can you?"

"I don't know either."

"The answer to the first question is no." She felt his involuntary flinch. "The answer to the second question is yes."

She stood up then, but he tugged on her dress, and she sat down again. "I'm a very good husband, Della," he told her, not pleading with her—he would never do that—but not giving up. "I hang up my clothes, I take a bath every day, I treat people kindly, I love my daughter." He paused a moment, as if considering, then plunged ahead. "I have it on good authority that I am a competent lover."

She looked away, shy. No man had ever spoken to her like that. "I have no idea what I am."

He laughed softly. "I have a strong suspicion that you are everything I just said I was." He gave her neck a little shake. "Ah, well. Up you get. I'm on afternoons for two weeks now. I know you can polka. Practice your waltz, Butterbean. We're going to the dance."

He stood up and walked away without a backward glance. She waited, listening. In a minute, she heard him singing, "'Nay, speak no ill, a kindly word, can never leave a sting behind,'" which made her laugh in spite of herself.

He hadn't asked her if Angharad could stay with them until he was out of the mine each evening, so the child walked home every afternoon with Myfanwy Jones and Mary Evans, her best friends. Miss Clayson stopped by her classroom after school one afternoon, curious to know what had happened.

"I heard you in your classroom on Sunday evening and then I heard someone else, so I stayed away, Della. Now you're so quiet. Can I help?"

Della regarded her principal, who had returned to her own silence in the months after Christmas, but at least not to her distrust and malice, if that's what it was. "Too quiet, eh? I don't know, Lavinia. My miner doesn't seem to be as compliant and fun-loving as Miss Forsyth's mining engineer. I won't be running off before the term ends."

"I knew that," Miss Clayson said with a laugh. "If you feel like talking . . ." She turned to go, then looked back. "I nearly forgot: I'll be getting next year's contracts any day now."

Della nodded and turned her attention to the letter she

was writing to the Phoenix School District. When she finished this one, supplying addresses of references, she mailed it. In the Wasatch Store, Clarence Nix glanced at the address and frowned.

"This had better not be what I think it is," he said. Word must have circulated about her uncharacteristic foul mood.

"Clarence, just mail it," she said patiently and handed over two cents. She gave him another penny. "And let me have a peppermint stick, a big one."

The candy was no remedy for heartache, but she sucked on it all the way home, past the homes that had just been pathetic shacks clinging to the rocky hillside when she first saw them months ago; past the mechanical buildings and the open-sided woodshed that still made her heart beat faster and thank the Lord for. When she came to the little pocket canyon with its trestle marking the Number Four incline, she looked in that direction as she always did when she knew Owen was under the mountain. She felt the muffled rumble more than heard it, knowing some crew was shooting down coal. The rush was on to finish a few smaller contracts before the US Navy contract.

She would have stopped at Mabli's, except that Eeva Koski caught up with her, and linked her arm through Della's.

"What's this I hear?" Eeva asked, keeping her walking toward Finn Town. "Victor Aho tells me Owen is chewing nails and growling. You're quiet and glum. And eating candy!" She nudged Della. "I eat sugar mints when I'm ready to murder Kari."

Della couldn't help the tears in her eyes. "He proposed, and I just can't marry a miner."

Eeva steered her into her home and shooed her children outside. She sat Della down. "You can't?" she asked, all kidding gone. "My dear, why not? I know you love him."

"He won't leave the mine for me. Eeva, my father died in a mine and the next years of my life were horrible beyond description." She looked away. "That ended when I came here. I dread that it would begin again, with another loss."

They sat together in silence. Trust Eeva not to give her any glib answers, even though her silence spoke volumes.

"Miners are strange creatures," Eeva said finally. "There's something called the lure of the mine. It seems to draw those men who like pitting themselves against impossible odds. Women don't do that. We nurture and try to avoid impossible odds." She chuckled. "It's a wonder there are any children in the world, considering how different we are."

Della nodded. She sat with her friend until she finished her peppermint stick, then rose quietly and left Finn Town.

Choir practice Tuesday night was equally subdued. The voices were as wonderful as usual, even though both Richard and Owen were in the mine. Will Pugh gave her a handful of letters.

"Questions about Eisteddfod," he told her. "See? We did need a secretary."

"Thanks, Will. I'll answer them."

He frowned, obviously not content with her quiet acceptance.

The singing calmed her, as it always did. By the end of the hour, she was smiling again, even when Martha Evans, with a merry expression, suggested they sing "Nay, Speak No Ill," followed by "Kind Words Are Sweet Tones."

"I especially like the chorus," Martha said. "You know, where we sing *in perfect harmony*, Della. 'Let us oft speak kind words to each other, kind words are sweet tones of the heart.'"

"You are all hopeless!" Della scolded, with a fair imitation of her usual asperity that earned her relieved smiles, except for Martha Evans, who was not even slightly fooled.

The library was still solace, which made her think about writing a letter to the Phoenix library, assuming anyone read in Arizona and there *was* a library.

She brushed through the next Sunday, sitting in her usual place in the choir next to Owen. She stood just far enough away from him to avoid his hand, which reached for her hand once or twice, then gave up. She had no similar defense against Angharad's frown and her drooping shoulders, which told her too much about the silence at the Davis residence.

"Miss Anders, I miss you," Angharad said after church as they walked home together, Owen walking behind with the Evanses. Mabli was in front again with William Goode, which gave Della the only lift to her heart. Angharad tugged on her hand. "Da isn't even carving."

"Oh, my dear," Della whispered. She pressed her fingers against the bridge of her nose. "He'll be all right. You will too."

"Will you?"

Angharad came to the library with the Evanses on Wednesday night, returning a book and wondering what to read next. Della steered her to Grimms' Fairy Tales. "It'll take some effort on your part, but your da will know the bigger words." She leaned closer. "Tell you what—you can check this one out for three weeks."

"You can *do* that?" Angharad asked, her eyes wide.

"Only for my best friends." She kissed Angharad and set the stamp for three weeks.

"Thank you, miss." Angharad handed her a folded piece of paper. "For you. Maybe you forgot how much you need one."

She waited until Angharad left with the Evanses to open the paper. It was a red dragon, paw raised, defiant. She looked closer. Angharad had drawn the dragon with tears in its eyes.

The end of the week couldn't have come soon enough to suit Della. She closed her door with a sigh that even Israel Bowman heard as he locked his own door.

"Della, Della, he's an unhappy fella," he said.

"Not you too! There is a vast conspiracy in this canyon full of busybodies!" she told him, exasperated.

He backed away, holding up both hands. "Steady now. Maybe I should talk to Owen. I discovered last year that if I do whatever Blanche wants, I'm a happy man. G'day, dearie. You'll figure it out. I'm off to Provo, as usual." He kissed her cheek in passing.

There wasn't a letter in sight from Arizona when she checked at the Wasatch Store. "It's been two weeks since I wrote to that school district," she grumbled. "Clarence, what is the matter with the US Postal Service?"

"Not a thing, Miss Anders." He handed her a folded note. "There's this. Don't look so suspicious! It's from Dr. Isgreen. He just dropped it by."

I am getting tired of myself, she thought as she opened the note. She read the note, hoping he wasn't going to cry off and leave her to pout and sulk alone. "Dear Della, I'm in a rush tomorrow. Could you just meet me at the restaurant? Doctor duties, you know. EI."

She did know, glad she still had a friend in the canyon. The weather was pleasingly warm, so she wore the green silk shirtwaist Aunt Amanda had sent from Provo for no particular reason. It went quite well with her brown skirt. She piled her curls on top of her head in a style found in this month's *McCall's Magazine*, frowned at the effect, and reverted to a simple braid down her back.

The solitary walk suited her mood, but nothing prepared her for the sight of Owen Davis seated at Emil Isgreen's usual corner table. She went to the table and stood there.

"He s-s-sent me a note. Something about doctor duties," she stammered. Owen wore a new white shirt and one of Angharad's Thanksgiving cravats. His hair was slicked back and he looked wonderful. "You are *not* a doctor duty."

"Beg to differ, Butterbean. I went to his office before my shift yesterday and told him to put a stethoscope to my heart. It worried him, so he gave up dinner. Sit down, please."

She sat, nodding to the waiter when he handed her a menu.

"Angharad told me the food is wonderful here," he said, when the silence grew. "Della, please smile."

"It's kind of hard," she told him simply. "I've lost to the mine. I could fight another woman, but I can't fight a mine."

"Do you love me?"

It was a good question; she hadn't thought he would be so bold to ask it in a restaurant. Did she love him? Even the thought of a summer away from him was impossible to fathom; he was talking about years, with an eternity thrown in on the side.

"I always will, Owen."

She ordered a bowl of soup she didn't want, and Owen ordered dinner. Drat the man for sitting there brooding and looking so handsome. The Welsh must be the most aggravating, duplicitous, infuriating band of Celts in all of known history.

"You won't take that scary step and marry me?"

She shook her head. "I told you I would never marry a miner. Aren't you listening?" She couldn't help her flash of anger.

He ignored it. "I'm listening. You're still sitting here, so I won't give up. It can end right here, Della. Just say the word."

She teared up again, distressed with herself. He made it worse by handing her a handkerchief smelling of soap and coal.

"Now then. If you decide you'd like more than vegetable soup, I'll share. I'll share anything with you: my food, my bed, my pathetic income, my daughter. My clothes won't fit you. Only one of us will fit in my tin tub at a time. A pity, that."

He cut into what looked like fork-tender beef, something

she had never eaten before at the restaurant. Trust even the cows to be part of some conspiracy to make her miserable. She pointed to a piece of beef on his plate. With only the barest smile, he forked it onto her paltry little plate of saltines.

"Tasty," she said and pointed to another piece.

His smile broader now, he handed it over, then batted away her fork when she gestured for another. She laughed and could have sworn everyone in the restaurant let out a sigh of relief.

After dinner, he walked her home to Mabli's. She was amazed how many people in Winter Quarters Canyon seemed to be out and about as the sun left the sky. It was no boardwalk in Atlantic City, but close to her suspicious mind.

He glanced at the woodshed as they strolled past and let out his breath in a puff. "I never walk by that without a prayer of thanksgiving, Butterbean."

"I don't either," she told him, her voice small. "It's been quite a year."

"Not over yet. It can be quite a life, Della. Maybe one to go down in the annals of best ideas since Moses parted the Red Sea."

"You are the world's worst exaggerator."

He tucked her arm through his and she let him. At Mabli's door, he kissed her good night, and she let him do that too, her arms around him because she found it hard to maintain her balance otherwise.

Sunday was a fair, windy day, one of many in the canyon. She went to church early, hoping to find Bishop Parmley there. He must have known she wanted to see him. When she knocked on his door, he said, "Come in, Sister Anders."

"You knew it was me," she accused, which made him hold up his hands. She plopped down in his office chair. "I've been terrible and disagreeable. Bishop, I don't know what to do."

He smiled at her and held out his hand across the desk. She put her hand in his. "You're the wrong man to talk to, Bishop. The last thing you want Owen to do is quit the mine because you're his employer and he's good. But you're his bishop too, and mine. Give me some advice, please."

"Fast and pray," he told her promptly. "If you haven't done that already, that tells me you don't want to listen to the answer you're going to get."

She sat back, surprised. "I haven't."

"Then get to it, Sister Anders. Start now."

She nodded and left his office. She listened with her whole heart that afternoon as Owen and Richard sang, "'How gentle God's commands! How kind his precepts are! Come, cast your burden on the Lord, and trust his constant care.'"

As the sacrament came around, she drank from the cup, her eyes on Owen, and then her heart. He seemed to sing the last line of the last verse to her alone, his eyes on her and so kind, "'I'll drop my burden at his feet and bear a song away.'"

Drop my burden, she thought as she shook her head at company on the walk home. "I need to think," she told the Evanses, who came up on each side of her. "Pray for me," she said, as an afterthought.

"We already do," Richard said.

She nodded, thanking him with her eyes, and hurried on, head down. As she passed the school, a motion caught her eye. She looked up to see Miss Clayson gesturing to her. Curious, she went up the steps and opened the door.

"Good! I was afraid I'd missed you," she said. "Goodness, you Mormons go to church so often."

"It's our bad habit," Della told her, amused. "What . . . ?"

Miss Clayson started down the steps to the basement. "I have something to show you."

As Della followed, the principal opened the door to

her living quarters. More curious now, Della followed her in, thinking of the times Israel Bowman had told her he thought Miss Clayson had a collection of snakes hidden down there.

The only light came from two small windows high on the wall, which allowed little sun in the front room. Della knew she could never live in a place of such low light and wondered what an effect this had on Miss Clayson through the years. *Not for me*, she told herself.

The most prominent object in the room was a photograph on the wall opposite the door. Della stepped closer, interested. It was a handsome man, looking like a banker or a teacher, perhaps. He had a closely trimmed beard and a slight smile. His suit was well-tailored and looked to her like clothing from the last Grant administration.

"This is Edwin Aldridge," Miss Clayson said, her voice surprisingly tender, as though she introduced them. "We knew each other as children in Boise. He went to the Rialto Mine in Butte, Montana Territory, a hard rock miner like your father."

Della sat down, her eyes on the photograph.

"He asked me to marry him, and I told her I would never marry a miner. He went back to Butte."

"Please don't, Lavinia," Della whispered.

"You're going to hear this, Della," she said, with steel in her voice. "One morning, there was some trouble with the cable in the hoist. The foremen went down to look at it. The flame from his head lamp caught the cloth insulation on fire and the shaft turned into a blaze. Fifty miners were trapped and could not escape. Edwin was one of them."

Della bowed her head, unable to look at Edwin, forever a young man.

"Many asphyxiated, but some survived for a day or more. Edwin was one of those. He wrote me a note while waiting to die." Her voice faltered then, and she made a guttural sound in her throat. "It took me ten years to work up the courage to read it. I came here vowing to do everything I could to make sure no child I taught ever went into a mine again."

Della sat back, understanding her principal as never before. Or not. She frowned, thinking about that debacle of a holiday dinner at the Anderses' house. "But you defended me. You defended miners. I don't understand."

Lavinia sat down beside her. "Della, you've been so absorbed in your own past that it might not occur to you that other people can change too. I have. I probably owe it to you."

"I still don't understand."

"Then pay attention! I have regretted every single day of my life since Edwin's death. If I had married my darling Edwin, I would have had six months with him. Six months!"

"But that's so sho—"

"Short? Compared to *nothing*? No memories, no child, nothing to look forward to. Della, think very carefully before you tell that fine man no."

Miss Clayson seemed to think she had overstepped her bounds. Her expression mellowed. "I don't mean to frighten you. You're probably tired of every well-meaning soul in this canyon telling you what to do."

"I am, and now you too!" Della said angrily. "You don't live my life!"

"True, we don't. You came here so unsure of yourself. You changed. Now you are resourceful, determined, and so much fun. Last week, your third graders got brave enough to slip a petition under my door, asking that you be moved to the upper primary grade with them this fall."

"We . . . did have a lesson on the power of common consent," Della said.

"Obviously they listened!" Miss Clayson said, with a touch of her usual asperity.

Della tried to gather her scattered thoughts. "You want

me to marry him, even if we only have a few years together. You're afraid I'll become the old Della if I say no."

"Oh, no. The old Della is gone. What I *don't* want is for you to turn into Lavinia Clayson. What a waste."

Chapter 36

❦

*T*hougtful, Della went home and apologized to Mabli for being so hard to live with. For penance, she volunteered to start the breakfast bread dough all by herself. Mabli laughed and told her aye and that she was forgiven.

"This will give you another hour at least in your front room with the shy William Goode," Della said as she put on her apron.

"He's on the verge," Mabli said.

"Of what?" Della asked, feeling frisky for the first time in a month. "Saying 'May I call you Mabli?'"

Determined not to think about Owen, she pounded the bread dough until she wore herself out.

Mabli's parlor was empty when Della returned, so she prepared for bed quietly, braiding her hair again in a long braid. In her bedroom, she unfolded Angharad's latest dragon, looked at it a long time, and put it in the carved box Angharad had made "with only a little help from Da."

She stayed on her knees a long time, hoping for some confirmation, some sign that her petitions to the Almighty had reached at least the waiting room of those celestial realms. Hadn't the bishop told her months ago that the Lord was mindful of her?

Della finally turned off her lamp and tried to sleep. It would have been easier, but a chorus was singing outside the house. They wouldn't go away. As she listened, alert now, the song became distinct. She threw back her covers and hunted for her robe, finding it and knotting the tie around her waist as she opened the front door.

"My goodness, you sillies," she murmured, looking at the men's section of the Pleasant Valley Ward choir delivering a remarkable rendition of "Daisy Bell," all the verses. She stood in the doorway as doors opened all over her end of the canyon and others listened too. After the last verse, there was a pause as Owen stepped forward and gestured to her.

"I'm in my nightgown!" she hissed at him.

"And it is a fetching nightgown."

"Flannel, you nod," she said, which made the men's chorus laugh.

She stood still when he put his hands on her shoulders, not drawing her closer but looking at her. "I once knew and loved a lady who asked me to sing for her when she was afraid. I'll sing for you now." He gave a little downbeat, and the chorus hummed while he sang the chorus, "'Della, Della, give me your answer do, I'm half crazy, all for the love of you. It won't be a stylish marriage, I can't afford a carriage, but you'll look sweet upon the seat of a bicycle built for two.'"

He rested his forehead against hers. "Just give me something to hope for."

There was her answer, coming simply and plainly, like most things the Lord engineered. She felt the same peace she had felt on the upper wagon road last fall. It seemed so long ago, but she had changed, just as Miss Clayson said.

"I can tell you this, Owen Davis: things are inclining more in your favor. What girl doesn't like a serenade?"

"Is that what it's called here?" he asked with a little smile. "In Wales, we call it a shameless act of total desperation. Go to bed."

"Aye, sir. Do me a favor. You pray too."

"We're still not together on this, are we?"

"No, we're not," she said, with all the dignity in her heart and soul, hoping he would hear what she could not say. "Good night, Owen. You'll get my answer Tuesday at the dance."

Monday morning, Della put her class through their paces. "School will be over in three weeks," she reminded them. "These are little tests before our big tests. Astound me, and after lunch, we'll spend the afternoon making tissue flowers for the Dewey Day dance."

They astounded her. During lunch, she looked over their tests, pleased. *You've learned so much this year*, she thought. *Almost as much as I have.*

By the time the final bell rang, her classroom was a garden of paper flowers of all shapes and sizes and levels of ability.

"Miss, this is a long way from our leaves on the bulletin board last autumn," Danny Padfield told her as he put another dozen tissue paper flowers to her desk.

"It is," she agreed. "Those all blew away, winter came, and now it is spring." Trust Danny to be so observant. A page in everyone's book of life had turned; soon it would be summer. She looked around her classroom, pleased with what she saw—a roomful of little scholars all working at or above grade level and ready for next year.

After the bell, Della's students stayed long enough to pile the flowers into a cardboard box Clarence had furnished from the Wasatch Store. He promised to retrieve it by noon tomorrow and send the flowers to Scofield School, where those students would finish decorating the new Odd Fellows Hall.

Satisfied, Della spent a quiet evening in the library, where all was order, idle chat, and the reassurance of pages turning regularly. The day's mail included a letter from Samuel Auerbach, complaining of rheumatoid twinges but eager to see her in a month.

The surprise of the evening was Miss Clayson, who came in, looked around, and sat down with a copy of the

Denver Post. Curious, Della glanced her way, noticing that she had turned to the back of the second section, where the classified ads resided. *Looking for a change of venue, Lavinia?* Della asked herself. *Looks like we're all going to step out of our easy place.*

Miss Clayson lingered after the last patron said good night. "Could I take this?" she asked, indicating that second section.

"Certainly. Are you thinking of somewhere else than the canyon for next year?"

"You're a busybody!" the principal said, true to form, but the sting in her words was gone. "I am, actually. What about you, Della?"

"I've decided to accept his offer of marriage," she said, trying out the sentence for the first time and liking the sound. "I believe you are right."

"One hundred percent staff turnover," Miss Clayson said. "We're not going to make the district office happy."

"Well, I'll be here," Della said. "If they get desperate enough, they'll have to let me teach, even if I am married." She held out her hand. "Thanks, Lavinia. I'll always owe you."

Miss Clayson shook her hand. "The debt's paid in full. You're a fine teacher." The starch went back into her voice. "Let's wish ourselves good luck *tomorrow*. It's going to be a test of our teaching abilities to keep our little scholars thinking of school and not Dewey Day!"

Dewey Day dawned without a cloud in the canyon. Della yawned, hungry. She had fasted since Sunday, made her decision, for good or ill, and wanted oatmeal. She followed it with two soft boiled eggs and toast, wondering which side of the bed Owen preferred. *The idle brain is the devil's playmate*, she reminded herself. Tomorrow, maybe she and Owen could stop by Bishop Parmley's house to make an appointment for temple recommend interviews for Manti.

The stake president was in Provo, so that would mean a trip there for his interview too, maybe next week. There wasn't much time for her to make temple garments, but she could probably enlist the skills of the Pleasant Valley Relief Society.

Mr. Auerbach wouldn't care much for the news coming his way, but he might not feel so bad if she and Owen could get to Salt Lake so he could meet her new husband. Better yet, they could invite the Auerbachs to Winter Quarters for the June Eisteddfod. Before leaving the house, she flipped the calendar page from April to May, where she had circled May 1 earlier, and penciled in "dance."

Della decided she was going to have more trouble than any of her students, keeping her mind on the day's work. Dewey Day was nothing compared to the reality that tonight she would put Owen out of his misery with the answer he wanted. Six days, six months, or sixty years. Whatever the Lord allotted her with Owen would be sufficient to the day. Miss Clayson was right.

"Now remember, students. We have work to do today," she told them when everyone was seated, hands folded the way she liked, eyes straight ahead. She pulled up the maps over the blackboard. "Same rules as always: Third graders at your level, but first and second graders anywhere you want. Use each word in a sentence."

Everyone worked quietly and efficiently, the balm of Gilead to any teacher's heart. She sat at her desk and day-dreamed, wondering if Owen would even go to sauna next winter with her.

After her students put their papers on her desk, she divided them into groups, the older children by the window in a group to read to each other, and the younger ones closer to her desk, where she could supervise. She knew that Mary Parmley was quite capable of keeping order in the older group.

She had just glanced at the Regulator, wishing time would go faster, when a monster roar bellowed across the canyon, vibrating the floor. The windows rattled and one started to bow. Della leaped to her feet and threw herself in front of her students' desks close to the window. Someone screamed.

"Steady, my dears," she said, breathless, waiting for the windows to break and shower glass on her back. "Get up and go to that wall." She pointed at the wall separating her classroom from Miss Clayson's. "Move!"

They obeyed her without question, their eyes huge and frightened.

"Someone's celebrating Dewey Day early," Juko Warela said, his voice unnaturally high.

"Maybe that's it." Della glanced out the window to see a billow of black rise over the canyon where the men of the Number Four worked the day shift. As she watched, another roar and then another rumbled through the canyon and more smoke belched. "My Lord and my God," she whispered, as the bottom dropped out of her stomach.

She started for the door of her classroom, but Israel was already there, more serious than she had ever seen him. "Get them in Miss Clayson's classroom. I don't want them looking across the canyon," he ordered.

She did as he said, gathering her children and shooing them next door. Miss Clayson, her face white, ushered them inside. In mere moments, all the children were crammed in her room, where the windows looked over the swings and sand lot. She touched Della's hand briefly, then assumed command, a small woman in total control, even though Della knew exactly how much it cost her, down to the last tear.

"Children, we're going to stay right here until we know what's going on," Miss Clayson said, her voice calm. "School policy is to send you to your homes, but we will wait until we know something. Am I understood?"

Everyone nodded. Della watched as the children silently grouped themselves into families, brothers and sisters holding their smaller brothers and sisters on their laps, arms around them. Angharad stood alone, eyes wide with terror, and no one to comfort her. Della picked her up and sat with her, her lips on her hair. She could feel the child's heart pounding like a trip hammer in her chest. Or maybe that was her own heart. "I'm here with you, my dear," she murmured. "I'll never let you go."

Then they heard it, farther away at first, then coming closer—the sound of women wailing and screaming. Israel's eyes locked on hers. He made a placating gesture with his hands and edged out of the room. When he came back, his face was as white as Miss Clayson's. "I don't know what to say," he told the principal, his lips close to her ear. "Something terrible has happened. It's the Number Four."

Della closed her eyes, her brain empty of everything except an enormous scream that wanted out so badly, even as she forced it down, whipping it back like a lion tamer with a cudgel and chair. The last thing these children needed was for their teacher to lose her mind in front of them. She took her cue from Miss Clayson and sat a little taller, pressed her lips a little firmer, turning herself into a bulwark when she wanted to crumble and die.

The room was absolutely silent. Then she heard, "Even though I walk through the valley of the shadow of death, I will fear no evil."

It was Miss Clayson, calm and comforting. "Israel, go see what you can do. Della, go to the women. I'll stay here with the children until we hear otherwise."

Della nodded and set Angharad down on the chair. The child clung to her, wrenching her heart, until Miss Clayson picked her up and sat down with her. "No one will leave you alone, Angharad," the principal said. "Miss Anders will find out what is going on, and we will know what to do."

Della stood on the school steps for a moment, at a loss. Israel was already on the wagon road, shouldering his way past the women, running toward Number Four. Della went down the steps toward the largest knot of women. She held out her arms to include them.

"What will you have us do with your children?" she called.

The faces that turned toward her were familiar to her but unfamiliar at the same time: Martha Evans, Eeva Koski, Tamris Powell, her baby clutched in her shawl, Annie Jones, Mabli Reese. With a start she realized they all looked like the same woman—eyes filled with all the terror in the world, mouths agape. Some of them were shaking visibly. Someone on the edge of the circle had vomited onto the road. Soon others were retching, and Della knew why. Drifting across the canyon from the tortured mine was the odor of burning flesh. She turned away too, raising her skirt to her face, unmindful that everyone in the road could see her petticoat. Other women hid their faces in their aprons. Even more were screaming again. One of the older women was pulling her hair out in hunks.

Della grabbed her, holding her arms tight as she fought back and then went limp. Della dragged her to the edge of the road, looking around for help. There was no one. Each wife and mother on the road was staring into her own soul and had no heart for anyone but their man underground, dead, burning, in peril, breathing his last, clawing to get out, trying to save each other, swearing, praying—the women stared at every imaginable terror without any knowledge of what was actually happening.

Della pulled the unconscious woman farther off the road, seeing that her dress was decently around her ankles, her hands folded. She ran into the road again, looking around for someone, anyone, to restore order. There was no one. She ran to the Wasatch Store and found Clarence Nix, his face white too, going through a box of cards, his hands shaking so badly that the cards were flying everywhere.

"Let me help you," Della said, trying to imitate Miss Clayson's awesome control. She pushed Clarence into a chair and stroked his cheek until he was calm. "It won't do for you to be this way," she said, keeping her voice conversational. "Let me alphabetize these again." She picked up the scattered cards and restored them to order, a librarian's task. They were the coupon books for each miner, to charge expenses against the payout at the end of the month.

The names were so familiar because their children were her special stewardship in Winter Quarters Canyon. She touched the books almost lovingly, knowing in the depths of her soul that more lives were going to be ruined this Tuesday than anywhere else in the world.

"There now, Clarence. Let's leave these here, shall we? What should you be doing?"

"I don't know," he said, and she heard the shame in his voice. "I just don't know." He grabbed her shoulder. "Miss Anders, I do know! When they pull the bodies out of the mine, it'll be my task to identify them because I know them all." He gestured toward the card box. "I issue their coupon books. I know them."

She shuddered inside and willed herself calm. "Then Mr. Parmley will need you to be quite brave. Do you have any white cards?"

He stared at her as though she spoke Swahili, then nodded slowly. "In the drawer there."

She pulled out a handful of cards and looked for a pencil, something permanent that would not smear. "I'll go back to my classroom and get my crayons, Clarence. When you have to identify the men, you will write their names on the card and attach it somehow." She faltered, then gathered herself together again.

She hurried up the road and ran into her classroom, pulling out two boxes of Rainbow Colors, wondering for a tiny moment what Mr. Auerbach would make of the pictures they could draw now—vacant-eyed women, terrified children, and dead men. "Owen, I love you," she whispered.

She ran back to the Wasatch Store and put the crayons

in the counter next to the coupon box. Clarence stood in the doorway now, some calm in his face.

"I have to tell you, Miss Anders. I did something I shouldn't have."

"It's probably not too important today," she said, desperate for news, like the gathering crowd of women.

"I tampered with the US mail," he confessed. "Those letters you gave me to mail to Arizona? I haven't mailed them yet. No one wants you to leave the canyon." He turned his head and looked out the window toward the tracks below. "I'm sorry." He looked at her again, bewildered. "Why on *earth* am I talking such nonsense?"

"That's all right, Clarence," she said gently. "I don't mind. Nothing needs to go to Arizona. I am going to tell Owen tonight that I'll marry him. Except I can't now, can I?" She sobbed and turned away, her skirt to her face again.

He patted her shoulder. They left the store together in time to see everyone surging up the road.

"What's happening?" Della asked, alarmed.

"I think everyone is headed to the Number One portal," he said, more calm now. "It connects with the Number Four and it's easier to get into. They'll start a rescue from that direction. Come on."

She picked up her skirts and kept up with him, reaching the milling mass of women, silent now and anxious. The look of terror had been replaced by hope. They reached the portal, which was level with the roadway, unlike the Number Four, which was up a steep incline. Standing on the edge of the circle, she watched as a crew of six or seven men started into the mine. The silence was almost palpable, everyone straining forward, eager to see living men.

Her eyes searched the edge of the crowd, where miners stood with their blackened faces, bent over, some of them retching, the survivors. They must have run from the Number One when they heard the explosion in Four. Some of the women in the crowd had run forward now with little cries of relief, grabbing their husbands and sons, trying to hold onto them everywhere, heedless of the carbon transferring to their clothing. Their men were alive. For the smallest moment, Della hated those women with a ferocity that left her shaking.

Her attention returned to the Number One portal, where the rescuers, barely in, came staggering out, two of them carrying a man between them. Another man was slung over someone's back. The portly man—she recognized Bishop Parmley—waved everyone away. "Afterdamp! Go back!"

The crowd edged back and watched as the rescuers lowered one man to the ground. He was clean and Della realized he must have been one of the rescuers who just went in. She watched in horror as another man breathed into his mouth, then turned away, shoulders sagging. Someone else covered the rescuer's face with his own jacket.

"No," Della whispered. She clutched the man standing next to her, one of the fanway engineers with a son in her class. "Afterdamp?"

"It's the gas that rises after an explosion," he explained, his voice oddly mechanical. "It's deadly quick and it's killing the rescuers." He turned bleak eyes on her. "Miss Anders, no one else is going to come out of these mines alive. I'm sorry to tell you that. Seems rude of me. My mother would not approve."

She shook her head at the odd disconnect of people saying the strangest things. Maybe that was what terror and shock did to ordinarily rational beings. Hadn't she run back to the school for Franklin Rainbow Colors when she knew there must be a drawer of lead pencils in the Wasatch Store?

The engineer forced his way through the crowd and went to Bishop Parmley, who nodded and pointed. A handful of men sprinted to the fan house, ready to do whatever it took to get the air circulating in the mine again.

The full horror of the last half hour descended on the

milling crowd of women. Della flinched and put her hands over her ears as the most unearthly wail rose, women keening for their dead, crying for their men who had kissed them good-bye that morning and walked into the Number Four and Number One, Utah's safest mines. Della felt her skin crawl at the age-old sound of mourning for the dead.

Feeling one hundred years old, Della walked back toward the schoolhouse. After a few feet, her legs failed her, and she sank to the road. All the pins in her hair were gone. Her black hair that Owen had fingered at least once, settled wild and curly around her face. She wanted to lie down and die, pulling the soil over her until she was deep underground herself. The only thing that got her to her feet was the thought of Angharad, alone and frightened.

"I will be your dragon," she said, her words distinct. "I *am* your dragon."

Chapter 37

Della returned to the school, turning around to look once at the mouth of the underworld. Funny that she could get used to the smell of charred flesh. So much smoke still poured from the little side canyon housing the Number Four portal that the sun had dimmed. She watched, her eyes dull, as women from Scofield began to run up the road, heading for the mines.

She turned away, already weary of their anxious expressions. "Heavenly Father, this is going to be the longest day of our lives," she prayed out loud. "Give us the strength to get through it in a manner pleasing to Thee."

Della squared her shoulders and walked toward Miss Clayson's classroom. The children looked up expectantly, hope on their faces because they knew teachers had all the answers. She gazed at them, drawing strength from some reservoir not of her own creation. She wanted to smile away their fears, but she couldn't. She glanced at Miss Clayson and cleared her throat.

"I won't tell you that things are good right now. They are not. There is great confusion, and we are better off here. Miss Clayson, I suggest that we go downstairs. I hope that those of you who brought lunches today will be willing to share them. Let's make ourselves as comfortable as possible downstairs."

She held out her arms for Angharad, who leaned against her.

"Da?"

"I haven't found him yet, my dearest. I *will* find him. Let me get my magic paper and crayons. We can all use them today. Go on downstairs. I'll be there soon."

Miss Clayson followed her into her classroom, taking the paper and crayons, while Della gathered lunch boxes.

"How bad is it?" Miss Clayson whispered.

"I do not know how it could be worse," Della said simply. "There appear to be very few survivors from Number One, and they have not even got into Number Four because of the debris from the explosion."

"Oh, my dear," Miss Clayson said.

Della just shook her head and walked ahead with all the lunch boxes she could carry. Downstairs, Miss Clayson and the older girls brought more food and utensils out of her little apartment, while the boys arranged chairs. Trust Miss Clayson to find something for everyone to do. Angharad helped her carry the last of the lunch boxes downstairs.

"We could get the rest of the tissue paper and wire twists and make more flowers," the child said.

"That is a wonderful idea," Della said.

"I'll help."

Della looked at Angharad, so willing and so determined to stay beside her. For a small moment etched forever in her mind, she saw herself after Papa died, eyes hollow, trying so hard to make sense out of the senseless. She saw a young girl with a tag around her neck, taking a train to Salt Lake City. As she watched her new daughter, Della said good-bye to that other girl so friendless. Angharad's story would be different; Della would spend her life making it different.

"Where is my da?" she asked, when they stood in the classroom again.

Della knelt beside her. The shrieks were growing louder as the scope of the disaster made itself clear to the newly arrived women from Scofield. For a moment she gently put her hands over Angharad's ears. Just as gently, Angharad removed them, awesome in her own dignity, a child of the mines.

"Da is dead, isn't he?"

"I fear so, dearest."

In tears, Angharad melted into Della's embrace. They sobbed together, holding tight, drowning out the terrible noise on the wagon road, mourning the man they loved. They cried every tear there was, ever since Eve first realized how much she was going to miss the Garden of Eden. When they finished, they looked into each other's eyes, a family still, or maybe a family in spite of unmanageable pain that would somehow be managed in the years ahead.

"My nose is running," Angharad said.

"So is mine. Here, I have a petticoat. Blow."

They both did. "Better now?" Della asked, smoothing down her dirty skirt. "We have work to do."

Angharad puffed out her cheeks and blew in perfect imitation of her father, and Della turned away to collect herself. When she looked back, she was Angharad's mother.

"You carry the wires and I'll get the paper. March, missy."

Downstairs, Miss Clayson had organized everyone to form a lunch line, while the older girls set out the food, mostly bread and butter.

"We'll have a blessing, Miss Clayson," Della said, folding her arms. "That's what these children do. Bow your heads, my dears."

In a voice that only faltered a few times, Della asked a blessing on their lunch, eaten two hours late, and asked the Lord to look with favor on their canyon. That was all she could say. After the children were served, she shook her head when Miss Clayson held out a sandwich.

Her lips tight, Miss Clayson put it in her hand and closed her fingers around it. "Eat," she insisted in the tone that meant no argument was allowed. Della ate, keeping it down by sheer willpower.

In a few minutes, Miss Clayson had organized the children into two groups. In one, the older girls took turns reading to the younger children. In the other, Angharad and her friends, their fingers sure and steady, taught the other grades how to make paper flowers. Della felt her heart start beating again to see the quiet order in the gymnasium.

A little later, she heard someone come down the stairs and looked around to see Israel Bowman. He was dirty, covered with carbon, and smelled like death. Moving slowly, so as not to frighten the children, Della and Miss Clayson walked a few steps up the stairs and sat him down.

While Della held his hand, Miss Clayson got a sandwich and a handful of dried apples she had been saving for him. When he shook his head, Miss Clayson gave him The Look. He ate, chewing so long that Della had to gently remind him to swallow.

"Here is what I know and what you must do," he said when he could speak. "So far there are fifty bodies in the Edwards boardinghouse, since it's the closest to the Number One portal. More are being brought out."

Without a word, Della and Miss Clayson joined hands.

"Bishop has organized a team of men to remove their clothes and wash them. They're wrapping them in brattice cloth." He hauled out his pocket watch as though it weighed fifty pounds. "He's having them brought here within the hour. The classrooms will become morgues. I need to get the older boys to help me shove the desks to one side or into the hall."

Miss Clayson nodded. "We can do that."

"We'll have to hurry. Sister Parmley is going from woman to woman, telling them to fetch their children and take them home. Andrew Hood will . . ."

"Oh, thank God," Della interrupted. "He's alive."

Israel nodded. "He was at the entrance to Number One and escaped the afterdamp. He's organizing volunteers to push back the benches in the chapel for another morgue."

Della couldn't help her inarticulate moan. She clapped her hand over her mouth and glanced at the children, who were still busy with paper flowers. Miss Clayson's grip tightened on her free hand.

"It won't be enough, Della," Israel said. "When things are sorted out here, I'm sure a lot of the . . . men will go to Scofield's school too."

They sat in silence a moment, then Della had to know. "What of the Number Four?"

He shook his head. "I came from there. The rescue team has cleared enough of the debris to open the mine." He leaned against her, and she smelled the death on him. "Oh, Della! They're only in about two hundred feet and everyone is burned to death. One man is alive, but who knows for how long."

She nodded, her eyes blurry with more tears. Israel stood up. "I have to go back to Number Four. We're putting those bodies in sacks and taking them to the boardinghouse." He shook his head. "And Clarence is looking at every dead man's face. He's even trying to identify the unidentifiable."

"He thought that would be his job," Della said. "Poor Clarence."

Israel managed the ghost of a smile. "He has white tags and crayons. I have to leave." He turned and walked back up the stairs. He stopped and looked at Della. "If it's any consolation, I think death was very quick in Number Four."

Della and Miss Clayson sat together for a moment more. "I wish we could keep them here reading and making flowers," the principal said, her voice wistful. "Our school year is now over. When we can—if it even matters—we'll compute their final scores from their last tests."

Della leaned against Miss Clayson, grateful for her arm around her. "I was going to tell him tonight at the dance that I would marry him anyway." She turned her face into Miss Clayson's black dress. "I didn't have a chance to tell him. I hope I can live with that."

"Angharad will help you."

They kept the children occupied until Della heard

footsteps overhead. She raced up the stairs to see the stark face of Sister Parmley, with the women trailing behind, their expressions either fearful or vacant.

"Della, I am so sorry," she whispered, her grip firm on her arm. "I can take Angharad with me. Thomas wants you to go to the houses and see what you can do."

Della closed her eyes in relief. "Yes, please, take Angharad, but only for now. I may have to convince her, but I'd rather have her with you this day. You're far enough away."

Sister Parmley shook her head. "No one is far enough away, but it's best." She released Della's arm, only to touch her cheek. "She's your child now."

Della hurried downstairs with the women, who went directly to their fatherless children, holding each one in turn, or gathering them all into a tearful embrace. She knelt by Angharad, who shook her head vigorously when she told her to go with Sister Parmley.

"Please, dearest, just for now," Della said. "Bishop wants me to help the ladies however I can, and I still need to find your father."

"You won't leave me?"

"Never. Go now, and help Sister Parmley. I'll get you before bedtime, and we'll go . . . home."

Soon the basement was empty. Their faces so stern, even the little ones, the children left, towed by their mothers, or in some cases, already in charge and helping their younger siblings. The older boys had already pushed back the desks in her room, crowding them against the far wall next to the box with paper flowers, ready for Clarence Nix—identifying dead men now—to take to the Odd Fellows Hall for tonight's dance. She doubted anyone would dance in Scofield for a long time, if ever.

Della found a tablet and a pencil. Indecisive, she stood a long moment on the school's front steps. The magnitude of the disaster seemed to grow by the minute. Last night's coal train was ready to go. Della turned away, appalled. How could the coal just keep coming? she asked herself.

She watched, eyes as dull as anyone's, as the train began to move toward the canyon mouth. She noticed a sudden flurry on the track and stared as a woman far along in pregnancy began to walk deliberately toward the moving engine. Della sucked in her breath. It was Mari Luoma, her blonde hair wild around her pale face.

Dropping her silly pad and pencil, Della ran down the front steps and slid down the embankment, calling Mari's name, ordering her to stop. She reached the distraught woman at the same time as Emil Isgreen. He shouldered Della aside and balanced on the rails, trying to reason with the crazed woman. As the train came closer, Mari fought back when he tried to snatch her from danger.

Della joined him, tugging on her free arm and trying to speak low words of comfort at the same time. She helped Emil pick her up and carry her to safety, even as she struggled to free herself. As the train rumbled past, Mari tried to scramble back onto the tracks, screaming. Della wrapped her arms around the woman, rocking back and forth until her screams turned to whimpers and then faded away.

"God bless you, Della," Emil said. He grabbed two men with headlamps. "Please help us take this woman to the hospital."

"The mine rescue—" one of them started to say.

"There is no mine rescue!" Emil hissed, in a voice Della had never heard. "They're all dead. This woman is alive, and she needs help. My nurse is there. Don't argue with me."

They didn't. They put Mari on her feet, and she crumpled to the ground. Della knelt beside her again, speaking into her ear. "Mari, you have to let these men help you. Heikki would not want to see you here like this. Think of his baby. *Please*, Mari."

Mari looked at her, wild-eyed. Her expression gradually settled into a weird sort of acceptance almost as disturbing as her wild grief of moments ago. "Yes, my baby," she said, her voice mechanical now, like the fan engineer at the Number One portal. "Miss Anders, did you know I am going to have a baby?"

Della shuddered inside at Mari's new world.

"Stand up, Mrs. Luoma," Emil said firmly. "You have to help us."

The men tried again, and she remained on her feet. They formed a human chair and carried her away. Emil draped both of his arms on Della's shoulders, weighing her down with his exhaustion.

"Please tell me she will regain her senses," Della pleaded.

Emil nodded. "I'll tell you anything you want to hear, Della." He took his arms off her shoulders, and she saw the tears in his eyes. "What's worse? To come upon a disaster and know there aren't enough trained people to handle it, or to come upon a disaster and not be needed because there are only dead men." He shook his head. "Miss Harroun came on last night's train to help me with a tonsillectomy today. She was looking forward to the dance."

He seemed to register in his mind just who she was. "And here I am, breaking your heart some more. Della, forgive me."

She shook her head and climbed the embankment, retrieving her puny tablet and pencil. She stared at them a moment, then tossed them away. She sat down in the open-sided woodshed, numb to the sounds of grief all around—women running, women moving as though sleepwalking, women pleading, demanding, disturbingly calm—everyone reacting to disaster according to their natures. The children, released from school, trailed after their mothers. Some of them saw her and sat down. She cuddled them close, wordless.

An hour passed, then two. The children left her finally to follow their mothers some more, little people treading water in an ocean of distress. She looked down the canyon toward the Number Four mine. The smoke had stopped, and she saw men with stretchers now, carrying body bags to the closer company boardinghouse. The Edward boarding-house must be full.

Weary, she stood up and walked toward Mabli's and the boardinghouse. As she came closer, she realized with horror that discarded clothing lay in a mountainous pile on one end of the building. Resolutely, she looked away and went into Mabli's house, stopping in the doorway at the sight before her.

Mabli sat on the floor, rocking rhythmically back and forth and moaning. Vomit flecked the front of her dress. Shocked, Della looked closer. Mabli had bitten through her lip and blood soaked her front.

"Oh my dear," Della said, kneeling and taking her in her arms.

"First Dafydd and now Owen," Mabli said, her head against Della's breast. "And William too, think on. When does it end?"

"I wish I knew," Della told her, relieved at least that Mabli was making sense. "Let's get you cleaned up."

Thank goodness for warm water. Her eyes listless, Mabli offered no objections when Della took off her ruined clothing, cleaned her, and put her into fresh clothing. Della found her something to eat, made sure she ate it, then settled her in the rocking chair, a warm mug of peppermint tea in her hand.

Della found a clean apron and put that over the ruin of her own clothes. She knelt by Mabli's chair. "I'm going to go see who else I can help. Just stay here."

Mabli nodded and closed her eyes. Della put her hand on the doorknob, unwilling to open it on more scenes of misery so acute that her breath started to come in little gasps. She leaned her forehead against the door until she fought down the shriek that threatened to turn her inside out.

She said a prayer with no words to it and opened the

door on a wagonload of white-shrouded bodies passing in the road. Men with stretchers carried more bodies from the boardinghouse until there was a parade of bodies as far as she could see. Shocked, she started to count them, but her overtaxed mind rebelled against trying to clamp order on top of terror. Her jaw started to ache, and she realized she was grinding her teeth. She made a conscious effort to stop but failed. It was as though her body was now working independently of her mind. Soon someone would have to remind her to breathe.

She glanced at the boardinghouse porch, groaning aloud as the volunteers set down more bodies to wait for the wagon's return. She looked beyond the bodies to the ever-growing pile of clothing. Her eyes filled with tears.

Head high, she stepped around the bodies now lying on the ground beside the porch, her eyes still focused on the clothing pile. The smell of death rose from the clothing, rank and musty. Tears streamed down her face now as she reached out and tugged at a blue and white pinstriped shirt on the pile. Only a sleeve was showing, but she knew that shirt. She had sold a lot of them last summer in Menswear.

Tenderly she cradled it in her arms, unmindful now of vomit and carbon and grease and mysterious stains. She put the shirt to her cheek and sobbed. Volunteers and rescuers hurried around her, moving fast. She wanted to tell them to slow down; there was no rush. Everyone was dead. She barely saw them as she knotted Owen's shirt around her waist and walked to Finn Town.

Chapter 38

*D*ella didn't leave Finn Town until dark, desperate to avoid the sights in the canyon. Darkness was like snow: it could hide a multitude of ugliness. She had spent the afternoon going from house to house as Bishop Parmley wanted, not with notepad and pencil to record anyone's needs. Everyone was in shock and had no idea what they needed. She sat with her children, just holding them on her lap as they sobbed, mingling her tears with theirs.

By some miracle, Kari Koski had stayed home that morning from Number Four with a toothache. As she saw that living, breathing man, Della finally snapped and turned on Eeva.

"How dare he be alive?" she raged.

Eeva and Kari had grabbed her, much as she and Emil had grabbed Mari hours ago. As Della struggled, they held her tight. Finally exhausted, Della sagged in Kari's arms.

God bless Eeva Koski. She gave Della little shake and put her face close to hers. "I want you to scream as loud as you can, and as long."

"I'm so ashamed," Della said. "Kari, I didn't mean . . ."

"I know that," he told her gently. "Do what Eeva says."

Della screamed. She screamed until her throat hurt, and then she screamed some more. She screamed until she retched. Finally she lay whimpering in Eeva's arms, drained.

"Now you pick yourself up and move on," Eeva told her. "Go find your little girl and take her home. Do you want Kari to help you?"

She did, afraid to go into the wagon road, but shook her head. "No. It's my task, and your hands are full here. How many from Finn Town, Kari?"

"At least sixty." He swallowed. "Two of them are my brothers."

"Oh, Kari, forgive me," she said.

He kissed her forehead.

The dark was a blessing, she decided as she walked slowly down the canyon. Lights were on in buildings that didn't usually have lights on: all the machine shops, the school. She stopped in front of the school, reluctant to go in, but compelled.

The door to her room was open, the smell of death everywhere. Aghast, she stared at the rows of cloth-covered men in the lower grades classroom. The bare feet of the taller ones were uncovered, looking oddly vulnerable. She walked down the rows. Some of the corpses' faces were uncovered. These were the men caught in the deadly gases that spilled from Number Four into Number One, killing quietly. They looked as though they slept.

She looked on the faces of her boardinghouse miners, thinking how they teased her, escorted her to and from the library, and shoveled snow from Mabli's door all winter. She stopped in front of Nicola Anselmo. A woman in Italy was waiting for him to send her the fare to America. "Nicola, strong man," she whispered. "I wish you had been stronger."

When she came to the end of the row, she noticed the box of paper flowers, still waiting for someone to take them to the Odd Fellows Hall for tonight's party. She took an armful of flowers from the box and walked down the rows again, placing a flower on each miner's shrouded chest. She left two for Nicola and two for her German.

As she gazed down at Herr Muller, she noticed soot dripping from his nose. She knelt and wiped his nostrils with the edge of her apron, dabbing lightly. "There now, there now," she whispered. "Thank you for being my escort."

She couldn't go any farther than the door into Israel Bowman's classroom. These must have been some of the men of Number Four. They were covered in brattice cloth, the odor of charred flesh still strong. Some of the cloth had slipped and she saw black forms underneath that used to be miners. Maybe Owen lay there. How could she tell? She turned away, tapping into her never-ending day's prayer to add, "Please God, I hope they did not suffer long."

But they deserved flowers. Resolute, she went back into her classroom and grabbed another handful of paper flowers for Israel's room. She walked the rows of carbonized men and left a flower on each man's chest. She did the same in Miss Clayson's classroom. When she finished, Miss Clayson stood in the doorway.

"I'm not that brave," the principal told her.

"Yes, you are. You're still here, aren't you?"

Miss Clayson gave her a faint smile. "I am, indeed. What will you do now?"

"I will take Angharad home."

She walked to the Parmleys' house, where all the downstairs lights were on, even though it was after midnight. On the sofa, Angharad leaned against her friend Mary, her eyes closed. Sister Parmley kissed Della's cheek. "She wouldn't let me take her upstairs to bed." She leaned closer. "My sister-in-law is here too and her children. William hasn't been found yet." Tears welled in her eyes, which looked as swollen as Della's.

Della looked away, giving her grief privacy. She knelt beside Angharad. "Wake up, my dear. Let's go home."

Owen Davis's house was dark. Della knew it would be, but it was still a jolt to know that he wasn't there and never would be again. *It's going to be the small things that hurt, too*, she told herself. *Dark houses, empty chairs, empty beds, empty lives, until we can rebuild elsewhere.* She thought of poor Clarence Nix, given the worst job in Winter Quarters, worried because he had robbed the US Postal Service of four cents. So irrational. So had she been irrational, trying to attack Eeva Koski because Kari was still alive.

While Angharad prepared for bed, Della lit the lamp in the kitchen and started a fire in the stove. She wanted warm water to wash the mine from her, even though she already knew she could scrub forever and never be free of it. There was enough warmth remaining from the morning, when Owen lit the fire, so she wiped Angharad's face with a washcloth.

"Will you stay with me until I go to sleep?" Angharad said.

"Certainly. Let's kneel and say our prayers."

They knelt; neither could speak. Della decided the Lord could rely on His particular powers to hear the prayers they could not say tonight. "In the name of Jesus Christ, Amen," she said finally and helped Angharad into bed.

"I don't think I can sing," Angharad said, her voice small.

"Let's hum, because I can't sing either." Della made her comfortable against her breast. "Words can wait."

She hummed, faltering when Angharad started to weep. "'Sleep, my child, and peace attend thee,'" Della managed to say. She was silent as Angharad cried, thinking her way through the rest of song. She paused longest on "my loving vigil keeping," because she knew it would give her life the purpose it craved, from this horrible day forward, now that Owen was gone. She had no intention of becoming Lavinia Clayson, sleeping tonight in a morgue.

Worn out with grief and tears, Angharad finally slept. Della got up, wishing she had a nightgown but not willing to return to Mabli's. She went into the kitchen and took off her apron and dress, paring down to her camisole and petticoat, relishing the feel of warm water on her skin as she washed. She sat a long time in the kitchen, too weary to move, her mind racing like a mouse on a wheel, unable to hop off.

She dreaded what she had to do next, but there was nowhere else to sleep. She went into Owen's room, vulnerable to the flood of feeling that washed over her. *Just do it, Della*, she told herself and climbed into Owen's bed. She wept again, knowing she would never share it with the man she loved. After a while, his scent would be gone too. She wondered if anyone had ever taken a picture of him. It seemed unlikely. In the greater scheme of things, coal miners were not photogenic.

She opened her eyes hours later, or maybe fifteen minutes later. She couldn't tell because the room was dark and there was no clock. *Della, go to sleep*, she told herself and rolled over, Owen's pillow close to her side. She yawned and put both hands under her cheek.

There it was again. Someone was definitely in the kitchen. She sat up, heart pounding, fearing for her reason as she distinctly heard someone shoveling coal into the kitchen range. Someone was building up the fire she had banked.

Della got out of bed quietly, groping for her shirtwaist, but not bothering with her skirt. She wore a petticoat and was probably hearing things anyway. She tiptoed from Owen's bedroom into the front room and stood there until her eyes adjusted to the gloom. When she was more sure of herself, she sidled along the wall and peered into the kitchen.

Backlit against the moon, a man bent over the firebox. She watched, curious, as he blew on the coals and waited for them to catch. As she watched, it began to slowly dawn on her tired brain that it was Owen Davis, risen from the dead or sent from the spirit world for one last visit.

She tried to speak, but her lips weren't working. She must have made a sound, because the man at the stove turned around.

"Butterbean?" he asked, as startled as she was. "I

thought you two were with Mabli. I couldn't go there dirty."

Della's eyes rolled back in her head as she fainted for the first time in her life.

Angharad's washrag on her face brought her around a few minutes later. She blinked. Owen was holding her. She reached up and felt his face. He was filthy, but he was real.

"What a fright you gave me," he said.

"*You?*" she gasped. She touched touch his face again, stunned. "You're dead."

"No," he said quickly. "Everyone else is." He sat her up, then helped her into a chair, getting to his feet to light the kerosene lamp. When it flared, she saw his face and put out her hand to touch him again.

"I found your blue-and-white shirt on the pile outside the boardinghouse," she told him, some part of her tired brain still not convinced.

"Aye, you did. After mucking around on my hands and knees after we got into Number Four, I had to throw it on the pile." He shuddered. "Everything I touched . . ." He tightened his grip on her fingers. "I was in that first group of rescuers to go into Number Four. We spent an hour pulling out timbers and moving machinery. You must not have gone to the Four portal. You might have seen me before we went in."

She shook her head. "Just the Number One. I was with the children, and then I helped some women and went to Finn Town. Angharad stayed with the Parmleys until I returned for her. Owen! *How* are you alive?"

He was still no more than a vague outline, but she didn't need to see his face to know embarrassment when she heard it. "Della, you're looking at a stupid man. I'm so stupid I don't know why the Ellis Island inspectors didn't send me back to Wales."

"Oh, for heaven's sake!" she declared, exasperated. She moved over and he crowded onto the same chair.

"Since I proposed and we argued, I've been fasting and praying for the Lord to make you see things my way. I'm a miner. I'm a good one. Why should I leave the mines?" He let out a breath of air. "I owe my life to Richard." He stopped, unable to continue.

Della put her hand on his neck, caressing him. "I'm so in the dark."

"I spent so long on my knees Sunday and Monday nights, pleading with the Lord for you to come around to *my* way of thinking. I was complaining about that to Richard this morning—yesterday morning—as we rode the mantrip to the Number Four." He sobbed out loud, and she understood from the depths of her heart what this explanation cost him. "I can tell this only once."

"Once is enough. If anyone else needs to tell it, I will," she assured him.

"He shook his finger at me and told me, 'All you're doing is wishing Della would change her mind. Is that any way to supplicate the Lord? Owen, I'm ashamed of you.' I need a handkerchief."

She held up her petticoat. "Go ahead. We've all used it today."

He blew his nose on her petticoat. She shuddered to see it all black.

"Della, we were on the mantrip! I closed my eyes and finally prayed for the Lord's will instead of mine. I didn't even say Dear Heavenly Father, or anything polite. I didn't even ask Him the time of day! I just said, 'Thy will, Lord.'"

Della kissed his cheek, dirty as it was, and smelling of death as he did.

"I heard the Holy Spirit tell me, 'Quit now.' He doesn't waste words, Della. When we got to the portal, I told Richard I'd see him at the dance and rode the mantrip back down."

They both cried then, hanging tight to each other. "There's a washrag somewhere," he muttered. "I can't keep blowing my nose on your petticoat. It isn't mannerly. My mam would be so disappointed in me."

She thought of all the things she had heard yesterday that made no logical sense, considering the chaos and destruction all around them. "You found Bishop Parmley?"

"He was in his office. I told him I was quitting as of right then. He tried to talk me out of it and reminded me of the navy contract. I told him what the Spirit had told me." He chuckled. "It bothered the superintendent in him, I know, but the bishop in him couldn't disagree. He shook my hand and said I'd have five days to vacate my house. He wished me well, and I came back here." He squeezed her hand until she wanted to cry out. "Della, I was twenty feet from walking into Number Four!" He loosened his grip and pulled her closer. "You and I . . . we are the luckiest two people in the world."

"Angharad too."

"Aye. I was going to tell you at the dance."

Della ran her hand across his face again, exploring the contours she never thought to see again, much less touch. She told him about Edwin Aldridge and the Rialto Mine. "Miss Clayson didn't want me to make her mistake. *I* prayed, but the Lord told me to marry you anyway. I was going to tell you at the dance."

They sat in silence for a long moment, then Della asked, "I have to know. Who is left of the tenors and basses?"

"You're looking at him."

She cried out. He swallowed audibly a few times, then leaped up and ran for the kitchen door, flinging it open. He went to his knees in the backyard, vomiting. She ran after him, standing by him to steady his head.

She looked down when he finished, horrified. "It's black!"

"I'll be vomiting up mine for days, I fear," he said, sitting back and leaning against her, exhausted. "We all will. It's terrible there. Butterbean, the explosion was so hot it coked the coal on the mine face! Men were thrown against the ribs and even the roof. I can't . . ."

"Then don't," she said, putting her hand over his eyes. She hesitated but had to know. "What . . . what caused it?"

"The only ones who can tell us are dead," he said, taking her hand off his eyes and kissing her fingers. "We keep black powder and giant powder in the mines. I don't know. Maybe someone was setting a charge and a headlamp flared or dripped. Maybe there was too much coal dust. I doubt we will ever know."

He shook his head. "So many lovely men gone—my friends. Farishes, Hunters, Pughs, Gatherums, all those Luomas, Victor Aho, Padfields, Pittmans, Koskis, Evanses. Oh, Della . . . Two hundred men may have died in Utah's safest mine. The only man who knows for sure what happened is our foreman William Parmley, and he's still in there somewhere." He didn't try to mask his bitterness.

"Stop now," she murmured, pulling him close to her breast as she leaned against the house. "Stop. Stop."

"I'll see them in my dreams," he whispered.

"Not if I can help it," she whispered back. "You wrote on my blackboard, 'Marry me.' My answer *now* is yes, and I expect it to be soon."

"I'm unemployed," he reminded her. "No house in five days."

"Not for long. We're going to Provo, and you have work there," she told him. "Stand up now. I'm going to help you into the kitchen, where you're going to strip and get in that tin tub. I'll scrub your back and wash your hair and the rest is your problem."

He smiled a little at that. "Good enough. I'll wake Angharad in the morning."

"You'll wake her once you're clean and in your nightshirt!"

"Della . . ."

She hauled him to his feet and looked him in the eyes.

"Owen Davis, I will never again put a little girl to bed with tears drying on her face because she thinks—knows!—her da is dead! You two will sleep together in your bed, close and tight, for the rest of this horrible night. And you are *not* going into the mine again, not to pull out one more friend."

"I am not. Miners from Clear Creek have already arrived to help. Miners from Castle Gate and Sunnyside will be here by sunrise. The state inspector might be here now." He sounded so grim. "I am no longer a miner. I am now a coffin maker."

In the gloom of the kitchen, he stood still while she unbuttoned his filthy shirt and started on the ties to his garments.

"Turn around and pour in the water. I'm a modest man, Butterbean, at least for another week and a wedding in Manti Temple."

She laughed when she had told herself after Angharad slept that she would never laugh again. Life was going to go on, even if the mountain had blown up and everything had changed.

He settled in the tub with a sigh that went all the way to the bottom of her heart. She scrubbed his back, singing to him, then humming because her tears flowed again. She cried onto his back and scrubbed away the coal dust with her tears.

"I have something to do tomorrow," he told her, when they both could speak. He took the washrag from her and soaped up his front. "You're going to help me take everything out of my great-grandfather's chest and take the bedding off my bed. I'm going to use them both to make a coffin for Richard Evans. A pine box furnished by the Pleasant Valley Coal Company isn't good enough for the sweetest singer in Israel."

"Save the lid, my love," she said. "You can make another box for it later."

He nodded. "I'll have enough if I can use your bed too."

Della thought of her red dragons, Richard's soon. When Owen's beautiful coffin went into the ground in Scofield's cemetery, only God would see it.

"I'll keep Angharad by me tomorrow. She's seen enough. She'll want to carve something on Richard's coffin too. Will you send a telegram to the Knights? Tell them you and Angharad will arrive in Provo on Thursday. You'll probably want to telegraph Mr. Auerbach, since he'll be worried. Today, there are widows for you to attend to in this canyon: Martha Evans, Annie Jones, Tamris Powell. Oh, Della . . ."

She closed her eyes to hear the names of her friends. She also sighed with relief, savoring the decisive sound to his voice. Owen was back.

"I have some money saved with all the boxes I have carved."

"I have money saved too."

"Good. Find us a place to live in Provo. I'm sure the Knights will help. I think the funerals will begin on Saturday. I'll stay through Sunday, then come to you and Angharad on Monday. Maybe by next Friday, we'll be in Manti at the temple, for our wedding."

He was silent a moment, as though gathering his feelings. "I have the strongest feeling that Angharad is already your daughter. Am I right?"

"She became my daughter the moment I thought you were dead," Della said, decisive too. "I was going to move to Arizona with her and start over. She would have my constant love and never, ever have a tag around her neck, sending her to a distant relative. Angharad is *mine*."

"You'll have me too, Della Olympia? We're a matched set, Angharad and I."

"If you'll have me, Owen."

"Aye, then."

Angharad gaped at her father for a long moment when he woke her, doing what Della had done, staring at him, feeling his face, then wrapping her arms around him. He carried her into his room and climbed in bed with her, holding her close as she sobbed in relief, murmuring to her in the musical language of his birth. Della tucked the covers around them. She kissed them and turned to leave. Owen took her hand.

"Not yet, *m cara*," he whispered. "I'm afraid. Sing to me."

She sat on the bed. "You pitch it."

He hummed her note and she sang. It was ragged, but she did her best. "'Sleep, my child, and peace attend thee, all through the night . . .'"

She sang the lullaby all the way through, even though they were both asleep by "my loving vigil keeping."

Her heart calm in the middle of this disaster, Della sat beside them all night, keeping her vigil. The eye of God was on them.

Afterword

The Winter Quarters Mine Disaster remains Utah's worst catastrophe. At the time, it was the worst such disaster in the United States. It now ranks fifth. At least 200 men and boys died, although some figures place the total as high as 246. The only one who knew for certain how many men were in the Number Four that day was foreman William Parmley, and he died.

The explosion in Number Four set off a perfect storm of disastrous consequences. Because the Number Four and the Number One mine connected, the deadly afterdamp that was a by-product of the explosion raced from Four to One, killing quietly and instantly. Some of the miners far back in the Number One tried to escape through the closer exit in Number Four, only to run right into the afterdamp.

Before May 1, 1900, Winter Quarters Mines were often referred to as the married men's mines because they were considered so safe. Family groups—fathers, sons, nephews, cousins, brothers—gravitated to Winter Quarters. Because of this, the tragedy was compounded. Of the more than 1,300 people living in Scofield and Winter Quarters, no family was left untouched by the events of May 1, because so many were related.

Pleasant Valley Coal Company managers purchased burial clothes from Zions Cooperative Mercantile Institution in Salt Lake City. The dead men who were endowed members of The Church of Jesus Christ of Latter-day Saints were buried in temple robes consistent with LDS funeral rites.

The tragedy was of such unprecedented dimension that only 125 coffins could be found along the Wasatch Front. Another 75 coffins had to be sent from Denver, Colorado, to meet the need. Some 150 miners were buried in Scofield Cemetery. Others were transported to Utah towns and cities and buried in family plots. A smaller number of miners were buried in other states. Most of the Finnish dead and other foreign nationals were buried in Scofield.

There was a great outpouring of monetary assistance from many organizations in Utah and in all parts of the United States. Pleasant Valley Coal Company officials canceled the April debts that the miners owed to the Wasatch Store, amounting to $8,000. Eventually each widow was awarded $500, minus $33 for taxes. Some fatherless families remained in the area; others drifted away. The 1900 US Census, conducted six weeks after the mine disaster, lists many widows and children still in the canyon.

Even before all the miners had been brought to the surface, Gomer Thomas, Utah's state mine inspector, began his investigation. While no one will ever know for certain just what happened, Thomas, an experienced Welsh coal miner, was able to reach likely conclusions. A common belief at the time was that coal dust—ever-present in mines—was not likely to explode in the absence of flammable gases. Winter Quarters mines were not gassy, so the presence of coal dust was not a particular worry until May 1.

Miners bought their own black powder and giant powder (dynamite) and stored much of it in One and Four. They shot down the coal while in the mine, a common practice. Gomer Thomas's conclusion was that miners working with giant powder accidentally set off a blast that exploded some of the stored powder. In turn, this created even more coal dust, which ignited and raced through the mine, touching off more of the stored explosives. Death in Number Four was violent and fast, by explosion, searing heat, and cave-in. Death in Number One was less violent, almost peaceful, as miners dropped dead from afterdamp. Photographs taken of these miners show men who appear to be asleep. There are no photographs of the dead from Number Four. Indeed, identification of these miners was problematic, although Clarence Nix did his best.

As is often the case with tragedy, change comes. Following the disaster, more emphasis was placed on watering down mines to keep coal dust at a minimum. Superintendents and foremen worked to improve the skills of men handling explosives. In Utah, at least, tag boards were placed in mine offices, with a man's number stamped on a metal tag that was clipped to his belt. The simple system is still used today to denote who is in the mine at any particular time.

More change came in the form of strikes. An early strike in Carbon County took place at Winter Quarters in January–February of 1901. Poorly organized, it petered out. Strikes in 1903 and 1904 were more violent, with labor organizers, including Mother Jones, advocating better pay, better working conditions, and an end to the scrip system of payment, which forced miners to buy from company stores. By the 1930s, the United Mine Workers of America had unionized most, if not all, of the mines in Utah. The battle was hard fought and continues.

Scofield Cemetery might be the saddest place in Utah. Rows and rows of weatherworn headstones all bear the same date: May 1, 1900, which is disturbing enough. Wind, rain, and snow continue to scour Pleasant Valley. This is not a lush and green resting place. Time has not erased any of the tragedy from that cemetery and never will.

As Welsh Owen Davis and Richard T. Evans, English Thomas Farish, and Finnish Heikki Luoma understood, it was their children who laid full claim to America's great promise. Many thousands of their descendants thrive in Utah and other parts of the United States. Many of those descendants return to that little cemetery to honor their ancestors who left the Old World to seek a better life in the New World.

May they rest in peace.

*A*cknowledgments

This is a work of fiction, based strongly on fact. I have woven true stories in with fiction. Many thanks go to friends and colleagues who helped in my research for this historical novel. Stephanie Fitzsimons, director of the Western Railroad and Mining Museum in Helper, Utah, provided photographs, insight, and camaraderie. Danny Price, in his nineties, remembers what his father told him about the disaster. Danny's father and grandfather ranched in Pleasant Valley and ran to the mine to help in recovering bodies. Danny's comments were about as close as it is possible to come to eyewitness history. I owe a particular debt to Delon Hardy, section mechanic in a mining crew in Deer Creek Mine. He answered my amateur's questions and read the manuscript to help spare me from stupid mistakes. Thanks, Delon. Thanks also to Brad Timothy, a fire boss in Deer Creek Mine. Brad is a seventh generation miner whose family came from those coalfields in Wales. His father, Perry, also taught me about mines. His mother, Carol, is a good example of the resilience of miner's wives. So is Brad's wife, Margaret. A big thanks to Dennis Gibson, surface superintendent, who kindly gave me permission to spend some interesting hours in the Rhino Mine in Huntington Canyon. That experience was more useful than I can ever say. Clyde Davis, an LDS seminary teacher in Eastern Utah, is a direct descendant of John T. Davis, Welsh coal miner who died with two of his sons in the Winter Quarters Disaster. Mary Ann Davis was left to raise eight children.

Clyde is the perfect Welsh descendant—he has a wonderful singing voice. Special thanks to Leena Herlevi Dawson, my own dear Finn, who told me about sauna. And thanks to you, Debbie Balzotti, for your advice, photographs, and knowledge. In a work where some of the details remain sketchy because of circumstances, I have probably made mistakes. They are mine alone.

About the Author

Photo by Marie Bryner-Bowles,
Bryner Photography

Carla Kelly is a veteran of the New York and international publishing world. The author of more than thirty novels and novellas for Donald I. Fine Co., Signet, and Harlequin, Carla is the recipient of two Rita Awards (think Oscars for romance writing) from Romance Writers of America and two Spur Awards (think Oscars for western fiction) from Western Writers of America. She is also a recipient of a Whitney Award for *Borrowed Light*.

Recently, she's been writing Regency romances (think *Pride and Prejudice*) set in the Royal Navy's Channel Fleet during the Napoleonic Wars between England and France. She comes by her love of the ocean from her childhood as a Navy brat.

Carla's history background makes her no stranger to footnote work, either. During her National Park Service days at the Fort Union Trading Post National Historic Site,

Carla edited Friedrich Kurz's fur trade journal. She recently completed a short history of Fort Buford, where Sitting Bull surrendered in 1881.

Following the "dumb luck" principle that has guided their lives, the Kellys recently moved to Wellington, Utah, from North Dakota and couldn't be happier in their new location. In her spare time, Carla volunteers at the Railroad and Mining Museum in Helper, Utah. She likes to visit her five children, who live here and there around the United States. Her favorite place in Utah is Manti, located after a drive on the scenic byway through Huntington Canyon.

And why is she so happy these days? Carla doesn't have to write in laundry rooms and furnace rooms now, because she has an actual office.